THE
WICKED
DEEP

THE SHEA ERNSHAW BINDUP

WINTERWOOD

THE
WICKED
DEEP

ALSO BY SHEA ERNSHAW

A Wilderness of Stars
A History of Wild Places

WINTERWOOD

THE
SHEA ERNSHAW
BINDUP

THE WICKED
DEEP

SIMON & SCHUSTER BFYR

NEW YORK LONDON TORONTO SYDNEY NEW DELHI

SIMON & SCHUSTER BFYR

An imprint of Simon & Schuster Children's Publishing Division
1230 Avenue of the Americas, New York, New York 10020

This book is a work of fiction. Any references to historical events, real people,
or real places are used fictitiously. Other names, characters, places, and events are
products of the author's imagination, and any resemblance to actual events
or places or persons, living or dead, is entirely coincidental.

For information about special discounts for bulk purchases, please contact Simon & Schuster
Special Sales at 1-866-506-1949 or business@simonandschuster.com.
The Simon & Schuster Speakers Bureau can bring authors to your live event.
For more information or to book an event, contact the Simon & Schuster Speakers Bureau
at 1-866-248-3049 or visit our website at www.simonspeakers.com.
Interior design by Tom Daly
The text for this book was set in Adobe Garamond Pro.
Manufactured in the United States of America
This Simon & Schuster Books for Young Readers paperback edition November 2022
2 4 6 8 10 9 7 5 3 1
CIP data for this book is available from the Library of Congress.
ISBN 9781665932257 (paperback)
ISBN 9781481497367 (*The Wicked Deep* ebook)
ISBN 9781534439436 (*Winterwood* ebook)

These titles were previously published individually.

CONTENTS:

Praise for *The Wicked Deep*

"A wickedly chilling debut about ghosts, witches, love, and revenge."
—*School Library Journal*

★ "Chilling both by the damp, briny streets of Sparrow and
by its residents' sudden fervor for vengeance."
—*BCCB*, starred review

"Readers will drown in this finely crafted, atmospheric book."
—*Kirkus Reviews*

"Complex and sweetly satisfying."
—*Booklist*

"*The Wicked Deep* is more than just a scary story, it is a tale with substance and depth, one of magic and curses, betrayal and revenge, but most importantly, it is a story about the redemptive power of love to make even the worst wrongs, right."
—Amber Smith,
New York Times bestselling author of *The Way I Used to Be*

"*The Wicked Deep* has both teeth and heart. It's a mystery and a ghost story and a love story, all woven together with evocative prose and unforgettable settings. This is the perfect book to curl up with on a rainy night, when the swirling mists and dancing shadows make the ghosts and magic leap off the pages. Prepare to be bewitched."
—Paula Stokes,
author of *Liars, Inc.* and *Girl Against the Universe*

"*The Wicked Deep* is eerie and enchanting. I was thoroughly under the spell of the Swan Sisters, and utterly captivated by Shea Ernshaw's gorgeous, haunting debut."
—Jessica Spotswood,
author of the Cahill Witch Chronicles and editor of *Toil & Trouble*

"A magical, haunted tale of the sea, spells, and secrets. *The Wicked Deep* will lure you in, ensnaring you in the twisted enchantment of true love and sacrifice. Beware!"
—S. M. Parker, author of *The Rattled Bones*

To my parents, for encouraging my reckless imagination

THE SEA

Three sisters arrived in Sparrow, Oregon, in 1822 aboard a fur trading ship named the *Lady Astor*, which sank later that year in the harbor just beyond the cape.

They were among the first to settle in the newly founded coastal town, and they strode onto the new land like thin-legged birds with wavy caramel hair and pastel skin. They were beautiful—too beautiful, the townspeople would later say. Marguerite, Aurora, and Hazel fell in love often and typically with the wrong men—those whose hearts already belonged to someone else. They were coquettes, temptresses, and men found them impossible to resist.

But the townspeople of Sparrow found the sisters to be much more: They believed them to be witches, casting spells on the men to make them unfaithful.

And so at the end of June, when the moon was nothing but a thin shard in the overcast sky, stones were tied to the sisters' ankles, and they were dropped into the ocean just beyond the cape, where they sank to the bottom and drowned. Just like the ship they arrived on.

1

ONE

I have an old black-and-white photograph taken in the 1920s of a woman at a traveling circus floating in a massive tank filled with water, blond hair billowing around her head, legs hidden by a false mermaid's fin made of metallic fabric and thread to look like scales. She is wispy and angelic, with thin lips pinched tightly together, holding her breath against the icy water. Several men stand in front of the glass tank, staring at her as if she were real. So easily fooled by the spectacle.

I think of this photograph every spring, when murmurs begin to circulate through the town of Sparrow about the three sisters who were drowned beyond the maw of the harbor, past Lumiere Island, where I live with my mother. I imagine the three sisters floating like delicate ghosts in the dark shadows beneath the water's surface, mercurial and preserved just like the sideshow mermaid. Did they struggle to stay above the waterline two centuries ago, when they were forced into the deep, or did they let the weight of each stone carry them swiftly to the cold, rocky bottom of the Pacific?'

A morning fog, somber and damp, slides over the surface of the ocean between Lumiere Island and the town of Sparrow. The water is calm as I walk down to the dock and begin untying the skiff—a flat-bottomed boat with two bench seats and an outboard motor. It's not ideal for maneuvering in storms or gales but fine as a runner into town and back. Otis and Olga, two orange tabby cats who mysteriously appeared on the island as kittens two years back, have followed me down to the water, mewing behind me as if lamenting my departure. I leave every morning at this time, motoring across the bay before the bell rings for first period—Global Economics class, a subject that I will never use—and every morning they follow me to the dock.

The intermittent beam of light from the lighthouse sweeps over the island, and for a moment it brushes across a silhouette standing on the rocky western shore atop the cliff: my mother. Her arms are crossed in her knobby camel-colored sweater wrapped tightly around her fragile torso, and she's staring out at the vast Pacific like she does each morning, waiting for someone who will never return: my father.

Olga rubs up against my jeans, arching her bony back and raising her tail, coaxing me to pick her up, but I don't have time. I pull the hood of my navy-blue rain slicker up over my head, step into the boat, and yank the cord on the motor until it sputters to life, then steer the boat out into the fog. I can't see the shore or the town of Sparrow through the dim layer of moisture, but I know it's there.

Tall, sawtooth masts rise up like swords from the water, land mines, shipwrecks of years past. If you didn't know your way, you could run your boat into any of the half-dozen wrecks still haunting these waters. Beneath me lies a web of barnacle-crusted metal, links of rusted chain trailing over broken bows, and fish making their homes in rotted port-holes, the rigging long since eaten away by the salty water. It's a grave-yard of ships. But like the local fishermen chugging out through the dreary fume into the open sea, I can navigate the bay with my eyes pinched shut against the cold. The water is deep here. Massive ships used to bring in supplies through this port, but not anymore. Now only small fishing boats and tourist barges sputter through. These waters are haunted, the seamen still say—and they're right.

The skiff bumps against the side of dock eleven, slip number four, where I park the boat while I'm in class. Most seventeen-year-olds have driver's licenses and rusted-out cars they found on Craigslist or that were handed down from older siblings. But instead, I have a boat. And no use for a car.

I sling my canvas bag over my shoulder, weighted down with textbooks, and jog up the gray, slick streets to Sparrow High School. The town of Sparrow was built where two ridges come together—tucked between the sea and mountains—making mudslides all too common here. One day it will likely be washed away completely. It will be pushed down into the water and buried beneath forty feet of rain and silt. There are no fast-food chains in Sparrow, no shopping malls or movie theaters, no Starbucks—although we do have a drive-through coffee hut. Our small town is sheltered from the outside world, trapped in time. We have a whopping total population of two thousand and twenty-four. But that number increases greatly every year on June first, when the tourists converge into town and overtake everything.

Rose is standing on the sloping front lawn of Sparrow High, typing on her cell phone. Her wild cinnamon-red hair springs from her

5

head in unruly curls that she loathes. But I've always envied the lively way her hair cannot be tamed or tied up or pinned down, while my straight, nut-brown hair cannot be coaxed into any sort of bouncy, cheerful configuration—and I've tried. But stick-straight hair is just stick-straight hair.

"You're not ditching me tonight, are you?" she asks when she sees me, tenting both eyebrows and dropping her cell into her once-white book bag that's been scribbled with Sharpie and colored markers so that it's now a collage of swirling midnight blues and grassy greens and bubblegum pinks—colorful graffiti art that has left no space untouched. Rose wants to be an artist—Rose *is* an artist. She's determined to move to Seattle and attend the Art Institute when we graduate. And she reminds me almost weekly of the fact that she doesn't want to go alone and I should come with her and be her roommate. To which I've skillfully avoided committing since freshmen year.

It's not that I don't want to escape this rainy, dreadful town, because I do. But I feel trapped, a weight of responsibility settled firmly over me. I can't leave my mother all alone on the island. I'm all she has left—the only thing still grounding her to reality. And perhaps it's foolish—naive even—but I also have hope that perhaps my father will return someday. He'll magically appear on the dock and stroll up to the house as if no time has passed. And I need to be here in case he does.

But as our junior year comes to an end and our senior year approaches, I'm forced to consider the rest of my life and the reality that my future might be right here in Sparrow. I might never leave this place. I might be stuck.

I'll stay on the island, reading fortunes from the smeared remains of tea leaves in white porcelain cups just like my mom used to before Dad vanished and never came back. Locals would steer their boats across the harbor, sometimes in secret under a ghost moon, sometimes in the middle of the day because they had an urgent question they needed answered, and they'd sit in our kitchen, fingers tapping on the wood-block table, waiting for Mom to tell them their fate. And afterward they'd leave folded or crumpled or flattened bills on the table just before they left. Mom would slide the money into a flour tin she kept on the shelf next to the stove. And maybe this is the life I'm destined for: sitting at the kitchen table, the sweet scent of chamomile or orange lavender tea settling into my hair, running my finger around the rim of a mug and finding messages in the swirling chaos of leaves.

I've glimpsed my own future in those leaves many times: a boy blowing in from across the sea, shipwrecked on the island. His heart beating wildly in his chest, his skin made of sand and wind. And my heart unable to resist. It's the same future I've seen in every cup of tea since I was five, when my mom first taught me to decipher leaves. *Your fate lies at the bottom of a teacup*, she had often whispered to me before shooing me off to bed. And the idea of this future stirs inside me whenever I think about leaving Sparrow—like the island is drawing me back, my fate rooted here.

"It's not ditching if I never said I'd go," I say in response to Rose's question.

"I won't allow you to miss another Swan party." She shifts her hips to the side, looping her right thumb around the strap of her book bag. "Last year I was stuck talking to Hannah Potts until sunrise, and I won't do it again."

"I'll think about it," I say. The Swan party has always served a double purpose: the start of the Swan season and also the end-of-the-school-year bash. It's a booze-fueled celebration that is an odd mix of excitement to be free of classes and teachers and pop quizzes, blended with the approaching dread of the Swan season. Typically, people get way too smashed and no one remembers any of it.

"No thinking, just doing. When you think about things too long, you just talk yourself out of them." She's right. I wish I wanted to go—I wish I cared about parties on the beach. But I've never felt comfortable at things like this. I'm the *girl who lives on Lumiere Island*, whose mom went mad and dad went missing, who never hangs out in town after school. Who would rather spend her evening reading tide charts and watching boats chug into port than chugging beers with people I barely know.

"You don't even have to dress up if you don't want to," she adds. Dressing up was never an option anyway. Unlike most locals in Sparrow, who keep a standby early 1800s costume tucked away in the back of their closet in preparation for the yearly Swan party, I do not.

The warning bell for first period rings, and we follow the parade of students through the main front doors. The hallway smells like floor wax and rotting wood. The windows are single-pane and drafty, the wind rattling the glass in the frames every afternoon. The light fixtures blink and buzz. None of the lockers close because the foundation has shifted several degrees off center. If I had known another town, another high school, I might find this place depressing. But instead, the rain that leaks through the roof and drips onto desks and hallway floors during winter storms just feels familiar. Like home.

Rose and I don't have first period together, so we walk to the end of A Hall, then pause beside the girls' bathroom before we part ways.

"I just don't know what I'll tell my mom," I say, scratching at a remnant of Blueberry Blitz nail polish on my left thumb that Rose made me paint on two weeks back at her house during one of our movie nights—when she decided that to fit in as a serious art major in Seattle she needed to watch classic Alfred Hitchcock movies. As if scary black-and-white films would somehow anoint her as a *serious* artist.

"Tell her you're going to a party—that you actually have a life. Or just sneak out. She probably won't even notice you're gone."

I bite the side of my lip and stop picking at my nail. The truth is, leaving my mom alone for even one night makes me uneasy. What if she woke up in the middle of the night and realized I was no longer asleep in my bed? Would she think I had disappeared just like my dad? Would she go looking for me? Would she do something reckless and stupid?

"She's stuck on that island anyway," Rose adds. "Where's she going to go? It's not like she's just going to walk out into the ocean." She pauses and we both stare at each other: Her walking out into the ocean is precisely what I'm afraid of. "What I mean," Rose corrects, "is that I don't think anything will happen if you leave her for *one* night. And you'll be back right after sunrise."

I look across the hall to the open doorway of my first-period Global Economics class, where nearly everyone is already in their seats. Mr. Gratton is standing at his desk, tapping a pen on a stack of papers, waiting for the final bell to ring.

"Please," Rose begs. "It's the biggest night of the year, and I don't want to be the loser who goes solo again." A slight lisp trails over the word "solo." When Rose was younger, she talked with a lisp. All her *Ss* sounded like *Th*s. In grade school, kids used to tease her whenever a teacher asked her to speak out loud in front of the class. But after regular visits to a speech therapist up in Newport three days a week during our first years of high school, suddenly it was like she stepped out of her old body and into a new one. My awkward, lisping best friend was now reborn: confident and fearless. And even though her appearance didn't really change, she now radiated like some beautiful exotic species of human that I didn't recognize, while I stayed exactly the same. I have this sense that someday we won't even remember why we were friends in the first place. She will float away like a brightly colored bird living in the wrong part of the world, and I will stay behind, gray-feathered and sodden and wingless.

"Fine," I relent, knowing that if I skip another Swan party she might actually disown me as her only friend.

She grins widely. "Thank God. I thought I was going to have to kidnap you and drag you there." She shifts her book bag higher onto her shoulder and says, "See you after class." She hurries down the hall just as the final bell chimes from the tinny overhead speakers.

Today is only a half day: first and second period, because today is also the last day of school before summer break. Tomorrow is June first. And although most high schools don't start their summer session so early, the town of Sparrow began the countdown months ago. Signs announcing festivals in honor of the Swan sisters have already been hung and draped across the town square and over storefront windows.

Tourist season starts tomorrow. And with it comes an influx of outsiders and the beginning of an eerie and deadly tradition that has plagued Sparrow since 1823—ever since the three Swan sisters were drowned in our harbor. Tonight's party is the start of a season that will bring more than just tourist dollars—it will bring folklore and speculation and doubt about the town's history. But always, every year without fail or falter, it also brings death.

A SONG

It starts as a low croon that rolls in with the tide, a sound so faint it might just be the wind blowing through the clapboard shutters, through the portholes of docked fishing boats, and into narrow cracks along sagging doorways. But after the first night, the harmony of voices becomes undeniable. An enchanting hymn sailing over the water's surface, cool and soft and alluring. The Swan sisters have awakened.

TWO

The doors of Sparrow High are flung open just before noon, and a raucous parade of students is set loose into the sticky midday air. Shouts and whoops of excitement echo across the school grounds, scattering the seagulls perched along the stone wall that borders the front lawn.

Only half the senior class even bothered to show up for the final day, but the ones who did tear out pages from their notebooks and let the wind carry them away—a tradition to mark their freedom from high school.

The sun sits lazy in the sky, having burned through the morning fog, and it now seems defeated and weary, unable to warm the ground or our chilled faces. Rose and I stomp down Canyon Street in our rain boots, jeans tucked inside to keep them dry, with our coats unzipped, hoping the day will brighten and warm the air before tonight's all-night bash, which I am still not entirely thrilled to attend.

On Ocean Avenue we turn right and then stop at the next corner, where Rose's mom owns a shop that sits like a little square cake with white-painted brick walls and pink eaves—and where Rose works every day after school. The sign above the glass door reads: ALBA'S FORGETFUL CAKES in pale pink frosting–swirled letters on a cream-colored background. Yet the wood sign has started to collect a greenish brine that will need to be scrubbed away. A constant battle against the salty, slimy air.

"I only have a two-hour shift," Rose says, hoisting her book bag over to the other shoulder. "Meet at nine on the dock?"

"Sure."

"You know, if you had a cell phone like a normal person, I could just text you later."

"Cell phones don't work on the island," I point out for the hundredth time.

She blows out an exasperated breath. "Which is catastrophically inconvenient for me." As if she were the one who has to endure the lack of cell service.

"You'll survive," I say with a smirk, and she smiles back, the freckles across her nose and upper cheeks catching the sunlight like constellations of golden sand.

The door behind her whips open with a fluttering of chimes and bells clanking against the glass. Her mom, Rosalie Alba, steps out into the sunlight, blocking her gaze with a hand as if she were seeing the sun for the first time since last summer.

"Penny," Mrs. Alba says, dropping her hand. "How is your mother?"

"The same," I admit. Mrs. Alba and my mom were friends once, in a very casual way. Sometimes they'd meet for tea on Saturday mornings, or Mrs. Alba would come out to Lumiere Island and she and my mom would bake biscuits or blackberry pie when the thorny

16

blackberry bushes began to overtake the island and my dad would threaten to burn them all down.

Mrs. Alba is also one of the only people in town who still asks about my mom—who still cares. It's been three years since my father disappeared, and it's as if the town has forgotten about him entirely. Like he never lived here at all. But it's far easier to endure their blank stares than it was to hear the rumors and speculation that spun through town in the days after he vanished. *John Talbot never belonged here in the first place*, people had whispered. *He abandoned his wife and daughter; he always hated living in Sparrow; he ran away with another woman; he went mad living on the island and waded out into the sea.*

He was an outsider, and he had never been fully accepted by the locals. They seemed relieved when he was gone. As if he deserved it. But Mom had grown up here, gone to Sparrow High, then met my father at college in Portland. They were in love, and I know he never would have abandoned us. We were happy. He was happy.

Something far stranger happened to him three years ago. One day he was here. The next he wasn't.

"Will you give this to her?" Mrs. Alba asks, extending her palm where she's holding a small pink box with white polka-dot ribbon.

I take it from her, running the ribbon through my fingertips. "What flavor?"

"Lemon and lavender. A new recipe I've been experimenting with." Mrs. Alba does not bake ordinary cakes for ordinary cravings. Her tiny forgetful cakes are intended to make you forget the worst thing that's ever happened to you—to wipe away bad memories. I'm not entirely convinced they actually work. But locals and summer tourists devour the tiny cakes as if they were a potent cure, a remedy for any unwanted thought. Mrs. Potts, who lives in a narrow house on Alabaster Street, claims that after eating a particularly decadent chocolate fig basil cake, she no longer could recall the day her neighbor Wayne Bailey's dog bit her in the calf and made her bleed, leaving a scar that looks like a spire of lightning. And Mr. Rivera, the town postman, says he only vaguely recollects the day his wife left him for a plumber who lives in Chestnut Bay an hour's drive north. Still, I suspect it might only be the heaping cups of sugar and peculiar flavors in Mrs. Alba's cakes that for a brief moment allow a person to think of nothing else but the intermixing earthiness of lavender and the tartness of lemon, which not even their worst memories can rise above.

When my father vanished, Mrs. Alba began sending me home with every flavor of cake imaginable—raspberry lime tart, hazelnut espresso, seaweed coconut—in hopes they might help my mother forget what had happened. But nothing has broken through her grief: a stiff cloud not easily carried away with the wind.

"Thank you," I say, and Mrs. Alba smiles her wide, toothy grin. Her eyes are like pools of warmth, of kindness. And I've always felt comforted by her. Mrs. Alba is Spanish, but Rose's father is true-blooded Irish, born in Dublin, and Rose managed to get all her father's features, much to her displeasure. "See you at nine," I say to Rose, and she and her mom vanish into the shop to bake as many forgetful cakes as they can before the tourists arrive tomorrow morning by the busload.

* * *

The eve before the start of Swan season has always felt burdensome to me. It's like a dark cloud I can't shake.

The knowing of what's coming, the death that creeps up over the town like fate clawing at the door of every shop and home. I can feel it in the air, in the spray of the sea, in the hollow spaces between raindrops. The sisters are coming.

Every room at the three bed-and-breakfasts along the bay front is booked solid for the next three weeks until the end of Swan season—which will come on midnight of the summer solstice. Rooms facing the sea go for twice what can be charged for the rooms facing inland. People like to push open their windows and step out onto their balconies to hear the beckoning call of the Swan sisters singing from the deep harbor.

A handful of early tourists have already found their way into Sparrow, dragging their luggage into lobbies or snapping photos of the harbor. Asking where to get the best coffee or hot cup of soup because their first day in town usually feels the coldest—a chill that settles between the bones and won't go away.

I hate this time of year, as do most locals. But it's not the influx of tourists that bothers me; it's the exploitation, the spectacle of a season that is a curse on this town.

At the dock, I toss my book bag onto one of the bench seats inside the skiff. All along the starboard side, dotted into the white paint are scrapes and dings like Morse code. My dad used to repaint the skiff every spring, but it's been neglected for the last three years. Sometimes I feel just like that hull: scarred and dented and left to rust since he vanished somewhere out at sea.

I place the small cake box onto the seat beside my bag, and then walk around to the bow, about to untie the front line when I hear the hollow *clomp* of footsteps moving down the dock behind me.

I'm still holding the bowline when I notice a boy standing several feet back, holding what looks like a crumpled piece of paper in his left hand. His face is partly obscured by the hood of his sweatshirt, and a backpack hangs heavy from his shoulders. "I'm looking for Penny Talbot," he says, his voice like cold water from the tap, his jaw a hardened line. "I was told I could find her down here."

I stand up fully, trying to see his eyes, but there is a shadow cutting over the top half of his face. "Why are you looking for her?" I ask, not entirely certain I want to tell him that *I* am Penny Talbot just yet.

"I found this up at the diner . . . the Chowder," he says with an edge of uncertainty, like he's not sure he's remembered the name right. The Chowder is a small diner at the end of Shipley Pier that extends out over the water, and has been voted Sparrow's "Best Diner" for the last ten years in the local *Catch* newspaper—a small print paper that employs a total of two people, one of which is Thor Grantson because his father owns the paper. Thor is in the same class as me. During the school year, local kids overtake the Chowder, but in the summer months we have to share the worn stools along the bar and the tables on the outdoor deck with the horde of tourists. "I'm looking for work," he adds, holding out the limp piece of paper for me to see, and then I realize what it is. I posted a note on the cork bulletin board inside the Chowder nearly a year ago, asking for help maintaining the lighthouse out on Lumiere Island, since my mom had become nearly incapable of doing anything and I couldn't manage on my own. I had forgotten about posting it, and when no one ever came looking to fill the position, and the scribbled, handwritten note was eventually buried beneath other flyers and business cards, I made do.

But now, somehow this outsider has found it among the clutter of papers tacked to the bulletin board. "I don't need the help anymore," I say flatly, tossing the bowline into the boat—and also inadvertently revealing that I am indeed Penny Talbot. I don't want an outsider working on the island—someone who I know nothing about. Who I can't trust. When I had posted the listing, I had hoped a laid-off fisherman or maybe someone from my school might have responded. But no one did.

"You found someone else?" he asks.

"No. I just don't need anyone now."

He scrubs a hand over his head, pushing back the hood that had shrouded his face, revealing stark, deep green eyes the color of the forest after it rains. He doesn't look like a drifter: grimy or like he's been showering in gas station bathrooms. He's my age, maybe a year or two older. But he still has the distinct look of an outsider: guarded and wary of his surroundings. He clenches his jaw and bites his lower lip, looking back over his shoulder to the shoreline, the town twinkling beneath the afternoon sun like it's been sprinkled with glitter.

"Are you here for the Swan season?" I ask, flattening my gaze on him.

"The what?" He looks back at me, a measure of hardness in every move he makes: the twitch of an eyelash, the shifting of his lips before he speaks.

"Then why are you here?" He obviously has no idea what the Swan season is.

21

"It was the last town on the bus line." This is true. Sparrow is the final stop on a bus route that meanders up the coast of Oregon, stopping in several quaint seaside villages until it meets a dead end in Sparrow. The rocky ridgeline blocks any roads from continuing up the shore, so traffic has to be diverted inland for several miles.

"You picked a bad time to end up in Sparrow," I say, unhooking the last rope but holding on to it to keep the skiff from drifting back from the dock.

He pushes his hands into his jean pockets. "Why's that?"

"Tomorrow is June first."

By his stiff, unaltered expression, I can tell he really has no idea what he's just stumbled into.

"Sorry I can't help you," I say, instead of trying to explain all the reasons why he'd be better off just catching tomorrow's bus back out of here. "You can look for work at the cannery or on one of the fishing boats, but they usually don't hire outsiders."

He nods, biting his lip again and looking past me to the ocean, to the island in the distance. "What about a place to stay?"

"You can try one of the bed-and-breakfasts, but they're usually booked this time of year. Tourist season starts tomorrow."

"June first?" he echoes, as if clarifying this mysterious date that obviously means something to me but nothing to him.

"Yeah." I step inside the boat and pull the engine cord. "Good luck." And I leave him standing on the dock as I motor across the bay toward the island. I look back several times and he's still there, watching the water as if unsure what to do next, until the final time I glance back and he's gone.

THREE

The bonfire throws sparks up into the silvery night sky. Rose and I scramble down the uneven trail to Coppers Beach, the only stretch of shore in Sparrow that isn't bound in by rocks and steep cliffs. It's a narrow length of speckled white and black sand that ends at an underwater cave that only a few of the bravest—and stupidest—boys have ever attempted to swim into and then back out of.

"Did you give her the forgetful cake?" Rose asks, like a doctor who's prescribed medication and wants to know if there were any ill side effects or positive results.

After returning to Lumiere Island, after showering in the drafty bathroom across the hall from my bedroom then staring at my small, rectangular closet, trying to decide what to wear to tonight's event—finally settling on white jeans and a thick black sweater that will keep out the night's chill—I went into the kitchen and presented my mom with Mrs. Alba's forgetful cake. She had been sitting at the table staring into a cup of tea.

"Another one?" she asked drearily when I slid the cake in front of her. In Sparrow, superstition holds as much weight as the law of gravity or the predictability of the tide charts, and for most locals

Mrs. Alba's cakes have the same likelihood of helping Mom as would a doctor's bottle of pills. So she obediently took small bites of the lavender and lemon petit four, careful to not spill a crumb onto her oversized tan sweater, the sleeves rolled halfway up her pale, bony forearms.

I don't think she even realized today is the last day of school, that I just finished my junior year of high school, and that tomorrow is June first. It's not like she's completely lost all sense of reality, but the edges of her world have dulled. Like hitting mute on the remote control. You can still see the picture buzzing on the TV; the colors are all there, but there's no sound.

"I thought I saw him today," she muttered. "Standing on the shore below the cliff, looking up at me." Her lips quivered slightly, her fingers dropping a few crumbs of cake onto the plate in front of her. "But it was just a shadow. A trick of the light," she amended.

"I'm sorry," I told her, touching her arm softly. I can still hear the sound of the screen door slamming shut the night my father left the house, recall the way he looked walking down the path toward the dock, his shoulders bent away from the spray of the sea, his gait weary. I watched him leave on that stormy night three years earlier, and he never came back.

He simply vanished from the island.

His sailboat was still at the dock, his wallet on the side table by the front door of the house. No trace. No note. No clues. "Sometimes I think I see him too," I tried to console her, but she stared at the cake in front of her, the features of her face soft and distant as she silently finished the last few bites.

Sitting beside her at the kitchen table, I couldn't help but see myself in her: the long straight brown hair, same liquid blue eyes and tragically pale skin that rarely sees the sun in this dreary place. But while she is polished and graceful with ballerina arms and gazelle legs, I have always felt knock-kneed and awkward. When I was younger, I used to walk bent forward, trying to appear shorter than the boys in my class. Even now, I often feel like a puppet whose master keeps pulling all the wrong strings so that I fumble and trip and hold my hands clumsily out in front of me.

"I don't think cake is going to fix her," I tell Rose as we walk single file down the path lined with dry grass and thorny bushes. "The memory of my dad's disappearance is so solidified in her mind that no amount of local remedies will strip it out."

"Well, I don't think my mom has given up yet. Today she was talking about a new mixture of bee pollen and primrose that she thinks might help unsnag the worst of memories." We finally reach the beach and Rose hooks her arm through mine, our feet kicking up sand as we make our way to the bonfire.

Most of the girls are wearing long, layered dresses with low necklines and ribbons tied in their hair. Even Rose has on a pale green gown made of lace and chiffon that sweeps across the sand when she moves, dragging bits of driftwood and shells along with her.

Olivia Greene and Lola Arthurs, best friends and the rulers of Sparrow's social elite, are dancing on the other side of the bonfire when we enter the crowd, obviously already intoxicated, which is no surprise to anyone. Their hair is an identical shade of gothic black with short, severe bangs, dyed and trimmed just two weeks ago for the Swan season. Normally, their locks are bleached white—long and beachy. Which will probably return in a month, when the Swan season is over and they aren't feeling the need to dress like death. But Olivia and Lola love the dramatic, love dressing up, love being the center of attention at any social gathering.

Last year they pierced each other's noses in defiance of their parents—Olivia's is a silver stud in her left nostril, Lola's is a hoop through the right. And their nails are painted a matching macabre black, a perfect complement to the hair. They spin in circles beside the bonfire, waving their arms in the air and lolling their heads from side to side as if to mimic the embodiment of a Swam sister. Although I doubt the Swan sisters ever did anything so idiotic-looking two hundred years ago.

Someone hands Rose a beer and she in turn hands it to me to take the first sip. On weekends, sometimes we'll sneak beers or a half-finished bottle of white wine from her parents' fridge then get buzzed while stretched out on her bedroom floor listening to music—lately it's been country hits, our most recent obsession—and flipping through last year's yearbook, speculating about who's going to hook up this year and who might be inhabited by a Swan sister come summer.

I take a swig and look through the crowd at all the faces I recognize, at people who I've gone to school with since grade school, and I have the sharp thought that I hardly know any of them. Not really. I've had passing conversations with a few: *Did you write down the chapters we're supposed to read tonight in Mr. Sullivan's third-period history? Can I borrow a pen? Do you have a cell phone charger I can use?* But to call any of them friends wouldn't just be a stretch, it would be an all-out lie. Maybe it's partly because I know most of them will leave this town eventually—they will go off to college and have lives far more interesting than mine. We're all just passing ships; no point forming friendships that won't last.

And while Rose is not exactly climbing the social hierarchy at Sparrow High, she at least makes an effort to be friendly. She smiles at people in the halls, starts chatty conversations with her locker neighbors, and this year Gigi Kline, cheerleading captain for our struggling basketball team, even invited her to try out for the squad. They were friends once—Gigi and Rose—in elementary school. Best friends, in fact. But friendships are more fluid in grade school; nothing feels as permanent. And though they aren't exactly close anymore, Rose and Gigi have remained friendly. A tribute to Rose's kind nature.

"To the Swan sisters!" someone shouts. "And to another fucking year of high school!" Arms rise into the air, holding cans of beer and red cups, and a chorus of hoots and whistles carries across the beach.

Music thumps from a stereo balanced on one of the logs near the bonfire. Rose takes the beer from me and shoves a larger bottle into my hand. Whiskey—it's being passed through the crowd. "It's awful," she confesses, her face still puckered. But then she smiles, wagging an eyebrow at me. I chug back a quick slog of the dark booze, and it burns my throat, sending goose bumps down my arms. I hand it off to my right, to Gigi Kline. She grins, not at me—she doesn't even seem to notice me—but down at the bottle as she takes it from my hands, tips it to her mouth, swallows down way more than I could ever manage, and then wipes at her perfect coral lips before passing the bottle to the girl on her right.

"Two hours until midnight," a boy across the bonfire announces, and another wave of whoops and hollers rolls through the group. And those next two hours pass in a fog of bonfire smoke and more beers and swigs of whiskey that burn less and less with each sip. I hadn't planned on drinking—or getting drunk—but the warmth radiating throughout my entire body makes me feel loose and floaty. Rose and I find ourselves swaying happily with people who we might normally never talk to. Who might normally never talk to us.

But when it's less than thirty minutes to midnight, the group begins to stagger down the beach to the water's edge. A few people, either too drunk or deep in conversation to leave the bonfire, stay behind, but the rest of us gather together as if forming a procession.

"Who's brave enough to go in first?" Davis McArthurs asks aloud so everyone can hear, his spiky blond hair pushed up from his forehead and his eyelids sagging lazily like he's about to take a nap.

A rumble of low furtive voices passes through the mob, and a few of the girls are pushed playfully forward, their feet splashing into the water only ankle deep before they scurry back out. As if a few inches of water were enough for the Swan sisters to steal their human bodies.

"I'll do it," a singsong, slurring voice announces. Everyone cranes their head to see who it is, and Olivia Greene steps forward, twirling in a circle so that her pastel yellow dress fans out around her like a parasol. She's obviously drunk, but the group cheers her on, and she bows forward as if greeting her adoring fans before turning to face the black, motionless harbor. Without any coaxing, she begins to wade out into the salty sea, arms outstretched. When she's waist deep, she does a very ungraceful dive forward, which looks more like a belly flop. She disappears from view for half a second before reappearing at the surface, laughing wildly with her tragic-black hair draped over her face like seaweed.

The crowd cheers and Lola steps into the water up to her knees, urging Olivia back to the shallows. Davis McArthurs calls again for volunteers, and this time there is only a half beat before a voice shouts, "I'll go in!"

I snap my gaze to the left where Rose has stepped out of the crowd, moving toward the water.

"Rose," I bark, reaching out and grabbing her arm. "What are you doing?"

"Going for a swim."

"No. You can't."

"I've never really believed in the Swan sisters anyway," she says with a wink. And the crowd pulls her from my grasp, ushering her toward the cold ocean. She smiles widely as she wades out into the water, past Olivia. She's barely up to her waist when she dives forward and slips beneath the surface. A ripple shudders out behind her, and everyone on the beach falls silent. The air constricts in my lungs. The water flattens again at the surface, and even Olivia—who's still calf deep in the shallows—turns to watch. But Rose doesn't reappear.

Fifteen seconds pass. Thirty. My hearts starts to clap against my chest—a painful certainty that something isn't right. I push out from the crowd, suddenly sober, watching for Rose's red hair to break through the surface. But there's not even a breeze. Not even a ripple.

I take a single step into the water—I have to go in after her. I don't have a choice. When beneath the bloodless half-moon, shattering the calm, she suddenly bursts above the waterline, reemerging several yards farther out into the harbor from where she went in, I let out a trembling sigh of relief and the crowd erupts in a collective cheer, raising their cups as if they just witnessed some impossible feat.

Rose flips onto her back and lifts her arms overhead in a fluid pinwheel, swimming toward shore—casual, as if she were doing laps in a pool. I expect Davis McArthurs to ask who else wants to go in, but the group has gotten rowdy and girls are now traipsing through the shallow ankle-deep water, but never actually going all the way in. People stretch out on the sand, some shotgun beers, and others do sloppy cartwheels into the water.

Rose finally reaches the beach, and I try to push over to her, but several senior guys have gathered around her, giving her high fives and offering her beers. I slink back from the group. She shouldn't have done that—gone into the water. Risked it. My cheeks blaze, watching her nonchalantly wipe the water from her arms as if she is pleased with herself, smiling up at the cluster of guys who've taken a sudden interest in her.

The moonlight makes a path up the beach, and I wander away from the noise of the party—not far, just enough to catch my breath. I drank too much, and the world is starting to buzz and crackle and tilt off axis. I think of my father vanishing on a night when there was no moon to see by, no stars to guide his way back from the dark. If there had been a moon, maybe he would have returned to us.

I consider heading back to the marina, ditching the party and returning to the island, when I hear the heavy breathing and staggered footsteps of someone stumbling up the sandy beach behind me. "Hey," a voice calls. I spin around and see Lon Whittamer—one of Sparrow High's notorious partiers—swaying toward me like I'm standing in his path.

"Hi," I answer softly, trying to step out of his way so he can continue his drunken walk up the beach.

"You're Pearl," he says. "No, Paisley." He laughs, tosses his head back, his brown eyes slipping closed briefly before focusing on me again. "Don't tell me," he says, holding up a finger in the air as if to stop me from giving away my name before he's had time to figure it out on his own. "Priscilla. Hmm, Pinstripe."

"You're just saying things that start with the letter *P*." I'm not in the mood for this; I just want to be left alone.

"Penny!" he shouts, cutting me off.

I take a step back as he leans forward, exhaling a boozy breath and almost falling into me. His dark brown hair is plastered to his forehead, and his narrow-set eyes seem unable to focus, blinking closed every couple seconds. He's wearing a neon orange shirt with palm trees and pink flamingos scattered across it. Lon likes to wear obnoxious Hawaiian shirts in all shades of bright tropical colors with exotic birds and pineapples and hula girls. I think it started as a joke or maybe a dare our sophomore year, and then it turned into his trademark style. It makes him look like an eighty-year-old man on permanent vacation in Palm Springs. And since I don't think he's ever been to Palm Springs, his mother must order them online. And tonight he's wearing one of his ugliest.

"I like you, Penny. I always have," he mumbles.

"Is that right?"

"Yup. You're my kind of girl."

"I doubt that. You didn't even know my name two seconds ago."

Lon Whittamer's parents own the only major grocery store in town: Lon's Grocery, which they named after him. And he's known for being a total narcissistic asshole. He considers himself a ladies' man—a self-proclaimed Casanova—only because he can offer his

31

girlfriends discounts on makeup in the meager cosmetics aisle at his parents' store, and he uses this like a gold trophy he only hands out to girls who are worthy. But he's also known for cheating on his girlfriends and has been caught numerous times making out with other girls in his jacked-up, chrome-rimmed, mud flap–accessorized red truck parked in the school parking lot. Basically, he's a moron who doesn't even deserve the breath it takes to tell him to get lost.

"Why didn't you go into the water?" he asks slyly, inching closer to me again. "Like your friend did?" He brushes his hair back from his forehead and it sticks straight up, either from sweat or seawater.

"I didn't want to."

"You're afraid of the Swan sisters?"

"Yeah, I am," I answer honestly.

His eyes slide partway closed, and a stupid grin curls across his lips. "Maybe you should swim with me?"

"No thanks. I'm going back to the party."

"You didn't even wear a dress," he points out, and his eyes slide down my body like he's shocked by my appearance.

"Sorry to disappoint you." I start to take a step around him, but he grabs hold of my arm and digs his fingers into my skin.

"You can't just walk away." He hiccups, closes his eyes again, then snaps them open like he's trying to stay awake. "We haven't swum yet."

"I told you, I'm not getting in the water."

"Sure you are." He smiles playfully, like I must be enjoying this as much as he is, and begins dragging me with him into the shallows.

"Stop it." I use my other hand to push against his chest. But he continues to lurch backward, deeper into the harbor. "Stop!" I shout this time. "Let me go." I look up the shore to the mass of people, but they're all too loud and drunk and distracted to hear me.

"Just one swim," he coos, still smiling, slurring each word as they tumble from his lips.

We've staggered calf deep into the water, and I slam my fist against his chest. He winces briefly and then his expression changes, turns angry, and his eyes go wide.

"Now you're going all the way in," he announces more crisply, yanking against my arm so that I stumble several steps deeper, up to my knees. Not deep enough to risk being taken by a Swan sister, but still my heart begins to thump, fear pushing the blood out to my extremities and sending panic racing down my veins. I raise my arm again, ready to punch him directly in the face to keep him from dragging me in any farther, when someone appears to my left; someone I don't recognize.

It all happens in an instant: The stranger shoves a hand against Lon's chest; Lon's throat lets out a short wheezing sound. His grip on my arm releases at the same time he loses his balance, and suddenly he's careening backward, falling all the way into the water, arms flailing.

I take a staggering step back, sucking in air, and the person who pushed Lon off of me touches my arm to steady me. "You okay?" he asks.

I nod, my heart rate not yet receding.

Lon, a few feet away, stands up from the waist-deep water, gagging and coughing and wiping seawater from his face. His bright orange shirt is now sopping wet. "What the fuck?" he yells, looking directly at the stranger standing beside me. "Who do you think you are?" Lon demands, marching toward us. And for the first time I really look up at the face of the stranger, trying to place him—the rigid angle of his cheekbones and the straight slope of his nose. And then I know: It's him, the boy from the dock who was looking for work—the outsider. He's wearing the same black sweatshirt and dark jeans, but he's standing closer now, and I can clearly see the features of his face. The small scar by his left eye; the way his lips come together in a flat line; his short dark hair flecked with droplets of mist from the sea air. His gaze is still hard and unflinching, but in the moonlight he seems more exposed, like I might be able to read some clue in the rim of his eyes or the shiver of his throat when he swallows.

But I don't have time to ask him what he's doing out here because Lon is suddenly in his face, shouting about what an asshole he is and how he's going to get his face punched in for having the nerve to shove Lon into the water like that. But the boy doesn't even flinch. His gaze looks down at Lon—who is a good six inches shorter than him—and even though the muscles in his neck tense, he seems wholly unconcerned by Lon's threats of an ass-kicking.

When Lon finally takes a breath, the boy raises an eyebrow, like he wants to be sure Lon is done babbling before he responds. "Forcing a girl to do anything she doesn't want to is reason enough to kick your ass," he begins, his voice level. "So I suggest you apologize to her and save yourself a trip to the ER for stitches and a raging headache in the morning."

Lon blinks, opens his mouth to speak—to spew some rebuttal that would probably involve more cuss words than actual substance—but then thinks better of it and snaps his jaw shut. Standing beside the two of them, it's obvious Lon is outweighed, outmuscled, and probably outexperienced. And he must see it too, because he turns his head to face me, swallows his pride, and mutters, "I'm sorry." I can tell it pains him to say it, his expression twisting in disgust, the words sharp and foreign in his mouth. He's probably never apologized to a girl in his life . . . maybe never apologized to anyone ever.

Then, he turns and slogs up the beach back to the group, trailing seawater from his soaked clothes.

"Thank you," I say, wading out of the shallow water. My shoes and the lower half of my white jeans are drenched.

The boy's shoulders relax for the first time. "That guy wasn't your boyfriend, was he?"

"God, no," I snap, shaking my head. "Just some self-entitled prick from school. I've never even talked to him before."

He gives me a half nod and glances past me to the party in full swing. Music thumps; girls squeal and skip along the edge of the waterline; boys wrestle and crush empty beer cans between their palms.

"What are you doing here?" I ask, squinting up at him, tracing the arc of his eyebrows where they pinch together.

"I came down to sleep on the beach. I didn't realize there was a party."

"You're sleeping out here?"

"Planned to, up beside the rocks." His eyes flick up the shoreline to where the cliff rises, steep and jagged—an abrupt end to the beach.

I assume he checked the bed-and-breakfasts in town but there were no vacancies, or perhaps he couldn't afford to rent a room. "You can't sleep out here," I tell him.

"Why not?"

"High tide will be in at two a.m., and that whole stretch of beach by the cliff will be underwater."

His dark green eyes taper at the edges. But instead of asking where he should move his makeshift campsite to, he asks, "What's with the party? Something to do with June first?"

"It's the Swan party, for the Swan sisters."

"Who are they?"

"You've really never heard of them?" I ask. I think it's truly the first time I've met an outsider who came to Sparrow with no clue about what goes on here.

He shakes his head then looks down at my waterlogged shoes, my toes swimming in seawater. "You should get dry by the fire," he says.

"You're soaked too," I point out. He went into the water just as far as I did.

"I'm fine."

"If you're sleeping outside tonight, you should probably get dry so you don't freeze to death."

He glances up the beach to the dark cliff wall, where he'd planned to sleep, then nods.

Together, we walk to the bonfire.

It's late.

Everyone is drunk.

The stars sway and slip out of alignment overhead, reconfiguring themselves. My head thrums; my skin itches from the salt water.

We find a place to sit on an open log, and I untie my shoes, leaning them against the ring of rocks encircling the bonfire. My cheeks already feel flushed, and my toes tingle as the blood circulates back through my feet. The fire licks at the sky, licks at my palms.

"Thank you again," I say, looking at him from the corner of my eye. "For the rescue."

"Right place at the right time, I guess."

"Most guys aren't so chivalrous around here." I rub my palms together, trying to warm them, my fingers cold to the bone. "The town might be required to give you a parade."

He smiles full and big for the first time, a softness in his eyes. "The hero requirements in this town must be pretty low."

"We just really like parades."

Again he smiles.

And it means something. I don't know what, only that I'm intrigued by him. This outsider. This boy who glances at me from the corner of his eye, who feels both familiar and new all at the same time.

Down near the water's edge, I can see Rose still talking to three boys who've taken a sudden interest in her after her swim, but at least she's safe and out of the water. Half of the crowd has wandered back up to the bonfire, and beers are handed around. My head still feels swimmy from all the whiskey, so I set the beer in the sand at my feet.

"What's your name?" I ask the boy as he takes a long sip of his beer.

"Bo." He holds the can loosely in his right hand, casual, noncommittal. He doesn't seem uneasy in this foreign social setting, in a new town surrounded by strangers. And no one seems to think he looks out of place.

"I'm Penny," I say, glancing at him, his eyes so green it's hard to look away. Then, twisting my hair over my shoulder to ring out the small amount of seawater from the ends, I ask, "How old are you?"

"Eighteen."

I press my hands together between my knees. Smoke from the fire swirls over us, and the music continues to blare. Olivia and Lola stumble up to the edge of the bonfire, hugging each other around the waist and looking completely trashed.

"Are those the Swan sisters?" Bo asks. Olivia and Lola do look alike, with their jet-black hair and matching piercings, so I can see why he might think they're related.

But I let out a short laugh. "No, just friends." I dig the toes of my right foot into the sand. "The Swan sisters are dead."

Bo turns back to me.

"Not recently," I amend. "They died two centuries ago— drowned in the harbor."

"Drowned on accident or by intention?"

Olivia, who is standing on the other side of Bo, laughs hard and sharp. She must have overheard his question. "It was murder," she answers for me, peering down at him. Her coral lips arch into a smile. She thinks Bo is cute—who wouldn't?

"It wasn't murder," Lola counters, swaying left then right. "It was an execution."

Olivia nods in agreement then looks across the bonfire. "Davis!" she calls. "Tell the legend."

Davis McArthurs, who has his arm around a girl with pixie-cut dark hair, grins and walks closer to the fire. It's tradition to recount the story of the Swan sisters, and Davis seems rather pleased with himself to be the one to do it. He finds an open stump and stands on top, peering down at everyone around the bonfire. "Two hundred years ago—" he begins, voice booming, far louder than is necessary.

"Start at the beginning," Lola interrupts.

"I am!" he shouts back. He takes a drink of his beer then licks his lips. "The Swan sisters"—he continues, glancing around the group to be sure everyone is watching, everyone is listening—"arrived in Sparrow on a ship named . . . something I can't remember." He raises an eyebrow and grins. "But that's not important. What's important is this one thing: They lied about who they were."

"They did not," Gigi Kline yells up at him.

Davis scowls at this second interruption. "All girls lie," he says with a wink.

Several guys around the fire laugh. But the girls boo. One even tosses an empty beer can at his head, which he just barely dodges by ducking.

Gigi snorts, her head shaking in disgust. "They were beautiful," she points out. "It wasn't their fault that all the men in this town couldn't resist them, couldn't help but fall in love, even the married ones."

They weren't just beautiful, I want to say. *They were elegant and charming and winsome. Unlike anything anyone in this town had ever seen before.* We grew up knowing the stories, the legend of the sisters. How the locals in Sparrow accused the three sisters of being witches, of possessing the minds of their husbands and brothers and boyfriends, even if the sisters didn't intentionally set out to make the men fall for them.

"It wasn't love," Davis barks. "It was lust."

"Maybe," Gigi agrees. "But they didn't deserve what happened to them."

Davis laughs, his face turning red from the heat of the fire. "They were witches!"

Gigi rolls her eyes. "Maybe this town just hated them because they were different. Because it was easier to kill them than to accept that the men in this place are thick-skulled, misogynistic assholes."

Two girls standing near me break out into laughter, spilling their drinks.

Bo looks at me, eyes piercing, then speaks low so only I can hear. "They were killed for being witches?"

"Drowned in the harbor with rocks tied to their ankles," I answer softly. "They didn't need a lot of evidence back then to find someone guilty of witchcraft; most of the townspeople already hated the Swan sisters, so it was a pretty swift verdict."

He stares at me intently, probably because he thinks we're making the whole thing up.

"If they weren't witches," Davis counters, staring down at Gigi, "why the hell did they return the following summer? And every summer since?"

Gigi shrugs like she doesn't want to have this argument with him anymore, and she tosses her beer can onto the flames, ignoring him. She staggers away from the bonfire down to the shore.

"Maybe you'll be taken by a Swan sister tonight!" Davis shouts after her. "Then we'll see if you still think they weren't witches."

Davis pounds the rest of his beer and crushes the can in his grip. He's apparently completely over the idea of retelling the story of the Swan sisters as he clumsily steps down from the stump and slings his arm back over the pixie-haircut girl.

"What did he mean 'return the following summer'?" Bo asks.

"On the first of June the summer after the sisters were drowned," I begin, staring at the flames working their way through the dry beach wood, "locals heard singing from the harbor. People thought they were imagining it, that it was only the horns of passing ships echoing off the ocean's surface, or the seagulls crying, or a trick of the wind. But over the next few days, three girls were lured into the water, wading out into the sea until they sank all the way under. The Swan sisters needed bodies to inhabit. And one by one, Marguerite, Aurora, and Hazel Swan slipped back into human form, disguised as local girls who emerged from the harbor, but not as themselves."

Abigail Kerns staggers up to the bonfire completely drenched, her usually frizzy, dark hair slicked back with seawater. She crouches down as close to the fire as she can get without tumbling into it.

"That explains all the soaking-wet girls," Bo says, looking from Abigail back to me.

"It's become a yearly tradition, to see who is brave enough to go out into the harbor and risk being stolen by one of the Swan sisters."

"Have you ever done it—gone into the water?"

I shake my head. "No."

"So you believe it could really happen—that you could be taken over by one of them?" He takes another drink of his beer, his face lit by the sudden burst of flames as someone tosses another log onto the coals.

"Yeah, I do. Because it happens every year."

"You've *seen* it happen?"

"Not exactly. It's not like the girls come out of the water and announce that they're Marguerite or Aurora or Hazel—they need to blend in, act normal."

"Why?"

"Because they don't inhabit bodies just to be alive again; they do it for revenge."

"Revenge on who?"

"The town."

He squints at me, the scar beneath his left eye tightening, then he asks the obvious question. "What kind of revenge?"

My stomach swirls a little. My head pulses at my temples. I wish I hadn't drunk so much. "The Swan sisters are collectors of boys," I say, pressing a finger to my right temple briefly. "Seducers. Once they have each taken a girl's body . . . the drowning begins." I pause for effect, but Bo doesn't even blink. His face is hardened suddenly, like he's stilled on a thought he can't shake. Maybe he wasn't expecting the story to involve actual death. "For the next three weeks, until midnight on the summer solstice, the sisters—disguised as three local girls—will lure boys out into the water and drown them in the harbor. They're collecting their souls, stealing them. Taking them from the town as revenge."

Someone to my right hiccups then drops their beer onto the sand near my feet, the brown liquid spilling out.

"Every year, boys drown in the harbor," I add, staring straight ahead into the flames. Even if you don't believe in the legend of the Swan sisters, you can't ignore the death that plagues Sparrow for nearly one month every summer. I've seen the boys' bodies being pulled from the harbor. I've watched my mom console grieving mothers who've come to have their fortunes read, pleading for a way to bring back their sons—my mom patting their hands and offering little more than the promise that their hurt would eventually dull. There is no way to bring back the boys who've been taken by the sisters. There is only acceptance.

And it's not just local boys; tourists are persuaded into the water as well. Some of the boys standing around the bonfire, whose faces are flushed from the heat and the alcohol in their bloodstreams, will be discovered floating facedown, having swallowed too much of the sea. But right now, they aren't thinking about that. Everyone believes they're immune. Until they're not.

It makes me nauseous, knowing some of these boys, who I've known most of my life, won't make it through the summer.

"Someone must see who drowns them," Bo says, his curiosity evident now. It's hard not to feel drawn in by a legend that repeats itself without falter or fail each season.

"No one has ever seen the moment when they're taken into the harbor—their bodies are always discovered after it's too late."

"Maybe they drown themselves?"

"That's what the police think. That it's some sort of suicide pact devised by high school students. That the boys sacrifice themselves for the sake of the legend—to keep it alive."

"But you don't believe that?"

"It's pretty severe, don't you think—kill yourself for the sake of a myth?" I feel my heart beat faster remembering summers past: bodies bloated with seawater, eyes and mouths caught open like gutted fish, as they were pulled onto the docks in the marina. A chill sweeps through my veins. "Once a Swan sister has whispered into your ear, promised the touch of her skin, you can't resist her. She will lure you into the water then pull you under until the life spills out of you."

Bo shakes his head and then finishes his beer in one gulp. "And people actually come to watch this happen?"

"Morbid tourism, we call it. And it usually turns into a witch hunt, locals and tourists all trying to figure out which three girls in town are inhabited by a Swan sister—trying to determine who is responsible for the killing."

"Isn't it dangerous to speculate about something you can't prove?"

"Exactly," I agree. "The first few years after the sisters were drowned, many local girls were hanged because they were suspected of being taken over by one of the sisters. But obviously they never hanged the right girls, because year after year the sisters kept returning."

"But if you were inhabited by one of these sisters, wouldn't you know it, remember it? Once it was all over?" He rubs his palms together and turns them toward the bonfire—worn hands, rough in places. I blink and look away.

"Some girls claim they have a cloudy recollection of summer, of kissing too many boys and swimming in the harbor, staying out past curfew. But that could be from too much booze and not because a Swan sister was inside them. People think that when a sister takes over a body, she absorbs all the girl's memories so the girl can resume her normal life, behave naturally, and no one will suspect she's not herself. And when the sister leaves the body, the sister blots out all the memories she doesn't want her host to recall. They need to blend in because if they were ever found out, the town might do something awful just to end the curse."

"Like kill them?" Bo asks.

"It would be the only way to keep them from returning to the sea." I press all my toes down into the warm sand, burying them. "Kill the girl whose body they inhabit."

Bo leans forward, staring into the flames like he's recalling some memory or place that I can't see. "And yet you celebrate it each year," he finally says, sitting up straight. "You get drunk and swim in the harbor, even when you know what's coming? Even though you know people are going to die? You've just accepted it?"

I understand why it seems odd to him, an outsider, but this is what we know. It's how it's always been. "It's our town's penance," I say. "We drowned three girls in the ocean two centuries ago, and we've suffered for it every summer since. We can't change it."

"But why don't people just move away?"

"Some have, but the families who've been here the longest choose to stay. Like it's an obligation they must endure."

A soft breeze rolls suddenly through the crowd, and the bonfire snaps and flickers, sending sparks up into the sky like angry fireflies.

"It's starting," someone calls from the waterline, and those clustered around the fire begin moving down to the beach.

I stand up, still in my bare feet.

"What's starting?" Bo asks.

"The singing."

FOUR

The moonlight makes an eerie path down to the water's edge.

Bo hesitates beside the bonfire, resting his hands on his knees, his mouth an even, unbreakable line. He doesn't believe any of this. But then he stands up, leaving his empty beer can in the sand, and follows me down to the shore where people are huddled together. Several girls are totally soaked, shivering, hair dripping down their backs.

"Shhh," a girl whispers, and the group falls totally silent. Totally still.

Several seconds pass, a cool wind slides across the water, and I find myself holding my breath. Each summer it's the same, yet I listen and wait like I'm about to hear it for the first time. The start of an orchestra, the seconds of anticipation before the curtain lifts.

And then it comes, soft and languid like a summer day, the murmuring of a song whose words are indistinguishable. Some say it's French, others Portuguese, but no one has ever translated it because it's not a real language. It's something else. It curls up off the ocean and slips into our ears. It's gentle and alluring, like a mother whispering a bedtime riddle to a child. And as if on cue, the two girls standing closest to the waterline take several staggering steps into the sea, unable to resist.

But a group of boys go in after them and drag them back out. The time for dares has passed. There will be no more coaxing girls into the harbor, no more taunts to swim all the way out then back again. The danger is suddenly stark and real.

The lulling melody coils around me, fingers sliding across my skin and down my throat, tugging at me. Begging me to respond. I close my eyes and take a step forward before I even realize what I've done. But a hand—solid and warm—grabs ahold of mine. "Where you going?" Bo asks in a hush as he pulls me back to his side.

I shake my head. I don't know.

He doesn't release my hand, but squeezes it tighter, like he's afraid to let me go. "Is it really coming from the water?" he asks, his voice low, still facing the dark, dangerous sea, like he doesn't believe his own ears.

I nod, drowsy suddenly. The alcohol in my body has made me weak, more susceptible to the call of their song. "Now you know why the tourists come: to hear the sisters' song, to see if it's real," I say. The warmth of his palm pulses against mine, and I feel myself leaning into him, his firm shoulder an anchor keeping me from toppling over.

"How long will it last?"

"Until each of the three sisters has lured a girl into the water and taken her body." I clench my jaw. "Day and night the ocean will sing. Sometimes it takes weeks, sometimes only a few days. All three sisters could find bodies tonight if girls keep wading out into the bay."

"Does it scare you?" I realize we're the last two people standing at the water's edge—everyone else has gone back up to the safety of the bonfire, away from the tempting harbor—but his hand is still in mine, keeping me rooted to shore.

"Yes," I admit, the word sending a shiver down to my tailbone. "I usually don't come to the Swan party. I stay home and lock myself in my room." When my dad was still alive, he would stay up all night sitting in a chair beside the front door to be sure I didn't get drawn from my room—in case the urge to swim out into the sea was too great for me to resist. And now that he's gone, I sleep with head-phones on and a pillow over my head each night until the singing finally stops.

I believe that I'm stronger than most girls—that I'm not so easily fooled by the sisters' ethereal voices. My mother used to say that we are like the Swan sisters—she and I. Misunderstood. Different. Out-casts living alone on the island, reading fortunes in the cosmos of tea leaves. But I wonder if it's even possible to be normal in a place like Sparrow. Perhaps we all have some oddity, some strangeness we keep hidden along our edges, things we see that we can't explain, things we wish for, things we run from.

"Some girls want to be taken," I say in a near whisper, because it's hard for me to imagine wanting something like that. "Like it's a badge of honor. Others claim that they've been taken in summers past, but there's no way to prove it. Most likely they just want the attention."

The Swan sisters have always stolen the bodies of girls my age—the same age the sisters were when they died. As if they desire to relive that moment in time, even if just briefly.

Bo blows out a breath then turns and looks back up at the

bonfire, where the party has resumed in full upheaval. The goal of tonight is to stay awake until sunrise, to mark the start of summer, and for all the girls to survive without being inhabited by a Swan sister. But I sense Bo's hesitation—that maybe he's had enough.

"I think I'll head back to my camp and find a new place to sleep." He releases my hand, and I rub my palms together, feeling the residual warmth. A spire of unnerving heat coils up the center of my chest into my rib cage.

"Are you still looking for work?" I ask.

His lips press flat, as if he's contemplating the next few words, sifting them around in his mouth. "You were right about no one wanting to hire an outsider."

"Well, maybe I was wrong about not needing any help." I let out a breath of air. Maybe it's because he's an outsider like my dad, because I know this town can be cruel and unaccepting. Maybe I know he won't last long without someone to keep him safely away from the harbor once all three sisters have found bodies and begin their revenge on the town. Or maybe it's because it would also be a relief to have some help with the lighthouse. I know almost nothing about him, but it feels as if he's always been here. And it might be nice having someone else on the island, someone who I can talk to—someone who isn't fading into a slow, numbing madness. Living with my mom is like living with a shadow. "We can't pay you much, but it's a free place to stay and free meals."

Dad has never officially been declared deceased, so there's never been a life insurance check waiting for us in the mailbox. And shortly after he vanished, Mom stopped reading tea leaves, so the money stopped coming in. Thankfully, Dad had some savings. Enough that we've been able to survive on it these last three years—and it will probably get us through another two before we'll need to find an alternative source of income.

Bo scratches at the back of his neck, turning his head slightly away. I know he doesn't have any other options, but still he's considering it.

"All right. No guarantees on how long I'll stay."

"Deal."

I grab my shoes from beside the fire and find Rose talking to Heath Belzer. "I'm going home," I tell her, and she reaches out for my arm.

"No," she says in an exaggerated slur. "You can't."

"If you want to come with me, I'll walk you home," I say. She lives only four blocks from here, but far enough in the dark that I don't want her doing it alone. And drunk.

"I can walk her," Heath offers, and I look up at the soft, agreeable features of his face. Loose grin, dark eyes, reddish-brown hair that's always spilling across his forehead so he's constantly brushing it back out of the way. He's cute, likable, even if the curves of his face have that mildly dopey look. Heath Belzer is one of the good ones. He has four older sisters who've all graduated and moved away from Sparrow, but his whole life he's been known as Baby Heath, the kid who was beaten up by girls his entire childhood. And I once saw him save a blue jay that got trapped in the science lab at school by spending his entire lunch period trying to catch it then finally setting it free through an open window.

"You won't ditch her?" I ask Heath.

50

"I'll make sure she gets home," he says, looking me square in the eyes. "I promise."

"If anything happens to her—" I warn.

"Nothing's going to happen to me," Rose mumbles, squeezing my hand and pulling me into a hug. "I'll call you tomorrow," she whispers with whiskey-stained breath into my ear.

"All right. And no swimming."

"No swimming!" she repeats loudly, lifting her beer into the air, and a chorus of echoes pass through the crowd as everyone begins shouting in unison, "*No swimming!*" I can hear the chant all the way down the beach as Bo and I walk toward the bluff to retrieve his backpack, intermixing with the singing of distant voices blowing in with the rising tide.

Otis and Olga are waiting on the dock when I steer the skiff slowly up alongside it and kill the engine. We motored across the harbor in the dark, without even a flashlight to mark our path through the wreckage, the inviting whispers of the Swan sisters sliding languidly over the water so that it felt like we were being swallowed by their song.

I secure the ropes to the dock then bend down to stroke each cat's slender back, both of them slightly damp and probably unhappy that I'm returning so late. "Did you wait all night?" I whisper down to them then lift my head to see Bo stepping onto the dock, carrying his backpack in one hand. He cranes his head up, looking across the island to the lighthouse. The beacon of light illuminates us briefly before continuing its clockwise cycle out over the Pacific.

In the dark, Lumiere Island feels eerie and macabre. A place of ghosts and mossy hollows, where long-dead sailors surely haunt the reeds and wind-scoured trees. But it's not the island you should fear— it's the waters surrounding it.

"It's not as creepy in daylight," I assure Bo, passing my father's old sailboat, the *Windsong*, bobbing on the other side of the wood dock, sails down, unmoved for the last three years. My father didn't name the boat. It was called the *Windsong* when he purchased it ten years ago from a man who moored it south of Sparrow in a small seaside harbor. But the name *Windsong* had always seemed fitting, considering the voices that rise up from the sea each summer.

Otis and Olga trot after me, and Bo falls into step behind them.

The island is shaped like a half-moon with the flat side facing inland and the opposite side curved by the endless waves crashing against its banks. A two-story, robin's-egg-blue house—where my mom and I live—stands near the lighthouse, and a collection of smaller buildings are scattered across the island, built and torn down and added on to over the years. There is a wood shed and a toolshed and a greenhouse long since abandoned, and there are two cottages that serve as living quarters—Old Fisherman's Cottage and Anchor Cottage—and I lead Bo to the newer of the two, a place where staff was once housed, cooks and maintenance men, when such people were required to keep this place up and running.

"Have you always lived on the island?" he asks from the darkness as we follow the winding, sometimes broken wood-slated path up through the interior of the island, the air foggy and cool.

"I was born here."

"On the island?" he asks.

"My mom would have preferred to have had me at the hospital in Newport an hour away or at least at the clinic in Sparrow, but out here fate is determined by the sea, and a winter storm blew in, covering the island with a foot of snow and making the harbor a complete whiteout. So she delivered me at the house." The dizzying swirl of alcohol still thumps through me, and my head feels roomy and unfocused. "My dad said I was meant for this place," I explain. "That the island didn't want to let me go."

I may belong here on the island, but my father never did. The town always hated that an outsider purchased the island and the lighthouse—even if my mom was a local.

Dad was a freelance architect. He designed summer homes along the coast, and even a new library up in Pacific Cove. Before that, he worked at an architectural firm in Portland after he and Mom got married. But Mom always missed Sparrow—her hometown—and she wanted desperately to move back. Even though she had no family here, her parents were long dead and she was an only child, it had always felt like home to her. So when they saw the listing for Lumiere Island for sale, including the lighthouse, which was going to be decommissioned by the state—no longer of use since Sparrow was not a large shipping harbor anymore—they both knew it was exactly what they wanted. The lighthouse was a historic structure—one of the first buildings in town—and local fishermen still needed it to navigate into the harbor. It was perfect. Dad had even planned to renovate the old farmhouse someday—fix it up when he had the time, make it ours—but he never got the chance.

When he disappeared, the police came out to the island, filed a report, and then did nothing. The townspeople didn't rally together, didn't organize search parties, didn't climb aboard their fishing boats to scan the harbor. To them, he had never belonged here in the first place. For this, a part of me hates this town, this place, and these people for being so callous. They fear anyone and anything that isn't them. Just like they feared the Swan sisters two hundred years ago . . . and they killed them for being different.

We turn right, away from the glowing lights of the main house, and walk deeper into the unlit center of the island, until we reach the small stone cottage.

ANCHOR COTTAGE is written in letters formed out of frayed fishing rope then nailed to the wood door. It isn't locked, and thankfully when I flick on the light switch just inside the front door, a floor lamp across the room blinks on.

Otis and Olga zip past my feet into the cottage, curious about the building, which they've rarely had the opportunity to explore. It's cold and dank and there is a mustiness that can't be cleaned away.

In the kitchen I flip on the switch beside the sink and a light shivers on overhead. I kneel down and grab the power cord for the refrigerator and plug it into an outlet in the wall. Instantly it begins to hum. A small bedroom is situated just off the living room; a peeling wood dresser is against one wall and a metal bed frame sits beneath a window. There is a mattress, but no pillows or blankets. "I'll bring you sheets and bedding tomorrow," I tell him.

"I have a sleeping bag." He drops his backpack on the floor just inside the bedroom doorway. "I'll be fine."

"There's wood inside the shed just up the path if you want to start a fire. There's no food in the kitchen, but we have plenty up at the main house. You can come up in the morning for breakfast."

"Thanks."

"I wish it weren't so . . ." I'm not sure what I want to say, how to apologize for it being so dark and mildewed.

"It's better than sleeping on the beach," he says before I can locate the right words, and I smile, feeling suddenly exhausted and light-headed and in need of sleep.

"See you in the morning," I say.

He doesn't say anything else, even though I stand mute for a moment too long, thinking he might. And then I turn, my head swaying, and slip out the door.

Otis and Olga follow me out, and we trudge up the slope to the main house, where I left the back porch light on.

THE ISLAND

The wind is constant.

It howls and tears at siding and rips shingles from roofs. It brings rain and salt air, and in the winter sometimes it brings snow. But for a time each spring, it carries in the lurid and seductive voices of three sisters held captive by the sea, aching to draw out the girls of Sparrow.

From the black waters of the harbor, their song sinks into dreams, permeates the brittle grass that grows along steep cliffs and rotting homes. It settles into the stones that hold up the lighthouse; it floats and swirls in the air until it's all you can taste and breathe.

This is what cajoles the weak-hearted from sleep, pulls them out of bed and beckons them down to the shore. Like fingers wrapped around their throats, it drags them into the deepest part of the bay among the wreckage of ships long abandoned, pulling them under until the air spills from their lungs and a new thing can slip inside.

This is how they do it—how the sisters are freed from their brackish grave. They steal three bodies and make them their own. And this season, they do it swiftly.

FIVE

I wake with the choking sense of seawater in my throat. I sit upright, fisting my white sheet in both hands. The feeling of drowning claws at my lungs, but it was only a nightmare.

My head throbs, temples pulse, the lingering taste of whiskey still on my tongue.

It takes a moment to orient myself, last night still whirling through my head. I push back the sheet and stretch my toes over the hardwood floor, feeling stiff and achy and like a hammer is cracking against my skull from the inside. Sunlight peeks through the daffodil-yellow curtains, reflecting off the white walls and the white dresser and the high white ceiling—blinding me.

I press my fingers to my eyes and yawn. In the full-length mirror mounted to the closet door, I catch my reflection. Dark circles rim both eyes, and my ponytail has slid partway free so that strands of coffee-brown hair drift across my face. I look horrible.

The floor is cold, but I plod to one of the massive windows overlooking the choppy sea and slide the window upward in its frame.

In the wind I can still hear it: the faint cry of a song.

* * *

The scent of powdered sugar and maple syrup hangs in the air like a soft winter snowfall. I find her in the kitchen standing at the stove—Mom—her dark hair tied in a braid down her back, a serpent of brown, folded and coiled. And I feel like I'm still caught in a dream, my head swirling, my body rocking side to side like it's being pushed inland by an invisible tide.

"Are you hungry?" she asks without turning around. I absorb her movements, the sedated way she slides the spatula under a doughy pancake and flips it in the pan. She doesn't normally make breakfast—not anymore—so this is a rare occurrence. Something's up. For a moment I let a memory materialize in my mind: her making waffles with homemade blackberry jam, her cheeks flushed from the heat of the stove, her eyes and lips smiling, the morning sun on her face. She was happy once.

I touch my stomach, clenched and queasy. "Not really," I answer. There's no way I could eat right now. And keep it down. I move past her to the counter, where a row of identical silver tins sit perfectly spaced. They are unmarked, but I know the contents of each one: Lavender Chamomile, Rose Earl Grey, Cardamom Chai, Moroccan Mint, and Jasmine Dragon Pearl. I boil water then set my tea to steep—Rose Earl Grey—and lean against the counter breathing in the rustic, sweet scent.

"We have guests," she says suddenly, sliding the lightly browned pancakes onto a white plate.

I glance around the kitchen then back at her. The house is silent. "Who?"

She looks over at me, examining the creases around my eyes from lack of sleep; the queasiness that comes in waves when I pinch my lips tightly together to keep from vomiting. She stares for a moment, eyes pinched like she doesn't quite recognize me. Then she drops her gaze. "That boy you brought to the island last night," she says. The memory pours back through me: the beach, Bo, and my offering him a job on the island. Again I press my palms to my eyes.

"Is he a local boy?" she asks.

"No." I recall the moment on the dock when he said he was looking for work. "He came into town yesterday."

"For the Swan season?" she asks, setting the skillet back on the stove and turning off the burner.

"No. He's not a tourist."

"Can we trust him?"

"I don't know," I answer honestly—I don't actually know anything about him.

"Well," she says, turning around to face me and sliding her hands down into the pockets of her thick black robe, "he's just waking up. Take him some breakfast. I don't want a stranger inside the house." This is one of her gifts: She knows when people are near, when they're coming to the island—she senses their arrival like a nagging in the pit of her stomach. And this explains why she decided to cook breakfast—what drove her from bed just after the sun rose, compelled her into the kitchen to turn on the stove and pull out her good skillet. She might not want a stranger in the house, she might not trust him, but she won't allow him to starve. It's just her nature. Even her grief can't keep her from kindness.

She pours maple syrup over the stack of warm pancakes then

hands me the plate. "And take him some blankets," she adds. "Or he'll freeze out there." She doesn't ask why he's here, why I brought him to the island—for what purpose. Maybe she just doesn't care.

I tug on the green rubber boots beside the front door and a black raincoat, then grab a set of sheets and a thick wool blanket from the hall closet. Holding a palm over the plate of pancakes to keep the rain from turning them into a soggy heap of sugar and flour, I step outside.

Pools of water collect in divots and holes beside the walkway, and sometimes the rain seems to rise up from the ground instead of from overhead—a snow globe effect, but with water. A swift wind crashes against my face as I make my way down to the cottage.

The sturdy wood door rattles when I knock, and Bo opens it almost instantly, as if he had been just about to step outside.

"Morning," I say. He's standing in jeans and a charcoal-gray rain-coat. A fire crackles in the fireplace behind him. And he looks rested, showered, and new. Nothing like how I feel. "How'd you sleep?"

"Fine." Yet his voice is weathered and deep, betraying perhaps a lack of sleep after all. His eyes stare unblinking, soaking me in, and my skin prickles with the intensity of it. He is not someone who looks through you, past you, like you're not even there. His gaze is sharp, incisive, and an itch settles behind my eyes, making me want to look away.

He shuts the door behind me, and I set the plate of pancakes on the small square wood table in the kitchen then brush my palm down my jeans even though there is nothing to wipe off. The cottage feels different with him inside it, and the glow from the fireplace smooths over all the hard, rough edges so that everything feels muted and soft.

I place the sheets and wool blanket on the musty gray couch facing the fireplace, and he sits at the table. "Can you show me the lighthouse today?" he asks, taking a bite of the pancakes. In this light, in the scarlet hue of the fire, he reminds me of the boys who come into town aboard fishing boats, green and wild looking, like they've been cast off by the winds, set adrift.

He reminds me of someone who has left his past behind.

"Sure." I bite the inside of my bottom lip. My eyes scan the cottage. The tall wood bookshelves beside the fireplace are crowded with books and old almanacs and tide-chart periodicals, all covered in a decade of dust. Lumps of aqua-blue sea glass, collected over the years from the island's rocky shores, are piled into a small porcelain dish. On the top shelf sits a large wood clock that probably once lived on the deck of a ship. This cottage has served as the living quarters for a variety of staff and hired laborers, men who stayed a week and others years, but almost all left something behind. Trinkets and mementos, hints about their lives, but never the full story.

When Bo finishes breakfast—so quickly that I know he must have been starving—we leave the warmth of the cottage and are submerged by the drizzling rain. The ash-gray sky presses down against us—a weight that is tangible. Water trickles through my hair.

We pass the small greenhouse where herbs and tomato plants and leafy greens were once tended and grown, the glass walls now tarnished and smudged so that you can no longer see inside. The island has taken back most of the structures, decaying walls and rot seeping up from below. Moss covers every surface: a weed that feeds off the constant moisture and cannot be contained. Rust and mildew. Slop and mud. Death has found its way into everything.

"The singing hasn't stopped," Bo says when we're halfway to the lighthouse, our feet making hollow clomping sounds that echo against the wood walkway. But in the wind, the voices are still there, sliding lazily in with the sea air. It's so familiar that I hardly discern it from the other sounds of the island.

"Not yet," I agree. I don't glance back at him. I don't let his eyes find mine again.

We reach the lighthouse, and I pull open the metal door, corroded at the hinges. Once inside the entryway, it takes a moment for our eyes to adjust to the dim. The air is stark and smells of moisture-soaked wood and stone. A rounded staircase serpents its way up the interior of the lighthouse, and I point out to Bo where not to step as we ascend—many steps have rotted away or broken—and at times I pause to catch my breath.

"Have you ever been taken?" Bo asks when we're almost to the top of the stairway.

"I wouldn't know if I had," I say between gasps for breath.

"Do you really believe that? If your body was inhabited by something else, you don't think you'd know?"

I stop on a solid step and look back at him. "I think it's easier for the mind to forget. To sink into the background." He doesn't seem satisfied, his jaw shifting to the left. "If it makes you feel better," I say with a partial grin, "if a Swan sister is ever inside me, I'll let you know if I can tell."

He raises an eyebrow and his eyes smile back at me. I turn and continue up the stairway.

The wind rattles the walls the higher we climb, and when we

finally reach the upper lantern room, a howling gust screams through cracks in the exterior.

"The first lighthouse keeper was a Frenchman," I explain. "He named the island Lumiere. It was a lot more work to keep the lighthouse running back then—maintaining the lanterns and the prisms. Now it's mostly automated."

"How did you learn all this?"

"My dad," I answer automatically. "He studied lighthouses after my parents bought the island." I swallow hard then continue. "We need to check the glass and the bulb each day. And everything needs to be cleaned a couple times a week to keep the salty air from building up. It's not hard. But during a storm or a thick fog, this lighthouse can save the lives of fishermen out at sea. So we have to keep it running."

He nods, walking to the windows to look out over the island.

I eye him, tracing the outline of his shoulders, the curve of his assured stance. Arms at his sides. *Who is he? What brought him here?* Fog has rolled in over the island, creating a sheer veil of gray so that we can't make out any features of the terrain below. After a few minutes of staring through the glass, he follows me back through the doorway and down the winding staircase.

Otis is sitting on the wood walkway outside, waiting with eyes blinking against the rain, and I pull the lighthouse door closed. Olga is several yards up the path, licking her orange-striped tail. They're both used to the relentless downpour, their cat instincts to escape wet weather have gone dormant.

We walk up the path to the high center of the island, through the old orchard, where rows of Braeburn apple and spindly Anjou pear trees grow in wild, unruly directions. People used to say that fruit trees couldn't grow in the sea air, but they've always thrived on Lumiere Island. An anomaly.

"What about the orchard?" Bo asks, pausing at the end of a row.

"What about it?"

"These trees haven't been trimmed in years." I squint at him and he reaches up to touch one of the bony, leafless branches, as if he can sense the tree's history just by touching it. "They need to be limbed and the dead ones cut down."

"How do you know?" I ask, shoving my hands into the pockets of my raincoat. They've started to go numb.

"I grew up on a farm," he answers vaguely.

"My mom doesn't really care about the trees," I say.

"Someone cared about them once." He releases the spindly branch from his fingers and it springs back into place. He's right; someone did care about this orchard once. And there used to be more rows and a variety of hardy apples and pears. But not anymore. The trees are overgrown and windswept, only producing small, often bitter fruit. "They could live another hundred years if someone maintains them," he says.

"You could really bring them back to life?"

"Sure, it will just take some work."

I smile a little, scanning the rows of trees. I've always loved the orchard, but it's been years since it's seen a real bloom. Just like the rest of the island, it's fallen into decay. But if the trees could be saved, maybe the whole island could too. "Okay," I say. "Let's do it."

He smiles faintly, and our eyes meet for an instant.

I show Bo the other buildings on the island, and we circle around the perimeter. He's careful not to walk too close to me, keeping his arm from brushing mine when we walk side by side, his steps deliberate and measured over the stony landscape. But his eyes flick over to me when he thinks I'm not looking. I swallow. I tighten my jaw. I look away.

When we reach the cliffs facing west, the ocean slamming against the shoreline in violent waves that spray water and foam against the rocks, he stops.

This close to the sea, the song of the sisters feels like a whisper in our ears. As if they were standing beside us, breath against our necks.

"How many people have died?" he asks.

"Excuse me?"

"During the months when the Swan sisters return?"

I cross my arms, the wind brushing the hair over my eyes. "They each drown one boy . . . usually."

"Usually?"

"More or less. It depends."

"On?"

I shrug, thinking about the summers when five or six boys were found tumbling with the waves against the shore. Sand in their hair. Salt water in their lungs. "How vengeful they're feeling . . . I suppose."

"How do they choose?"

"Choose what?"

"Who they're going to kill?"

A breath sticks in my throat, trapped like a hook in a fish's mouth. "Probably the same way they chose lovers when they were alive."

"So they love the boys they drown?" I think maybe he's being sarcastic, but when I tilt my gaze to look at him, his dark eyes and punctuated full lips have stiffened.

"No. I don't know. I doubt it. It's not about love."

"Revenge, then?" he asks, echoing my words from last night.

"Revenge."

"The perfect justification for murder," he adds, his stare slipping away from mine to look out over the hazy brume rising up from the sea like smoke.

"It's not . . ." But I stop myself. *Murder.* That's precisely what it is. Calling it a curse does not unmake the truth of what happens here each year: murder. Premeditated. Violent, cruel, barbaric. Monstrous even. Two hundred years' worth of killing. A town reliving a past it can't change, paying the price year after year. An eye for an eye. I swallow, feeling a pain in my chest, in my gut.

It's as predictable as the tide and the moon. It ebbs and flows. Death comes and it goes.

Bo doesn't press me to finish my thought. And I don't offer to. My mind is now twisting like a snake into a deep dark hole. I lift my shoulders and shiver, the cold seething through me.

We peer out at the churning sea, and then I ask, "Why are you really here?"

"It was the last stop on the bus line," he repeats. "I needed work."

"And you've never heard of Sparrow before?"

His eyes slide to mine and the rain catches on his lashes, lingers on his chin, and spills from his dark hair. "No."

Then something changes on the wind.

An abrupt hush breaks over the island and sends a quick chill across the nape of my neck.

The singing has stopped.

Bo takes a step closer to the edge of the cliff, like he's straining to hear what is no longer there. "It's gone," he says.

"The sisters have all found bodies." The words seem pulled from my throat. The quiet settles between each of my ribs, it expands my lungs, it reminds me of what's to come. "They've all returned." I close my eyes, focusing on the silence. It's the fastest it's ever happened before.

Now the drowning will begin.

A WARNING

We wait for death. We hold our breath.
We know it's coming, and still we flinch when it claws at our throats
and pulls us under.

—Plaque located on the stone bench on Ocean Avenue,
facing the harbor (commissioned in 1925)

SIX

The soil squishes away beneath my rain boots. A steady, uninterrupted drizzle collects on the waterproof sleeves of my raincoat as I move back down the rows of the orchard.

Bo is back in his cottage. We parted ways an hour ago. And even though I thought about going back to bed—my head still pounding, my skin rattling against my bones—I decided I wanted to be outside, alone.

I find the familiar old oak tree that grows at the center of the orchard, where Bo and I passed by not long ago. But we didn't stop here.

This is my favorite place on the island—where I feel protected and hidden among the old, rotted fruit trees. Where I let memories slide over me like a cool stream. This oak tree stands alone among the rest, ancient and weathered from the sea air—its growth stunted. But it's been here since the beginning, nearly two hundred years, back when the Swan sisters first stepped onto land, when they were still alive.

I run my fingers along the crude heart etched into the wood, cut there by lovers long ago dead. But the heart remains, the bark fallen away, permanent.

I slide down against the trunk of the tree and sit at its base, leaning my head back to look up at the sky, speckled with dark clouds caught in the fickle ocean winds.

The Swan season has begun. And this little town tucked along the shore will not come out unharmed.

A storm is blowing in from the ocean.

The clock beside my bed reads eleven p.m. Then midnight. I can't sleep.

I walk from my bedroom into the bathroom across the hall, my thoughts straying to Bo. He's not safe, even on the island.

I can hear Mom's fan blowing in her room two doors down while she sleeps. She likes to feel a breeze, even in winter; she says she has nightmares without it. I flick on the bathroom light and look at myself in the mirror. My lips are pale, hair lying flat across my shoulders. I look like I haven't slept in days.

And then a sliver of light blinks through the bathroom window and reflects back at me in the mirror. I lift a hand to block it. It's not the beam of light from the lighthouse. It's something else.

I squint through the rain-streaked window. A boat is pulling up to the dock down on the lower bank.

Someone is here.

I shrug into my raincoat and boots and slip out the front door quietly. The wind howls over the rocky outcroppings on the island, blowing the hardy sea grass sideways and swirling my hair across my face.

As I get closer, I see a light pass over the dock—a large flashlight—the kind used to see into the fog when you're trying to pick your way through the wreckage of the harbor back to port. There is a low exchange of voices and the stomping of feet on the wood dock. Whoever it is, they aren't trying to be quiet or covert.

I lift a hand over my face to block the wind. And then I hear my name. "Penny?"

In the dark, I make out Rose's wild hair caught up in a gust. "Rose—what are you doing out here?"

"We brought wine," says Heath Belzer—the boy who walked Rose home from the Swan party last night, and who is now standing beside her, holding up a bottle for me to see.

The boat behind him has been secured sloppily to the dock, ropes hanging down into the water, and I assume it must be Heath's parents' boat.

"The singing stopped," Rose says in a hush, like she doesn't want the island to hear.

"I know."

She takes several steps toward me, swaying a bit, obviously already a little intoxicated. Heath looks back at the harbor, the sea lapping against the dock. Out there, in the darkness, is where at least three boys' lives will be taken.

"Can we go up in the lighthouse?" Rose asks, changing the subject. "I want to show Heath." Her eyebrows lift, and she bites the side of her cheek—looking like a cherub all rosy-cheeked and saucer-eyed. I can't help but love her—the way she always brightens the air around her as if she were a light bulb. Like she were a summer day and a cool breeze all in one.

"Okay," I say, and she smiles big and dopey, tugging me up the boardwalk with Heath following.

"I seem to recall a boy with you last night," she whispers in my ear, her breath hot and sharp with alcohol.

"Bo," I answer. "I gave him a job on the island. He's staying in Anchor Cottage."

"You did what?" Her mouth drops open.

"He needed work."

"You must have been drunk if you were willing to take in an outsider. You realize he's probably just a tourist."

"I don't think so."

"Then why's he here?"

"I'm not sure."

"Penny," she says, slowing her pace up the path. "He's living on the island with you. . . . He could murder you in your sleep."

"I think he has more to fear than I do."

"True," she agrees, pulling down the sleeves of her white sweater so her fingers are tucked in out of the cold wind. "He couldn't have shown up at a worse time. We'll see if he makes it until summer solstice."

A chill shuttles down my spine.

Once we reach the lighthouse, Rose giggles as she sways unsteadily up the spiral staircase, and Heath keeps grabbing on to her to prevent her from tumbling backward.

At the top of the stairs, I push through the door into the lantern room. But it's not dark like I was expecting. The lamp resting on the white desk on the right-side wall has been switched on, and a silhouette is standing at the glass, one shoulder leaning against it.

"Bo?" I ask.

"Hey." He turns around, and I notice a book held in his right hand. "I came up to watch the storm."

"Us too," Rose squeaks. She steps forward to introduce herself. "I'm Rose."

"Bo."

Rose grins and looks back at me, mouthing *he's cute* so no one else will see.

Bo and Heath shake hands, then Heath holds up the bottle. "Looks like we have a small party."

"I should probably head down," Bo offers, tucking the book under his arm.

"No way," Rose says, grinning. "You're staying. Three isn't a party, but four is perfect."

Bo glances at me, as if looking for permission, but I stare back at him blankly, unsure what to think about him up here all alone, reading or watching the storm. Whatever the truth might be.

"All right," he agrees, a hint of reluctance in his eyes.

Heath produces an opener from his coat pocket and begins uncorking the bottle.

"Heath stole two bottles from his parents' B and B," Rose says. "We drank one on the way over." Which explains why she's already so tipsy.

There aren't any glasses, so Heath takes a swig, but before he passes it around, he says, "Should we take bets?"

"On what?" Rose asks.

"How long until the first body turns up in the harbor."

"That's morbid," Rose says with a grimace.

"Maybe. But it's going to happen whether we want it to or not."

Bo and I exchange a look.

Rose exhales a breath through her nose. "Three days," she says meekly, grabbing the bottle from Heath's hands and taking a drink.

"Three and a half," Heath guesses, eyeing her. But I think he only says it to be cute, playing off her number.

Rose hands the bottle to Bo and he holds it low, looking down at it like the answer is somewhere inside. "I hope it doesn't happen at all," he finally says.

"That's not really a guess," Rose points out, lifting an eyebrow.

"Sure it is," Heath defends. "He's guessing no days. Which has never happened, but I suppose it's possible. Maybe no one will drown this summer."

"Unlikely," Rose adds, looking a little disgusted with this whole game.

Bo takes a quick slug of the red wine then holds it out for me. I take it carefully, sliding my thumb down the neck of the bottle, then look up at the group. "Tonight," I say, tipping the bottle to my lips and taking a full swig.

Rose shivers slightly and Heath wraps an arm around her. "Let's talk about something else," she suggests.

"Whatever you want." And he smiles down at her.

"I want to count ghosts!" she chirps, her mood returned.

Heath releases her and frowns, confused. "You want to do what?"

"It's a game Penny and I used to play when we were kids, remember Penny?" She looks to me and I nod. "We'd look for ghosts in the beam of light from the lighthouse as it circled around the island. You get points for every one that you see. One point if you see it on the island and two points if you see one out on the water."

"And you actually see these ghosts?" Heath asks, one eyebrow scrunching up into his forehead.

"Yes. They're everywhere," Rose answers with an artful smirk. "You just have to know where to look."

"Show me," Heath says. And even though he's obviously skeptical, he smiles as she drags him to the window. It's a childish game, but they press their palms against the glass, laughing already.

I hand the bottle back to Bo, and he takes another drink.

"What are you reading?" I ask.

"A book I found in the cottage."

"About what?"

He slides it out from under his arm and sets it on the white desk. *The History and Legend of Sparrow, Oregon.* The front cover is an old photograph of the harbor taken from Ocean Avenue. A cobblestone sidewalk is in the foreground, and the harbor is crowded with old fishing boats and massive steamships. It's more of a pamphlet than a real book, and you can find it at just about every coffee shop and restaurant, and in the lobby of each bed-and-breakfast in town. It's a tourist's guide to everything that happened in Sparrow two centuries ago and everything that has occurred since. It was written by Anderson Fotts, an artist and poet who used to live in Sparrow until his son drowned seven years ago and then he moved away.

"Brushing up on our town's history, huh?"

"Not much else to do in the evening around here." He has a point.

I stare down at the book, knowing its contents all too well. On page thirty-seven is a portrait of the three Swan sisters sketched by Thomas Renshaw, a man who claimed to have met the sisters before

79

they were drowned. Marguerite stands on the left, the tallest of the three, with long auburn hair, full lips, and a sharp jaw, her eyes staring straight ahead. Aurora is in the middle with soft waves of hair and bright full-moon eyes. Hazel, on the right, has plain, smaller features and a braid twisted across her shoulder. Her eyes are focused away, like she's looking at something in the distance. They are all beautiful—captivating, as if they were shifting slightly on the page.

"So you believe in the sisters now?" I ask.

"I haven't decided."

The beam of light slides across his face, and I follow it out to sea, where it cuts through the storm and the impending rain, warning sailors and fishermen that an island lies in their path. "You shouldn't go into town if you don't have to from now on," I tell him.

Both his eyebrows lift. "Why not?"

"It's safer if you stay here on the island. You can't trust anyone in town. . . . Any girl you meet could be one of them."

His eyelids lower, partly concealing the dark tint of his green eyes. Verdant and rueful. He is familiar in a way I can't pin down. Like seeing someone you knew a long time ago, but they've changed in the passing years, become someone different and new. "Even you?" he asks, like I'm joking.

"Even me." I want him to understand how serious I am.

"So no talking to girls?" he clarifies.

"Precisely."

The right side of his mouth turns up into a grin, a fractional parting of lips, and he looks like he might laugh, but then he takes a sip from the bottle instead. I know it sounds absurd, maybe even a little irrational, to warn him against speaking to any girls. But I wouldn't say it if I didn't mean it. Most local boys—if they truly believe in the legend—will steer clear of all girls until the summer solstice. Better to minimize the risk. But Bo, like most outsiders, won't take it seriously. He's in danger just by being in this town.

"That's three!" Rose bellows from the window, and Heath shakes his head. Apparently, Rose is winning the ghost-hunting game. As usual.

"Where are you from?" I ask Bo, after the beam of light passes around the lighthouse a full three times.

"Washington."

I arch an eyebrow at him, expecting him to narrow it down to a city or county or nearest proximity to a Starbucks. But he doesn't. "That's extremely vague," I say. "Can you be more specific?"

His cheekbones tighten, a rivulet of tension. "Near the middle" is all he offers up.

"I can see this won't be easy." I rub my tongue along the roof of my mouth.

"What?"

"Figuring out who you really are."

He taps his fingers against the side of the bottle, a rhythm to a song, I think. "What do you want to know?" he asks.

"Did you go to high school in this fictional, *near-the-middle* town?"

Again I think he's going to smile, but he stifles it before it escapes his lips. "Yeah. I graduated this year."

"So you graduated then promptly escaped your make-believe town?"

"Basically."

"Why'd you leave?"

He ceases the tapping against the bottle. "My brother died."

A blast of wind and sideways rain sprays the windows, and I flinch. "I'm . . . sorry." Bo shakes his head and tips the bottle to his lips. The minutes pass, and the question resting inside my throat starts to feel strangled, cutting off the air to my lungs. "How did he die?"

"It was an accident." He swirls the bottle, and the carmine wine spins up the sides. A mini cyclone.

He looks away from me, like he's considering heading for the door and leaving. Saying good night and vanishing into the storm.

And although I'm curious exactly what kind of accident, I don't press it any further. I can tell he doesn't want to talk about it. And I don't want him to leave, even though our conversation feels tightened along the edges, tugged and constrained because he's holding things in. I'm also not quite ready for this night to be over. There are things I like about him—*no*, that's not right. It's not him exactly. It's me. I like how I feel standing beside him. Eased by his presence. The steady buzz along my thoughts, the ache in my chest tamped down. Softened.

So I take the bottle from him and sit cross-legged on the cold floor, staring out at the storm. I know what it is to lose the people around you. And I take a long, slow drink of the wine, warming my stomach and making my head swim, wiping away the hangover. Bo sits beside me, forearms resting on his bent knees.

"Have you been in a lot of fights before?" I ask after a stretch of silence.

"What?"

"On the beach last night, with Lon, you seemed like you weren't afraid to fight him."

"I don't like fighting, if that's what you mean. But yeah, I've been in a few. Although not because I wanted to." He exhales slowly, and I think he's going to change the subject. His lips stall partway open. "My brother was always getting himself into trouble," he continues. "He liked taking risks—jumping into rivers in the middle of winter, climbing bridges to watch the sunrise, driving his truck too fast down the centerline just for the rush. Things like that. And sometimes he'd say things he shouldn't, or hit on girls he shouldn't, and find himself in a fistfight." Bo shakes his head. "He thought it was funny, but I was always the one who had to step in and save him, keep him from getting his ass kicked. He was my older brother, but my parents were always asking me to keep an eye on him. But since he died . . ." His gaze dips to the floor, voice trailing, memories sliding through him. "I haven't had to defend him." I hand him the bottle of wine, and he takes a long drink. Holding it between his knees with both hands, he asks, "Do you ever think about leaving this town?"

I lift my chin. "Of course."

"But?"

"It's complicated."

His thumb taps the neck of the bottle. "Isn't that what people say when they just don't want to admit the truth?"

"Probably . . . but the truth is complicated. My life is complicated."

"So after you graduate, you're not going to leave Sparrow— you're not going to college somewhere?"

I shrug. "Maybe. It's not something I think about." I shift uneasily on the floor, wishing we could change the subject back to him.

"What's keeping you here?"

I almost laugh but don't, because the answer isn't funny. Nothing about the reasons why I'm stuck here is funny. "My family," I finally say, because I have to say something. "My mom."

"She doesn't want you to leave?"

"It's not that. She's just . . . she's not well." I look away from him, shaking my head. The truth slips between the edges of the lies.

"You don't want to talk about it?" he asks.

"Just like you don't want to talk about where you're from," I say softly. "Or what happened to . . ." I almost bring up his brother again but stop myself.

He makes a low exhaling sound then hands the bottle back to me. We're swapping sips of wine instead of sharing the truth. Like a drinking game we just invented: If you don't want to talk about something, take a drink.

"There're always reasons to stay," he says. "You just need to find one reason to leave." His eyes hold mine, and something familiar stirs inside me—something I want to pretend isn't there. A flicker that illuminates the darkest part of my insides. And I absorb it like sunlight.

"I guess I haven't found that reason yet," I say. I know my cheeks are blazing pink, I can feel the heat against my skin, but I don't look away from him.

The storm blows against the windows, rattling the glass in the casings.

Bo looks out at the rain, and I watch his gaze, wishing I could pluck more thoughts from his head. Pain rests behind his eyes, and I feel myself suddenly wanting to touch his face, his skin, his fingertips.

Then, like a machine being switched off, the wind outside stops, the rain scatters and turns to mist, and the moody black clouds begin to push farther south, revealing a backdrop of black sky with pinhole pricks for stars.

Rose hops up from the floor and twirls herself in a circle. "We need to go make wishes," she announces. "Tonight."

"The shipwreck?" Heath asks from his place still sprawled out on the floor.

"The shipwreck!" she repeats.

"What's the shipwreck?" Bo asks, flinching his gaze away from mine for the first time.

"You'll see," Rose answers.

We tromp through the darkness and down the wood path to the dock. Heath insists we take his boat, and we pile into the small, narrow dinghy. Bo takes my hand, even though I don't need it to keep my balance—I'm as steady on the water as I am on land—and he doesn't let go until I'm seated beside him on one of the benches.

The interior is sparse and tidy, a stack of orange life vests strapped to the gunwale. Heath pulls on the engine cord once, and the motor revs to life.

Maybe I shouldn't go with them. It's late, and my head rocks gently with the sloppiness of wine purring through my bloodstream. But the looseness is also addictive; it rounds out the rough edges of my mind, the worry that is constant there, that lives beneath my fingernails and at the base of my neck.

So I grip the edge of the bench seat, and slowly we chug across the eerily calm harbor. It's as if the water has died, surrendered after the storm. The ruins of sunken ships are like tombstones jutting up from the water ahead of us, jagged spikes of metal, rusted, turning to sand from the relentless tide.

"I wish we had more wine," Rose murmurs, but her voice is soft and unconcerned, so no one responds.

The green mast, covered in a layer of moss and algae, rises the tallest of all the wreckage in the harbor, the flag that once hung from its peak long ago disintegrated and blown away.

Heath slows the boat as we approach then kills the engine entirely so that we drift within only a few feet of the mast. Dark, murky outlines of the rest of the ship sit beneath us, close enough to tear apart the propeller on Heath's boat if he didn't shut off the motor when he did. It's dangerous to be this close to wreckage, but it's also why kids come out here, to test their nerve. If it weren't dangerous, it wouldn't be fun.

"Did anyone bring coins?" Rose asks.

Bo looks from Rose to me. "For what?"

"To make a wish," I tell him.

"This was a pirate ship," Heath explains. "The legend says that if you drop a coin down to the dead pirates who still haunt the ship, they will grant you a wish."

"There's probably hundreds—no, thousands of dollars in quarters down there," Rose says, waving a hand in the air as if she were a magician.

"Or just a pile of pennies," I say.

Heath checks his pockets and produces a dime and a quarter. Bo pulls out three quarters and several pennies. "The higher denomination the coin, the greater the chance that they'll grant your wish.

Pirates are greedy, obviously," Rose says as she snatches the quarter from Heath's palm.

Bo and I each take a penny, and Heath holds the dime. Apparently, Bo and I aren't very optimistic about our wishes actually coming true.

But still, I know what my wish will be—the same wish I've always had.

We each extend our arms over the side of the boat, fists clenched, and Rose counts us down from three. "Two . . . one," she says, and we all open our palms and let our coins plop into the water. They flit down quickly, reflective at first as they sink among the serrated, cavernous angles of wreckage, and then they're gone.

We are still for a moment, holding our breath . . . waiting for something immediate to happen. But when nothing does, Bo lets out a breath of air, and I cross my arms, feeling chilled. Anxious even.

We shouldn't be here, I think suddenly. Out on the water so soon after the sisters have returned. It's dangerous, risky for Heath and Bo. And something doesn't feel right. "We should head back to the island," I suggest, trying not to sound panicked, looking up at Heath, hoping he'll start the engine.

The ocean seems too calm. The singing now gone, the storm passed. Only a ripple laps up against the side of the boat.

I sense it even before I see it: The temperature drops; the sky yawns open so huge that the stars could swallow us like a whale drinking down a school of fish. The sea vibrates.

My eyes lock on something dark swaying with the current. A body is drifting faceup only a couple yards from the boat, eyes open but lost of all color. The first dead boy.

* * *

"Oh my God," Rose screeches, eyes bursting to globes, finger pointing at the corpse.

The arms are spread wide, the legs half-sunk beneath the water, and a navy-blue sweatshirt hangs from the torso like it's two sizes too big.

"Shit," Heath mutters under his breath, like he's afraid to speak too loudly or he might wake the dead.

The moon breaks through the clouds, shining over the water. But it's not a milky white, it's a pale red. Blood on the moon—a bad omen. We shouldn't have come out here.

"Who is it?" Rose asks, her voice trembling, fingers reaching for something to grab on to. Like she's reaching for the body.

The face comes into view: ashen, hollow cheeks. Short blond hair swaying outward from a pale scalp. "Gregory Dunn," Heath answers, wiping a palm over his face. "He graduated this year. Was going to college out east in the fall. Boston, I think."

Bo and I are completely silent. He touches the side of the boat, blinks, but doesn't speak.

"We have to do something!" Rose says, standing up suddenly. "We can't leave him in the water." She takes a step forward, toward the starboard side of the dinghy, which has now drifted closer to the body. But her movements shift the boat off center, and it rocks toward the water.

"Rose," I bark, reaching out for her. Heath makes an attempt to grab for her too, but the momentum has tipped the boat too far and she stumbles, her legs unbalanced, hands scrambling to brace herself on something. She pitches headfirst into the icy water.

Bo, for the first time, reacts. He's at the side of the boat before I've even had time to process what's happened. Ripples cascade outward toward the corpse of Gregory Dunn. Thankfully, Rose didn't land *on* him when she went over.

Bo leans over the starboard side of the boat, plunges his arms down into the frigid water, wrapping his hands beneath Rose's arms, and hoists her in one swift motion back into the boat. She collapses instantly, knees pulled up, shaking and convulsing uncontrollably. Health grabs a blanket from under one of the seats and wraps it around her. "We need to get her to shore," Bo says in a rush, and Heath starts the motor again. I crouch down next to Rose, an arm wrapped around her, and we race toward the marina, leaving the body of Gregory Dunn behind.

When we reach the shore, I walk quickly up the docks to the metal bell that hangs from a wood archway facing the harbor. The Death Bell, everyone calls it. Whenever a body is discovered, someone will ring the bell to alert the town that a body has been found. It was installed twenty years ago. And during the month of June, up until the summer solstice, the bell becomes the tolling sound of death.

Each time it rings, locals wince and the tourists grab their cameras.

I reach for the rough fiber of the rope and clank it twice against the inside of the bell. A hollow tolling sound echoes up through town, bouncing among the damp walls of shops and homes, waking everyone from sleep.

It takes an hour for the police and local fisherman to finally head back into port, having retrieved the body of Gregory Dunn from the water. They took their time collecting any evidence, of which there will be none. No blood, no marks, no sign of a struggle. There never is.

Rose is shivering beside me, sipping numbly on a cup of hot chocolate that Heath retrieved from the Chowder, which opened early—three a.m.—to serve the townspeople who awoke to come see the first body pulled from the sea.

We all wait on the docks, watching the parade of boats slice through the water. People stand in their pajamas and wool caps and rain boots. Even children have been pulled from bed, stumbling down with blankets slung over their shoulders to see this annual, gruesome event.

But the local police have learned to minimize the spectacle. And when they move the body onto a stretcher on the dock, they make sure it's completely covered. But people still snap photos, kids still begin to cry, and people gasp then cover their mouths with gloved hands.

"You were right," Bo whispers against my ear when the ambulance whirls away with Gregory Dunn's body strapped onto a cold metal stretcher in the back. "You said it would happen tonight, and it did."

I shake my head. It's not a contest I wanted to win.

The crowd around us slowly dissolves, and people begin tromping back to their beds or to the Chowder to discuss this first drowning. Heath approaches, eyebrows cut sharply into a grave frown. "I'm going to take Rose home," he says. "She's pretty shook up."

"Okay." I glance to Rose, who has already slipped away from my side and is walking up the dock, the striped red-and-gray blanket from Heath's boat falling from her shoulders. She looks stunned, and I know I should probably go with her, but she seems to only want Heath right now, so I let him take her.

"I'll come back to take you guys over to the island," Heath says before walking after Rose.

I nod. Then Bo and I follow the drowsy stream of people to Shipley Pier, where a waitress at the Chowder is wearing blue polka-dot pajamas and fuzzy Ugg boots. "Coffee?" she asks us. I scan her face, settling on her eyes, but she looks normal. Human.

"Sure," Bo answers.

"Black tea, please," I tell her.

She frowns briefly and makes a snort sound, like my request for tea will require more effort than she's willing to give at this hour, but she shuffles away in her boots, and Bo and I stand at the end of the pier, leaning against the railing and facing out to sea, waiting for the sunrise.

Voices murmur all around us, and speculation begins to circulate almost immediately. Over the next couple weeks, we will be in the middle of an all-out witch hunt.

Several girls from school have gathered on the outdoor deck, sipping coffee and popping bits of blueberry muffin and biscotti into their mouths, chatting loudly even though it's the middle of the night and they can't possibly be fully awake. I examine their features, the hue of their eyes, the chalky porcelain of their skin. I am looking for something unnatural, a gossamer creature suspended behind human flesh. But I don't see it.

The waitress brings us our drinks without even a smile. "How could Gregory Dunn have been led into the harbor without anyone seeing?" Bo asks, keeping his voice low, holding his coffee between his hands but not yet taking a drink.

I lift my shoulders, biting my lower lip. "The Swan sisters don't *want* to be seen," I say. "They've been doing this for two hundred years; they're good at it. They're good at not getting caught." I circle a finger around the rim of my white cup.

"You say it like you don't want them to get caught, like the town deserves it."

"Maybe it does." The anger I feel for this town, these people, burns inside me—it beats against my skull. So many injustices—so much death. They've always treated outsiders cruelly, cast them off because they didn't belong. "The sisters were killed by the people of this town," I say, my voice weighted with something that doesn't sound quite like me. "Drowned unfairly because they fell in love with the wrong men. Maybe they have a right to their revenge."

"To kill innocent people?"

"How do you know Gregory Dunn didn't deserve it?" I can hardly believe my own words.

"I don't," he says sharply. "But I doubt every person who's been drowned did deserve it."

I know he's right, yet I feel inclined to argue the point. I just want him to understand *why* it happens. Why the sisters return every year. It's not without cause. "It's their retribution," I say.

Bo stands up straight and takes a sip of his coffee.

"Look, I'm not saying it's right," I add. "But you can't start thinking that you can prevent it or change what happens here. Gregory Dunn was just the first. There will be more. Trying to stop it has only ever made things worse."

"What do you mean?"

"The town has killed innocent girls because they thought they were inhabited by one of the sisters. It's just better to leave it alone. There's nothing you can do."

The sun starts to edge up from the east, dull and pink at first. At the marina, fishermen begin slogging down the docks to their boats. And then I spot Heath, walking down Ocean Avenue, returned to give us a ride back to the island.

Bo doesn't speak, his mind likely wheeling over thoughts that don't line up: trying to resolve what he's seen tonight. A dead body. A two centuries–long curse. A town that has accepted its fate.

It's a lot to take in. And he only just got here. It's going to get worse.

We start down the pier, the light changing, turning pale orange as it streaks over the town. Two girls are walking toward us, headed to the Chowder. My gaze slides over them briefly.

It's Olivia and Lola—the best friends who danced around the bonfire at the Swan party shortly after the singing started. They are both fully dressed, no pj's or messy hair, as if the death of Gregory Dunn were a social event they wouldn't dare miss. One they were expecting. Lola's dyed-black hair is woven back in a French braid. Olivia's is loose across her shoulders, long and wavy. Her nose ring glints against the encroaching sun.

And when my eyes meet hers, I know: Marguerite Swan is occupying her body.

The white, spectral image of Marguerite hovers beneath Olivia's soft skin. Like looking through a thin pane of glass, or beneath the surface of a lake all the way down to the sandy bottom. It isn't a clear, crisp outline of Marguerite, but like a memory of her, wavy and unsettled, drifting inside this poor girl's body.

I've found her.

A part of me had dared to hope I wouldn't see them this year, that I could avoid the sisters, avoid the ritual of death that befalls this town. But I won't be so lucky after all.

I wish I weren't staring through Olivia's snow-white skin at Marguerite hidden beneath. But I am. And I'm the only one standing on Shipley Pier who can. This is the secret I can't tell Bo—the reason why I know the Swan sisters are real.

Her lurid gaze settles on me, not Olivia's—Olivia is gone—but Marguerite's, and then she smiles faintly at me as they stride past.

I feel briefly paralyzed. My upper lip twitches. They continue down the pier, Lola chatting about something that my ears can't seem to focus on, oblivious that her best friend is no longer her best friend. Just before they reach the Chowder, I glance over my shoulder at them. Olivia's hair swings effortlessly over her shoulders and down her back. "You all right?" Bo asks, turning to look at Olivia and Lola.

"We need to get back to the island," I say, spinning back around. "It's not safe here."

Marguerite has found a host in the body of Olivia Greene. And Marguerite is always the first to make a kill. Gregory Dunn was hers. The drowning season has started.

PERFUMERY

The Swan sisters might have dabbled in witchcraft in the years before they arrived in Sparrow—an occasional hex or potion to detour jealous wives or bad spirits—but they certainly wouldn't call themselves witches, as the people of Sparrow had accused.

They were businesswomen, shop owners, and when they arrived in Sparrow two centuries ago, they brought with them an array of exotic scents to be crafted into delicate perfumes and fragrant balms. At first the women in town gathered together inside the Swan Perfumery, swooning over scents that reminded them of the civilized world. They purchased small glass bottles of rose water and honey, lemongrass and gardenia. All perfectly blended, subtle and intricate.

It wasn't until Marguerite, the oldest of the sisters at nineteen, was caught in bed with a ship's captain, that everything began to crumble. The sisters couldn't be blamed. It wasn't witchcraft that seduced the men of Sparrow—it was something much simpler. The Swan sisters had a charm that was born into their blood, like their mother: Men could not resist the softness of their skin or the gleam of their aquamarine eyes.

Love came easily and often for them. While Marguerite liked

older men with money and power, Aurora fell for boys who others said couldn't be seduced—she liked a challenge, typically falling for more than one boy at a time. Hazel was more particular. Precise. She didn't delight in the affection of numerous men, like her sisters, yet they adored her anyway, a trail of heartbroken boys often left in her wake.

The sisters brought about their fate like someone stumbling into a poison ivy bush in the dark, unaware of the consequences that would befall them by morning.

SEVEN

For three awful weeks, tourists and locals will accuse nearly every girl of being a Swan sister. Any offense, any deviation in behavior—a sudden interest in boys they used to despise, spending too many nights out late, a twitch or flick of an eye that seems out of place—will make you a suspect.

But I know who the sisters really are.

Heath gives us a ride across the harbor, and when we reach the island, we all say a swift good-bye, and then Heath chugs back to town.

Bo and I don't speak as we walk up the path, until we reach the place where the walkway splits. A mound of old buoys and crab pots that have washed ashore over the years sit just to the left of the walkway. A decomposing heap. A reminder that this place has more death than life.

"I'm sorry," I say. "We never should have gone out there." I'm used to the gruesome shock of death, but Bo isn't. And I'm sure he's starting to consider leaving this place as soon as possible. And I wouldn't blame him if he did.

"It wasn't your fault." His eyelashes lower, and he kicks a pebble from the walkway. It lands in a patch of yellow grass and vanishes.

"You should get some sleep." We've both been awake all night, and the delirium of exhaustion is starting to feel like a freight train clamoring back and forth between my ears.

He nods, removes his hands from his coat pockets, and heads up the path to Anchor Cottage. He doesn't even say good-bye.

I won't be surprised if he starts packing as soon as he gets back to the cottage.

Mom is already awake and listening to the radio in the kitchen when I walk through the back door. It's a local station that announces storm warnings and tide reports, and today the host, Buddy Kogens, is talking about the body that authorities pulled from the water early this morning.

"This town is black with death," she says morosely, facing the kitchen sink, her hands gripping the white tile edge. "It's saturated with it." I don't answer her. I'm too tired. So I slip out into the hall and upstairs to my bedroom. From the window, I see Bo moving up the path, almost to Anchor Cottage near the center of the island. His gait is slow and deliberate. He looks back once, as if he feels me watching him, and I duck back from the window.

Something nags at me. I just can't put my finger on it.

The afternoon sky shatters apart, revealing a swath of milky blue.

Last night we found Gregory Dunn's body in the harbor.

This morning we watched the sunrise from the pier as his body was brought ashore.

Day one of the Swan season: one boy dead.

I slip from bed, rubbing my eyes, still groggy even though the sun has been up for hours, and dress in an old pair of faded jeans and a navy-blue sweater. I take my time. I stand at the dresser, not meeting my own gaze in the mirror on the wall, running my fingers over a meager collection of things. A bottle of old perfume—Mom's—which I bring to my nose. The vanilla scent has turned sharp and musty, taken on the tinge of alcohol. There's a silver dish filled with pebbles gathered from the shore: aqua and coral and emerald green. Two candles sit at one corner of the dresser, the wicks hardly burned down. And hanging by a length of yellow ribbon from the top of the mirror is a triangle piece of glass with flowers pressed between it. I can't dredge up the memory of where it came from. A birthday gift, maybe? Something Rose gave me? I stare at it, the small pink flowers flattened and dried, preserved for eternity.

I turn and lean against the dresser, taking stock of the room. Sparse and tidy. White walls. White everything. Clean. No bright colors anywhere. My room says little about me. Or maybe it says it all. A room easily abandoned. Left behind with hardly a hint that a girl ever lived here at all.

Mom is not in the house. The floorboards groan as I walk down the stairs into the kitchen. A plate of freshly baked orange muffins sits on the table. That's two mornings in a row she's made breakfast. The two mornings that Bo's been on the island. She can't help herself, she won't let a stranger starve, even though she'd easily let herself or me go hungry. Old habits. The social decorum of a small town—feed anyone who comes to visit.

I grab two muffins then head out onto the front porch.

The air is warm. Calm and placated. Seagulls spin in dizzying circles overhead, swooping down to the steep shoreline and snatching up fish caught in the tide pools. I catch the silhouette of Mom inside the greenhouse, walking among the decomposing plants.

I peer across the island to Anchor Cottage. Is Bo still inside? Or did he pack his bag and find a way off the island while I slept? A knot tightens in my stomach. If I find the cottage empty, cold, and dark, how will I feel? Despair? Like my gut has been ripped out?

But at least I'll know he's safe, escaped this town before he wound up like Gregory Dunn.

A noise draws my focus away from the cottage. A low sawing sound—the cutting of wood. It echoes over the island. And it's coming from the orchard.

I follow the wood-slat path deeper into the island, but before I've even stepped into the rows of perfectly spaced trees, I can tell that things are different. The wood ladder that normally rests at the farthest row against a half-dead Anjou tree, protected from the wind, has been moved closer to the center of the grove and has been positioned beside one of the Braeburn trees. And standing on the highest rung, leaning into the thicket of branches, is Bo.

He didn't leave after all. He didn't do the smart thing and flee when he had the opportunity. Relief swells inside my chest.

"Hey," he says down to me, holding on to one of the low branches. The sun makes long shadows through the trees. "Is everything okay?"

He takes several steps down the ladder, his hat turned backward on his head.

"Fine," I answer. "I just thought maybe you'd . . ." My voice dissipates.

"What?"

"Nothing. I'm just glad you're still here."

He squints and wipes at his forehead. "You thought I would leave?"

"Maybe."

The sunlight catches his eyes, making the dark green seem like pieces of emerald glass, an entire world contained within them. His gray T-shirt sticks to his chest and arms. His cheeks are flushed. I watch him a moment too long.

"Have you slept?" I ask.

"Not yet." He smiles from one side of his mouth—his mood seems to have lifted slightly since this morning. While I was curled up in bed, sheets pulled over my head to block out the sun, he's been out here working. Sleep probably seemed like an impossibility after last night, after what he saw. "I wanted to get started on the orchard." He hooks a wide-toothed handsaw over a low, crooked limb then climbs down the ladder, brushing his hands across his jeans.

I hand him one of the freshly baked orange muffins. "What are you doing exactly?"

He cranes his head up to the tangled limbs above us, squinting. The scar beneath his left eye pinches together. "Cutting out any new growth. We only want the oldest limbs to stay because those are the ones that produce fruit. And see how some of the branches grow straight up or down? Those also need to go." He blinks away from the sun then looks at me.

"Can I help?"

He sets the muffin on a rung of the ladder then lifts the hat from his head and scrubs a hand through his short hair. "If you want to."

"I do."

He drags out a second ladder from the old woodshed and finds another, smaller handsaw. He places the ladder against the tree next to the one he had been pruning and I climb carefully to the top, a little unsteady at first as it wobbles beneath me. Once I feel settled, I realize I'm shrouded by a veil of limbs, hidden in a world of branches, and then Bo climbs up behind me, standing one rung down. He extends the handsaw up to me and then wraps his arms around my waist, gripping the ladder to keep me from falling.

"What do you see?" he asks, his voice at my neck, my ear, and I shiver slightly at the feeling of his breath against my skin.

"I'm not sure," I say truthfully.

"The trees haven't bloomed yet," he explains. "But they will soon, so we have to take out all the branches that are crowding the older limbs—the *old wood*, it's called."

"This small one," I say, tapping it with my finger. "It's growing straight up from a thicker branch, and it still looks a little green."

"Exactly," he praises. And I lift the saw, holding it to the limb. On my first stroke across the branch, the saw slips out, and I lurch forward to keep from dropping it. Bo tightens his arms around me, and the ladder teeters beneath us. My heartbeat spikes upward. "The saw takes some getting used to," Bo adds.

I nod, gripping the top of the ladder. And then I feel the sharp stinging in my left index finger. I turn my palm up so I can examine it, and blood beads to the surface along the outer edge of my finger. When the blade slipped, it must have cut into my skin where my hand was holding the branch. Bo notices it at the same time, and he leans closer into me, reaching around to grab my finger.

"You're cut," he says. The blood drips down the tip of my finger and plummets all the way to the ground, six feet below. I notice Otis and Olga sitting in the swath of sun between rows, orange-and-white heads titled upward, watching us.

"It's okay," I say. But he yanks out a white handkerchief from his back pocket and presses it to the cut, staunching the bleeding. "It's not that deep," I add, even though it stings pretty good. The white fabric turns red almost instantly.

"We should clean it out," he says.

"No. Really, I'm fine."

This close, with his face directly beside mine, I can feel each breath as it rises in his chest, see his lips move as he exhales. His heart is racing faster than it should. Like he was worried I might have just cut my entire hand off, and it would have been his fault for allowing me to wield a saw.

He lifts the handkerchief away to inspect the cut, leaning into me.

"Do we need to amputate?" I ask lightheartedly.

"Most likely." His eyes slide to mine, the corner of his mouth lifting. He tears off a small strip of the handkerchief, holding my hand in his, then ties the narrow piece of fabric around my finger like a makeshift tourniquet. "This should keep the finger from falling off until we operate."

"Thanks," I say, smiling even though it still burns. My lips so close to his I can almost taste the saltiness of his skin.

He slides what's left of his handkerchief into his back pocket and straightens up behind me so that his chest is no longer against my back. "It's probably safer with just one person on the ladder," he amends.

I nod, agreeing, and he climbs down, jumping the last couple feet to the ground and leaving me weightless atop the ladder without him.

He scales back up his ladder, and we work side by side, sawing away the unwanted limbs on each tree. I'm careful to keep my fingers out of the way, and soon I feel confident with the saw. It's a tedious, slow process, but gradually we work our way down the first row.

This becomes our routine.

Each morning we meet in the orchard, moving our ladders to a new row. Bringing the fruit trees back to life. I don't mind the work. It feels purposeful. And by the end of the week my hands have a roughness like I've never felt before. My skin has browned, and my eyes taper away from the midday sun. It hasn't rained once all week, and the summer air feels light and buoyant and sweet.

On Saturday we collect all the sawn limbs and pile them at the north end of the orchard. And just after sunset we set them ablaze.

The sooty night sky sparks and shivers, the stars dulled by the inferno we've created on land.

"Tomorrow we'll cut down the dead trees," Bo says, arms crossed and staring into the fire.

"How?" I ask.

"We'll saw them down to stumps then burn them out from the ground."

"How long will that take?"

"A couple days."

I feel like I've been suspended in time this last week, protected from a season that comes each year like a violent squall. In moments, I've even forgotten entirely about the world outside this little island. But I know it will find a way in. It always does.

* * *

It takes three days to trim the two dead apple trees and one pear tree down to only stumps. And by the end of the third day, my arms can barely move. They ache just lifting them through my T-shirt in the morning.

We walk through the orchard, examining our hard work—today we will torch the three tree stumps—when Bo stops beside the single oak tree at the center of the grove, the one with the heart cut into the trunk. It looks like a ghost tree, white moss dripping from the limbs, two hundred years of history hidden in its trunk. "Maybe we should burn this one down too," he comments, surveying the limbs. "It's pretty old and not that healthy. We could plant an apple tree in its place."

I press my palm against the trunk, over the etched heart. "No. I want to leave it."

He lifts a hand to block the sun.

"It feels wrong to cut it down," I add. "This tree meant something to someone." A gentle wind blows my ponytail across my shoulder.

"I doubt whoever carved that heart is still alive to care," he points out.

"Maybe not, but I still want to keep it."

He pats the trunk of the tree. "All right. It's your orchard."

Bo is careful and precise before he lights the three dead trees on fire, making sure we have several buckets of water and a shovel at each tree in case we need to dampen the flames. He strikes a match and instantly the first stump ignites. He does the same to the next two trees, and we watch the flames slowly work their way through the wood.

The sun fades, and the flames lick upward from the tall stumps like arms reaching for the stars.

I make two mugs of hot black tea with cardamom then carry them down to the orchard, and we stay up to watch the fires burn through the night. The air is smoky and sweet with apples that will never bloom because these trees have reached their end.

We sit on a stack of cut logs watching the fires burn for nearly an hour.

"I heard your mom used to read tea leaves," Bo says, blowing on his tea to cool it.

"Where did you hear that?"

"In town, when I was looking for work and found the flyer. I had asked someone how to get to the island, and they thought I was looking to have my fortune read."

"She doesn't do it anymore, not since my dad left." I lean forward and pull up a clump of brittle beach grass at my feet then roll it between my palms to crush it, feeling the broken fibers before I scatter the fragments back across the ground. I have a memory of my dad walking across the island, kneeling down occasionally to pull up a gathering of dandelions or clover or moss, then rubbing them between his worn hands. He liked the way the world felt. Loam and green. The earth giving up things we often ignored. I wipe the memory away with a quick closing of my eyes. It hurts to think of him. Pain skipping through my chest.

"Do you read tea leaves?" He asks with a quirk of an eyebrow.

"Not really." A short laugh escapes my throat. "So don't get your hopes up. I won't be revealing your future any time soon."

"But you *can* do it?"

"Used to. But I'm out of practice."

He holds out his mug for me to take.

"You don't fully believe in the Swan sisters, but you believe that fortunes can be seen in tea leaves?" I ask, not accepting his mug.

"I'm unpredictable."

I smile and raise both eyebrows at him. "I can't read the leaves with liquid still in the cup. You have to finish it and then the pattern of leaves left inside is where your fortune lives."

He looks down into his mug like he might be able to read his own future. "Spoken like a true witch."

I shake my head and smile. It's hardly witchcraft. It doesn't involve spells or potions or anything quite so intriguing. But I don't correct him.

He takes a long drink of his tea and finishes it in one gulp, then extends it out to me.

I hesitate. I really don't want to do this. But he's looking at me with such anticipation that I take the cup and hold it between both palms. I tilt it to one side, then the other, examining the whirl of leaves around the edges. "Hmm," I say, as if I were considering something important, then peek at him from the corner of my eye. He looks like he's moved closer to the edge of the log, about to fall off if I don't tell him immediately what I see. I lift my head and look at him fully. "Long life, true love, piles of gold," I say, then set the mug on the log between us.

One of his eyebrows lifts. He glances at the mug then at me. I try to keep a straight face, but my lips start to tug upward. "Very astute reading," he says, smiling back then laughing. "Perhaps you shouldn't make a career of reading tea leaves," he says. "But I do hope you're right about my future on all accounts."

"Oh, I'm right," I say, still grinning. "The leaves don't lie."

He laughs again, and I take a sip of my own tea.

Sparks dance and writhe up into the sky. And I realize how at ease I am sitting here with Bo. How normal it feels. As if this were something we do each evening: set trees on fire and laugh together in the dark.

I don't feel the gnawing at the base of my skull that usually plagues me each summer—a ticking clock counting down the days until the summer solstice and the end of the Swan season. Bo has distracted me from all the awful things lurking in this town, in the harbor, and in my mind.

"People used to say that the apples and pears that grew on the island had magical healing properties," I tell him, tilting my head back to watch the waves of smoke spiral upward like mini tornados. "They thought they could heal ailments like a bee sting or hay fever or even a broken heart. They would sell for twice the normal price in town."

"Did your family used to sell them?" he asks.

"No. This was long before my family lived here. But if the orchards could produce edible fruit again, maybe we could sell it."

"By next summer, you should be able to harvest ten to twenty pounds from each tree. It'll be a lot of work, so you'll probably need to hire more help."

He says "you," like he won't be around to see it.

"Thank you for doing this," I say, "for bringing them back to life."

He nods and I touch my index finger, now wrapped with a

Band-Aid. The stinging is gone, the cut almost healed. But it will probably leave a tiny scar. My gaze slides to Bo, to the scar beneath his left eye, and I have to ask, "How did you get that?" I nod to the smooth, waxy line of skin.

He blinks, the scar puckering together, as if he feels the pain of it again. "I jumped out of a tree when I was nine. A branch cut me open."

"Did you get stitches?"

"Five. I remember it hurting like hell."

"Why'd you jump out of a tree?"

"My brother dared me. For a week he had been trying to convince me that I could fly if I had enough speed." His eyes smile at the memory. "I believed him. And I also probably just wanted to impress him since he was my older brother. So I jumped."

He tilts his head back to look up at the sky, sewn together with stars.

"Maybe you didn't have enough speed," I suggest, smiling and craning my head back to look up at the same stars.

"Probably not. But I don't think I'll test the theory again." His smile fades. "My brother felt terrible," he goes on. "He carried me all the way back to our house while I sobbed. And after I got stitches, he sat beside my bed and read me comics for a week. You'd think I lost a leg, he felt so guilty."

"He sounds like a good brother," I say.

"Yeah. He was."

A breath of silence weaves between us.

Sparks swirl up from the charred tree trunk into the dark. Bo clears his throat, still staring into the flames. "How long has that sailboat been sitting down by the dock?"

The question surprises me. I wasn't expecting it. "A few years, I guess."

"Who does it belong to?" His tone is careful, as though he's unsure if he should be asking. The focus has quickly shifted from him to me. From one loss to another.

I let the words tumble around inside my skull before I answer, conjuring up a past that lies dormant in my mind. "My father."

He waits before he speaks again, sensing that he's venturing into delicate territory. "Does it still sail?"

"I think so."

I stare down into the mug held between my palms, absorbing its warmth.

"I'd like to take it out sometime," Bo says cautiously, "see if it still sails."

"You know how to sail?"

His lips part open—a gentle smile—and he looks down at his feet like he's about to reveal a secret. "I spent almost every summer sailing on Lake Washington growing up."

"Did you live in Seattle?" I ask, hoping to narrow down the city where he's from.

"Near there." His answer is just as vague as the last time I asked. "But a much smaller town."

"You realize I have more questions about you than answers." He was built to conceal secrets, his face revealing not even a hint of what's buried inside. It's both intriguing and infuriating.

"I can say the same about you."

I draw my lips to one side and squeeze the mug tighter between my hands. He's right. We're deadlocked in a strange battle of secrecy.

Neither of us is willing to tell the truth. Neither of us is willing to let the other one in. "You can take the sailboat out if you want," I say, standing up and tucking a loose strand of hair back behind my ear. "It's late. I think I'll head up to the house." The flames burning in each stump have been reduced to hot embers, slowly chewing through the last of the wood.

"I'll stay up and make sure the fires are out completely."

"Good night," I say, pausing to look back at him.

"Night."

EIGHT

The orchard looks different. Pruned and tidy, like a manicured English garden. It reminds me of how it used to be in summers past, when ripe fruit would hang bright and vibrant beneath the sun, beckoning the birds to pick at the ones that had fallen to the ground. The air always smelled of sweet and salt. Fruit and sea.

In the early morning I walk down the rows. The three burned stumps send out thin strands of smoke even though they are now nothing but piles of ash.

I wonder how late Bo stayed up, watching the last of the embers turn black. I wonder if he slept at all. I walk to his cottage and stand facing the door. I lift my fist, about to knock, when the door swings open, and I suck in a startled breath.

"Hey," he says reflexively.

"Hi . . . sorry. I was just about to knock," I stammer. "I came to say . . . good morning." A dumb explanation. I'm not even sure why I've come.

His eyebrows screw into a confused line, but his lips form an easy half grin. He's wearing a plain white shirt and jeans that sag low over his hips, and his hair is pressed to one side like he's just woken up. "I was coming out to check on the trees," he says. "Make sure they didn't reignite in the last couple hours."

"They're only smoldering," I tell him. "I was just up there."

He nods then extends his arm to open the door wider. "You want to come inside? I can make coffee."

I step past him, feeling the warmth of the cottage fold over me.

Otis and Olga are already inside, curled up on the couch as if this was their new home. As if they now belonged to Bo. There is no fire, but the windows are all open, a warm breeze purring through the cottage. The weather has shifted, turned mild and buoyant—the air blowing in from the sea stirs up the dust motes and scares away the ghosts. Every day that he's here on the island, in the cottage, I can feel the space changing, becoming brighter.

Bo stands in the kitchen, his back to me, and turns on the faucet in the sink, filling the coffeepot with water. He's tan after a week outside under the sun. And the muscles in his shoulders flex beneath the thin cotton of his shirt.

"How do you like your coffee?" he asks, turning around to face me, and I quickly flick my eyes away so he doesn't catch me staring.

"Black is fine."

"Good . . . because I don't have anything else." I wonder if he bought coffee grounds in town before I invited him out to the island. Brought it with him in his backpack? Since I doubt there was coffee here when he moved in.

A stack of books sits on the low table in front of the couch and more books are lined up on the floor, all pulled from the shelves. I pick up a book resting on the arm of the couch. *Encyclopedia: Celtic Myths and Fables Vol. 2.*

"What are all these?" I ask.

Bo dries his hands on a kitchen towel then walks into the living room. Otis wakes up and begins rubbing a paw over one ear.

"All the books in here are about legends and folklore," he answers.

I run a finger over a row of books on the bookshelf beside the fireplace. The spines are printed with titles like *Native American Legends of the Northwest*, *How to Break an Unwanted Curse*, and *Witches and Warlocks: A Guide to Understanding*. They are all like this—a library of books on topics of the unnatural, the mystical, similar to what's happening in Sparrow. Collected by someone and stored in the cottage . . . *but who?*

"You didn't know?" Bo asks. Coffee begins streaming into the glass pot behind him, the warm roasted scent filling the room.

I shake my head. *No, I didn't know these were in here. I had no idea.* I sink down onto the couch, touching the page of a book left open on one of the cushions. "Why are you reading them?" I ask, closing the book with a *thud* then setting it on the coffee table.

"I don't know. Because they're here, I guess."

Olga hops down from the couch and coils herself around Bo's leg, purring up at him, and he bends down to scratch gently behind her ear. "And what about the Swan sisters—do you believe in them now?" I ask.

"Not exactly. But I also don't believe people drown themselves for no reason."

"Then why are they drowning?"

"I'm not sure."

My foot taps against the floor, my heart thuds inside my rib cage—a scratching at my thoughts. *So many books. All these books.*

Placed here—hidden in here. "And what about the singing from the harbor—how do you explain that?"

"I can't," he answers. "But it doesn't mean it won't eventually be explained. Have you seen those rocks in Death Valley that move across the desert floor on their own? For years people didn't understand how it happened. Some of the rocks weighed over six hundred pounds, and they left trails in the sand as if they were being pushed. People thought it might be UFOs or some other bizarre cosmic event. But researchers finally discovered it's just ice. The desert floor freezes, and then strong winds slide these massive boulders across the sand. Maybe the Swan sisters' legend is like this. The singing and the drownings just haven't been explained yet. But there's some perfectly logical reason why it happens."

The coffeepot has stopped sputtering behind him, but he makes no move to walk back into the small kitchen.

"Ice?" I repeat, looking at him like I've never heard anything so absurd in my life.

"I'm just saying that maybe someday they'll discover that none of this has anything to do with three sisters who were killed two hundred years ago."

"But you've seen firsthand what happens here; you saw Gregory Dunn's body in the harbor."

"I saw a body. A boy who drowned. That's it."

I tighten my lips together. My fingernails dig into the fabric edge of the couch. "Did you really come to Sparrow by accident?" I ask— the question piercing the air between us. Splitting it apart. It's been nagging me since he showed up, a needle at the very base of my neck, a question I've wanted to ask but felt I shouldn't. Like the answer didn't matter. But maybe it does. Maybe it matters more than anything else. There's something he's not telling me. A part of his past or maybe his present, a thing that rests between the ribs, a purpose—a reason why he's here. I sense it. And although I don't want to push him away, I need to know.

The sunlight through the window spills over half of his face: light and dark. "I already told you," he says, his voice sounding a little hurt.

But I shake my head, not believing. "You didn't just come here by accident, because it was the last stop on the bus. There's another reason. You're . . . you're hiding something." I try to see into his eyes, into his thoughts, but he is carved by stone and brick. Solid as the rocks bordering the island.

His lips part, his jaw tenses. "So are you." He says it quickly, like it's been on his mind for a while, and I shift uncomfortably on the couch.

I can't meet his eyes. He sees the same thing in me: a chasm of secrets so deep and wide and unending that it bleeds from me like sweat. We both carry it. A mark on our skin, a brand burned into flesh from the weight of our past. Perhaps only those with similar scars can recognize it in others. The fear rimming our eyes.

But if he knew the truth—what I see what I peer through Olivia Greene, the creature hidden inside. If he knew the things that haunt my waking dreams. If he saw what I saw. If he *saw*. He'd leave this island and never come back. He'd leave this town. And I don't want to be alone on the island again. There have only ever been ghosts here, shadows of people that once were, until he arrived. I can't lose him. So I don't tell him.

I stand up before our words tear apart the fragile air between us. Before he demands truths I can't give. I never should have asked him why he came to Sparrow, unless I was willing to give up something of myself. Otis blinks at me from the gray cushion, stirred by my movement. I walk past Bo to the door, and for a moment I think he's going to reach out for me, to stop me, but he never actually touches me, and my heart wrenches. Spills onto the floor, seeps into the cracks between the wood boards.

A burst of bright morning sun pours into the cottage when I open the door. Otis and Olga don't even attempt to follow me. But before I can pull the door closed behind me, I hear something in the distance, beyond the edges of the island. There is no wind to carry it across the water, but the stillness makes it audible.

The bell at the marina in Sparrow is ringing.

A second body has been found.

TAVERN

The Swan sisters were never ordinary, even at birth.

All three were born on June first, exactly one year apart. First Marguerite, then came Aurora a year later, and Hazel the year after that. They did not share the same father, yet fate would bring them into this world on precisely the same day. Their mother had said they were destined for one another, bound by the stars to be sisters.

And so upon their birthday, during their first year in Sparrow, they closed up their shop early and strode down to the White Horse Inn and Tavern. They ordered pints and a bottle of brandy wine. The liquid was dark and red and bittersweet, and they passed it among them, drinking straight from the bottle. The men in the tavern shook their heads and whispered of the sisters' boldness—women rarely entered the tavern, but the sisters were not like other women in town. They laughed and spilled wine onto the damp wood floor. They sang songs they had heard the fishermen bellow when heading out to sea, enticing the winds to be calm and kind. They tipped in their chairs. They toasted their mother, who they hardly remembered now, for bringing them into this world, one year apart from each other, but on precisely the same day.

The moon shone bright over the harbor, and the whale-oil lamps flickered from atop each table inside the tavern. Marguerite stood from her chair, scanning the musty room filled with fishermen and farmers and seamen who would be here for only a week or two before they set out again. She grinned, eyeing them with the heat of booze in her cheeks. "They all think we're witches," she hissed down to her sisters, waving the bottle of brandy wine around the room. The rumors had been seething through town for months, suspicion rooting itself in the framework of homes along the seaport, passing from lips to ears until each tale became more vile than the last. The people of Sparrow had begun to hate the sisters.

"Yes, witches." Aurora laughed. She tilted her head back and nearly toppled from her chair.

"No, they don't," Hazel protested, frowning.

But Aurora and Marguerite laughed even harder, for they knew what their youngest sister didn't want to believe: that the entire town had already decided they were witches. A coven of three sisters, come to Sparrow to unleash treachery and ill deeds.

"You all think we are witches, yes?" Marguerite shouted.

The men seated at the bar turned to look. The barkeep set down the bottle of whiskey in his hand. But no one answered her.

"Then I hex you all," she announced, still smiling, lips ruddy from the wine. She circled a finger in the air then pointed it at a man seated at a nearby table. "You will grow a beard made of sea snakes." She roared with laughter then swayed her finger to a man leaning against the wall. "You will trip and fall on your way home tonight, hit your head, and see your future death." Her eyes, it would be said later, seemed alight with fire, like she was casting spells from an inferno that would burn alive anyone caught in her stare. "You will marry a mermaid," she told another man. "You will taste fish, no matter what you eat, for the rest of your life," she said to a man hunched over the bar. And as Marguerite's finger waved around the room, calling out imaginary spells, the men began to flee, certain her hexes would come true. Aurora laughed from deep within her belly, watching her sister frighten even the toughest men in Sparrow. But Hazel, horrified by the looks on the men's faces, grabbed her sisters and dragged them from the tavern as Marguerite continued to shout nonsense into the salty night air.

Once outside, the three sisters locked arms and even Hazel laughed as they staggered up Ocean Avenue, past the docks, to the small living space they shared behind the perfumery. "You can't do that," Hazel said through her laughter. "They'll think us real witches."

"They already do, my sweet sister," Aurora told her.

"They just don't understand us," Hazel offered, and Marguerite kissed her on the cheek.

"Believe what you want," Marguerite murmured, tilting her head to the starry sky, to the moon, which seemed to await her command. "But one day they will come for us." They all fell silent, the wind brushing through their hair, making it weightless. "But until then, we drink." She still had the bottle of wine and they passed it among them, letting the constellations guide them home.

Later, when Arthur Helm hit his head, he swore he saw his death as Marguerite predicted. Even though he didn't actually fall on his way home from the tavern—he was struck in the jaw by his plow horse a week later—the town still believed Marguerite had caused it. And when Murrey Coats married a woman with long ribbons of hair the color of wheat, people said she was once a mermaid he had caught in his fishing net—proof of Marguerite's spell coming true.

Four weeks later, on the summer solstice of 1823—a day chosen by the townspeople because a solstice was said to guarantee a witch's death—the three sisters were drowned for their accused witchery. Marguerite was the oldest at nineteen on the day of her death, Aurora eighteen, Hazel seventeen.

Born on the same day. Died on the same day.

NINE

Bo appears behind me in the doorway just as the tolling bell from across the harbor begins to fade. "Another one?" he asks, hand lifted as if he could see out over the water all the way to the docks.

"Another one."

He sidesteps around me, his shoulder grazing mine, then starts down the path.

"Where are you going?"

"Town," he answers.

"You're safer here," I call after him, but he doesn't stop. I have no choice but to follow—I can't let him go alone. Marguerite is in the body of Olivia Greene. And this latest kill is likely Aurora's. But I haven't seen her yet—don't yet know whose body she has stolen. So when Bo reaches the skiff, I climb in after him and start the motor.

A cluster of boats have gathered in the harbor just offshore from Coppers Beach.

I can't see the body from this distance, but I know there must be one, newly discovered, floating, being pulled aboard one of the boats—so we motor over to the marina, Bo's face hardened against the blustery wind.

We dock the skiff, and see that a crowd has already assembled on Ocean Avenue awaiting the return of the harbor police boats, cameras ready. There are signs at the top of the marina that read: DOCK MEMBERS ONLY, NO TOURISTS ALLOWED. But there are always people who ignore the signs and tromp down to the docks anyway, especially after the bell has been rung.

I push through the clot of tourists, past the stone bench facing the harbor, when someone grabs my arm. It's Rose. Heath is standing beside her.

"There's two of them," she says with shaking breath, her blue eyes magnified. She still looks pale and weak, like she hasn't yet shaken off the chill of falling into the water over a week ago, only inches from Gregory Dunn's corpse.

"Two bodies?" Bo asks, stepping in beside me so the four of us form a tight circle on the sidewalk, our breath coming out in bursts of steamy white.

Rose nods her head.

Aurora, I think. She's greedy and impulsive, can never decide, and so she will take two boys at once.

"That's not all," Heath says. "They saw one of the Swan sisters."

"Who did?" I ask.

Heath and Rose exchange a look. "Lon Whittamer was out on his dad's boat this morning, patrolling the harbor. He and Davis decided to take shifts, like vigilantes; they thought they could catch one of the sisters in the act. Apparently, Lon was the first to spot the two bodies in the harbor. Then he saw something else: a girl swimming, her head just above the waterline. She was kicking frantically back to Coppers Beach." Heath pauses and it feels like time stops, all of us holding our breath.

"Who did Lon see?" I press, my heartbeat rising into my throat, about to burst.

"Gigi Kline," he answers in one swift exhale.

I blink, a cold spire of ice slipping down the length of my spine.

"Who's Gigi Kline?" Bo asks.

"A girl from my school," I answer, my voice a near hush. "She was at the Swan party on the beach."

"Did she go in the water?"

"I'm not sure."

I glance up Ocean Avenue, where the mass of people has grown larger, tourists pressed together, trying to get a better view of the docks where the bodies will be brought ashore. *This* is what they came for—to glimpse death, proof that the legend of the Swan sisters is real.

"Who knows about Gigi?" I ask, looking back at Heath.

"I don't know. I saw Lon when he reached the docks, and he told me what he saw. Now he and Davis are searching for her."

"Shit," I mutter. If they find her, who knows what they'll do.

"Do you think it's true?" Rose asks. "Could Gigi be one of them?" Her expression seems tight and anxious. She's never fully believed in the Swan sisters before—it scares her, I think, the idea that they could be real, that she could be taken and not even know it. It's a survival mechanism for her, and I understand why she does it. But now the waver in her voice makes me think she's not so sure what she believes anymore.

"I don't know," I answer. *I won't know for sure until I see her.*

"They already found her," Heath interrupts, his cell phone in his hand, the screen lit a vibrant blue.

"What?" I ask.

"Davis and Lon, they have her." His throat catches. "And they're taking her to the old boathouse past Coppers Beach. Everyone's headed over there." Word is traveling fast, at least among the inner circle of Sparrow High students. "I'm going down there," Heath adds, clicking off his phone.

Bo nods and Rose twines her fingers through Heath's. We're all going, apparently. Everyone will want to see if Gigi Kline—last year's homecoming princess and star cheerleader—has been inhabited by a Swan sister. But I'm the only one who will know for sure.

The harbor police boats are just starting to motor into port, carrying two bodies whose identities we don't yet know, when the four of us push through the crowds toward the edge of town. We pass Coppers Beach then turn down a dirt road almost completely overgrown by blackberry bushes and a tangle of wind-beaten shrubs.

The air smells green here, damp and sodden, even with the sunlight glaring down. No cars pass down this road. The property is abandoned. And when we emerge from the dense thicket of green, the boathouse comes into view at the edge of the waterline. The old stone walls of the structure are slowly turning brownish green from the algae inching its way up the sides, and the wood-shingled roof is covered in a slimy layer of moss. A sheer cliff stands to the right of the boathouse and a rocky embankment to the left. You can't see the town or the beach from here; it's completely secluded. Which is why kids come here to smoke or make out or ditch classes. But it's not exactly a pleasant place to spend longer than an afternoon.

As we get closer, I notice that the small door into the boathouse is ajar several inches, and voices echo out from inside.

Heath is the first to step into the dark interior, and several faces turn to look at us as we shuffle in behind him. It smells worse inside. The room has a rectangle cut out of the floor near the far doors where a boat once sat protected from the weather, and seawater laps up into the interior, making reflective patterns across the walls. The stench of fuel, fish guts, and seaweed permeates the space.

Davis McArthurs and Lon Whittamer are standing against the right side wall on the narrow three-foot-wide walkway that stretches down either side of the boathouse. Three other girls who I recognize from school—but whose names I can't recall—are crowded just inside the door, as if they're afraid to get too close to the water splashing up from the floor with each wave that rolls in. And sitting in a plastic lawn chair between Davis and Lon, zip ties around her wrists and a red-and-white-checkered bandanna tied over her mouth, is Gigi Kline.

We seem to have walked into the middle of a discussion already unfolding, because one of the girls, wearing a bright pink parka, says, "You don't know for sure. She looks fine to me."

"That's the point," Davis says, jutting out his square jaw. Davis reminds me of a slab of meat, broad and thick. With a nose like a bull. There is nothing delicate about him. Or especially kind, for that matter. He's a bully. And he gets away with it because of his size. "They look like everyone else," he continues, firming his glare on the pink-parka girl. "She killed those two guys in the harbor. Lon saw her."

"You can't keep her tied up," another girl interjects, her smooth dark hair pulled up into a ponytail, and she points to Gigi with one long, sharp finger.

"We sure fucking can," Lon snaps back, while Davis scowls at the girl. Lon is wearing one of his standard Hawaiian shirts—light blue with neon yellow anchors and parrots. I feel Bo shift closer to me, like he wants to protect me from whatever is unfolding in front of us. And I wonder if he recognizes Lon from the night at the Swan party, when he was wasted and Bo pushed him into the sea.

"There's no way to prove she did anything," ponytail girl points out.

"Look at her fucking clothes and hair," Lon says sharply. "She's soaking wet."

"Maybe she . . ." But ponytail girl's voice trails off.

"Maybe she fell in," pink-parka girl offers. But everyone knows that's a weak excuse, and unlikely considering the circumstances. Two boys are being hauled from the harbor as we speak, and Gigi Kline is found completely drenched—it's not hard to put the pieces together.

Davis uncrosses his arms and takes a step toward the group. "She's one of them," he says coldly, his deep-set eyes unblinking. "And you all know it's true." He says it with such finality that everyone falls silent.

My eyes slide over Gigi Kline, her cropped blond hair dripping water onto the wood-plank floor. Eyes bloodshot like she's been crying, lips parted to accommodate the bandanna stretched across her mouth and tied at the back of her head. She looks cold, miserable, terrified. But while everyone speculates as to whether she might no longer be Gigi Kline, I know the truth. I can see right through the delicate features of her face, through her tear-streaked skin, right down into her center.

A pearlescent, threadlike creature resides just beneath the surface—

silky, atmospheric, shifting behind her human eyes. The ghost of a girl long dead.

Gigi Kline is now Aurora Swan.

Her gaze circles around the room, like she's looking for someone to help her, to untie her, to speak up, but when her eyes settle on mine, I look quickly away.

"And now," Davis says, rolling his tongue along the inside of his lower lip, "we're going to find the other two." I think of Olivia Greene, now inhabited by Marguerite Swan. But she will be harder to catch—Marguerite is careful, precise, and she won't allow these boys to discover what she really is.

And no sooner have I thought her name than Olivia and Lola step into the boathouse through the little door behind us. Hardly anyone takes notice of their arrival.

"How are we going to find them?" the third girl asks, chomping on a piece of gum and speaking up for the first time. If she only knew—if all of them only knew—how close they really are.

"We set a trap," Lon says, grinning like he's about to crush an insect beneath the sole of his shoe. "We have one of them now. The other two sisters will come for her. Gigi is our bait."

A short laugh at the back of the group breaks apart Lon's words. "You think the Swan sisters would be stupid enough to fall for that?" It's Marguerite who's spoken, and she rolls her eyes when everyone turns to look at her.

"They're not just going to leave her here," Davis points out.

"Maybe they'll think she deserves to be tied up for being dumb enough to get caught. Maybe they'll want her to learn her lesson." Marguerite stares directly at Gigi when she says it, her gaze penetrating deeply so that Aurora knows she's speaking to her: one Swan sister to another. It's a threat. Marguerite is upset that Aurora allowed herself to be captured.

"I guess we'll find out," Davis says. "And until then, we don't let any girls near the boathouse."

"That's not fair," pink-parka girl asserts. "Gigi's my friend and—"

"And maybe you're one of them," Davis snaps, cutting her off.

"That's insane." She snorts. "I didn't even get in the water at the Swan party."

"Then we should question everyone who did."

The girl with the perfect ponytail drops her gaze to the floor. "Almost everyone swam that night."

"Not everyone," Lon adds, "but you did." His eyes are harpooned on her. "And so did Rose." He nods to Rose, who is standing a half step behind me, next to Heath.

"This is ridiculous," Heath pipes up. "You idiots can't start blaming every girl who was at the party that night. It might not have even happened at the party—the sisters might have stolen bodies later, after everyone was too wasted to remember anything. Or even the next morning."

Lon and Davis exchange a look, but they're obviously undeterred, because Davis says, "Everyone is a suspect. And Gigi is staying in here until we find the other two."

"She can't stay in here until the summer solstice; it's over a week away," parka girl says, her voice pitched.

"Well, we sure as shit can't let her go," Davis rebukes. "She'll just kill someone else. Probably *us*, for tying her up." Davis slaps Lon against the shoulder, and Lon cringes a little, like he hadn't considered this—that he and Davis might be next on the drowning kill list for capturing a Swan sister.

Gigi tries to shake her head, to make a sound, but only muffled, garbled noises manage to make it through. The bandanna is tied too tightly.

Gigi's parents will certainly get suspicious when she doesn't come home; the police will be called, a search party sent to look for her. But the boys did get one thing right: Gigi Kline *is* a Swan sister—the only problem is that they can't prove it. And I'm not about to tell them the truth.

Still, this is bad. Aurora has been captured. Marguerite knows it. And the summer solstice will be here soon—things are getting complicated. Aurora's capture has made it complicated. And I just want to stay as far away from them and this mess as I can.

Heath has had enough, and I see him grab Rose's hand. "Come on," he whispers to her, then leads her out of the boathouse.

A new group of three guys—one I recognize as Thor Grantson, whose father owns the *Catch* newspaper—and one girl shuffle in through the doorway, coming to see Gigi Kline and determine for themselves if they think she's been infected by a Swan sister.

The room suddenly feels claustrophobic.

"Hell no!" Davis says loudly, pointing a finger at Thor. "You'd better not write about this in your shitty paper, Thor, or tell your father."

Thor lifts both hands in the air in a gesture of innocence. "I just came to see her," he says amiably. "That's it."

"You're a fucking snitch and everyone knows it," Lon chimes in.

Pink-parka girl starts arguing with Davis in Thor's defense, and soon the room is a cacophony of voices, all the while Gigi Kline sits tied to a chair and Olivia Greene stands calmly at the back of the group, leaning against the wall.

I can't stay in here anymore, so I slip through the new group of people and stumble back out into the daylight, opening my mouth to breathe in the warm, salty air.

Rose and Heath are standing a couple yards away, but Rose's arms are crossed. "They're bullies," I hear her say. "They can't do this. It's not right."

"There's nothing we can do," Heath says. "It's going to be a witch hunt. And they could just as easily lock you up in there."

"He's right," I say, and they both look up. "None of us are safe."

"So we just let them keep her locked up and accuse whoever they want?"

"For now," I say, "yeah, we do."

The door to the boathouse swings open and Bo steps out behind me, blinking away the sunlight.

"Maybe they're right," Heath offers, reaching out to touch Rose's arm. "Maybe Gigi did drown those two boys. Maybe she's one of them. It's better if she's in there, where she can't kill anyone else."

"You don't really believe that girl could be dangerous?" Bo asks, crossing his arms. I glance over my shoulder at him and a stillness settles over the four of us—each of us considering how dangerous she could really be, picturing her hands around a boy's throat, her eyes wicked with revenge as she forced him below the waterline, waiting for bubbles to escape his nostrils and break at the surface.

Then Rose says, "Penny?" as if she's hoping I might have an answer. As if I might know how to fix everything and make it all okay. And suddenly I feel the urge to tell her the truth: that Gigi is indeed occupied by Aurora Swan, and that the town is safer with her tied up inside the old boathouse. That setting a trap to catch the remaining two Swan sisters might be a smart move.

But instead I tell her, "We need to be careful. Act normal. Don't give them any reason to suspect we could be one of them."

"But we aren't one of them!" Rose says sharply.

My eyes feel dry, unable to blink. Rose sounds so certain, she's so sure that she understands the world around her, that she'd be able to see something as villainous as a Swan sister if it were tucked inside of Gigi Kline. She trusts her eyes to tell her the truth. But she can't see a thing. "They don't know that," I say. "We shouldn't even be here; we shouldn't be anywhere near Gigi."

I have a flash of a memory, of Rose talking with Gigi in C hall last year. They were laughing about something, I can't seem to recall what exactly. It doesn't matter. But it reminds me that they were friends once, in grade school, and perhaps Rose is more upset by what's happened because it's happening to Gigi. Someone who she was once so close with. And if it can happen to Gigi, it can happen to her, or to me, even.

The boathouse door opens again and several people spill out, all chatting in low voices. Lola walks out by herself, staring down at her cell phone, probably sending out more text messages about Gigi's current incarceration inside the boathouse.

"I want to get out of here," Rose murmurs, and Heath twines his fingers through hers and starts leading her back up the road.

"You're really okay just leaving that girl gagged and tied to a chair in there?" Bo asks me.

"We don't have a choice right now."

"It's kidnapping and wrongful imprisonment. We could call the cops."

"But what if they're right?" I pose. "What if she's a Swan sister and just killed those two boys?"

"Then the cops will arrest her."

From the corner of my eye, I see Olivia Greene finally exit the boathouse, her onyx hair shimmering in the light, her skin papery and transparent so that I can see the inhuman thing resting inside. A watery, grayish-white image that flickers and shifts, similar to an old black-and-white film. Never solidifying or taking shape, always liquid—drifting elegantly but cruelly beneath the features of Olivia's face. The dark, inky eyes of Marguerite flicker out from behind Olivia's skull and settle on me.

"Let's go," I say to Bo, touching his forearm to urge him to follow me. We start back up the road, Rose and Heath a good distance ahead of us, already pushing through the bramble and overgrown brush.

"What's wrong?" Bo asks, sensing my unease.

But before I can answer, I hear Olivia's voice cut through the crashing waves and the cawing of seagulls circling over the tide pools on the rocky shore. "Penny Talbot!" she calls.

I try to keep walking, but Bo stops and turns around.

Olivia has already broken away from the group gathered outside the boathouse and is walking toward us.

"Don't stop," I hiss to Bo, but he looks at me like I'm not making any sense. He doesn't realize he's in danger just by being close to her.

"Leaving already?" Olivia asks, coming to a stop in front of us with a hand planted smugly on her hip, nails still painted a shiny, morbid black. Marguerite has fully embraced this body. It suits her, fits her already vain, indignant personality.

"We've seen enough," I answer, willing Bo not to speak, not to make eye contact with Olivia or allow her to touch him.

"But I haven't met your new friend," she says with a vampish grin, her pale blue eyes sliding over Bo like she could devour him. "I'm Olivia Greene," she lies, holding out her hand. She smells like black licorice.

Bo lifts his arm to shake her hand, but I grab onto his wrist just before they touch and pull it back down. He frowns at me, but I ignore it. "We really have to go," I say, more to him than to Olivia. And I take a couple steps up the road, hoping he'll follow.

"Oh, Penny," Olivia says blithely, moving forward so she's only a few inches from Bo, her eyes pouring through him. "You can't keep him all to yourself on that island." Before I can stop her, she slides her fingers up to his collarbone, holding his gaze steady on hers. And I know he has no choice, he can't look away. He's captured in her stare. She leans in close so her face is next to his, her lips hovering against his ear. I can't make out what she's saying, but she's whispering something to him, serpentine words that can't be undone. Promises and vows, her voice twining around his heart, drawing it forth from his chest, making him want her—crave her. A *need* that will be planted deep inside him, that won't be satiated until he sees her again, can feel her skin against his. Her fingertips trail up his neck to his cheekbone, and a fury of emotions spark straight down into my gut. Not just fear but something else: jealousy.

"Bo," I say sharply, grabbing his arm again, and Olivia releases him from her snare. He blinks, still watching her like she were a goddess formed of silks and sunsets and gold. Like he has never seen anything so perfect or mesmerizing in his entire life. "Bo," I say again, still holding on to him and trying to snap him from his reverie.

"When you get bored on that island," Olivia says, winking at him, "when you get bored with her . . . come find me." Then she spins around, sauntering back to the group.

She touched him. She wove words together against his ear, enticing him. She wants to make him hers for eternity, pull him into the sea and drown him. She is collecting boys, and now she's dug her delicate, bewitching claws into Bo.

TEN

I start a fire in Bo's cottage.

I know I shouldn't trust this feeling, this unraveling in my heart. It will only end up in a tangled heap. But I need to protect him. Watching Olivia run her fingers up his throat, touching the hard line of his jaw, a sickening lump of dread wretched up from my stomach. *Don't let yourself care*, I recite in my mind. Boys die all too often in this town. But maybe Marguerite's words didn't work, didn't stick. Maybe he resisted. I just need to keep him safe until the summer solstice, keep him from wandering out into the sea in search of her, and then he will leave the island and this town, and we'll never see each other again. Simple. Uncomplicated.

I stand up once the flames have ignited over the logs, sending sparks in a cyclone up the chimney. Bo is sitting on the couch, elbows on his knees, forehead pressed into his palms.

"What did Olivia whisper to you?" I ask, sitting down beside him.

He drops his hands, forehead lined with confusion. "I don't know."

"Do you remember anything?"

His thumb taps against the side of his knee. "I remember her."

His eyes lift, staring into the fire. I don't think I want to hear what he remembers about her, but he tells me anyway. "She was so close, it was like her voice was inside my head. And she was . . . beautiful." He swallows immediately after he says it, like he can't believe his own words.

I push up from the couch and cross my arms beside the fire.

"I can't stop thinking about her," he adds, shaking his head, squinting like he could squeeze her from his mind. But it's not that easy.

"That's how it works," I say, bending down to put another log on the growing flames.

He stares up at me. "You think she's one of them?"

"I know you don't believe any of this, but how can you explain that you can't remember what she said to you? And that you can't stop thinking about her; that you're suddenly so captivated by her?"

"I'm not—" But his words break off. He knows I'm right: He knows his mind keeps slipping back to thoughts of Olivia Greene. Her fingertips against his skin, her eyes sinking so deeply into his, it was like she was looking at the exact center of his soul. A part of him craves her now, wants her as much as she wants him. And it tears at him. He won't be able to stop thinking about her until they're together again. "I don't know anymore. I don't trust my own thoughts."

I pace across the room. *How do I undo this? How do I rid Olivia from his mind?* I don't think it's ever been done before—I don't think it's even possible. He belongs to her now.

I run my tongue along the inside of my teeth. "You have to get away from here. You have to leave town."

Bo stands up from the couch, and the movement makes me

flinch. He walks to the fireplace, stepping in front of me, willing me to look up at him, but I can't. He unsettles me, cracks apart my insides, and I bite down on the feeling, willing it away.

From beneath my eyelashes, I see his lips flatten together, and our breathing seems to settle into the same rhythm. I want him to speak, to cut through the silence, and all at once I feel light-headed, like I might reach out for him to steady myself. But then his lips open and he says, almost like a confession: "My brother was drowned in Sparrow." His eyes cease to blink, his body a stone outline in front of me.

"What?" I lift my gaze.

"That's why I'm here. Why I can't leave . . . not yet. I told you he died, but I didn't tell you how. He drowned here in the harbor."

"When?" My fingertips begin to tingle; the hairs on the back of my neck rise on end as if a cool breeze were gliding across my skin.

"Last summer."

"That's why you came to Sparrow?"

"I didn't know about the Swan sisters. I didn't know about any of it. The police told us that he'd committed suicide, that he'd drowned himself. But I never believed it."

I shake my head a fraction of an inch, trying to understand.

"His name was Kyle," he starts. It's the first time he's said his name out loud to me. "After he graduated high school last year, he and two of his friends took a road trip down the coast. It was supposed to be a surf trip; they planned to drive all the way to Southern California, but they never made it that far." He chokes back something, an emotion threatening to spill past his bulletproof veneer. "They stopped in Sparrow for a night. I don't think they had any idea about the town, about the drownings. They were staying at the

Whaler Bed-and-Breakfast. Kyle left his room sometime just after sunset . . . and he never came back. His body was found the next morning tangled in a fishing net not far from shore."

"I'm . . . sorry," I manage, barely above a whisper. A ripple of something shudders through me. A pain that I crush back down.

"He had a scholarship to Montana State in the fall. He had a girlfriend who he wanted to marry. It didn't make any sense. I know he didn't commit suicide. And he was a good swimmer. He surfed every summer; it's not like he would have accidentally drowned."

He takes a step back, unmooring me, and I let out a swift breath I didn't even realize I had been holding in. "None of them committed suicide," I say, thinking of all the boys who've waded out into the harbor, lured to their death.

We look at each other, the seconds stretching out between us.

"Maybe you're wrong about the Swan sisters," he says, extending an arm to touch the mantel over the fireplace, index finger brushing over a scratch in the wood. The heat from the fire has made his cheeks flushed, his lips pink. "Maybe it's just a story that locals tell to explain why so many people have drowned. Maybe someone really is killing them; maybe that girl in the boathouse, Gigi Kline, did do it. Not because she has some ancient witch inside her who's seeking revenge, but because she's just a murderer. And maybe she's not the only one; maybe there are other girls who are killing too . . . who killed my brother."

"But that doesn't explain why boys have drowned in Sparrow for the last two centuries." I need him to believe—to know the Swan sisters exist.

"Maybe it's like a cult," he answers, refusing to accept the truth, "and every generation, its members drown people for some unexplained sacrifice or something."

"A cult?"

"Look, I don't know how cults work. I'm just trying to figure this all out as I go."

"So if you really believe it's just some cult . . . then what?"

"Then I have to stop them from killing anyone else."

"I thought you wanted to go to the police and tell them about Gigi Kline locked in the boathouse? Let them handle it?"

"Maybe that's not enough. Maybe that's not justice—for my brother, for everyone else who's been killed."

"Then what? What would justice be?"

"Putting an end to whatever is happening in this town."

"Killing a Swan sister, you mean? Killing Gigi?"

"Maybe there's no other way," he says.

I shake my head. "There is another way—you can leave Sparrow," I say. "You can go and never come back, and maybe someday you'll even start to forget this place, as if you were never here at all." I don't mean the words I say. I don't want him to leave. Not really. Except I need him to leave so he doesn't get hurt, so he doesn't end up like his brother.

A storm builds in the features of his face, a coldness in his eyes I haven't seen before. "You don't know what it feels like—this pain that won't go away," he says. "I know my brother would do this for me; he wouldn't stop until he found out who was responsible for my death. And he would get revenge."

"This town was built on revenge," I say. "And it's never made anything better or right."

"I'm not leaving," he says with such finality that I feel my throat tighten.

I look up at him like I'm seeing him for the first time, the resoluteness in his eyes, the anger in his jaw. He's searching for a way to rid himself of the pain of losing his brother, and he's willing to sacrifice everything, do whatever it takes, pay any price. Even end someone else's life. "It wasn't those girls," I tell him, pleading with him to understand. "It was the thing inside them."

"Maybe," he answers, lifting his gaze. "But maybe there's no difference between the girl and whatever evil makes them commit murder."

The fire crackles, spitting out sparks onto the wood floor that darken and turn to ash. I walk to the bookshelf beside the fireplace, examining the spines of each book, looking for a way to make him understand without telling him what I know—what I can see.

"Why are you so certain it's real?" he asks, reading my thoughts, and I let my hand fall away from one of the books. I shift onto my heels and turn to face him. He's stepped closer to me, so close I could reach out and touch his chest with the tips of my fingers. I could take one swift step forward and tell him everything, tell him all my secrets, or I could press my lips to his and silence the turmoil rattling around inside my head. But instead I ignore every urge snapping through my veins.

I draw in my lips before I speak, careful to control each word. "I want to tell you," I say, a thousand tons of stones sinking into my stomach. "But I can't."

His eyes flatten on me at the same moment the fire ignites over a dry log and floods the room with a sudden burst of glowing orange light. I was right about Bo, and I was also wrong: He didn't end up in Sparrow by accident. But he's also not a tourist. He came for his brother—to find out what happened to him. And what he found here is far worse than anything he could have imagined.

The pressure in my head expands, the cottage walls start to rotate off axis like a carnival ride out of control, and I feel like I might be sick. I can't stay in here with him. I don't trust myself. I don't trust my heart, thumping wildly like I might do something reckless that I can't take back. I don't know what I'm supposed to feel, supposed to say. *I shouldn't allow myself to feel anything.* It's dangerous, these emotions, the fear pumping through my chest, cracking along each rib. My head isn't thinking straight; it's tangled up with my heart, and I can't trust it.

So I walk to the door and touch the knob, running my fingers around the smooth metal. I close my eyes for a half second and listen to the sounds of the fireplace behind me—warmth and fury, the same exploding conflict happening inside my head—then I open the door and steal out into the evening light.

Bo doesn't try to stop me.

THE OUTSIDER

A year earlier, five days into the start of Swan season, Kyle Carter left the Whaler Bed-and-Breakfast just as the rain lifted. The sidewalks were slick and dark, the sky muted by a cloak of soft white clouds. He had no destination. But the allure of the marina drew him closer.

He reached the metal gangway that led to the marina, rows of boats lined up like sardines in a tin can, and he spotted a girl walking down one of the docks, ebony brown hair loose and sweeping across her back. She looked over her shoulder at him, settled her deep, ocean-blue eyes on his, and then he found himself stumbling after her.

She was the most stunning thing he had ever seen—graceful and enticing. A rare species of girl. And when he reached her, she stroked a hand through his dark hair and pulled him close into a kiss. She wanted him, desired him. And he couldn't resist. So he let her spool her fingers between his and pull him out into the sea. Their bodies entwined, languid and insatiable. He didn't even feel the water when it entered his lungs. All he could think about was her: warm fingers against his skin, lips so soft they melted his flesh, eyes seeing into his thoughts, unraveling his mind.

And then the ocean drew him under and never let go.

ELEVEN

My mind stirs and rattles with all the secrets held captive inside it. I won't be able to sleep. Not now that I know the truth about Bo, about his brother's death.

And I need to keep him safe.

I make a cup of lavender tea, turn on the radio, and sit at the kitchen table. The announcer repeats the same information every twenty minutes: The identity of the two drowned boys has not yet been released, but the police don't believe them to be locals—they're tourists. Eventually, the drone of the announcer's voice bleeds into a slow, drowsy song—a piano melody. Guilt slithers through me, a thousand regrets, and I wish for things I can't have: a way to undo all the deaths, to save the people who've been lost. Boys die all around me. And I do nothing.

I don't realize I've dozed off until I hear the ringing of the telephone mounted to the kitchen wall.

I jerk upright in the stiff wood chair and look to the window over the sink. The sun is barely up—it's morning—the sky still a subdued, pastel gray. I stand and fumble for the phone. "Hello?"

"Did I wake you?" It's Rose's voice on the other end.

"No," I lie.

"I stayed up all night," she says. "Mom kept feeding me cakes, hoping it would help me forget everything that's happened in the last week, but I was so jittery from all the sugar that it made it worse."

I feel distracted, and Rose's words slip ineffectually through my mind. I keep thinking of Bo and his brother.

"Anyway," Rose continues after I don't respond, "I wanted to tell you not to come into town today."

"Why?"

"Davis and Lon are on some kind of crusade. They're questioning everyone; they even cornered Ella Garcia in the girls' bathroom at the Chowder, wouldn't let her leave until she proved she wasn't a Swan sister."

"How'd she prove it?"

"Who knows. But Heath heard that she just started bawling, and Davis didn't think a Swan sister would cry so hysterically."

"Isn't anyone stopping them?"

"You know how it is," Rose says, her voice drifting away from the phone briefly like she's reaching for something. "As long as they don't break any laws, everyone would be relieved if Davis and Lon actually figured out who the sisters were—then maybe they could put an end to all of this."

"There's no ending it, Rose," I reply, thinking back to my conversation with Bo last night in his cottage. He wants to end this too—an eye for an eye. One death for another. But he's never taken a life before—it isn't who he is. It will change him. I hear a *ding* pass through Rose's phone.

"Heath is texting me," she says. "I'm supposed to meet him at his house."

"Maybe you shouldn't leave your house either," I warn.

"My mom doesn't know about Heath yet, so I can't invite him over here. She thinks I'm meeting you for coffee."

"Just be careful."

"I will."

"I mean be careful with Heath."

"Why?"

"You never know what will happen. We still have a week to go."

"He might drown, you mean?" she asks.

"I don't want you to lose someone you care about."

"And what about Bo? Aren't you worried you're going to lose him?"

"No," I say too quickly. "He's not my boyfriend, so I don't . . ." But I feel the lie churning inside my chest and it takes the weight out of my words. I am worried—and I wish I weren't.

Another text chimes through her phone. "I gotta go," she says. "But I'm serious about not coming into town."

"Rose, wait," I say, as if I have something else I need to tell her: some warning, some advice to keep her and Heath safe from the Swan sisters. But she hangs up before I can.

I pick up my mug of cold tea from the table and walk to the sink. I'm about to pour it out when I hear the creaking of floorboards.

"Were you practicing reading the leaves?" she asks from the doorway.

I turn on the faucet. "No."

"You should practice every day." She's chewing on the side of her lip, wearing the black robe that hangs loose across her frame. Soon she'll be so tiny that the wind will carry her away when she stands on the cliff's edge. Maybe that's what she wants.

When I meet her eyes, she's looking at me like I'm a stranger, a girl she no longer recognizes. Not her daughter, but merely a memory.

"Why don't you read the leaves anymore?" I ask, rinsing out the mug and watching the amber tea spiral down the sink. I know this question might stir up bad memories for her . . . but I also wonder if talking about the past might bring her back, shake her loose from her misery.

"Fate has abandoned me," she answers. A shiver passes through her, and her head tilts to the side like she's listening for voices that aren't really there. "I don't trust the leaves anymore. They didn't warn me."

The old silver radio sitting on the kitchen counter is still on—I never shut it off before I fell asleep last night at the table—and music quietly crackles through the speakers. But then the song ends and the announcer promptly returns. "*She has been identified as Gigi Kline,*" he is saying. "*She left her home on Woodlawn Street on Tuesday morning and hasn't been seen since. There is some speculation that her disappearance may have something to do with the Swan season, but local police are asking anyone who may have seen her to contact the Sparrow Police Department.*"

"Do you know Gigi?" Her voice shakes as she asks it, her eyes penetrating the radio. The announcer repeats the same information again then fades to a commercial.

"Not really." I think of Gigi spending the night inside the boat-house, probably hungry and cold. But it's not Gigi who will remember being tied to a chair; only Aurora—the thing inside her—will recall these frigid, shivering nights for years to come. And she will probably seek her revenge on Davis and Lon—if not in the body of Gigi Kline, then next year, inside the body of another girl. Assuming they let Gigi go eventually, and Aurora is able to return to the sea before the Swan season ends.

"When your father disappeared, they announced it on the radio too," she adds, walking to the sink and staring out the window, pushing her hands down into the deep pockets of her robe. "They asked for volunteers to search the harbor and the banks for any sign of him. But no one came out to help. The people in this town never accepted him—their hearts are cold, just like that ocean." Her voice wavers then finds strength again. "It didn't matter, though; I knew he wasn't in the harbor. He was farther out at sea—he was gone, and they'd never find him." This is the first I've heard her speak of him as if he was dead, as if he wasn't ever coming back.

I clear my throat, trying not to lose myself in a wave of emotion. "Let me make you some breakfast," I offer, walking past her. The sunlight is spilling across her face, turning it an unnatural ashen white. I open a cupboard and set one of the white bowls on the counter. "Do you want oatmeal?" I ask, thinking that she needs something warm to shake off the chill in the house.

But her eyes sweep over me and she grabs on to my wrist with her right hand, her fingers coiling around my skin. "I knew," she says coldly. "I knew the truth about what happened to him. I always have." I want to look away from her, but I can't. She's looking through me, into the past, to a time we'd both like to forget.

"What truth?" I ask.

Her dark hair is tangled and knotted, and she looks like she hasn't slept. Then her eyes slide away from mine, like a patient slipping back into a coma, unable to recall what had stirred them from unconsciousness in the first place.

Gently, I pull my arm away from her, and I can see that she's already forgotten what she said.

"Maybe you should go back to bed," I suggest. She nods, and without any protest, she turns and shuffles across the white tile kitchen floor, out into the hall. I can hear her slow, almost weightless footsteps as she makes her way up the staircase and down to her room, where she will likely sleep for the rest of the day.

I lean against the edge of the counter, pinching my eyes shut then opening them again. Against the butter-yellow wallpaper on the far wall of the kitchen is a distorted, stretched-out shadow of me, formed by the morning sunlight spilling in through the window over the sink. I stare at it for a moment, trying to match up elbows and legs and feet. But the more I look at the gray outline against the sun-bleached daffodil wallpaper, the more unnatural it seems. Like an artist's abstract sketch.

I push away from the counter and head for the front door. I can't get out of the house fast enough.

The skiff floats perfectly still against the dock. Not a ripple of water or gust of wind blows across the harbor. The sun is hot overhead, and a fish jumps from the surface of the water then splashes back into the deep.

I've just begun untying the boat and tossing the lines over the side when I sense someone watching me. I whip around and Bo is standing on the starboard side of the sailboat—the *Windsong*—one arm raised, holding on to the mast.

"How long have you been out here?" I ask, startled.

"Since sunrise. I couldn't sleep—my mind wouldn't turn off. I needed to do something."

I imagine him out here, climbing aboard the sailboat, the sun not fully risen, checking the sails and the rigging and the hull to see what's still intact after all these years and what will need to be repaired. His mind working over the problems—anything to keep him from thinking about yesterday at the boathouse, about last night in his cottage. *I have to stop them from killing anyone else*, he had said to me. A promise—a threat—that he would find his brother's killer.

"Are you going into town?" he asks, his jade eyes shivering against the early sunlight.

"Yeah. I have to go do something."

"I'm coming with you," he says.

I shake my head, tossing the last rope into the bow of the boat. "I need to do this by myself."

He drops his arm from the mast and steps over the side rail of the sailboat then hops down onto the dock in one fluid motion. "I need to talk to that girl in the boathouse—Gigi," he says. "I need to ask her about my brother, see if she remembers him."

"That's not a good idea."

"Why not?"

"Olivia might be waiting for you."

"I'm not worried about Olivia."

"You should be," I say.

"I think I can resist whatever powers of seduction you think she has over me."

I let out a short laugh. "Have you been able to stop thinking about her since she touched you yesterday?"

His silence is the only answer I need. But I also feel a sharp stab in the core of my heart, knowing he's been thinking about her all night, all morning, unable to shake the image of her. Only her.

"You're safer here," I tell him, stepping onto the skiff as it begins to drift away from the dock.

"I didn't come here to be trapped on an island," he says.

"Sorry." I start the engine with a swift pull on the cord.

"Wait," he calls, but I shift the boat into gear and pull away from the dock, out of reach.

I can't risk bringing him with me. I need to do this alone. And if Marguerite sees him in town, she might try to take him into the harbor, and I don't know if I can stop her.

Today is the annual Swan Festival in town.

Balloons bounce and swerve across the skyline. Children squeal for shaved ice and saltwater taffy. A red-and-yellow banner stretches across Ocean Avenue announcing the festival, with cartoon cobwebs and full moons and owls printed at the corners.

It's the busiest day of the year—when people drive in from neighboring towns up and down the coast or board buses that shuttle them into Sparrow early in the morning, then haul them back out in the evening. Each year attendance grows, and this year the town feels close to bursting.

Ocean Avenue has been closed off to traffic and is lined with booths and stands selling all manner of both witchy and unwitchy items: wind chimes and wind socks and local boysenberry jam. There is a beer garden selling old-style craft beers in large steins, a woman dressed as a Swan sister reading palms, and even a booth selling perfumes claiming to be some of the original fragrances the sisters once sold at their perfumery—although everyone in Sparrow knows they aren't authentic. Much of the crowd is dressed for the period in high-waisted gowns with ruffles at the sleeves and low necklines. Later tonight, at the stage set up near the pier, there will be a reenactment of the day the sisters were found guilty and drowned—an event I avoid each year. I can't bear to watch it. I can't stand the spectacle it's become.

I push through the crowds, winding my way up Ocean Avenue. I keep my head down. I don't want to be seen by Davis or Lon—I don't need an interrogation from them right now. I leave town and the bustle of the festival, reaching the road that winds through the brambles to the boathouse. There's no way to access it except from this road; I don't have a choice but to walk straight down it.

Seagulls turn and spiral overhead like vultures waiting for death, sensing it.

When the road widens and the ocean comes into view, flat and glittery, the boathouse seems small and plain, more sunken into the earth than it did yesterday. Lon is sitting on a stump against the right side of the boathouse. At first I think he's staring up at the sky, soaking up the sun, but as I inch closer I realize he's asleep, his head canted back against the outer wall. He's probably been out here all night guarding Gigi, one leg stretched out in front of him, arms

155

hanging limp at his sides, jaw hung slightly open. He's wearing one of his stupid floral-print shirts, teal with purple flowers, and if it weren't for the dreary backdrop he'd almost look like he was on a tropical beach somewhere, working on his nonexistent tan.

I move quietly, careful not to step on a twig or dried leaf that might give me away, and when I reach the boathouse, I pause to look down at Lon. For a brief moment, I think maybe he's not breathing, but then I see his chest rise and his throat swallow.

The wood door isn't locked, and I push it easily inward.

Gigi is still sitting in the white plastic chair, arms tied, chin to chest like she's sleeping. But her eyes are open, and she slides them up to meet mine as soon as I step inside.

I walk toward her and pull the gag out of her mouth then take a swift step back.

"What are you doing here?" she asks, lifting her chin, her cropped blond hair falling back from her face. She stares at me through her lashes, and her tone is not sweet, but low, almost guttural. The waspy, flickering outline of Aurora shifts lazily beneath her skin. But her emerald-green eyes, the same inherited color of each Swan sister, blink serpent-like out at me.

"I'm not here to save you, if that's what you think," I tell her, keeping my distance back from the white chair that has become her cage.

"Then what do you want?"

"You killed those two boys they pulled from the harbor, didn't you?" She eyes me like she's trying to understand the real motivation behind my question. What purpose I have for asking it.

"Maybe." Her lips tug at the edges. She's holding back a smile—she finds this amusing.

"I doubt it was Marguerite." At this her eyes broaden to perfect orbs. "Only you would drown two boys at once."

She shifts her jawbone side to side then wriggles her fingers like she's trying to stretch them, her wrists confined by zip ties. The lime-green polish on her fingernails is starting to chip, and her hands look waterlogged and pale. "You came here just to accuse me of killing those boys?" she asks.

I stare through her sheer exterior, beyond Gigi, finding the monster inside her—meeting Aurora's gaze. And she knows it. Knows I'm looking at the real her.

Her expression changes. She grins, revealing Gigi's bleached white and perfectly aligned teeth. "You want something," she says pointedly.

I take a deep breath. *What do I want?* I want her to stop. Stop killing. Stop seeking revenge. Stop this vicious game she's been playing for too long. I'm a fool to believe she would listen to me. Hear my words. But I try anyway. For Bo. For me. "Stop this," I finally say.

"Stop?" Her tongue pushes against the inside of her cheek, and she examines me through lowered eyelashes.

"Stop drowning boys."

"I can't do much drowning tied up in here, can I?" She sucks in a long breath through her nostrils, and I'm surprised when she doesn't grimace—the boathouse smells fouler than I remember. Her eyes narrow. "If you untie me, then perhaps we can discuss this little idea of yours."

I examine the zip ties around her wrists and ankles. A quick yank, and I might be able to break them free. If I had a knife, I could easily slice through the plastic. But I won't do that. I won't set her loose on Sparrow again.

I shake my head. "I can't."

"You don't trust me?" She doesn't even try to hide the wicked curl of her upper lip or the playful arch of her left eyebrow. She knows I don't trust her—why would I? "'Trust' is an irrelevant word anyway," she sneers when I don't respond. "Merely a lie we tell each other. I've learned not to trust anyone—a symptom of two centuries of existence. You have the time to consider such things." She tilts her head, looking at me from the side. "I wonder who you trust? Who you would trust with your life?"

I stare at the thing beneath Gigi's skin, eyes milky white and watching me.

"Who would you trust with yours?" I counter.

This forces a laugh from deep within her gut, eyes watering. I take a step back. Then her laughter stops, blond hair sliding forward to cover part of her face. Her arms stiffen against her restraints and her real eyes cut through me. Her mouth twists into a snarl. "No one."

The door behind me suddenly bangs open and Lon bursts into the room. "What the fuck are you doing in here?" His eyes are huge.

I glance from Gigi back to him. "Just asking her a couple questions."

"No one's allowed in here. She'll trick you into letting her go."

"That only works on the weak-minded male specimen," I tell him.

His lips stiffen together, and he takes a quick step toward me. "Get the hell out of here. Unless you want to confess to being one of them, then I'll gladly lock you up too."

I glance at Gigi, who sits defiantly blinking back at me, the side of her lip turned upward. She looks like she might even dare to laugh—she finds his threat amusing—but she holds it in. Then I step back out the door into the daylight.

"You realize the police are looking for Gigi," I tell Lon when he follows me out, closing the door behind him with a loud clatter.

"The police in this town are idiots."

"Maybe. But it's only a matter of time before they check the boathouse."

He waves a hand in the air dismissively, his floral shirtsleeve flapping with the motion, and returns to his post on the stump, leaning back against the wall and closing his eyes, obviously not concerned about Gigi escaping. "And tell your friend Rose not to come back either."

I stop midstride. "What?"

"Rose . . . your friend," he says mockingly, as if I don't know who she is. "She was here twenty minutes ago, caught her sneaking through the brush."

"Did she talk to Gigi?"

"My job is to keep people out, so no, I didn't let her talk to Gigi."

"What did she want?" I ask, although I'm certain whatever she told him was a lie.

"Hell if I know. Said she felt bad for Gigi or some crap, that it was cruel to keep her locked up. But you both had better stay away unless you want to be suspects." His voice lowers a bit like he's telling me a secret, like he's trying to help me. "We're going to find all the Swan sisters one way or another."

I turn and hurry up the road.

* * *

Alba's Forgetful Cakes smells like vanilla bean frosting and lemon cake when I step through the door. A dozen people crowd the small store—some wearing festival costumes, kids with faces painted in glitter and gold—picking out tiny cakes from the glass cases to be boxed up and tied with bubblegum-pink ribbon. Mrs. Alba stands behind one of the deli cases helping a customer, carefully placing petit fours into white boxes. Two other employees are also moving quickly around the shop, ringing people up and answering questions about the effectiveness of the cakes at wiping away old, stagnant memories.

But Rose is not in the store, and I wait several minutes before Mrs. Alba is free.

I press my fingertips against a glass case, hoping to get her attention. "Penny," Mrs. Alba chirps when she sees me, her grin stretching wide across the soft features of her face. "How are you?"

"I'm looking for Rose," I say quickly.

Her expression sags and then her eyes pinch flat. "I thought she was with you." On the phone, Rose told me that she had lied to her mother, saying that she was meeting me for coffee when she was really meeting Heath. But since she obviously wasn't meeting Heath, either, unless they went to the boathouse together to see Gigi, I thought Mrs. Alba might actually have seen her.

"I think I just got the time wrong, or where we were supposed to meet," I say with an easy smile—I don't want to get Rose into trouble. "I thought maybe she'd be here."

"You can check the apartment," she says, turning her gaze as several more customers enter the shop.

"Thank you," I answer, but she's already shuffled away to help the new patrons.

Back outside, I turn right and climb the covered stairs up to the second floor. The gray-shingled walls of the building are protected from the rain under a narrow roof, and at the top of the stairs there is a red door under a white archway. I press my finger against the doorbell, and the ring echoes through the spacious apartment. Their dog, Marco, begins yapping furiously, and I can hear the clatter of his paws as he races to the door, barking from the other side. I wait, but no one comes. And there's no way Rose could be inside and not know someone was at the door.

I head back down the stairs and push through the crowds across Ocean Avenue. I start down Shipley Pier toward the Chowder, when I spot Davis McArthurs. He's standing halfway down the pier among the throngs of people, talking to a girl I recognize from the boat-house when they first caught Gigi. She had argued with Davis about keeping Gigi locked up. His arms are crossed, his eyes surveying the outdoor tables like he's looking for any girl he's missed—who he hasn't yet interrogated for being a Swan sister.

A burning fury rises inside me at seeing Davis. But there's nothing I can do.

Rose wouldn't be on the pier anyway, not with Davis strutting around. She's probably back at Heath's house, but I don't know where he lives—and I'm not about to ask around and make myself known. So I hurry back to the marina before Davis sees me, and I motor across the harbor to the island.

FORETELLING

A woman stepped through the door of the Swan Perfumery early one morning on a Thursday, a week after the sisters' night at the tavern.

Aurora was sweeping the shop floor, Marguerite was leaning against the counter daydreaming about a boy she had seen working the rigging on a ship in the harbor the day before, and Hazel was scribbling notes on a piece of paper for a new scent she had been imagining: myrrh, tansy, and rose hips. A fragrance to ease sadness and clear away mistrust in others.

When the woman entered, Marguerite straightened and smiled pleasingly as she did whenever a new customer visited the shop. "Good morning," Marguerite spoke elegantly, as if she were raised by royals, when in fact all three sisters were raised by a woman who'd lewdly dabbed perfume between her thighs to entice her lovers.

The woman did not respond, but walked to a wall of bottled perfumes all containing hues of citrus and other fruit, meant for daytime wear, often cajoling memories of late summer winds and warm evenings. "A perfume shop seems a tad presumptuous in this town," the woman finally spoke. "Illicit even."

"Women in any town deserve the allure of a good scent,"

Marguerite responded, raising an eyebrow. Marguerite did not show it, but she recognized the woman—she was the wife of a man Marguerite had flirted with outside the Collins & Gray General Store three days earlier.

"*Allure*," the woman repeated. "An interesting choice of words. And this allure—" She paused. "It comes from the spells you cast in your scents?"

Marguerite's mouth quirked sharply upward on one side. "No spells, madam. Just perfectly arranged fragrances, I assure you."

The woman glared at Marguerite then swiftly moved toward the door. "Your devious work will not go unnoticed for long. We see what you really are." And in a whir of salty sea air, she opened the door and hurried back out to the street, leaving the three sisters staring after her.

"They really do think we're witches, don't they?" Hazel said aloud.

"Let them think it. It gives us power over them," Marguerite answered.

"Or gives them reason to hang us," Aurora added.

Marguerite sauntered to the center of the store, winking back at her sisters. "The boys all seem to like it," she replied with a sway of her hips.

Both Hazel and Aurora laughed. Marguerite had always been unabashed and they admired this quality in her, even if at times it got her into trouble. The three sisters were close, devoted to one another. Their lives interwoven as tightly as a sailor's knot.

They didn't yet know the things that would divide them.

For in a place like Sparrow, rumors spread quickly, like small pox or cholera, confusing the mind, rooting itself into the fabric of a town until there's no telling truth from speculation.

TWELVE

I dial Rose's cell when I get back to the house, but she doesn't answer, so I leave a message: "Call me when you get this."

I don't know why she went to see Gigi at the boathouse, but whatever the reason, I need to tell her to stay away.

Through the kitchen window, I see Mom standing out on the cliff, her black robe billowing around her legs with an updraft of wind. She didn't stay in bed all day after all.

I wait by the phone for most of the day, but Rose never calls. I dial her number three more times, but she doesn't answer. *Where is she?*

When the sun starts to settle over the ocean, I curl up in bed, knees to chest. I fall asleep with the wind rattling the glass in the windows, the sea air driving against the house.

Just after dawn it starts raining, gently pattering against the roof. The sky is painted in brushstroke ribbons of violet and coral pink. I stay in my room, but still no word from Rose. The rain keeps everyone inside. Mom locks herself in her bedroom, and I don't see Bo leave the cottage all day. There are things I should say to him—confessions buried inside me. The way my heart feels unmoored when I'm with him. My head loose with thoughts I can't explain. I should say I'm sorry. I should walk down through the rain and beat my fist against his door. I should touch his skin with my fingertips and tell him there are things I want, I crave. But how do you let yourself unravel in front of someone, knowing your armor is the only thing keeping you safe?

So I don't say anything. I keep my heart hidden deep and dark in my chest.

Evening eventually presses down and I slump in the chair beside my bedroom window, watching the sky peel apart and the rainclouds fade. Stars illuminate the dark. But I feel anxious, wishing Rose would just call, explain why she went to the boathouse. She's acting suspicious—making herself seem like one of them. Why?

And then I see something through the window.

Movement down on the path, a silhouette passing beneath the cascade of blue moonlight. It's Bo, and he's heading toward the dock.

And in my gut, I sense that something isn't right.

I pull on a long black sweater over my cotton shorts and tank top and hurry down the stairs to the front door. The air hits me as soon as I step outside, a blast of cold that cuts straight down to my marrow.

I lose sight of him for a moment, the darkness absorbing him, but when I reach the point in the path where it slopes down toward the water, I see him again. And he's almost to the dock.

The evening wind has stirred up from the west, and it pushes waves against the shore in intervals, spilling up over the rocks and leaving behind a layer of foam. Everything smells soggy from the rain. My bare feet are slapping against the wood walkway, but I still catch up to him just as he stops at the far end of the dock.

"Bo?" I ask. But he doesn't move, doesn't turn to look at me. Like he can't even hear me. And I already know. Under the dark sky and the pale, swollen moon, I can tell he's not himself.

I take two careful steps toward him. "Bo," I say again, trying to get his attention. But in one swift motion, he steps forward and falls straight off the edge of the dock and down into the water. "No!" I yell, scrambling forward.

The harbor heaves and churns. He's already gone under, sunk beneath the waves. I hold my breath, counting the seconds—how long does he have until there's no more air left in his lungs? I scan the water, afraid to blink. Then, ten yards out, he appears, sucking in a breath of air as he breaks through the surface. But he doesn't turn back for shore. He doesn't even look over his shoulder. He keeps going, swimming farther out into the harbor.

No, no, no. This is bad.

I strip out of my black sweater and drop it onto the dock. I draw in a deep breath, reach my arms over my head, and dive in after him.

The cold water cuts through my skin like needles, and when I gulp in the night air, it stings the inner walls of my lungs. But I start swimming.

He is already a good distance ahead of me, determined, being beckoned deeper into the bay. But my arms and legs find a fluid rhythm that is faster than his. His feet, still in his shoes, kick little explosions of water out behind him. When I'm finally within reach, I grab on to his T-shirt and pull hard. His arms stop circling overhead, and his legs pause their kicking. He lifts his head, hair slicked sideways over his forehead, lips parted, and looks at me.

"Bo," I say, meeting his stony eyes. His eyelashes drip with sea-water, his expression slack, unaware of where he is or what he's doing. "We need to go back," I yell over the wind.

He doesn't shake his head, doesn't protest, but he also doesn't seem to register anything I've said, because he drops his gaze and roughly pulls away, resuming his swim across the harbor. I suck in a few quick breaths. The beam of light from the lighthouse circles around, sweeping over the harbor and illuminating the masts of sunken ships. He's being summoned to the wreckage, by *her*.

"Shit." My skin is chilled and weighted from my clothes. But I push my legs out behind me and swim after him, through the dark, knowing that a boat passing through the harbor likely wouldn't see us in time. We'd be forced under by the bow, churned up by the prop, and might never come back up again. But if I let him go, I know what will happen. I will lose him for good.

I kick hard, my arms cutting through the water, the cold starting to slow my heartbeat and the blood pumping out to my extremities. But after several more rotations of the lighthouse—the only thing marking time—I manage to catch up to him again. I wrap my fist around the hem of his shirt and yank him back toward me. He turns to look at me, the same expression etched permanently on his face.

"You need to wake up," I scream at him. "You can't do this!"

His eyebrows pucker a fraction of an inch. He hears me, but he's also lost to Marguerite—her voice cycling through his mind, calling to him, begging him to find her somewhere out there.

"Bo," I say, harder this time, twisting my other fist around his shirt and pulling him closer to me. My legs kick quickly beneath me to keep from sinking under. "Wake up!"

He blinks. His lips are ghostly, lost of all color. He opens his mouth, squints slightly, and a word forms softly against his lips. "What?"

"She's in your head, making you do this. You need to get her out, ignore what she's telling you. It's not real."

Several yards ahead, toward the mouth of the harbor, the bell buoy rings against the force of the waves. An eerie sound that rolls across the water.

"I need to find her," he says, voice slurred. I know the image she has placed in his mind: of her, swimming in a pearl-white dress, fabric thin and transparent swirling around her body, hair long and silken, her beguiling voice slipping into his ears. Her words promise warmth, the velvet of her kiss and her body pressed to his. He is caught in her spell.

She will drown him like all the others.

"Please," I beg, staring into eyes that can't focus—that only see her. "Come back with me."

He shakes his head slowly. "I . . . can't."

I clench my jaw and wrap my hands around the back of his neck, forcing him so close that our bodies slide weightlessly together. I do it without thinking, without breathing. I crush my lips to his. Water spills between us, and I taste the sea on his skin. I dig my nails into the base of his neck, trying to spur him from his waking dream. My heartbeat drives against my chest, and I press my lips harder. I open my mouth to feel the warmth of his breath, but he doesn't move, doesn't react. Maybe this won't work—maybe it was a mistake.

But then one of his arms slides around me, bracing against my shoulder blades. His mouth parts open, and the heat from his body suddenly pours into me. His other hand finds my cheekbone and then weaves through my hair. He draws me in deeper, folding me in the circle of his arms. And with my lips, I wipe away the memory of Marguerite Swan from his mind. I take him from her, and he lets me. He kisses me like he wants me more than he's ever wanted anything. And for a second, none of it feels real. I am not swimming in the harbor, wrapped in Bo's arms, his mouth sweeping over mine, my heart pattering wildly against the cage of my chest. We are somewhere else, far away from here, coiled against each other under a warm sun with warm sand at our backs and warm breath on our lips. Two bodies bound together. Fearing nothing.

And then he pulls his mouth away, slowly, water dripping between us, and everything focuses into a single narrow pinprick. I expect him to release me, to resume his swim across the harbor, but he keeps a hand tangled at the back of my skull and the other against my back, our legs kicking rhythmically beneath us. "Why did you do that?" he asks, his voice raw and near breaking.

"To save you."

His eyes glance out at the dark forbidding sea, as if waking up from an all-too-real nightmare.

"We need to get back to shore," I tell him, and he nods understanding, his eyes still bleary and unfocused, like he's still not entirely sure where he is or why.

We swim side by side back to the dock. We've drifted farther away from it than I realized, the current drawing us out to sea, and after several minutes of swimming hard, we finally reach it. He wraps his hands around my waist and hoists me up to the edge of the dock, and then he pulls himself up after. We're too cold to speak, collapsing onto our backs on the dock, heaving in the chilled night air. I know we need to get inside and get warm before hypothermia sets in—a real possibility out here. So I touch his hand and we both rise, jogging up the wood path to his cottage.

We tug off our shoes and Bo kneels down beside the fireplace—a few embers are still alive beneath the charred logs—while I curl up on the couch with two wool blankets held tightly over my shoulders. Otis and Olga appear from the bedroom, stretching and looking sleepy. They've been spending all their time in here with Bo; they like him. Maybe more than they like me.

Bo adds more logs to the fire, and I crawl onto the floor beside him, stretching out my arms to warm my palms against the meager flames. My teeth chatter, and my fingertips are wrinkled. "You're freezing," he says, looking down at my trembling body beneath the blankets. "You need to get out of those clothes." He stands up and walks back into his bedroom, returning a moment later with a plain white T-shirt and a pair of green boxer shorts. "Here," he says. "You can wear these."

I consider telling him that I'm fine, but I'm not fine. My shorts and tank top are so drenched that they're starting to soak the blankets as well. So I stand up, thank him, and take the clothes into the bathroom.

The white tile floor is cold beneath my feet, and for a moment I stand scanning the tiny bathroom. A razor and a toothbrush sit beside the sink. A towel hangs from the rack. Hints that someone has been living in this cottage after so many years vacant. I slog out of my clothes then drop them heavily onto the floor in a pile. I don't even bother folding them.

Bo's shirt and boxers smell like him, minty and sweet, but also like a forest. I take in a deep breath and close my eyes before stepping back out into the living room. The fire now crackles and flames spark up the chimney, filling the cottage with warmth.

I sit on the floor beside Bo and pull the blankets around me. He doesn't turn to look at me; he is staring into the flames, biting his lower lip. While I was in the bathroom, he changed into dry jeans and a dark blue T-shirt. Both of us are now rid of our waterlogged clothes. "What happened out there?" he asks.

I tighten the blankets across my chest. The rain batters against the roof; the wind howls. "You were being led into the harbor."

"How?"

"You know how."

"Olivia," he says, as if the name has been trapped on his lips for days. "I could see her . . . out in the water."

"She was calling to you. Her voice infiltrated your mind."

"How?" he asks again.

"At the boathouse she whispered something in your ear. She claimed you as hers, making it impossible for you to think of anything or anyone else. It was only a matter of time until she beckoned you. Since you've remained on the island, hidden, she couldn't physically pull you out into the water, so she had to slip her voice into your mind and make you come in search of her."

He shakes his head, unable to rectify what has just happened to him.

"Olivia Greene," I tell him bluntly, "is Marguerite Swan. She was waiting for you out in the harbor; she would have pulled you to her, her lips on yours, and then she would have drowned you."

He leans forward against his knees, teeth clamped shut. I stare at the scar beside his left eye, his cheekbones are starting to blaze from the heat of the fire. My focus slides back to his lips, to the way they felt pressed to mine. "But how do you know that?" he asks. "How can you be so sure it's Marguerite Swan who's taken over Olivia's body? And not one of the other sisters?" He squints, like he can't believe his own question, that he's even asking it.

"You just need to trust me," I say. "Marguerite wants to kill you. And she won't stop until she finds a way to do it."

"Why me?" he asks.

"Because she saw you with me at the boathouse."

"What does that have to do with anything?"

My fingers tremble slightly; my heart pushes against my ribs, warning me not to tell him the truth. But the truth tastes like letting go, like the sharpness of sunlight on a spring day, and my head begins to pulse with every heartbeat. "I can see them," I confess, the words tumbling out before I can catch them.

"Them?"

"The sisters. I can see Aurora inside of Gigi Kline and Marguerite inside of Olivia Greene. I know whose bodies they've taken."

He straightens, lifting his elbows away from his knees. "How's that even possible?"

I shake my head, the air gone from my lungs, and a shiver races up my entire body.

"You can see them and you haven't said anything?"

"No one knows."

"But . . ." His mouth dips open, eyes narrowed on me. "You can see what they really are?"

"Yes."

I stand up, crossing my arms. I can tell he's trying to piece it all together, make everything fit. But his mind is fighting him. He doesn't want to believe what I'm telling him could be true. "How long have you been able to do this?"

"Always."

"But how?"

I lift my shoulders. "I don't know. I mean . . . it's just something I've always been able to do. . . . I . . ." I'm rambling, getting lost in the explanation. In the deception beneath the truth.

"Can your mom see them too?"

I shake my head.

He frowns and looks down into the fire, rubbing the back of his neck with his right hand. "Do they know . . . do the sisters know you can see them?"

"Yes."

Again his mouth parts open, searching for words, for the right question to make this all make sense. "What about the third one—the third sister?"

"Hazel," I answer for him.

"Where is she? Whose body has she stolen?"

"I don't know."

"You haven't seen her yet?"

"No."

"But she's out there somewhere?"

"Yes."

"And she hasn't killed anyone yet?"

I shake my head. "Not yet."

"So there's still time to find her and stop her."

"There's no stopping them," I answer.

"Have you tried?"

I can't meet his eyes. "No. It's pointless to try." I think about my encounter with Gigi in the boathouse. I had thought—foolishly—maybe I could talk to her, the *real* her. Aurora. Maybe some part of her was still human, still had a beating heart that would be tired of the killing. But Lon interrupted us. And I sense she's too far gone anyway. My words would never be enough.

Bo drops his palm from the back of his neck. And I can see in his eyes that he's starting to believe me. "Fuck, Penny," he says, standing up and taking a step toward me. "So Lon and Davis were right? They do have a Swan sister locked in that boathouse?"

I nod.

"And Olivia . . . or Marguerite—whatever her name is—is trying to kill me?"

"She's already slipped into your mind. She can make you see things that aren't there, feel things that aren't real."

"When I saw her," he says, "in the water . . . waiting for me. It felt like I needed her, like I'd die if I didn't get to her. Like . . ." He swallows back the words, choking on them.

"Like you loved her?" I finish for him.

"Yeah." His eyes find mine.

"She can convince you that you've never loved anyone quite so much or ever will again."

He clenches his fists together at his sides and I watch the motion, his forearms flexing, his temples pulsing.

"And then you were there," he says, recounting the moment

when I jumped into the ocean after him. "I could hear you but I couldn't focus on you. You seemed so far away. But then I felt your hands. You were right in front of me." He looks up, the darkest centers of his eyes like the darkest depths of the ocean. "And then you kissed me."

"I . . ." My voice feels strangled in my throat. "I had to stop you."

A beat of silence. My heart stumbles, catches, restarts again.

"After that," he says, "I didn't feel her calling me anymore. I still don't."

"Maybe we broke her hold on you," I say, my voice feeling small.

"*You* broke her hold on me."

Words tangle up on my tongue. All the things I want to say. "I needed to bring you back. I couldn't let you go; I couldn't lose you. I couldn't let . . ." The weight of my honesty rattles the very center of my ribs, my stomach, the place just behind my eyes. "I couldn't let her have you."

I don't allow myself to look away from him—I need him to speak, to wash over my words with his own. In his eyes, a storm waits at the edges. His hand lifts, and his fingers slide up the ridge of my cheekbone and behind my ear. The sensation of his fingertips against my skin unweaves the stone knitted together at the base of my heart. I close my eyes briefly then open them again, a craving rising up inside me, pure and uncorrupt. He pulls me forward, and I pause only a feather's width from his mouth. I look into his eyes, trying to root myself in the moment. And then he kisses me like he needs me to root him here too.

His lips are warm and his fingertips cold. All at once I am wrapped up in him: his heart battering just beneath his chest, his hands in my hair, his mouth searching my lower lip. He is everywhere, filling my lungs and the space between each breath. And I feel myself falling, tumbling like a star dropping from the sky and spinning toward Earth. My heart stretches outward, becomes light and jittery.

This moment—this boy—could tear me apart and upend everything. But in the heat of the cottage, wind rattling the glass in the windows, rain pelting the roof, with our skin flecked with salt water, I don't care. I let his hands roam my chilled flesh and my fingers weave up the back of his neck. I don't want to be anywhere else. I only want him. *Him.*

Love is an enchantress—devious and wild.

It sneaks up behind you, soft and gentle and quiet, just before it slits your throat.

I wake on the hardwood floor beside the fireplace, Bo asleep next to me, his arm folded over my hip bone. He is breathing softly against my hair. My eyes skirt across the living room, remembering where I am: his cottage. The fire has turned to coals, all the logs burned down, so I shimmy from beneath his arm—his fingers twitching—and slide a fresh log into the fireplace, pushing it through the coals. It takes only a moment for the flames to reignite.

I cross my legs and run my fingers through my hair. I smell like him, his T-shirt still against my skin. I know I can't leave him alone now. Marguerite will try again. And I won't let her have him. This thing I feel for him is working its way into my bones, like water through cracks in my surface. When it freezes, it will either shatter me into a million pieces or make me stronger.

I pick up one of the books sitting on the floor next to me, flipping through the pages. There are notes in the margins, paragraphs high-lighted, corners dog-eared. The ink is faded and smeared in places.

"I think they were your father's books," Bo says. His eyes are open, but he's still lying on the floor, watching me. He must have heard me sit up.

"Why do you think that?"

"They were purchased from a bookstore in town. And there's a name in the front of that one." I flip back to the front cover where a piece of paper sits tucked into the crease. Handwritten with black ink on the paper is the name JOHN TALBOT. It was a book he had special ordered, or maybe put on hold. And an employee wrote his name on a slip of paper until he came to pay for it. "Your father was John Talbot, right?"

"Yeah." Beneath the paper is a folded receipt from the Olive Street Tea & Bookhouse. It's dated June fifth, three years earlier. Only a week before he disappeared.

"He must have been researching the Swan sisters," Bo says. "Maybe he was looking for a way to stop them."

A scattering of memories crack through me, of the night I saw him moving down to the dock in the dark. The night he vanished. The rain fell sideways, and the wind ripped shingles from the roof of the house. But he would never return to repair them.

He had been collecting these books all along, in secret, looking for a way to end the Swan season.

"Are you all right?" Bo sits up, creases formed between his brows.

"Fine." I close the cover of the book and set it back on the floor. "And you've read most of them?" I ask.

He nods, stretching upright.

"And what did you find?"

"Mostly speculation about witches and curses—nothing definitive."

"Anything about how to end a curse?"

He shifts his gaze to me, exhaling. "Only the obvious."

"Which is?"

"Destroy the purveyors of it."

"The sisters."

"The only way to end it would be to kill them," he says.

"But then both the Swan sister and the girl whose body they stole would die."

He nods.

"And you still want to kill Gigi Kline?" I ask.

"I want whoever killed my brother to pay for it. And if the only way to do that is to destroy both the girl and the monster, then that's what I'll do."

I brush both hands through my hair, catching on knots that my fingers must work through before I can twist my mass of hair over my shoulder. "Does this mean you believe in the Swan sisters now?"

"I don't think I have a choice," he says. "One of them is trying to kill me." The fullness of his lips seems amplified as he pushes them together, a rivulet of tension passing over his expression. It can't be easy knowing someone—some*thing*—wants you dead.

But what's even harder is knowing it's your fault. Marguerite wouldn't want Bo so badly if he were just some random tourist. It's because of me that she's so intrigued by him. She loves a challenge. And Bo is the perfect prey.

I stand up from the floor. Otis and Olga had been sleeping on the couch, curled up together at one end. But now Olga is awake, her ears alert, head turned toward the door.

"I'm sorry you're here," I say, rubbing my palms down my arms. "I'm sorry you got dragged into this."

"It's not your fault." His voice is deep, his eyebrows angled downward, softening the hard edges of his face. "I came here because of my brother. I did this; not you."

"If you weren't on this island with me," I tell him, forcing the tears down so they don't rise up. "Then she wouldn't want you. I was wrong when I thought keeping you here on the island would make you safe. She'll find you wherever you are."

"No." He stands up too but doesn't touch me, doesn't run his hands up my arms to comfort me—not yet. "She's not in my head anymore," he says. "I don't hear her voice, feel her thoughts. You broke whatever hold she had on me."

"For now. But she'll try again. She'll come for you, here to the island if she has to. She'll physically drag you out into the water. She won't give up."

"If I'm not safe, then you're not safe."

"It doesn't work like that," I tell him. "It's you she will drown. Not me." My stomach begins to wrench and turn.

"If you can see them, and they know it, then you're in danger too."

I think of Marguerite out in the harbor, waiting for Bo, beckoning him with the promise of her lips skimming delicately over his. She is a wraith dredged up from the seafloor. She is vengeful and clever. She is single-minded in her hatred for this town. And she won't stop.

"You can't protect me," I tell him. "Just like I can't protect you."

Olga hops down from the couch and trots between us to the front door, stretching up on her hind legs to scratch at the wood. She begins to mew, and it wakes Otis.

"I can try," Bo says, moving closer, and in his eyes I see the ocean, and it draws me into him like the tide against the sand.

His hands find me in the firelight, grazing my wrists, my arms, then his palms slide up to my jaw, through my hair, fingerprints on my skin, and for a moment I believe him. Maybe he can keep me safe; maybe this thing threading between us is enough to keep all the terrors at bay. I suck in a breath and try to steady the two halves of my heart, but when his lips brush against mine, I lose all rooting to the earth. My heart turns wild. His fingers pull me closer, and I press myself against him, needing the steadiness of his heartbeat inside his chest and the balance of his arms. My own fingers slide up beneath his shirt: feeling the firmness of his torso, air filling his lungs. He is strong, stronger than most. Maybe he can survive this town, survive Marguerite. Survive me. I dig my fingers into his skin, his shoulders, losing myself to him. He feels like everything—all that's left. The world has been shredded around me. But this, *this*, might be enough to smooth the brittle edges of my once-beating heart.

The fire makes the heat between us almost unbearable. But we fold ourselves together among the pages of books and the blankets scattered across the floor. The wind roars outside. His fingers trace the moons of my hip bones, my thighs, my shivering heartbeat. He kisses down my throat, the place where my secrets are kept. He kisses my collarbone, where the skin is thin and delicate, patterns of freckles like a sailor's map. He kisses so softly it feels like wings or a whisper. He kisses and I slip, slip, slip beneath his touch. Crumbling.

His lips inch beneath my shirt, along the curves of my body. Valleys and hills. Breathing promises he'll keep against my skin. My clothes feel burdensome and heavy—clothes that belong to him, boxers and a T-shirt—so I peel them away.

My mind spins, my breathing catches then rises again. My skin crackles, set alight, and his touch feels infinite, fathomless, a wave that rolls ashore but never ends. He is gentle and sweet, and I never want his hands, his lips, to be anywhere else but against me. The morning sunlight is just starting to break above the horizon, soft pinks sifting through the windows, but I am breaking here on the floor, shattering into pieces as he whispers my name and I see only flecks of light shivering across my vision. And after, he holds his lips above mine, breathing the same air, my skin shimmering from the heat. Sweat dewing the curves of my body. He kisses my nose, my forehead, my earlobes.

I have doomed him, kept him here, made him the prey of Marguerite Swan. He is caught in the tempest of a season that could kill him. He needs to leave Sparrow, escape this wretched place. Yet I need him to stay. I *need* him.

JOHN TALBOT

On June fifth, a week before he vanished, John Talbot entered the Olive Street Tea & Bookhouse. He had special ordered four books a week earlier, titles he had researched online that contained real-life accounts of hexes and curses that had been documented in other unfortunate towns.

It was not unusual for locals in Sparrow to take an interest in the Swan sisters. They often collected newspaper clippings and old photographs of the town from when the sisters were still alive. They shared stories at the Silver Dollar Pub over too many beers, and then stumbled down to the docks and shouted into the night about their sons and brothers who they've lost. And sometimes they even became obsessed. Sorrow and desperation can make cracks along the mind.

But John Talbot never shared his theories. He never got drunk and lamented the tragedy of Sparrow over a pint. He never told anyone about the collection of books he kept stashed in Anchor Cottage. Not even his wife.

And on that bright, warm afternoon, as he left the bookstore, there was frenzy in his shadowed eyes, lines of worry carved along his forehead. His gaze darted side to side, as if the sunlight were unbearable, and he pushed through the horde of tourists back down to the skiff waiting at the dock.

Those who saw him that day would later say he had the look of someone overcome with sea madness. The island had been known to drive people insane. The salt air, the isolation. It had finally gotten to him.

John Talbot had lost his mind.

THIRTEEN

Two days slip by uncounted.

Bo's fingers coil through my hair, he watches me sleep, and he keeps me warm when the wind tears through the cracks in the cottage windows in the early hours of morning. He slides himself beside me beneath the wool blanket and runs his fingertips down my arm. I've forgotten about everything else but this little room, this fireplace, this spot in my heart that aches to the point of bursting.

On the third day, we wake and walk down the rows of the newly revived orchard trees under a tepid afternoon sky; the leaves are beginning to unfurl and the flowers just starting to break open. This season's apples and pears might still be stunted and hard and inedible. But by next year, hopefully our hard work will produce fat, sun-sweetened fruit.

"What were you like in school?" I ask, craning my head upward to soak up the sun. Little white spots dance across my closed eyelids.

"What do you mean?"

"Were you popular?"

He reaches out a hand and touches the craggy end of a branch, small green leaves sliding through his palm. "No."

185

"But you had friends?"

"A few." He glances at me, his jade-green eyes spearing a hole straight through my center.

"Did you play sports?" I'm trying to piece together the person he was, the person he is, and I find it hard to imagine him anywhere else but here in Sparrow, on this island with me.

He shakes his head, smiling a little, like he finds it funny that I would even ask this. "I worked for my parents every day after school, so I didn't have much time for friends or group sports."

"Your parents' farm?"

"It's actually a vineyard."

I pause near the end of a row. "A vineyard?" I repeat. "Like grapes?"

"Yeah. It's just a small family winery, but it does pretty well." It's not exactly the farm where I imagined him toiling: hands-in-the-earth, greasy, cow-manure type of farming. But I'm sure it was still hard work.

"It's not what I pictured," I tell him.

"Why not?"

"I don't know." I examine him, eyeing his faded gray sweatshirt and jeans. "Do your parents know where you are?"

"No. They didn't want me to come here. They said I just needed to let Kyle go. That's how they coped with his death, by ignoring it. But I knew I had to come. So when I graduated this year, I hitch-hiked down the coast. I never told them I was leaving."

"Have you talked to them since you left?"

He shakes his head, pushing his hands into his jean pockets.

"They're probably worried about you," I say.

"I can't call them. I don't know what I'd say." He looks at me. "How do I explain what's going on here? That Kyle didn't kill himself but was drowned by one of three sisters who died two centuries ago?"

"Maybe you don't tell them that," I offer. "But you should probably let them know you're okay . . . tell them something. Even a lie."

"Yeah." His voice dips low. "Maybe."

We reach the end of the orchard, where one of the dead apple trees is now gone, torched down to its roots.

"When this is all over," I say, "after the summer solstice, will you go home?"

"No." He pauses to look back down the rows of perfectly spaced fruit trees. A small gray bird bursts out from the limbs of one tree and lands on the branch of another. "I won't go back there. Not now. Before Kyle died, I always thought I'd stay and work for my parents after high school. Take over the family business. It was what they expected of me. My brother would be the one to move away and live a different life, to escape. And I was okay with that. But after he died . . ." He draws in his lips and looks up through the limbs of an apple tree, buds pushing out from the green stalks. "I knew I wanted something different. Something that was mine. I had always been the one who would stay behind while Kyle saw the world. But not anymore."

"So now what do you want?" I ask, my voice soft, not wanting to crack apart his thoughts.

"I want to be out there." He nods to the western edge of the island. "On the water." He looks back at me like he's not sure I'll understand. "When my dad taught me to sail, I knew I loved it, but I didn't think I'd ever have the chance to really do it. Maybe now I can. I could buy a sailboat, leave—maybe I won't ever come back."

"Sounds like an escape plan. Like you want to start a whole new life."

His eyes flicker, and he squares his shoulders to face me. "I do. I have money; I've been saving most of my life." His stare turns cool and serious. "You could come with me."

I draw in both my lips, holding back a betraying smile.

"You don't have to stay in this town—you could escape too, leave this place behind if it's what you want."

"I have school."

"I'll wait for you." And he says it like he actually means it.

"But my mom," I say. . . . Just another excuse.

His mouth hardens in place.

"It's just not that easy for me," I explain. I feel wrenched into halves, torn between the *wanting* and the prison that is this island. "It's not a no. But I also can't say yes."

I can see the hurt in his eyes, that he doesn't understand even if he wants to. But he slides his fingers around my waist, gently, like he's afraid I'll spook like one of the island birds, and he pulls me to him. "Someday you'll find a worthy enough reason to leave this place," he says.

I once read a poem about love being fragile, as thin as glass and easily broken.

But that is not the kind of love that survives in a place like this. It must be hardy and enduring. It must have grit.

He's strong, I think, the same thought I had the other night. I blink up at him, the sunlight scattering through the trees, making the features of his face soft at the edges. *Stronger than most boys.* He could survive this place. He's made of something different, his heart weathered and battered just like mine, forged of hard metals and earth. We've both lost things, lost people. We are broken but fighting to stay alive. Maybe that's why I need him—he *feels* like I feel, *wants* like I want. He's stirred loose something inside my chest, a cold center where blood now pumps, a hint of life, of green pushing up toward sunlight.

I might love him.

And it has tilted my universe off center, the frayed edges of my life starting to unravel. Loving someone is dangerous. It gives you something to lose.

I lift up to my tiptoes, his lips hovering over mine, and I know he's looking for answers in the steady calm of my stare. But he won't find them there, so he presses his mouth to mine, as if he might press some truth out of me. But I can only give him this moment, and I climb my fingers up his chest, breathing him in, tasting the salt air on his lips.

I wish suddenly that I could promise him forever, promise him *me*. But it would be a lie.

I try to call Rose. I leave messages on her phone. I tell her mom to have her call me back, but she never does.

Where is she? Why won't she call me? But I can't leave the island. I can't risk leaving Bo alone—I'm afraid Olivia might try to lure him into the harbor again.

But after several days, I can't take it anymore. The not knowing is making me edgy and nervous.

I wake up early, hoping to slip out of the cottage before Bo sees me. Olga trails me to the door; her eyes are watery from the cold, and she blinks, as if curious about what I'm doing awake at this hour.

I pull on my raincoat hanging from a metal hook beside the door then turn the knob; a swift breeze rips into the cottage, spraying raindrops over my face. Olga zips past my feet and trots up the boardwalk. But then she stops short, ears alert, tail swishing back and forth. Something has caught her attention.

It's still an hour or so before sunrise, but the sky has turned aqueous and lucid, morning pressing down, breaking apart the night clouds and sheering the island terrain in a hue of blush pink. And in the distance, I see what Olga sees: A light is wavering across the water, and an engine is sputtering toward the island dock.

"What is it?" Bo asks, his voice a shock to my ears. I wasn't expecting him to be awake. The door is partway open, and I glance back inside. He's standing up, rubbing his face.

"Someone's here," I say.

FOURTEEN

A boat knocks loudly against the dock, motoring too fast across the water. It's Heath's boat; I recognize it as the same one we took out into the harbor to make wishes at the pirates' ship when we found the first body.

But Heath is not driving it. It's Rose.

And someone is with her: a girl.

Bo grabs my arm, stopping me from getting any closer to the boat as Rose struggles to tie a rope around one of the cleats on the dock. He recognizes the girl before I do. It's Gigi Kline.

"Rose?" I ask. And she notices us for the first time.

"I didn't have anywhere else to go," she says frantically when her eyes meet mine. She looks scared, in a state of shock, and her red wavy hair is windblown like a person who's recently escaped from an asylum.

"What did you do?" I ask.

"I had to help her. And I couldn't hide her in town, they'd find her. So I brought her here. I thought she'd be safe. You could hide her in the lighthouse or the other cottage. I don't know—I panicked. I didn't know what else to do." She's speaking too fast, and her eyes keep flicking from Gigi back to me.

"You broke Gigi out of the boathouse?" Bo asks.

Gigi is sitting silently in the boat, meekly, innocently. Her façade is well practiced as she makes slow, measured movements. Each blink of an eyelash looks rehearsed.

"I . . . I had to."

"No, you didn't," I snap. "This was a very bad idea, Rose."

"I couldn't just let them keep her locked up like that. It was cruel! And they could just as easily do it to anyone else. To me—to us."

"And they probably will when they find out what you've done."

"Penny, please," she says, stepping from the boat, palms lifted in the air. "You have to help her."

I didn't realize Gigi's imprisonment upset Rose this deeply, enough that she would break her out and bring her here. I know they were friends once, years ago, but I never imagined she'd do this. She couldn't stand to see someone she once cared about tied up and suffering. Made to be a cruel spectacle. It didn't seem right to Rose from the start. And I can't fault her for that.

"This is dangerous, Rose. You shouldn't have freed her." I lock eyes with Gigi, and with Aurora tucked inside her—watching like an animal waiting until it's safe to come out of its hiding place. She didn't have to enchant Davis or Lon to save her, Rose did it out of the goodness of her heart. But she's set loose a monster, and she doesn't even realize it.

"Maybe it's better that she's here," Bo whispers to me, out of earshot of Rose and Gigi.

I feel my eyebrows slant into a scowl. "What are you talking about?"

"We can keep an eye on her, lock her up, make sure she doesn't kill anyone else."

I know why he wants to do this: He wants to ask Gigi about his brother. And if he decides that it was Aurora—hidden inside of Gigi—who killed his brother, then what? Will he try to kill her? This is a mistake, I can feel it, but both Bo and Rose are staring at me, waiting for me to decide what to do.

This can't be happening.

"Fine. Get her out of the boat. We'll take her to Old Fisherman's Cottage. Then we'll decide what to do next."

Sometimes I think this island is a magnet for bad things, the center of it all. Like a black hole pulling us toward a fate we can't prevent. And other times I think this island is the only thing keeping me sane, the only familiar thing I have left.

Or maybe it's me that's the black hole. And everyone around me can't help but be swallowed up, drowned and trapped in my orbit. But I also know that there's nothing I can do to change it. The island and I are the same.

I lead the way to Old Fisherman's Cottage, Rose trailing behind me, then Gigi, and Bo bringing up the back. He wants to make sure Gigi doesn't make a run for it.

The door is unlocked, and the interior is darker and damper and colder than Bo's cottage. I flip on a light switch, but nothing happens. I walk across the living room, furnished with a single wood rocking chair and a burgundy upholstered ottoman that doesn't match anything else in the room. I find a floor lamp, kneel down to plug it in, and it immediately blinks on.

But the light does little to brighten the appearance of the cottage.

"It's only temporary," Rose assures Gigi. But I'm not sure what Rose thinks will happen to change the current circumstances. Kidnapping Gigi from the boathouse will only make Davis and Lon more suspicious. They will assume one of the Swan sisters broke her out, and now they'll be looking for her. And Rose and I will likely be their first suspects since both she and I were caught sneaking into the boathouse—and now I know why Rose was there. She was planning this all along.

"We'll bring you wood for the fireplace," I say to Gigi, but her eyes don't lift from the floor. She's staring at a corner of the living room rug, the edges frayed—probably chewed up by mice.

"And I'll find you some new clothes," Rose offers, looking down at Gigi's stained shirt and jeans.

I tug at the only two windows in the cottage, seeing if they'll slide up in their casings, but they don't even budge—both are rusted shut. This cottage is much older than the one Bo is staying in. And these windows probably haven't been opened in two decades. I walk back to the door, not wanting to be in the same room as Gigi any longer than I have to.

"You're safe here," I hear Rose tell her, and Bo steps through the doorway, shooting me a sideways glance. We both know what she really is, and I can tell Bo is itching to interrogate her.

"Can I have something to eat?" Gigi asks.

Rose nods. "Of course. We'll bring you food too." She has no idea who she has just invited to the island. "Try to get some rest, I'm sure you're exhausted."

Once Rose has stepped through the doorway, I shut the door and Bo drags over a warped wood board that had been stacked along the backside of the cottage. He jams it up under the doorknob, locking it in place.

"What are you doing?" Rose asks, making a move to grab the board. "She's not a prisoner."

"If you want me to hide her here, then this is how it has to be," I explain.

"You don't actually think she did anything wrong—that she's one of them—do you?" Rose might not believe in the Swan sisters, but she knows that I do.

"You don't have any reason to think she's innocent," I say. "So for now, she stays locked in there. At least it's better than the boathouse."

"Hardly," Rose counters, but she crosses her arms and steps back from the door, reluctantly agreeing to our rules.

"Does Heath know what you did?" I ask.

She shakes her head. "No. But I borrowed his parents' boat, so I'll probably have to tell him where I've been."

"He can't say anything to anyone about this."

"He won't."

"And no one saw you take her?" Bo asks.

"It was dark, and Lon was completely passed out. He probably hasn't even realized she's gone yet."

Again I'm struck by what a horrible idea this is. I'm not even sure if we're hiding Gigi from Lon and Davis or if we're holding her hostage just like they did. Whatever this is that we're doing, I'm fairly certain it's going to end catastrophically.

"Just be careful in town," I say.

"I will." And she presses her hands down deep into her coat pockets, as if she were fighting off a sudden chill. "Thank you," she adds, just before she heads down the walkway back to the dock.

Bo and I look at each other once she's out of sight. "Now what?" he asks.

Back at the house, I make two peanut butter and jelly sandwiches for Gigi, wrap them in foil, then grab a blanket from the hall closet.

When I reach the door of Old Fisherman's Cottage, the wood board has been removed and the door is slightly ajar. At first my heart jumps upward with panic—Gigi must have gotten out—but then I hear Bo's voice inside. He went to collect logs to start a fire for her while I went to make food, and he's returned before me.

I pause, listening to the crackling of flames in the fireplace.

"I know what you are," I hear Bo say.

"Do you?" Gigi answers, her voice farther away, across the living room maybe, sitting in the only chair. I touch the doorknob with my fingers then pause. Maybe I owe him this: the chance to question her about his brother. So I wait before entering.

"You're not Gigi Kline," he says coolly, his voice measured and precise. "You're something else."

"And who told you that? Your girlfriend, Penny?"

I swallow down a jagged lump.

"Did you kill my brother?"

"Your brother?" Her voice changes, dips to an octave that is no longer Gigi's but is Aurora's. "You expect me to remember your brother, one boy from the thousands who've fallen in love with me?" She says it with a laugh, as if to fall in love is the first step toward death.

"It was last summer. June eleventh," he tries, hoping this will jog her memory. But even if she did remember, she would never confess. Not to him.

"Doesn't ring a bell."

I hear footsteps move across the room: Bo's. And his voice is farther away now. "Did you drown anyone on June eleventh?"

"Hmm, let me think." Her tone takes on an upswing, like she's shifting between Gigi's voice and Aurora's, playing a game with Bo that he will lose. "Nope," she finally concludes. "Pretty sure I took that day off. A girl gets tired with so many boys fawning over her." I'm surprised she's being so candid with him, even if her answers are still veiled by untruths. She must recognize that he's not fooled by her little act. He sees right through Gigi Kline, even if he can't actually *see* the thing inside her.

"I can make you tell me," he says, his voice like a steel nail driving into wood, and I push open the door, unable to stay quiet any longer. Gigi isn't sitting like I thought—she's standing at the far wall beside one of the windows, leaning against it like she's watching the ocean for a ship sailing into the harbor that might rescue her. And Bo is only a couple feet away, shoulders drawn back, hands halfway flexed at his sides like he's about to reach forward and wrap them around her throat.

"Bo," I hiss.

He doesn't turn around right away. He stares at her, like maybe he'll see a flicker of his brother in her eyes—of the moment right before he was killed. Gigi lifts a hand, smiling a little. "Poor boy," she says in her smoothest, most condescending tone. "I can't help you find your brother . . . but I *can* show you exactly what he felt." Her

197

fingers rise toward his face, her eyes piercing into his. "It won't hurt, I promise. In fact, you'll beg me for more." The tips of her fingers are only an inch away, about to touch his cheekbone. "I can show you things your girlfriend, Penny, can't. She's too afraid to really love you."

And just when her hand is almost to his jaw, he grabs her wrist, coiling his fingers around her skin. She winces slightly, and then he forces her arm away, where it falls to her side.

Her eyebrows rise in unison, and she glances over at me from across the room, like she wants to make sure I saw how close she was to making him hers. "I like the ones that play hard to get," she says with a wink.

I drop the blanket and two sandwiches onto the small kitchen table with a thump then turn for the door. And Bo is suddenly right behind me.

"If you miss me, Bo," she cajoles, smirking as she watches us leave, "you know where to find me." But Bo slams the door shut then slides the board back into place.

"You were right," he says. "She's one of them."

Bo and I walk the perimeter of the island like we're surveying it, watchmen on duty, scanning the boundary for marauders—as if the Swan sisters were going to swim ashore by the thousands and take over our small island. I am on edge. Fidgety. Certain none of this will end well.

Gigi Kline is locked in the boathouse. People will be looking for her. Davis and Lon want her dead; the Sparrow police are trying to locate her and return her to her parents. And we are somehow right in the middle of it.

I'm still not entirely sure what we're going to do with her.

"Do you want to come up to the house for dinner?" I ask Bo when the sun starts to set. We've spent most of our time in his cottage, alone, never in the main house.

He lifts his hat to brush a hand through his hair before placing it back on his head, lower this time, so it's hard to see his eyes. "What about your mom?"

"She won't mind. And it wasn't really a request but a demand. I'm not about to leave you alone; you might decide to go for a swim again." I say it with a grin, even though it's not funny. He smirks, looking across the island to Old Fisherman's Cottage, where Gigi is locked up. The wood board is still in place.

"All right," he agrees.

I heat a can of tomato soup and make two grilled cheese sandwiches on the stove—a simple meal. There aren't a lot of options anyway. I need to go into town for more supplies . . . eventually. But I'm not in a rush to leave the island.

We eat quickly, and then Bo follows me up the stairs. When we reach my bedroom, I can hear the fan blowing down the hall. Mom's already in bed.

"Do you think your mom knows I'm here?" Bo asks once we're inside my room.

"She knows. She senses when anyone is in the house or on the island."

"What about Gigi?"

"I'm sure Mom knows she's here too. But she won't say anything.

She hasn't talked to anyone outside the island for a couple years. I don't think she could muster the strength to call the cops about a missing girl even if she wanted to."

"Is she like that because of your dad?"

I give a swift nod then sit down on the edge of the bed while he settles into the cushioned chair beside the window. "After he vanished three years ago, she sort of lost her mind."

He nods understanding. "I'm sorry."

A light rain has started to fall, sprinkling the glass and pattering against the roof. A chorus that soothes the eaves and sharp angles of the old house. "Apparently, love is the worst kind of madness."

I go to the window and touch my palm to the glass. I can feel the coolness of the rain on the other side.

"Have you ever been in love before?" Bo braves to ask.

I look back at him, absorbing the drowsy slant of his eyes. "Once," I confess, the four-letter word spilling out. It's something I don't like to talk about—with anyone.

"And?"

"It didn't last. Circumstances beyond our control."

"But you think about him still?" he asks.

"Only sometimes."

"Are you afraid?"

"Of what?"

"To fall in love again?" His hands are resting on the arms of the chair, relaxed, but his gaze seems far more intent.

"No." I swallow down the heartbeat climbing up inside my throat. Can he see what I'm thinking, what I'm feeling? That my heart is already pooling in my stomach, that my mind can hardly think of anything but him? That when we're together, I almost believe nothing else matters? That maybe he could save me and I could save him? "I used to be afraid that I wouldn't get another chance to."

He stands up from the chair and walks to the window, pressing his shoulder against the wood frame, a hard line from his jaw up to his temple. "How did you know you were in love?"

His question makes my fingertips tingle with the need to touch his face, show him the feeling bursting from my seams. "It felt like sinking," I say. I know it might be an odd way to describe it, considering the prevailing death in this town, but it's how it comes out. "Like you're drowning, but it doesn't matter, because you don't need air anymore, you just need the other person."

His eyes flick to mine, searching them, looking to see if I'm drowning. And I am. The clock beside my bed ticks through the seconds; the rain keeps time.

"Penny," he says softly, tilting his gaze on me. "I didn't come here, to this town, expecting any of this." He looks to the floor then back up again. "If I hadn't met you, it probably would have been easier—less complicated. Maybe I would have left days ago." I frown, and he clears his throat. His words break apart then reform. This is hard for him. "But now I know . . ." He lets out a breath, eyes looking through me—turned wild and unwavering. "I'm not leaving here without you. Even if it means I have to wait. I'll wait. I'll wait in this miserable place for as long as it takes. And if you want me to stay, then I'll stay. I'll fucking stay here forever if you ask me to."

He shakes his head and opens his mouth like he's going to continue, but I don't let him. I take one swift step forward and crush my lips to his, pressing away his thoughts, his words. He tastes like a summer wind far away from here, like absolution, like a boy from a different life. Like we could make memories that belong only to us. Memories that have nothing to do with this place. A life, maybe. A real life.

I open my eyes. I trace his lips with mine. He looks at me like I am a girl brought in with the tide, rare and scarred and broken. A girl found in the roughest waters, in the farthest reaches of a dark fairy tale. He is looking at me like he might love me.

"I'm scared," I whisper up at him.

"Of what?"

"Of letting myself love you then feeling my insides collapse when I lose you."

"I'm not going anywhere without you."

Promises are easy to make, I think but don't say. Because I know he believes his own words. He believes that what we feel right now will rescue us in the end. But I know—*I know*. Endings are never so simple.

I sink back against the wall. His hand still touches my forearm, not letting me go.

"How does it end?" he asks, as if his thoughts trailed mine. "What will happen on the summer solstice?"

Memories cascade through me, all the years past, the summers that slid to a close, dead bodies left in their wake. "There will be a party, just like the one on the beach." I pull my arm away from his grip, tugging the sleeves of my sweater down over my hands and crossing my arms, feeling suddenly chilled. "Before midnight, the sisters will wade back out into the harbor, relinquishing the bodies they've stolen."

"And if they don't go into the water? If Gigi stays locked up during the solstice?"

My lungs stop drawing in air. *She will die. She will be trapped inside Gigi's body indefinitely, pushed down into the dark, dark, dark recesses of Gigi's mind. She will see and hear and witness the world, but Gigi will resume control, unaware that a Swan sister is now imprisoned inside her, buried deep within. A ghost inside a girl. The worst kind of existence. A punishment befitting the torment the sisters have caused.* But I don't tell this to Bo. Because I can't be sure it's true, since it's never happened before. A Swan sister has never stayed inside a body past midnight on the summer solstice.

"I'm not sure," I answer truthfully.

Bo's eyes have strayed to the window, he's considering something. "I have to kill her," he finally says. "Even if she didn't kill my brother, she's killed others. She doesn't deserve to live."

"You'd be killing Gigi, too," I say.

"I know, but you told me before how the town has killed girls in the past, hoping to stop the sisters, but that they always got it wrong." His eyes search mine. "This time we won't get it wrong. You can see them. You know who they are. We can find out where the third one is and we can end this for good. No one else has to die."

"Except three innocent girls."

"Better than a hundred more boys. Or two hundred. How many more centuries do they keep returning to this town before someone stops them? They never got it right in the past because they never knew for sure which girls were inhabited. But *we* know. And there's one right down there, locked up." He points to the window and his sudden urgency scares me. I never thought he'd be this serious, that he'd really want to do it. But now he's talking like we could march down there and end her life right now, all based on my ability to see what she really is.

"And you could live with yourself after that?" I ask. "Knowing you killed three people?"

"My brother is dead," he says coldly. "I came here to find out what happened to him, and I did. I can't just walk away now." He removes the hat from his head and drops it onto the chair. "I have to do this, Penny."

"You don't." I move closer to him. "At least not right now . . . not tonight. Maybe we can find another way."

He exhales then leans into the window frame. "There isn't another way."

I reach out and touch his arm, forcing him to look at me. "Please," I say, tilting my chin up at him. He smells like the earth; he smells wild and fearless and I know he could also be dangerous, but when I'm this close to him I don't care what he is. "We still have a few days until the solstice. There's time to figure something out. All those books in your cottage—maybe there really is a way to stop the sisters without killing the girls they've taken. We have to look; we have to try." My fingers slide down to his hand, the warmth of his palm burning me, setting me on fire, making me dizzy.

"Okay," he answers, tightening his fingers through mine. "We'll look for another way. But if we don't find one . . ."

"I know," I say before he can finish. *He will kill Gigi Kline just to get to Aurora.* But he doesn't fully understand what that will mean: taking a life. It will change him. It's not something he can take back.

The sun has managed to sink into the ocean in the span of time that we've been in my room, and I switch on the lamps on either side of my bed. "One of us should stay up to watch the cottage, make sure she doesn't sneak out," Bo says.

I doubt she'll try to escape, but I nod anyway, agreeing. Her odds aren't good back in town. Lon and Davis are surely looking for her. And I'm guessing she knows she's safer here—hidden in the cottage. Her mistake is that she thinks we'll protect her from them. Especially with Rose on her side. When, in fact, we're plotting ways in which to end her life.

SISTERS

Magic is not always formed from words, from cauldrons brewing spices or black cats strolling down dark alleys. Some curses are manifested from desire or injustice.

When she was alive, Aurora Swan would sometimes leave shards of broken glass or a rat's tail on the doorstep of a woman who hated her—hoping an illness might befall the woman or she might stumble on a loose stone while strolling down Ocean Avenue and break her neck. They were merely small omens, common hexes of the day to bend fate in her favor. Not real magic.

Hazel Swan could often be found whispering wishes onto a blood moon, her lips as swift as a hummingbird in flight. She enchanted the moon, wishing for things she craved—a real love to wipe all the others away.

Marguerite was more direct in her efforts. She would slide her fingers along her lovers' throats, tell them that they were hers, and if they refused her she would ensure they never loved anyone else ever again. She promised revenge and torment and the full wrath of her fury if they dared deny her. She swished through town as if she were made of the finest French silk, arrogant and imperious. She wanted power, and everyone knew it.

But their hubris would eventually catch up to them.

The sisters might have portrayed themselves scandalously, wicked and witchy. But they never practiced magic in a way that justified their demise. They were not witches, in a historical sense, but they did have a gravity about them—a thing that pulled you in.

They moved with a graceful ease, as though they were trained ballerinas from the Académie Royale de Danse in France; their hair was a hue that wavered between caramel and carmine, depending on the sunlight; and their voices had the singsong of a whistling thrush, each word a fascination.

They never stole the souls of newborn babies or cast potent spells to make the rains unending or the fish in the harbor uncatchable. Nor had they the skills to spin a curse as everlasting as the one that bound them now.

But magic was not always so linear. It was born from odium. From love. From revenge.

FIFTEEN

At two a.m. on the dot, my eyelids flutter open. The room is dark except for the angular shape of moonlight spilling across the floor from the window. The rain clouds are gone and the sky has split open. Bo is awake, sitting in the chair, finger tapping slowly and rhythmically on the armrest. He turns his head when I sit up in bed.

"You should have woken me sooner," I say drowsily.

"You seemed like you needed sleep."

I'm still fully dressed under the blankets, and I kick back the layers and stretch my arms in the air. "I'll take the next shift," I say. The wood floor is cold and creaking beneath the weight of my feet. "You must be tired."

He yawns and stands up. We bump shoulders as we try to move around one another, both of us sleepy. And when he gets to the bed, he collapses onto his back, one hand on his chest, the other stretched out at his side. He pulls his hat down over his face. I'm tempted to crawl back onto the bed beside him, rest my head on his shoulder and doze back into my dreams. It would be easy to let myself surrender to him, both in this moment and forever . . . let the days flit away until there are no more days left to count. I could leave this island with him and not look back. And maybe, possibly, I could be happy.

It doesn't take long for Bo's hands to relax, his head to shift slightly to the left, and I know he's asleep. But I don't settle into the chair. I walk to the door, opening it just wide enough to slip out into the hall. I move silently down the stairs to the front door.

A few intermittent clouds pass beneath the moon then reveal it again. A ballet of clear sky mixed with low clouds, washed in moonlight.

I wrestle into my raincoat, trying to move quickly, and then hurry out into the night, headed to Old Fisherman's Cottage.

It takes several tries before I'm able to dislodge the board from under the doorknob. My hands are wet; the wood board is wet. And when the door creaks open, the only light inside the cottage is from the fireplace across the room.

It smells like mildew and mothballs and a little like vinegar. And for a half second I feel bad for Gigi being trapped inside this place.

She is standing across the small room, awake, holding her palms over the fire for warmth. "Hello, Penny," she says without turning around. I close the door behind me, shaking the rain from my coat. "I didn't kill his brother."

"Maybe not," I answer. "But he's determined to find out who did." Instinctively, I want to move to the fire for warmth, but I also don't want to be any nearer to her than I already am. On the couch, I notice the folded-up blanket I brought her earlier. She hasn't slept at all.

"Did you come to invite me up to your house for tea and a shower? I could really use a shower."

"No."

"Then why are you here?" She pivots around, her shoulder-length, straight blond hair hanging frayed and dirty like the bristles on a broom. Again I stifle back the sensation of feeling sorry for her. She blinks, and the flickering, silvery-gray outline of Aurora Swan beneath her skin blinks too. They are like two girls transposed over top of each other. Two photo images developed all wrong, one hovering over the other. But when Gigi turns away from the firelight, I almost can't see Aurora inside her; the outlines of her face fade and turn shadowy. I could fool myself into believing that Aurora is no longer there and Gigi is just a normal girl.

"I need to talk to you."

"Without your boyfriend?" she asks, the left side of her lip arching up at the edge.

"He wants to kill you. . . . The whole town does."

"They always have; that's nothing new." In the corner of the ceiling behind her is a cobweb, partly decayed, dark specks—flies and moths—trapped in the sticky remains. Doomed. Legs and wings stuck. The spider is long dead, but the web keeps on killing.

"But this time they caught you swimming back to shore after drowning two boys. They're certain you're one of them."

Her eyebrows come together, forming a line that rises up into her forehead. "And I'm sure you've done nothing to encourage that idea." She's implying that I've said something, revealed that she is indeed a Swan sister, but I've only told Bo.

"Aren't you tired of this?" I ask. "Of killing people year after year?" This is what I had wanted to say when I confronted her at the boathouse, before Lon caught me talking to her.

She looks intrigued, and her head tilts to the left. "You say it like we have a choice."

"What if we do?"

"Don't forget," she says crisply, "it's your fault we ended up like this in the first place."

I drop my gaze to the floor. Dust motes have collected around the legs of the kitchen table and against the walls.

She smiles then rolls her tongue against her cheek. "Let me guess, you're falling in love with that boy?" Her mouth turns up again, grinning with satisfaction that she's hit on something that makes me uncomfortable. "And you're starting to think that maybe there's a way to keep this body you're in, to stay human forever?" She steps away from the fire, pushing her lower jaw out like she might laugh. "You're fucking naive, Hazel. You always have been. Even back then, you thought this town wouldn't actually kill us. You thought we could be saved. But you were wrong."

"Stop it," I tell her, my lips trembling.

"This isn't your town. That isn't your body. These people hate us; they want us dead all over again, and you're pretending that you're one of them." She lifts her chin in the air like she's trying to see me from a new angle, spy the thing inside me. "And that boy . . . Bo. He doesn't love you, he loves who he thinks you are: Penny Talbot, the girl whose body you stole." The words are spit from her lips like they taste vile on her tongue. "And now you've locked up your own sister in this disgusting cottage. You've betrayed us—your own family."

"You're dangerous," I manage to say.

"So are you." She laughs. "Tell me, were you planning on going the whole season without drowning a single boy? The solstice is coming."

"I'm done with that," I say. "I don't want to kill anymore." Even though the urge gnaws at me, tugging at my soul—the need like a thorn at the back of my throat, always pricking the skin, reminding me of what I'm here to do. But I have resisted. At times I've even forgotten. With Bo, the desire for revenge has been dulled. He's made me believe I can be someone else . . . not just the monster I've become.

"You have to. It's what we do." She twirls a strand of blond hair through her thumb and index finger, pressing her lips together into a pout. Aurora's face seems to push against the inside of Gigi's skull, like she's trying to find more space, stretch her neck a little within the confines of her body. I know the feeling. Sometimes I feel trapped in Penny's body as well—imprisoned by the outline of her skin.

"We've been living like this for too long," I say, my voice stronger now, finding purpose in the words. "Two centuries of torturing this town, and what has it gotten us?"

"You fall for some boy, who's not even a local, and now suddenly you want to protect this town?" She folds her arms over her chest, still wearing the same soiled white blouse as when she drowned those boys in the water. "And besides, I like coming back. I like making boys fall in love with me, controlling them . . . collecting them like little trophies."

"You like killing them, you mean."

"I make them mine, and I deserve to keep them," she snaps. "It's not my fault they're so trusting and gullible. Boys are weak—they were two centuries ago, and they still are."

"When will it be enough?"

"Never." She cants her head to the side, cracking her neck.

I exhale. What did I expect coming in here? What was I hoping for? I should have known: My sisters will never stop. They have become just like the sea, breaking apart ships and lives without remorse. And they'll keep on killing for another two centuries if they have their way.

I turn for the door.

"Haven't you learned your lesson, Hazel?" she says from across the room. "You were betrayed by the boy you loved once before; what makes you think Bo won't betray you too?"

I bite down on the fury boiling inside me. She doesn't know anything about what happened before—two centuries ago. "This is different," I say. "Bo is different."

"Unlikely. But he *is* cute." She smirks. "Maybe too cute for you. I think I should have him."

"Stay away from him," I bark.

Her eyes turn to slits, narrowed on me. "What exactly do you plan on doing with him?"

"I won't kill him." I won't take him into the sea and drown him. I don't want that for him—a dark, watery existence, his soul trapped in the harbor. A prisoner shifting with the tide.

"You realize that you're just going to have to leave him behind in a few days. And he will have fallen in love with a ghost and be left with the body of this girl Penny, who won't remember a thing." She lets out a short laugh. "Won't that be hilarious? He will be in love with Penny, not you."

A rattling of nausea starts to rise in my gut. "He loves me . . . not this body." But the words sound feeble and broken.

"Sure," she says, and her eyes roll in her head—such a Gigi thing

214

to do. We can't help but take on the mannerisms of the bodies we inhabit. Just as I have taken on the traits of Penny Talbot—all of her memories sit dormant in my mind, waiting to be plucked like a flower from the ground. I am playing the part of Penny Talbot, and I do it well. I've had practice.

I touch the doorknob. "I meant what I said," I say back to her. "Stay away from him or I'll make sure those boys in town get the opportunity to do exactly what they've been dying to do—kill you."

She chuckles, but then her gaze turns serious, watching me as I slip out the door and kick it shut behind me.

HAZEL SWAN

Hazel was walking swiftly down Ocean Avenue, a small package containing a vial of rosewater and myrrh perfume held delicately between her hands. She was on her way to deliver it to Mrs. Campbell on Alder Hill.

She had glanced down at the package, expertly wrapped in brown butcher paper, when she smacked right into the hard shoulder of someone standing on the sidewalk. The package slipped from her fingers and broke on the cobblestone street. The scent of rose and myrrh evaporated swiftly into the soggy, seaside air.

Owen Clement knelt down to scoop up the remains of the package, and Hazel did the same, her arm grazing his, their fingers touching and soaking up the perfume.

Hazel had always avoided the fervent affections of men, unlike her sisters. And so she wasn't prepared for the desire that twined through her upon meeting Owen Clement, the son of the first lighthouse keeper who lived on Lumiere Island. He was French, like his father, and words rolled from his tongue like a sanguine breeze.

Nightly, Hazel began sneaking across the harbor to the island—hands pressed to skin and tangled in each other's hair; bodies formed as one; waking each morning in the loft above the barn that stood near the main farmhouse, the air smelling of hay and sweat. The chickens clucked from their pen below. And in the evenings, with only the moonlight to reveal their faces, they wandered the single row of young apple tree saplings that Owen's father had planted that spring. It would still be several years before they would turn a harvest. But the promise of what they would bring felt ripe and sharp in the air.

Together they explored the rocky coastline; they let the water lap against their feet. They imagined a new life together, farther south. California, maybe. They threw flat stones into the water, and they made wishes for impossible things.

But Owen's father distrusted the Swan sisters, who were rumored to be witches—temptresses who lured boys into their beds just for amusement—and when he discovered his son and Hazel folded together in the loft one morning, he swore he would make sure they never saw each other again.

It was Owen's father who mounted the inquisition into the three sisters. It was Owen's father who tied the stones around their ankles that pulled the three girls to the bottom of the harbor. It was Owen's father who was responsible for their deaths.

And year after year, summer after summer, Hazel feels drawn back to Lumiere Island, reminded of the boy who she loved in that place, who she forged promises with, and who she lost two centuries ago.

SIXTEEN

B o is still asleep on the bed when I get back to the room.

The sky turned dark on my way back to the house, rain once again blowing across the island.

His chest expands with each breath; his lips fall open. I watch him, wishing I could tell him the truth without destroying everything. Without destroying him. But he thinks I'm someone else. When he looks at me, he sees Penny Talbot, not Hazel Swan. I have carried the lie around as if it were the truth, pretended that this body could actually be mine and that I wouldn't have to return to the sea at the end of June if I believed it hard enough. Maybe this feeling blooming inside my chest will save me; maybe the way Bo looks at me will make me real and whole. Not the girl who drowned two hundred years ago.

But Gigi's laugh rings in my ear. *It's what we do.* We're killers. Our revenge will never be satiated. And I can never have Bo, not really. I'm trapped in another girl's body. I've been repeating the same endless cycle summer after summer. I am not me.

I hardly know who I am anymore.

I walk to the white dresser against the far wall and run a finger along the surface. A collection of items lie scattered like fragments of a story: vanilla perfume that once belonged to Penny's mom, beach pebbles and shells in a dish, her favorite books by John Steinbeck and Herman Melville and Neil Gaiman. Her past rests unprotected in the open, so easily stolen. I can make these things mine. I can make her life mine. This home, this bedroom—including the boy asleep on her bed.

A photograph is tucked at the bottom corner of the mirror above the dresser. I pull it out. It's an image of a woman floating in a tank of water, a fake mermaid's tail fastened at her waist to conceal her legs. Men are gathered in front of the tank, staring in at her while she holds her breath, her expression soft and unstrained. She is a lie. An invention used to sell tickets at a traveling carnival.

I am her. A lie. But when the carnival closes for the night—all the lights flicked off and the water drained from the tank—I do not get to remove my fabric mermaid fin. I do not get to have a normal life outside of the illusion. I will always be someone else.

My deception has lasted two hundred years.

I place the photo back at the edge of the mirror and rub my palms over my eyes. *How did I become this thing?* A spectacle. A sideshow curiosity. I didn't want any of this—this prolonged, unnatural life.

I blow out a breath, keeping the tears from seeping to the surface, and turn to face Bo, who's still asleep.

He twitches on the bed then opens his eyes, as if he felt me watching him in his dreams. I flick my gaze away to the window.

"You all right?" He sits up, pressing his palms into the mattress.

"Fine." But I'm not. This guilt is burying me alive. I'm choking on it, suffocating, swallowing down mouthfuls of each gravelly lie.

"Did you go outside?" he asks.

I touch my hair, wet from the rain. "Just for a minute."

"To Gigi's cottage?"

I shake my head, pulling in my lips to hide the truth. "I just wanted some fresh air."

He believes me. Or maybe he's only pretending to believe me. "I'll stay up for a bit so you can sleep," he says. I start to tell him no then realize how exhausted I am, so I crawl onto the bed, knees drawn close to my chest.

But I can't sleep. I watch him standing at the window, looking out at a world that I don't belong in.

The sun will be up soon. The sky made new. And maybe I'll be made new too.

Three days whirl by in fast-forward. Rose comes to the island to check on Gigi—her freed prisoner. She brings forgetful cakes from her mom's shop: blackberry mocha and sea salt caramel with crushed pistachio.

She tells us that Davis and Lon are searching for Gigi, that they're worried they'll get in trouble if she goes to the police and rats them out for keeping her locked up in the boathouse. Somehow no one seems to suspect that she might be on Lumiere Island, secretly incarcerated in one of the cottages.

Bo spreads out books on the floor of his cottage each evening, fire blazing, his eyes watering and tired from reading late into the night. He is searching for a way to kill the Swan sisters but save the bodies they inhabit—a pointless endeavor. I know things he doesn't.

And I, secretly, am hoping for a way to keep this body forever.

I read books too, curled up on the old couch, the wind rattling the cottage windows. But I'm looking for something else: a way to remain, to exist above the sea indefinitely—to live. There are legends of mermaids who fall in love with sailors, their devotion granting them a human form. I read about the Irish tales of selkies shedding their sealskins, marrying a human man, and staying on land forever.

Perhaps this one thing is enough—to fall in love? If love can bind something, can it also undo it?

On the eve of the summer solstice, Bo passes out beside the fire with an open book on his chest. But I can't sleep. So I leave his cottage and wander up to the orchard alone.

From the rows of trees, I can just barely make out Mom—Penny's mom—standing out on the cliff's edge, the shadow of a woman waiting for a husband who won't return. Seeing her out there, alone, her heart cleaved in half by pain, I could easily let the grief buried inside this body rise up to the surface. Not only are memories stored in the bodies we take, but emotions as well. I can feel them, resting broad and deep inside Penny's chest. If I look too close, if I peer into that darkness, I can feel the gaping sadness of losing her father. My eyes will swell with tears, an ache twisting in my heart, a longing so vast it could swallow me. So I keep it stuffed down. I don't let that part of the host body overcome me. But my sisters have always been better at it than me. They can ignore whatever past emotions have ruled the body, while I tend to feel the sorrow and grief creeping through my veins, up my throat, trying to choke me.

I stop at the old oak tree at the center of the grove—the ghost tree, its leaves shivering in the wind. I press my palm against the heart carved into the trunk. I stare up through the limbs, a theater of stars blinking back at me. It reminds me of the night so many years ago, lying beneath this tree with the boy I once loved: Owen Clement. He held a knife in his hand and carved the heart there to mark our place in the world. Our hearts bound together. Eternity pumping through our veins. It was on that same night that he asked me to marry him. He had no ring or money or anything to offer except himself. But I said yes.

A week later my sisters and I were drowned in the harbor.

INQUISITION

A gust blew in through the open door of the perfumery, scattering dead leaves across the wood floor.

Four men stood in the doorway of the shop, muddy boots and filthy hands. Stinking of fish and tobacco. Against the stark white walls and the air tinged with the delicate intermingling of perfumes, their presence was alarming.

Hazel stared at their filthy boots and not their faces, thinking only of the soap and water she would need to scour the floor clean once they had left. She did not yet realize the men's intent or that she would never see the perfumery again.

The men grabbed the sisters by their forearms and dragged them from the shop.

The Swan sisters were being arrested.

They were hauled down Ocean Avenue for everyone to see; fat drops of rain spat down from the sky; muck from the street stained the hems of their dresses; the townspeople stopped to gawk. Some followed them all the way to the small town hall that was used for town meetings, a gathering place during bad storms, and occasionally but quite rarely, also for legal disputes. A squabble over a missing goat, disagreements over dock anchorage, or property lines with neighbors.

Never before had an accused witch been brought into the building, let alone three.

A group of selectmen and town elders had already gathered, awaiting the Swan sisters' arrival. Marguerite, Aurora, and Hazel were brought before them and made to sit in three wood chairs at the front of the room, their hands tied behind them.

A bird fluttered in the rafters, a yellow finch, trapped just like the sisters.

Quickly, the women of Sparrow came forward, pointing fingers at Marguerite and occasionally Aurora, telling lurid tales of their misdeeds, their infidelity with the husbands and brothers and sons of this town. And how no woman could be so enchanting on her own—it surely must be witchcraft that made the Swan sisters so irresistible to the poor, unwilling men in town. They were merely the victims of the sisters' black magic.

"Witches," they hissed.

The sisters weren't allowed to speak, even though Aurora tried more than once. Their words could not be trusted. Too easily spells could be uttered from their lips to charm those in the room and then they could use their power to demand they be released. They were lucky, one of the selectmen said, that they hadn't been gagged.

But there was another voice, one of the elders, a man who was blind in one eye and would often be seen standing on the docks staring out at the Pacific, longing for the days he once spent at sea. His voice rose above the others: "Proof!" he called. "We must have proof."

This single demand forced silence through the courthouse, over-flowing with spectators. A crowd pushed against the doors outside, straining to hear the first-ever witch trial in the town of Sparrow.

"I've seen Marguerite's mark," a man called from the back of the room. "On her left thigh, there is a birthmark shaped as a raven." This man, who had emboldened himself to speak at the urging of his wife, had shared a bed with Marguerite some months back. Marguerite's eyes went wide, and fury brewed behind them. She did in fact have a birthmark, but to call it the shape of a raven was the result of a clever imagination. The mark was more of an inkblot, but it made no difference; a mark of nearly any kind was considered the brand of a witch—proof she belonged to a coven. And Marguerite could not wipe away that which she was born with.

"What of the other two?" the half-blind elder called.

"Aurora," spoke a much quieter voice, a boy of only eighteen. "Has a mark on her shoulder. I've seen it." And he had, as he had claimed, seen the collection of freckles on her right shoulder. His lips had pressed against her flesh on several nights previous, tracing the freckles that dotted much of Aurora's skin. She was like a galaxy, speckled with stars.

Aurora's gaze met the boy's. She could see the fear obvious in his eyes. He believed Aurora might in truth be a witch as the town had claimed, and perhaps she had used dark magic on him, making his heart race whenever she was near.

"Two honorable men have stepped forward with proof of guilt for two of the accused before us," said one of the selectmen. "What of the last sister? Hazel Swan? Surely someone has spied the mark of a coven on this enchantress's skin?"

A stir of whispers carried through the room and echoed off the steep ceiling, voices trying to discern whom among them might have found themselves ensnared by Hazel, coaxed to her bed unwittingly.

"My son will tell you." A man's deep voice broke through the chatter.

Owen's father appeared at the back of the courthouse, and trailing behind him, head down, was Owen. "My son has been with her. He has seen what marks she conceals."

The air inside the room condensed, the damp walls stiffened. The yellow finch caught in the rafters fell quiet. Not even the floorboards creaked as Owen was pulled by his father to the front of the courthouse. Hazel Swan looked as if she might faint, her complexion drained of all color. Not from fear for herself, but fear for Owen.

"Tell them!" his father barked.

Owen stood stone-faced, eyes locked on Hazel. He would not.

His father marched up to where the sisters sat in a row, hands bound by rope. He drew a large knife from the sheath at his waist and placed it to Hazel's throat, blade pressing against her alabaster skin. Her breath hitched; her eyes quivered but did not stray from Owen's gaze.

"Stop!" Owen cried, stepping toward Hazel. Two men grabbed his arms and held him in place.

"Tell us what you've seen," his father demanded. "Tell us of the marks that riddle this girl's body."

"There are no marks," Owen shouted back.

"Her spell on you has made you weak. Now tell us, or I will cut her throat and you will watch her bleed out, here in front of everyone. A painful death, I assure you."

"You will kill her anyway," Owen said. "If I speak, you will accuse her of being a witch."

"So you *have* seen something?" the half-blind elder asked.

Those in the room that day would later say it was as if Hazel Swan was conjuring a spell before their eyes, the way she peered at Owen, forcing his lips to remain silent. But others, the few who had known real love, saw something else: the look of two people whose love was about to destroy them. It was not witchcraft in Hazel's eyes; it was her heart splitting in half.

And then Hazel spoke, a soft series of words that sounded almost like tears streaming down cheeks: "It's all right. Tell them."

"No," Owen answered back. He was still being held by the two men, his arms tensed against their grip.

"Please," she whispered. Because she feared he might be punished for protecting her. She knew it was already too late; the town had decided—they were witches. The selectmen just needed Owen to say it, to prove what they already believed. He only needed to tell them of one little mark; any imperfection on the skin would do.

His eyes watered, and his lips fell open, the air hanging there for several breaths, several heartbeats, until he uttered: "There is a small half-moon on her left ribs."

A perfect freckle, he had once whispered against her skin in that very spot, his lips hovering over it, his breath tickling her flesh. She had laughed, her voice bouncing along the eaves of the barn loft, her fingers slipping through his hair. He had wished on that half-moon many times, silent desires that someday he and Hazel would leave Sparrow, steal away on a ship bound for San Francisco. A new life far away from this town. Maybe if she really had been a witch, his wish muttered softly against her flesh might have come true. But it did not.

A gasp passed through the room, and his father lowered the knife from Hazel's throat. "There it is," his father proclaimed, satisfied. "Proof that she, too, is a witch."

Hazel felt her heart sink into her gut. The room echoed with murmurs. The finch resumed its chirping.

The half-blind elder cleared his throat, speaking loudly enough so that even those outside the town hall with their ears pressed to the doors would hear. "In our small town, where the ocean brings us life, it shall also take it. The Swan sisters are found guilty of witchcraft and sentenced to death by drowning. To be carried out at three o'clock this afternoon, on the summer solstice. An auspicious day for the assurance that their wicked souls will be extinguished permanently."

"No!" shouted Aurora.

But Marguerite's lips pinched shut, her cold stare enough to curse anyone who dared look at her. Hazel remained quiet, not because she wasn't afraid, but because she couldn't pull her eyes away from Owen. She could see his regret, his guilt. It wrenched him apart.

But he did not condemn her—she and her sisters were doomed the day they arrived in this town.

The men seized the three sisters before Hazel could mutter a word to Owen, leading them into a back room where five women stripped them naked of their clothes, verified the marks that had been claimed against them, and then dressed them in white gowns to purify their souls and ensure their eternal and absolute death.

But absolute, their death was not.

SEVENTEEN

The cottage rattles from the wind, and I wake, gripping for something that isn't there. I had been dreaming of the sea, of the weight of stones pulling me under, water so cold I coughed at first but then couldn't fight it as it spilled into my lungs. A bleak, lonely death. My sisters only a finger's width away as we all plummeted to the bottom of the harbor.

I rub my eyes, crushing away the memory and the dream.

It's early, the light outside the cottage still a watercolor of grays, and Bo is stoking the fire.

"What time is it?" I ask, turning over from my place on the floor where I managed to fall asleep. He's added several new logs to the fire, and the heat sears my cheeks and tingles my lips.

"Early. Just after six."

Today is the summer solstice. Tonight, at midnight, everything will change.

Bo has been unsuccessful in finding a way to kill the Swan sisters without also killing the bodies where we reside. There is nothing in any of the books. But I knew there wouldn't be.

And I know what he's thinking as he faces the fireplace: Today he will get his revenge for his brother's death. Even if it means killing an innocent girl. He won't allow Aurora to keep on killing. He will end her life.

But I've also made a decision. I'm not going back into the water tonight; I won't return to the sea. I'm going to fight to keep this body. I want to stay Penny Talbot, even if it means she no longer gets to exist. Even if it might be impossible—painful and severe and terrifying—I have to try.

Each summer, my sisters and I are given only a few short weeks inside the bodies we've stolen, making each day, each hour, precious and fleeting. And so we have a habit of lingering inside our bodies until the final seconds before midnight on the summer solstice. We want to feel every last moment above the waterline: breathe in our last gulps of air; peer up at the sky, dark and gray and infinite; touch the soil beneath our feet and savor the feeling of being alive.

Even when the draw of the harbor begins to pulse behind our eyes, coaxing us back to its cold depth, we resist until it becomes unbearable. We hold on to those final seconds for as long as we can.

And there have been summers past when we've pushed it too far, waited too long to return to the sea. It's happened to each of us at least once.

In those times, in those seconds that ticked past midnight, a flash of bright pain whipped through our skulls.

But the pain isn't all you feel; there is something else: a pressure. Like being stuffed down into the dark, into the deepest shadows of the body we occupied. When it happened to me many years back, I could sense the girl rising once again to the surface, and I was being crushed. We were swapping places. Wherever she had been—

hidden, stifled, and suppressed inside the body—I was now sinking into that very place. It was only when I returned to the sea that I slipped free from the girl's skin. The relief was immediate. I swore I would never cut it that close again. I would never risk being trapped in a body after midnight.

But this year, this summer solstice, I'm going to try. Maybe I can fight it. Resist the pain and the grinding force pushing me down. Maybe I'm stronger now, more deserving even. Maybe this year will be different. I haven't taken a single boy's life—perhaps the curse will release me, allow me this one thing.

Just like in the books I've read, about the mermaids and selkies who found a way to be human and exist above the sea, I'm going to stay in this body.

Even if Penny will be stifled indefinitely, I'm willing to be selfish to have this.

"I need to go into town," I say, my voice scratchy. Last night, sitting beside the oak tree, I realized that if I truly want to have this life with Bo—if I love him—then I need to let go of the one thing I've been holding on to.

"For what?" he asks.

"There's something I need to do."

"You can't go by yourself. It's too dangerous."

I pull down the royal-blue T-shirt that wrapped itself around my torso while I slept, tossing and turning fitfully as I battled my night-mares. "I have to do this alone." I yank on the dark gray sweatshirt I was using as a pillow then stand up.

"What if one of those guys—Davis or Lon—sees you? They might question you about Gigi."

"I'll be fine," I tell him. "And someone needs to stay here—keep an eye on Gigi." He knows I'm right, but the green of his eyes settles on me like he is trying to hold me in place with his stare. "Promise me you'll stay away from her while I'm gone."

"Time is running out," he reminds me.

"I know. I won't be gone long. Just don't do anything until I get back."

He nods. But it's a weak, uncommitted nod. The longer I'm off the island, the greater the risk that something bad will happen: Bo will kill Gigi; Gigi will seduce Bo and coax him into the ocean, where she'll drown him. Either way, someone will die.

I leave the cottage, closing the door behind me. And then another thought, a new fear rises inside my gut: What if Gigi tells Bo what I really am? Would he even believe her? Doubtful. But it might edge a sliver of suspicion into his mind. I have to go quickly. And hope nothing happens before I get back.

The harbor is crowded, fishing boats and tour barges chugging out past the lighthouse. The clouds are low and heavy, so close it feels like I could reach up and touch them, swirl them with my fingertip. But no rain spills from their bloated bellies. It waits. Just like everyone is waiting for the next drowned body to be found—the last of the season. But I'm the only sister who has yet to make a kill, and I refuse to do the thing I know both Aurora and Marguerite want me to do: drown Bo.

It's never happened before: a summer where one of us didn't make a single kill. I don't know what will happen, how it will change things—change me—if at all.

I feel the sea already, tugging at me, calling me back into the water. The need to return will grow stronger as the day wears on. It happens every year, a pulse behind my eyes, a twitch inside my ribs, drawing me back to the harbor, back into the deep where I belong. But I ignore the sensation.

The skiff motors past the orange buoys and through the marina, gliding into place at the dock.

Sparrow is teeming with tourists. Along the boardwalk kids run with rainbow-colored kites, struggling to get them airborne without any breeze; one is even tangled around a street lamp with a little girl tugging against the string trying to pull it down. Seagulls peck along the concrete for scraps of popcorn and cotton candy. People stroll the shops; they buy saltwater taffy by the pound; they take pictures beside the marina; they know the end is near. Today is the last day. The season is coming to a close. They will return to their normal lives, their normal homes in normal towns where bad things never happen. But I live in a place where bad things surround me, where *I* am a bad thing.

I don't want to be that anymore.

I move in the opposite direction of Coppers Beach and the boathouse, and I head up to Alder Hill at the south end of town. The same part of Sparrow where I was supposed to deliver a vial of rosewater and myrrh perfume the day I met Owen Clement. I never made the delivery.

Blackbirds circle above, eyes roving the ground, following me. Like they know where I'm headed.

Alder Hill is also the location of the Sparrow Cemetery.

The graveyard is a broad, grassy plot of land encircled by a partially fallen-down metal fence overlooking the bay so that the fisherman buried here can watch over the sea and protect the town.

I haven't been here in a very long time. I've avoided this place for the last century. But I find my way to the tombstone easily, my feet guiding me even after all these years, past graves covered in flowers and graves covered in moss and graves left bare.

It's one of the oldest stone markers in the cemetery. The only reason it hasn't turned to dust is because for the first century I made sure to keep the weeds from growing over it and the earth from pulling it under. But then it became too hard to come. I was holding on to someone who I would never see again. It was my past. And the person I had become—a murderer—was not who he had loved. I was someone else.

It's a simple marker. Rounded sandstone. The name and date carved into the rock have long ago been smoothed away by wind and rain. But I know what it used say; I know it by heart: OWEN CLEMENT. DIED 1823.

After the day his father caught us together in the barn's loft, Owen wasn't allowed to leave the island. I tried to see him, I rowed across the bay, I pleaded with his father, but he forced me away. He was so certain I had cast a spell on Owen to make him love me. That no boy could love a Swan sister without the sway of some hex or wicked enchantment.

If only love were so easily conjured, there wouldn't be so many broken hearts, I remember Marguerite saying once, back when we were alive.

I didn't realize what was coming—what Owen's father was plotting. If I had known, I wouldn't have stayed in Sparrow.

Clouds hung heavy over the town the day my sisters and I were led from the courthouse down to the docks. Aurora wailed, screaming at the men as they forced us aboard a boat. Marguerite spit curses into their faces, but I remained still, scanning the crowd of gathered spectators for Owen. I had lost sight of him after we were taken into a small dark room at the back of the courthouse, stripped bare, and forced into simple white gowns. Our death gowns.

They knotted rope around our wrists and ankles. Aurora continued to weep, tears making lines down her cheeks. And then just as the boat pushed back from the dock, I saw him.

Owen.

It took three men to restrain him. He yelled my name, scrambling to the end of the dock. But the boat was already drifting too far away, with his father and several other men steering us out to the deepest part of the harbor.

I lost sight of him in the low fog that settled over the water, muffling all sound and obscuring the dock where he stood.

My sisters and I sat together on a single wood bench at the bow of the boat, shoulders pressed together, hands bound in front of us. Prisoners being led to their death. The sea spray stung our faces as the boat pushed farther out into the harbor. I closed my eyes, feeling its cool relief. I listened to the harbor bell buoy ringing at long intervals, the wind and waves gone nearly still. One last moment to breathe the sharp air. The seconds stretched out, and I felt as if I could slip into a dream and never wake—like none of it was real. It's rare to know your death is approaching, waiting for you, death's fingers already grasping for your soul. I felt it reaching out for me. I was already half-gone.

The boat drifted to a stop, and I opened my eyes to the sky. A seagull slipped out from the clouds then vanished again.

The men tied burlap sacks filled with stones to our ankles—the stones likely pulled up from a farmer's rocky fields behind town, donated for the occasion of our death. We were forced to stand then pushed to the edge of the boat. Marguerite eyed one of the younger boys, her gaze clawing into him, as if she might be able to convince him to free her. But we would not be spared. My sisters and I were finally being punished: adultery, lust, and even true love would find atonement at the bottom of the sea.

I sucked in a breath of air, bracing myself for what would come next, when I saw the bow of another boat breaking through the fog. "What the hell?" I heard one of the men say behind us. It was a small boat, oars driving fast through the water.

Aurora turned and looked at me—she realized who it was before I did.

He stole a boat.

A second later, I felt the swift push of two hands against my back.

The water shattered around my body like razors, knocking the air from my lungs. Death is not a fire, death is a cold so fierce it feels like it will peel the skin away from your bones. I sank quickly. My sisters plummeting just as swiftly through the murky water beside me.

I thought death would take me quickly, a second, maybe two, but then there was movement above me: an explosion of bubbles, and a hand wrapping around my waist.

I opened my eyes and focused through the dark, speckled with bits of shell and sand and green. A haze dividing us. But *he* was there—Owen.

He grabbed hold of my arms and began tugging me upward toward the surface, fighting the cold and the weight of rocks around my feet. His legs kicked furiously while mine hung limp, tied together. His face strained, eyes wide. He was desperate, trying to save me before the water found its way down my throat and into my lungs. But the stones around my ankles were too heavy. His fingers worked at the rope, but the tension was too great, the knots too stiff.

Our eyes met, only inches apart as we sank deeper to the bottom of the harbor. There was nothing he could do. I shook my head frantically—pleading with him to give up, to release me. I tried to pry his hands off of me, but he refused to let go. He was falling too deep, too far. He wouldn't have enough air to make it back up. But he pulled me against him and kissed his frigid lips to mine. I closed my eyes and felt him against me. It's the last thing I remember before I drew in a breath and the water spilled down my throat.

He never let me go. Even when it was too late. Even when he knew he couldn't save me.

We both lost our lives in the harbor that day.

The following summer, when I returned to the town for the first time—hidden in the body of a local girl—I walked up the steep slope to Sparrow Cemetery and stood on the cliff over his grave. No one knew who I really was: Hazel Swan, come to see the boy she loved now buried in the ground.

The day we both drowned, his body eventually drifted to the surface of the harbor and his father was forced to pull his only son from the sea. A fate that he had set in motion.

Guilt seethed through my veins as I stood over his freshly dug grave so long ago. His life had ended because of me. And that guilt quickly turned to hatred for the town. All these years, my sisters sought revenge for their own death, but I wanted revenge for Owen's.

He sacrificed himself to try to save me, maybe because he felt he had betrayed me—for the trial, for confessing to having seen the mark of a witch on my skin. He believed he caused my death.

But I caused his.

I should have died that day—I should have drowned. But I didn't. And I've never forgiven myself for what happened to him. For the life we never got to have.

I kneel down beside the grave, brushing away the leaves and dirt. "I'm sorry. . . ." I begin then stop myself. It's not enough. He's been gone for nearly two hundred years, and I've never said good-bye. Not really. Not until now. I lower my head, unsure how any words will ever feel like enough. "I never wanted to live this long," I say. "I'd always hoped that someday the sea would finally take me. Or old age would bury me in the ground next to you." I swallow down a deep breath. "But things have changed. . . . *I* have changed." I lift my head and look out at the sea, a perfect view of the harbor and Lumiere Island, where Bo is waiting. "I think I love him," I confess. "But maybe it's too late. Maybe I don't deserve him or a normal life after everything I've done, all the lives I've taken. He doesn't know who I really am. And so maybe what I feel for him is also a lie." The wind brushes my cheeks, and a light rain starts to scatter over the cemetery. Confessing this to Owen's grave feels like a penance, like I owe him this. "But I have to try," I say. "I have to know if loving him is enough to save both of us."

I wipe a palm over the face of the tombstone, where his name was once etched. Now just a smooth surface. A grave without a name. I close my eyes, the tears falling in slow, measured rhythm with the raindrops.

Maybe I did die that day. Hazel Swan, the girl I once was, is gone. Her life taken on the same day as Owen's. My voice trembles as the last word slips out—I say it to him as much as to myself. "Good-bye."

I stand before my legs are too weak to carry me, and I leave the graveyard, knowing that I'll never come back here again. The people I loved are gone.

But I won't lose the one I love now.

EIGHTEEN

Memories can settle into a place: fog that lingers long after it should have blown out to sea, voices from the past that take root in the foundation of a town, whispers and accusations that grow in the moss along the sidewalks and up the walls of old homes.

This town, this small cluster of houses and shops and boats clinging to the shoreline, has never escaped its past—the thing it did two hundred years ago. Ghosts remain. But sometimes, the past is the only thing keeping a place alive. Without it, this fragile town may have long ago been washed out with the tide, sunken into the harbor in defeat. But it persists, because it must. Penance is a long, unforgiving thing. It endures, for without it, the past is forgotten.

I stop in front of the old stone building that sits squat and low on a street corner facing the sea. Rain pings off my forehead and shoulders. The sign above the door reads: ALBA'S FORGETFUL CAKES. But it didn't used to. A sign with bold black swirling letters hand-painted by Aurora once hung across the sidewalk, clattering with the afternoon breeze. This was once the Swan Perfumery. Although I've walked past it thousands of times in the summers since our death, seen countless businesses occupy it, and even watched in dismay during a fifteen-year period when it sat abandoned and crumbling before it was restored, sometimes, like today, it still strikes me that after all this time it has endured . . . just as we have.

A woman steps out through the glass door, her rain boots splashing through a shallow puddle as she walks to her red SUV holding a pink pastry box surely filled with tiny frosted cakes intended to wipe away some sticky memory caught in her mind.

I spent nearly every day inside that shop, concocting new scents made of rare herbs and flowers, my hair and fingers and skin always bursting with scents that couldn't be washed away. The oils soaked into everything they touched. Marguerite was the saleswoman, and she was good at it, a natural peddler. Aurora was the bookkeeper; she paid bills and tallied profits from a small, wobbly wood desk behind the front counter. And I was the perfumist, working out of a windowless back room that should have been a storage closet—a place for brooms and metal buckets. But I loved my work. And in the evening my sisters and I shared a tiny home behind the shop.

"It doesn't even look like the same place," a voice says beside me. I flinch. Olivia Greene is standing next to me, a black umbrella held over her head to protect her sleek, charcoal-black hair from the rain. My eyes pass through her fair skin to Marguerite underneath.

"The windows are the same," I say, looking back to the building.

"Replicas," she answers, her voice more somber than usual. "Everything it used to be is now gone."

"Just like us."

"Nothing that lives this long can stay the same."

"Nothing *should* live this long," I point out.

"But we did," she says, as if it were an accomplishment to be proud of.

"Maybe two hundred years is enough."

She blows out a quick breath through her nostrils. "You want to give up eternal life?"

"It's not eternal," I say. Marguerite and I have never viewed our imprisonment the same way. She sees it as our good fortune, a lucky draw of the card that we should live on for centuries, indefinitely perhaps. But she didn't lose anything the day we were drowned. I did. She wasn't in love with a boy who loved her back—not real love, like what Owen and I had. With each passing year we spent beneath the waves, each summer we rose again to claim our revenge on the town by taking their boys and making them ours, we lost a part of who we once were. We lost our humanity. I watched my sisters' cruelty grow, their ability to kill sharpen, until I barely recognized them.

My wickedness grew too, but not to a place I couldn't come back from. Because there was a thread that bound me to who I used to be—that thread was Owen. The memory of him kept me from slipping completely into the dark. And now that thread ties me to Bo. To the real world, to the present.

"We've spent most of our lives trapped in the sea," I say. "Cold and dark and miserable. That's not a real life."

"I block it out," she rebukes swiftly. "You should too. It's better to sleep, let your mind drift away until summer arrives."

"It's not that easy for me."

"You've always made things harder for yourself."

"What does that mean?"

"This thing you have with that boy, Bo. You're only dragging out the inevitable. Just kill him and get it over with."

"No." I turn to look at her, a shadow settled over her face beneath the domed umbrella. "I know you tried to lure him into the harbor."

Her eyes twinkle, as if delighted by the memory of almost drowning the boy I love. "I just wanted to help you finish what you started. If you like him so much, then take him into the sea, and you will have him for eternity."

"I don't want him like that. His soul trapped down there just like ours."

"Then how *do* you want him?"

"Real. Here—on land."

She laughs loud and full, and a man and woman strolling past us turn to look at her. "That's absurd and not possible. Tonight's the last night to make him yours."

I shake my head. *I won't do it.* "I'm not like you," I say.

"You're exactly like me. We're sisters. And you're just as cold-blooded as I am."

"No, you're wrong about that."

"Have you forgotten about Owen? How he betrayed you? Maybe if he hadn't spoken up about the mark on your skin, you wouldn't have been found guilty. You wouldn't have drowned with us. You might have lived a normal life. But no"—her lips curl up at the edges, a wolf baring her teeth—"boys cannot be trusted. They will always do whatever they can to save themselves. They are the cruel ones, not us."

"Owen wasn't cruel," I snap. "He had to tell them about the mark."

"Did he?"

I bite down on the rage building in my chest. "If he hadn't, they would have believed he was one of us, helping us. They would have killed him."

"And yet he died anyway." One of her eyebrows arches upward.

I can't stand here anymore, listening to Marguerite. She's never known real love. Even her infatuations with men when we were alive were all about her: the attention, the pursuit, the satisfaction of winning something that wasn't hers to start with. "Owen tried to save me that day, and he lost his life. He loved me," I tell her. "And Bo loves me now. But you wouldn't know what that's like because you're incapable of love."

I turn away from her and start up the sidewalk.

"Did you hear?" she calls after me. "Our dear sister Aurora has been sprung from her jail in the boathouse. It seems someone decided she was innocent after all."

I look back at her over my shoulder. "She's not innocent," I say. Marguerite squirms inside Olivia's body. "None of us are."

The dock is slick from the rain. Waves push into the marina at steady intervals, a ballet choreographed by the wind and tide. I climb into the skiff and start the motor. A few persistent rays of sun break through the dark clouds, spilling light over the bow of the boat.

Tonight, the summer solstice party will happen on Coppers Beach, marking the end of Swan season. But I won't be there. I'm staying on the island with Bo. I'm staying in this body—whatever it takes, no matter how painful, I'm going to fight it.

Yet I have the acute, anxious feeling that something bad is stirring out on those waters, in that approaching storm, and none of us will be the same after tonight.

SHIP

The *Lady Astor*, a 290-ton merchant ship owned by the Pacific Fur Company, left New York City in November of 1821 for its five-month passage around Cape Horn and up the west coast to Sparrow, Oregon.

It carried mostly supplies and grain to be delivered to the rugged western coastline, but it also carried two dozen passengers—those brave enough to venture west to the wilds of Oregon, where much of the land was undeveloped and dangerous. Aboard the ship were three sisters: Marguerite, Aurora, and Hazel.

Four months into the voyage, they had encountered mostly storms, dark seas, and sleepless nights when the ship rocked so violently that nearly everyone aboard, including the crew, was ill with seasickness. But the sisters did not clutch their stomachs and heave over the side of the boat; they did not press their palms to their eyes and beg the ocean to cease its churning. They'd brought herbs to sooth their swirling stomachs and balms to rub into their temples. And each evening they walked the deck even in the rain and wind to stare out across the Pacific, yearning for the land that would eventually rise up on the horizon.

"Only a month remains," Aurora said on one of those nights as the three sisters stood at the bow of the ship, leaning against the railing, the stars spinning bright above them in a clear, boundless sky. "Do you think it will be how we've imagined?" she asked.

"I don't think it matters what it's like, because it will be ours," Hazel mused. "A new town and a new life."

They had always craved to leave the hurried panic of New York City, to leave behind the reminder of their callous mother, to start anew in a land so far away, it could have been the moon. The west, a place said to be uncivilized and brutal. But that's exactly what they wanted: a territory so unfamiliar that their hearts raced and their minds whirled with fear and excitement.

"We can be anyone we want," Marguerite said, her wild, dark hair unspooling from its pins and cascading out behind her.

Aurora smiled, feeling the salt wind on her cheeks, and closed her eyes. Hazel stuck out her tongue to taste the sea, imagining a perfume that smelled just like the open ocean—crisp and clean.

"And no matter what," Marguerite added, "we'll be together. The three of us, always."

The sisters leaned into the railing, urging the ship forward as it pushed on into the night, through gales and strong currents and unfavorable winds, the moon chasing them. They saw something out in that vast sea, in the dark as the ship speared across the Pacific: the promise of something better.

They didn't know their fate.

But perhaps it wouldn't have mattered even if they had. They would have come anyway. They needed to see it, to step onto soil that was rich and dark and all theirs. They had been unmoored since birth, brave and fearless and wild just like that boundless unknown land.

They wouldn't have changed course even if they'd known what was awaiting them. They had to come. It was where they belonged—in Sparrow.

NINETEEN

Puddles have collected in the overly saturated soil, and my feet slap against the bent and warped wood boards of the walkway. I hurry up to the main house and fumble out of my boots.

I feel rattled after seeing Marguerite, after returning from the graveyard, knowing what I'm about to do. I need to settle my nerves before I go back to Bo's cottage.

I pace across the kitchen floor in my bare feet, weaving my hands into knots. My head pounds, crackling like Penny's body is trying to rid itself of me already. Trying to reclaim control. And there's another sensation building inside me: like a string being pulled from the very center of my chest. It's starting already, the gnawing beneath my fingernails, the desire weaving up my spine—the sea is calling to me. It wants me back. It beckons me; it begs.

But I'm not going back, not tonight, not ever.

The phone rings from the wall, clattering the bones down every limb of my body.

I pick it up without even registering the motion.

"They're coming!" Rose barks from the other end.

"Who?" My mind careens back into focus.

"Everyone—they're all coming to the island." Her voice is pan-icked, on the edge of breaking. "Olivia and Davis and Lon and everyone who got the text."

"What text?"

"Olivia said the summer solstice party is happening on the island this year. She texted everyone." Rose is flustered, and her *S*'s slur into *Th*'s. An old habit sneaking back in.

"Shit." My eyes dart around the kitchen, settling on nothing. *Why would Olivia do this?* What does she have to gain by bringing everyone to the island . . . and risking Gigi being found?

"We can't let them find Gigi," Rose says, echoing my thoughts.

"I know."

"I'm coming to the island right now. Heath will bring me."

"Okay." And she hangs up the phone.

I hold the receiver in my hand, squeezing it until my knuckles turn white.

I hear the back door bang shut, and I nearly drop the phone. There's the sound of feet shuffling slowly across the hardwood floor, and then Mom appears on the other side of the kitchen doorway, her robe hanging loose over her silt-gray pajamas, the belt dragging across the floor behind her. "People are coming," she says, her right thumb and index finger tapping together at her side. "They're all coming."

"Yeah, they are," I agree.

"I'm going up to my room until it's over." She won't look at me.

"I'm sorry," I tell her . . . for more than I can explain.

Memories of my real mother—Fiona Swan—shiver through me.

A quick burst of images. She was beautiful but vicious. Captivating and cunning and deceitful. She flitted through New York City in the early 1800s with an infectious attraction that men could not resist. She used them for money and status and power. My sisters and I were born to three different fathers who we never knew. And when I was only nine, she abandoned us for a man who promised to whisk her off to Paris—the city she had always envisioned would be her home someday. Where she would be adored. I don't know what happened to her after that: if she did cross the Atlantic to France, when she died, or if she had other children. My sisters and I have lived long enough to forget about her almost entirely. And I close my eyes briefly to squeeze back the memories of her.

Penny's mom pauses in the doorway, her fingers trembling where her left hand is holding tightly to the collar of her robe. Her voice comes out shaky but exact, a pinprick of words that have resided in her chest for too long. "I know you're not my Penny."

My eyes snap to hers, my heart drops down into my kneecaps. "Excuse me?"

"I've known all along."

I start to clear my throat but can't; my entire body has dried up and petrified. "I . . . ," I begin, but nothing else comes out.

"She's my daughter," she adds, her voice settling into a cool pace that wavers against the threat of tears. "I knew the moment she became something else . . . when she became you."

She's known the whole time. I find myself struggling for air.

But of course she's known. This is her talent—her gift. She's always sensed when people are on the island—strangers who've come unannounced—so she must have sensed when *I* arrived. Yet she's allowed me to pretend to be her daughter, to live on this island with her, knowing that at the end of this month, upon the summer solstice, I would leave.

"She's all I have left." Her blue-green eyes lift, penetrating mine, more lucid than I've ever seen them before, like she's just woken from a thousand-year dream. "Please don't take her from me."

She must sense that I have no intention of leaving. That I plan to steal this body permanently and make it my own. I'm not going back into the sea. "I can't promise that," I answer truthfully, a cloud of guilt growing inside me. She has been the closest thing to a real mom I've ever had—even with her madness. And maybe it's foolish to feel this way, desperate even, but I've allowed myself to think that this is my home, my bedroom up those stairs, my life. And that she could be my mom.

I recognize in her a part of myself: the sadness that darkens her eyes, the heartbreak that has unraveled the loose threads woven inside her mind. I could be her. I could slip into madness and let it overtake me just like she has. Turn into a shadow.

She and I are the same. We've both lost people we love. Both crushed by this town. Both know that the ocean takes more than it gives.

I wish I could undo her misery, the pain skittering behind her eyes. But I can't.

"I'm sorry," I tell her now. "I'm sorry for what's happened to you. You deserved a better life, far away from here. This town destroys everyone eventually. Like it destroyed my sisters and me. We weren't always this way," I say, wanting her to understand that I was good once, decent and kind. "But this place destroys hearts and throws them into the sea.

We are all at the mercy of that ocean out there—we'll never escape it."

We stare at each other, a streak of broken sunlight falling in through the kitchen window, the truth sliding like a crisp winter breeze between us.

"Go back into the water tonight," she pleads, tears slipping down her cheeks. "Let her have her life back."

I cross my arms, rubbing my hands down the sleeves of my coat. "But I deserve a life too," I counter, hardening my gaze on her.

"You've already had a life. You've had the longest life of anyone. Please."

I have stolen her daughter, the last thing she has left in this entire world—even her sanity has slipped away from her—but I can't release this body. It's my only chance at a real life. Surely she can understand that. Surely she knows what it is to be trapped, to be willing to do anything to escape, to crave normalcy in this tormented, messed-up town. To finally feel settled.

This is my second chance. And I'm not going to let it get away.

"I'm sorry." I back step through the kitchen, knowing she isn't strong enough to stop me, and I dart through the doorway into the hall, nearly bumping into a side table, then out the front door.

I pause on the front porch, hoping that Rose was wrong. A wall of black clouds has materialized several miles out at sea, dense and wide, laden with rain and maybe lightning.

But still no sign of boats converging toward the island.

I hurry down the porch steps, my heartbeat thudding against my ribs, and I move toward Old Fisherman's Cottage, where Gigi is still locked up. When I reach the door, I yank the board out of the way and step inside. Gigi's standing at the window, staring down toward the dock.

"People are coming to the island," I tell her, breathing heavily. "The summer solstice party is happening here. Olivia invited everyone. You need to stay inside and lock the door."

"First I was locked in, now you want me to lock you out? This is a very confusing situation for a prisoner."

"If any of them find you in here . . ."

"Yeah, yeah," she interrupts. "They want me dead. I get it."

"I'm serious."

She lifts her palms in the air. "You think I want to be hanged or strangled or shot? Trust me, I don't want them to find me either. I'll stay put like a good evil sister."

I tilt my head at her—I don't find her funny right now—but she smirks. I open the door a crack, letting in a sliver of wind that brushes my dark hair off my shoulders, and I'm about to step back outside when she asks, "Why are you helping me?"

"You're my sister." I gulp down the word, knowing that no matter what she and Marguerite have done, they will always be my sisters. "I don't want you dead . . . at least not like this."

She crosses her arms and looks back to the window. "Thank you," she answers, and then, in a voice that reminds me of Aurora when she was younger, tiny and sweet, "Will you be back before midnight to let me out?"

I nod, meeting her stony blue eyes—like snow under moonlight— sister to sister, letting her know that I won't abandon her. And I only hope I can keep my promise.

* * *

Once you've experienced death, living never feels quite the same.

The divide between the dark wretched sea and the bright places above the waterline begin to saturate your mind, until all you can think about is clawing your way to the surface, where you'll suck in deep, choking breaths of air. Feel the sun on your cheekbones. The breeze against your eyelashes. And never suffocate again.

I head straight for Bo's cottage, open the door, and step inside. But he's not here.

I start to turn back for the door and then a hand is on my shoulder. I whip around, nearly clocking him in the face. "What's wrong?" he asks, standing just outside the doorway, recognizing the panic in my eyes.

"They're coming," I say.

"Who?"

"Olivia and . . . everyone."

"They're coming here?"

"Olivia told them the summer solstice party is on the island. I don't think we have much time until they get here." Bo glances up the path to Old Fisherman's Cottage. "I already told Gigi to lock herself inside."

"If they find out she's here, they'll think you're protecting her . . . that you're one of them." Hearing him say this—knowing that he's so certain I couldn't possibly be a Swan sister—sends sharp pangs straight into my heart. He would defend me if he had to; he would probably bet his life that I am not one of them. And he would be wrong.

"They won't find her," I say to assure him, but I have no reason to think they won't. I can only hope she stays holed up in the cottage. Keeps quiet. And doesn't do anything stupid. But it's Aurora, and she's always taken risks—like drowning two boys in the harbor at once.

"We have to do it now," Bo says, his temples pulsing. "Before they get here."

I shake my head out of reflex and grab his arm, holding him in place. "No," I say.

"Penny, we might not have another chance. Tonight she'll go back into the ocean; then it'll be too late."

"We can't do it," I say weakly. "We can't kill her." *She's my sister, and even after everything she's done, I can't let him take her life.*

"We have to. She's drowned innocent people," he says like I've forgotten. "And she'll keep doing it unless we stop her." And then the worst crime, the one that nags at him for revenge. "My brother is dead, Penny. I need to end this."

The echo of quick footsteps rattles the air, and Bo and I turn at the same time. Rose is scrambling up the walkway, Heath a few paces behind. "There's still time," I say in a hush to Bo. "We'll figure something out before midnight." But it's only to stall him.

Rose is out of breath when she reaches us, her cheeks a fevered pink and her hair sticking out from under the hood of her raincoat, ruddy-red curls bursting to be set free. "They're coming," she says, the very same two words she told me on the phone, but this time she points out over the water. "They're piling into boats back at the marina. And there's a lot of them."

Heath reaches us and nods at Bo, a quick hello. His dusty blond hair is plastered to his forehead, but he doesn't make a move to brush it away.

"What are we going to do?" Rose asks, still sucking in air between each word.

"Keep Gigi hidden and act normal, whatever happens." I look straight at Rose. "And you can't tell anyone that you brought her here. If they find out you're responsible, they'll suspect you of being one of them."

She nods, but her lips start to tremble, like she's just now realizing the seriousness of what she's done by freeing Gigi from the boathouse and bringing her here.

The sun is coasting low over the water, forming dazzling slivers of light that play against the choppy sea, and then I spot them: a parade of boats sputtering across the harbor, making their way to the island.

The boats thump against the dock and some anchor just off shore, casting their lines down to the stony bottom.

And then there are voices. Dozens. Excited and pitched as they file up the boardwalk. Many of them have never been to the island before, and there is a sense of curiosity that permeates the air. And leading the mob, raven-black hair whipping out behind her, is Olivia Greene.

They carry cases of cheap beer and bottles of wine stolen from their parents' cellars. Without permission, they construct a bonfire just outside the old greenhouse, and under Olivia's command they take over the glassed-in structure, removing potted plants and replacing them with stacks and stacks of beer. Music begins to thump from inside, and as the sun begins to vanish past the horizon, a string of lights illuminates the interior—Christmas lights that someone brought and strung along the eaves. The bonfire sparks and grows larger as more and more people converge on the island.

We watch from Bo's cottage, keeping our distance, wary of anyone who strays away from the party.

Luckily, Gigi's cottage is tucked away on the north side of the island, the farthest structure from the main house and the dock and the greenhouse. Someone would have to go investigating to stumble across it. But from Bo's cottage we can see everything. And as Olivia waves her arms in the air, instructing a group of boys where to place several logs, which were taken from he woodshed, around the bonfire, I can't handle it anymore.

"What are you doing?" Bo asks when I open the cottage door.

"I have to talk to Olivia."

Rose stands up. "I can't stay in here anymore either. I'm going to check on Gigi."

I want to tell her it's better if she doesn't, that she should keep her distance, not draw attention to Gigi's cottage, but she and Heath are already out the door and hurrying up the path to Old Fisherman's Cottage.

Bo eyes me, then follows me outside and up to the bonfire.

Olivia spots us as we approach, and she saunters over. "Bo," she says in a singsong, reaching out to touch him, but I smack her hand away. She rubs it with her other hand and makes a pouty face. "Very protective, aren't you, Penny?" she says. "And perhaps a little jealous, too." She winks at Bo, like she's trying to give me something to really be jealous of. But Bo's gaze remains stiff and unwavering. He doesn't find her amusing—not after what she did to him. In fact, he looks like he wants to murder her right here, in front of everyone.

"What are you doing?" I ask.

"Decorating," she says with a flourish, sweeping an arm over her head. "I've always loved throwing parties—you know this." I do know, but I don't acknowledge it.

Behind her, Lola Arthurs and two of her friends are making cocktails in red plastic cups using a makeshift table constructed of plywood set on top of two empty flowerpots. They generously slosh vodka into each cup, followed by a splash of club soda. They've set up a full bar, and people are going to get drunk fast.

"Why here—why did you bring everyone to the island?" I ask her, making sure to stare through Olivia and down to Marguerite, her real eyes unblinking as they keep sliding over to settle on Bo. This is the last night, her last chance. But I won't let her have him.

"It's just a party," she says with an air of superiority, her bright blue eyes shimmering like she is taunting fate to bring our secret crashing down around us. With so many people here, how will she slip into the sea unnoticed? How can she be sure Gigi won't be discovered? "You used to love parties." She winks then puckers her lips together, a sly, furtive gesture. She wants Bo to figure out the truth, she wants him to know what I really am. She won't say it out loud, yet she'll gladly sprinkle hints along the razor's edge.

"This isn't going to end well," I whisper to Olivia, my eyes meeting hers, then penetrating deep to focus on the wispy mirage of my sister nestled down beneath Olivia's skin.

"We'll see," she counters.

A wind slides over the surface of the island, seeming to push a new group of uninvited guests up the gentle slope to the greenhouse.

TWENTY

It was high tide when the party began. When beers were pounded and shots guzzled into warm bellies, when the music started at a medium volume and conversations were had without the occasional hiccup. But as the tide recedes, so does the party. People stumble over the bonfire, melting the rubber from the bottom of their shoes; girls spill their drinks between their cleavage; boys vomit in the beach grass down near the dock. And Olivia grins from her place at the entrance to the greenhouse, like a queen overseeing a gala held in her honor.

And as it nears ten o'clock, only two hours until midnight, decisions will have to be made. Sacrifices allotted. Like Cinderella, at the stroke of midnight all magic will be revoked. And these bodies we inhabit will have to be given back. Or maybe, if my plan works, I'll keep this one for eternity. It's never been done before. We've never attempted to stay in a body indefinitely—I'll be the first to try. When the clock ticks past midnight, I won't wade out into the sea; I will resist the urge, the beckoning call of the ocean. I will endure whatever pain rips through me; I will fight the transition. I will stay in this body.

And I will watch the sunrise as Penny Talbot.

Rose and Heath reappeared a few minutes after checking on Gigi. Now they stand next to Bo and me near the bonfire, Rose's eyes always flashing across the island to the path that leads to Old Fisherman's Cottage. She's anxious, her fingers tapping against her thigh, afraid someone is going to find Gigi. And like the rest of us, she wishes everyone would just leave the island and go home.

But the party wears on. Boys are enticed down to the water's edge by the girls, dared to enter the harbor one last time before midnight. At the Swan party several weeks earlier, it was the girls who were braving the waters, risking being stolen by a Swan sister. Now it's the boys being persuaded to wade out into the sea, where they risk being drowned by a Swan sister looking for a final kill. It's a game to them.

But I can feel the sway of the sea, the changing tide, the magnetic draw of the harbor. It wants me back; it wants all three of us back. I know my sisters feel it too. I press my fingers against my temples, trying to silence it, keep it at bay. But at times it pulls against me so fiercely I feel dizzy.

"It's getting late," Rose says beside me, worry lines cutting deep into the space between her eyes. The countdown to the end drawing near.

Gigi will need to be let out of the cottage by midnight if she's going to sneak back into the sea. I will need to do it without Bo seeing, without anyone seeing.

And I will need to slip away, find somewhere to be alone, to fight the rising force of Penny, who will start to take back her body come midnight. I can't go to the main house because Penny's mom will hear my screams of pain. I had thought I could hide among the orchard rows, or perhaps the far rocky shore of the island where the crashing waves would conceal my cries. I will need to decide soon.

I turn to Bo.

Earlier, I promised him we would decide what to do with Gigi before midnight. Now there's only an hour left, and I need to tell him something, some reason why he can't take her life. *Because taking a life comes with consequences.*

But when I shift my gaze, Bo is no longer standing beside me. I scan the crowd of faces, searching for him. But he's nowhere within the ring of firelight. He's gone.

"Fuck," I say out loud. *How long has he been gone? How did I not notice when he slipped away?*

"What's wrong?" Rose asks, dropping her hand where she had been chewing on a fingernail.

"I—I think Bo went back to his cottage. I'm going to go check," I lie. I don't want her to know where he really is, what I realize in a sudden flash that he's gone to do: kill Gigi. He couldn't wait any longer, he couldn't let me talk him out of it, so he snuck away.

It might already be too late.

"I'll come with you," Rose offers quickly.

"No. You guys stay here, keep an eye on everyone."

Heath nods, but Rose doesn't look so sure.

I spin around, about to cut through the mob of people gathered around the bonfire, when I'm hit with both relief and horror. Gigi isn't dead, at least not yet, because she's strutting up the pathway, heading straight for the bonfire and the party. She got out.

My lungs cease to draw in air. My heart ratchets up so that it's beating against the back of my throat.

"Holy shit," I hear Heath say behind me.

And then Rose asks, "What is she doing?"

She's come for revenge.

Gigi escaped the cottage.

She must have broken through a window or forced her way past the barricaded door. She was tired of waiting for me to come release her. She's already feeling the pull of the tide, just like me. The sea in our blood, in our minds, begging us to sink into the darkness and be purged from these bodies. It will only get harder to resist.

But now Gigi's free. She's out. And she's surely really pissed off.

But where's Bo? Maybe he didn't go to kill her after all. Maybe I was wrong.

Gigi strides into the group, hair falling out of her ponytail, plain blue T-shirt and white drawstring pants one size too big because they're clothes that Rose brought for her to wear. Most people don't notice her as she pushes past them; they're already too drunk. But as she winds her way through the dwindling crowd, I can tell she's looking for something: someone.

Davis and Lon are standing just inside the doors of the greenhouse, hovering where the cases of beer and a nearly empty keg have been placed. Gigi spots them, mouth leveled into a sharp, determined line. She cuts swiftly up to the greenhouse. Davis sees her first, then Lon catches sight of her and actually takes a step back. He's wearing one of his loudest, most obnoxious shirts tonight: pink and teal with rainbow-colored peacocks and hula girls. It's actually hard to look directly at it.

Davis and Lon are the only ones in the greenhouse, and they could make a run for it, sprint out through the door on the far side of the glassed-in building. But they seem frozen, stupefied into inaction, which is exactly how I feel.

Rose and Heath, still standing near me, stare at Gigi with their mouths slightly agape.

Gigi slides in between Davis and Lon, fluttering her eyelashes up at Lon and tilting her head to the side. She grazes a finger around the rim of his cup, smiling, licking her lips. Still, the rest of the party has no clue what's happening: that Gigi Kline has suddenly reemerged. A few drunk girls on the other side of the fire pit giggle loudly then stumble backward, arms looped together. Another guy who is standing the closest to the greenhouse has a cigarette between his lips and is taking long drags as if he were actually smoking, but the cigarette isn't even lit. He's too trashed to notice anything around him.

I can see Gigi's lips moving, but she's whispering so softly, I can't make out the words. Her voice is slipping into Lon's ears; she wants to take him with her, one last kill before she retreats into the sea for the winter. She wants her revenge for what he and Davis did to her. Then her gaze snaps to Davis, biting her bottom lip. She wants them both.

But before she's able to brush her fingers across his cheek, he grabs her wrist and bends it away. "You fucking witch," I hear Davis bark. Lon already looks entranced, staring at her meekly, like a dog waiting to be told what to do. But Davis has stopped her before she's infiltrated the cracks in his mind. "I knew you were one of them," he says, loud enough that we can hear. He towers over her, broad meaty shoulders, holding her arm locked at her side. But she doesn't seem afraid. She smiles from the left side of her lips, amused. Her gaze penetrates his, and with his hand around her wrist, it's enough to seduce him into falling desperately in love with her. I watch as his expression melts, turns sappy at the edges until his thick, bushy eyebrows fold downward, and he releases his hold on her. She runs her fingers up his jaw then lifts onto her tiptoes. She brushes her lips against his ear, whispering things that will make him hers.

And when she's done, she threads her fingers through both Davis's and Lon's hands and begins leading them from the greenhouse. As she meanders past us, around the bonfire, her eyes glide over mine, but I don't move.

Rose looks baffled. She doesn't fully understand what's happening. "Gigi?" she says when Gigi and Davis and Lon stride past. "What are you doing?"

"Thanks for saving me," Gigi says to Rose, her tone guileful and distant. She's already thinking about the sea, about leaving Gigi's body and becoming part of the Pacific. "But they were right about me. . . ." She nods to Davis and Lon, standing obediently behind her. "See you next summer."

"Gigi, don't do this," I hiss, and her eyes snap to mine. Our real eyes meet, beneath these human exteriors. And there is a warning in hers, a threat that I can read in my sister's expression: If I try to stop her, if I do anything to prevent her from taking Davis and Lon, she will reveal who I really am. Right here. Right now. In front of everyone.

She tugs against Davis's and Lon's hands, pulling them toward the dock. But then a voice bellows from behind me. "It's Gigi!" I look over my shoulder, and Rose has taken several steps away from the firelight, pointing down the path to where Gigi has stopped, Davis and Lon standing obediently on either side of her.

The crowd encircling the fire stalls their conversations in almost perfect unison. They stop laughing and slurping beers and swaying dangerously close to the flames. And instead, they all turn to look at Rose, following her outstretched arm down to Gigi.

There is a pause, a delayed moment while everyone processes what's happening, their brains chugging forward at half speed. And then a girl shouts, "She has Davis and Lon!"

As if choreographed, several guys standing around the bonfire drop their beers into the flames then break into a sprint after Gigi. They know what she is—at least they think they do. And seeing her leading Davis and Lon down toward the water, on the last night of the summer solstice, after she's been missing for weeks, is proof enough that they've been right all along.

Gigi waits a half beat; her gaze sweeps over the crowd then back to me as she registers what's happening, and then her hands release their hold on Davis and Lon. She won't be able to take them with her. She has to run now. And she does.

Her blond hair shivers against the moonlight as she veers down the path to the dock. The boys shout after her, darting past Davis and Lon, both numbed to the commotion. And when the small mob reaches the dock, there is more shouting, and what sounds like people clamoring into boats and engines rumbling to life. Gigi must have dove straight into the water. It was her only escape.

She will have to swim; she will have to hide. Or maybe she will dip safely beneath the surface of the harbor, quickly relinquishing the body she's stolen to spend another winter in the cold and dark.

By morning, the real Gigi will wake as if from a hangover, floating in the harbor perhaps, forced to swim ashore and pull herself onto land. Only foggy images will surface in her mind from the last few weeks, when she was no longer Gigi Kline but was Aurora Swan. But we will all know the truth.

And that's assuming the crowd chasing after her doesn't catch her first.

Rose shakes her head in disbelief, staring down the path where Gigi has fled, where the rest of the party has descended to climb into boats and assist in the search for Aurora Swan.

I feel a wave of sympathy for Rose. She thought she was doing the right thing by rescuing Gigi. She thought she could see what was right in front of her—the truth—but she can't. She's blind, just like everyone else in this town.

She doesn't even know what I am.

Her best friend has been turned into something else. And for a sliver of a split second, I consider telling her the truth. Getting it over with. One night to shatter her entire world—to tear apart her reality.

But then I remember Bo.

He wasn't with Gigi in the cottage. He didn't go to kill her after all.

And then I realize . . . Olivia is nowhere in the crowd. She wasn't even here when Gigi appeared.

They're both missing.

"Where are you going?" Rose asks. She and Heath and I are the last remaining people standing beside the bonfire. Everyone else has gone in pursuit of Gigi.

269

"To find Bo," I tell her. "You guys should go back to town."

A slight rain has begun to fall, and a wall of bruise-black clouds pushes beneath the stars and blocks out the moon.

I walk to Rose. I hope this isn't the last time I'll see her, but just in case, I say, "You did the right thing helping Gigi. You didn't know what she really was." I want her to understand that even though she was wrong about Gigi, she shouldn't doubt herself. She wanted to protect Gigi, keep her safe, and I admire her for it.

"But I should have known," she says, her eyes turning glassy with tears, her cheeks flushed. And in this instant, I know I can't tell her what I really am. It will destroy her. And after tonight, if I'm still Penny Talbot, I will continue pretending to be her best friend. I will let her believe I am the same person she grew up with. Even if the real Penny Talbot will be gone—lost in the trenches of a body and mind that I have stolen.

"Please," I say to her and Heath. "Go back to town. There's nothing more you can do tonight. Gigi's gone."

Heath reaches forward and touches Rose's hand. He knows it's time to go.

"Call me tomorrow?" she asks. I hug her, smelling the sweet cinnamon-and-nutmeg scent that lingers in her wavy hair from her mother's shop.

"Of course." No matter what, if I'm still Penny tomorrow, I'll call her. If I'm not, I'm certain the real Penny will call her anyway. And Rose will hopefully never know the difference.

Heath pulls her away, back to the dock, and my chest aches watching them leave.

A deluge of rain begins falling from the dark, funeral-black sky, making the bonfire pop and sizzle.

I pick my way through the sharp beach grass and large boulders, the rain blowing steadily now. I will check Bo's cottage first and then the orchard. But I don't even make it that far when I notice something atop the lighthouse. Two silhouettes block the beam of light as it sweeps clockwise around the lantern room.

Bo and Olivia. It has to be them. They're in the lighthouse.

The metal door into the lighthouse has been left open by whoever was the last to enter, and it taps lightly against the wall behind it, the gusting wind blowing rain onto the stone floor.

Otis and Olga are standing just inside, mewing softly up at me, eyes watery and wide. *What are they doing out here?* I pause beside the stairwell, listening for voices. But the storm beating against the outer walls is louder than anything else. Bo must be inside. Otis and Olga have been attached to him since he arrived, following him around the island, sleeping in his cottage most nights. I think they've known I'm not really Penny since the start; they sensed the moment I took up residence inside her body. And they prefer Bo over me.

"Go back to the house," I urge them, but the two orange tabbies blink away from me, staring out into the gloomy night, uninterested in leaving the lighthouse.

I take the stairs two at a time, my breathing ragged. I use the railing to propel myself up the interior of the lighthouse. My legs are on fire. Sweat ripples down my temples. But I keep going. My heart feels like it's burning a hole through my chest. But I reach the top in record speed, pulling myself up over the last step and sucking in deep, quick breaths.

I inch along the stone wall, trying to steady my crazed heartbeat, then peek around the corner into the lantern room. Bo and Olivia are no longer inside. But I can see them through the glass. They are standing outside on the narrow walkway that encircles the lighthouse. Bo has something in his hand. It glints as he moves closer to Olivia.

It's a knife.

TWENTY-ONE

The small door that leads out to the walkway bangs open when I turn the knob, sucked out by the wind. Both Bo and Olivia jerk around to face me.

"You shouldn't be out here, Penny," Bo yells over the storm, his gaze quickly whipping back around to Olivia. Like he's afraid she might vanish into the air if he doesn't keep an eye on her.

The walkway hasn't been used in decades; the metal is rotted and rusted, and it creaks as I shuffle out onto it. "You don't have to do this," I say. The wind is blinding, rain stinging my face and eyes.

"You know that I do," he answers, his tone calm, resolute.

I'm trying to piece together the series of events that brought the two of them up here—who ambushed who? "Where did you get the knife?" I ask. The blade is large, a hunting knife, and not one I immediately recognize.

"Dresser drawer, in the cottage."

"And you're just going to stab her with it?" I ask. Olivia's eyes widen, and beyond the thin surface of her skin, Marguerite seems to be squirming.

"No," Bo answers. "I'm going to force her over the edge."

273

Eighty feet below us, rocky outcroppings lie in jagged, toothy mounds. A quick, abrupt death. No final gasps. No twitch of a finger. Just lights out, for both Olivia Greene and Marguerite Swan. At least it'll be painless.

"How did you get her up here?" I ask, inching closer to Bo. Olivia is leaning against the metal railing, and the entire walkway shudders when I take a step.

"I didn't. I saw her walking to the lighthouse." He swallows and grips the knife tighter in his hand, held firmly out in front of him. The blade glints with rainwater. "I knew it was my only chance." So it was Marguerite who lured him. Maybe she thought she could seduce him, prove to me that she could have him if she wanted. But instead Bo hunted her. She never had a chance to even touch him. And now he's going to force her over the ledge. It will look like suicide, like sweet, popular Olivia Greene took her own life by flinging herself from the town's lighthouse.

"Please," I say, stepping closer to Bo. The walkway shivers beneath me. "Doing this won't bring your brother back." At this, Olivia's expression changes. She didn't know about Bo's brother, that he was drowned in the harbor last summer, but her eyes light up and her lips tease into a smile.

"Your brother?" she asks inquisitively.

"Don't fucking talk," Bo snaps.

"Your brother was drowned, wasn't he?" she prods.

I can just barely see the side of Bo's face, and his temple pulses, rain spilling off his chin. "Was it you?" he asks with gravel in his voice, taking a single, swift step forward and pressing the blade against Olivia's stomach. He might just gut her right here if she gives him the wrong answer. He wants his vengeance, even if it means spilling her blood instead of forcing her over the railing. Murder instead of suicide.

Again Olivia smiles, eyes swaying over to me as if she were bored. She can see it in my face, in the tense outline of the real me hovering beneath Penny's skin. Marguerite is my sister, after all—she knows me, can read the truth better than anyone. "Of course not," she answers sweetly to Bo. "But you should ask your girlfriend; maybe she knows who it was."

I feel my chest seize up, ribs closing in around my heart and lungs, making it hard to draw in air and pump blood to my brain. "Don't," I say too softly, hardly loud enough for her to hear.

"You probably want to know why I brought all those people to your island, why I wanted the summer solstice to happen here."

I don't respond, even though I do want to know.

"I wanted you to see that no matter what we do, no matter how many times we steal a body and pretend that we are one of them . . . we never will be. We're their enemies. They hate us. And if given the chance, they will kill us." She nods her head at Bo, as if he were the proof. "You have been playing house for too long—too many summers in that body. You think you have friends here; you think you could make a real life in this town. You think that you can fall in love—as if you were entitled to it." She sneers, left eyebrow raised. And even though the rain cascades down her face, she still looks beautiful. "But they only like you because they don't know what you really are. If they did, they would hate you. Despise you . . . they'd want you dead." She says this last word as if it tastes like metal. "He"—she flashes her gaze at Bo—"would want you dead."

The knife is still pressed to her belly, but she leans into it, staring at Bo. "Ask your girlfriend what her real name is."

My heart stops completely. My eyes blur over. *No. Please*, I want to beg. *Don't do this. Don't ruin everything.*

"She's been lying to you," she adds. "Go ahead, ask her."

Bo turns just enough to look me in the eye where I'm pressed up against the wall of the lighthouse, palms flattened against the stone.

"It doesn't change anything. . . ." I start to say, trying to keep the truth from spilling up to the surface.

"Doesn't change what?" he asks.

"How I feel about you . . . how you feel. You know me."

"What the hell are you talking about?"

Olivia's smirk reaches her eyes. She's enjoying this. This is what she's wanted all along: for me to realize that we can't change what we are. We're killers. And I can never have Bo. Not like this, in this body. The only way a Swan sister can truly keep someone is by drowning them, trapping their soul in the sea with us.

"My name isn't Penny," I say, the confession ripping at my insides. My lips quiver, rainwater dripping over them and catching on my tongue.

The knife in his hand starts to lower, and his gaze cuts through me. The realization of what's coming next is already settling into his eyes.

"My name is Hazel."

He shakes his head a fraction of an inch. The knife is now lowered at his side, his mouth forming a hard, unyielding line.

"Hazel Swan," I concede.

His eyes sway briefly and his jawline tightens, and then he goes perfectly still, like he's solidified into a statue right in front of me.

"I should have told you before. But I didn't know how. And then when I found out why you came here, I knew you'd hate me. And I just couldn't—"

"When?" he asks matter-of-factly.

"When?" I repeat, not sure what he means.

"When did you stop being Penny Talbot?"

I try to swallow, but my body rejects the motion. As if Penny's body and mine are battling each other. Fighting for control. "The first night we met." I brush a wet clump of hair away from my forehead. "After the Swan party on the beach, Penny brought you back to the island. That night, she woke from sleep and came down to the dock before sunrise. It was a dream to her. She waded into the water, and I took her body."

"So that night on the beach, when we talked by the bonfire and you told me about the Swan sisters . . . that was Penny? Not you?"

I nod.

"But everything after that night . . . has been you?"

Again I nod.

"But you remembered talking to me on the beach, and things about Penny's life."

"I absorb the memories of the body I inhabit. I know everything about Penny."

"That's not the only reason," Olivia chimes in, happy to fill in the holes I'd like to avoid.

I close my eyes then open them. Bo has turned fully away from Olivia and is now staring at me. I'm the threat now. I've hurt him. Lied to him. Made him trust me and even love me. "I've taken Penny's body every summer for the last three years," I confess.

A blast of wind barrels into us, sending a surge of rain against the windows of the lighthouse.

"Why?" Bo manages to ask, though his voice sounds strangled.

"I like her life," I say, the first time I've admitted it aloud. "I like being here on the island."

"Oh, Hazel, if you're going to tell the truth, you might as well tell him everything," Olivia interjects.

I shoot daggers at her, wishing she'd just shut up. I should have let Bo push her over the edge. I shouldn't have stopped him. But now here she stands, bringing up every lurid detail of my past. And calling me by my real name.

"I used to come here when I was still—"

"Alive," Olivia finishes for me, raising both eyebrows.

"You lived here before?" Bo asks.

"No." I don't want to tell him about Owen. About my life before. It doesn't matter now. I'm not that girl anymore. That girl drowned in the harbor two centuries ago . . . and this girl is here, alive, right in front of him.

"The first lighthouse keeper had a son," Olivia fills in for me. "His name was Owen Clement. He was handsome; I'll give him that. But I never understood what she saw in him. He had no money, no estate, no lucrative future. Yet she loved him anyway. And she was going to marry him. That is, if his father hadn't accused us of being witches and drowned us in the harbor."

I cringe at her sharp account of Owen and me. As if it could be summed up so crisply. A single breath to tell our story.

"Now Owen is buried up on Alder Hill in the Sparrow Cemetery. That's where she went this morning—to his grave." She says it like an accusation, like I have betrayed Bo with this single act. And maybe I have. But it's not the worst offense, not by a mile.

Bo looks stunned. He's staring at me like I have ripped his heart from his chest, squeezed it between my clawed fingers, and crushed it until it stopped pumping.

Where he once saw a girl, he now sees a monster.

"It wasn't like that," I say. "I went to say good-bye to him." But my words seem frail and ineffectual. They don't mean anything anymore. Not to him.

"So you see, Bo," Olivia continues, hair whirling about her face, Marguerite Swan grinning and swaying beneath her skin as if she were suspended in midair. "Your sweet Penny is not who she says she is. She is a murderer like me, like Aurora—her sisters. And she only comes back to this island because it reminds her of the boy she used to love. And if you think you care about her, love her even, you might want to consider that she is a Swan sister, and seducing boys is what we do. You might only love her because she has spun a spell to make you think you do. It's not real." Olivia licks her lips.

"That's not true," I bark.

"Oh, no? Perhaps you should tell him about his brother. Tell him how good you are at seducing unsuspecting outsiders."

My knees buckle, and I dig my fingernails into the wall of the lighthouse to keep from collapsing. *I can't do this.*

"What was your brother's name?" Olivia ponders. "Doesn't matter. I'm sure you resemble each other, and how could my sister resist the chance to seduce two brothers? It's just so perfect."

"Stop it," I tell her, but Bo has taken a step back against the railing, and it rattles beneath him. His hair is soaked, his clothes soaked.

We all look like we've been swimming in the ocean, drenched, the three of us trapped together on this walkway, caught by the wind and whatever fate has brought us here to this point. Centuries of deceit now tearing me apart. The truth more painful than anything I've ever felt. Even more painful than drowning.

"Was it you?" Bo asks, and the way he says it feels like he's just thrust the knife straight into my gut.

"I didn't know at first," I say, fighting through the heat of tears that push against the rim of my eyes. "But when you told me what happened to your brother, I started to remember him. You look so much alike." I clear my throat. "I didn't want to believe it. I was different last summer. I didn't care whose life I took—I didn't care about anything. But I do now. You helped me see that. I don't want to hurt anyone anymore, especially not you."

"This entire time, you knew I was trying to figure out who killed him. . . ." He gets tangled up on the words. Then he finds them again. "It was you?"

"I'm sorry." Another breath.

He looks away, not even listening to me anymore. "This is why you could see what Gigi really is, and Olivia?" His eyes shift to look at Olivia and then me, like he's trying to see what lies inside us. "You could see them because you're one of them?"

"Bo," I plead, my voice sounding weak.

"You drowned my brother," he says, and he takes one quick step forward and locks his body around mine. His breath is low and shallow, and he brings the knife up to my throat, pressing it just beneath my chin. My eyelids flutter. I lean my head back against the wall. His gaze tears through me. Not with lust but rage. And I sense in the fury pumping through his stare, through his fingertips where they hold the knife, that he wants to kill me.

Olivia's eyes flash to the doorway. This is her chance to flee. But for some reason she stays. Maybe she wants to see him slit my throat. Or maybe she just wants to see how this plays out.

"How many have you killed this year?" Bo asks, like he's looking for another reason to slide the blade across my throat and let the life drain out of me.

"None," I mutter.

"My brother was the last one?"

I nod, just barely.

"Why?"

"I don't want to be that person anymore." My voice is a whisper.

"But it's what you are," he spits back.

"No." I shake my head. "It's not. I can't do it anymore. I won't. I want a different life. I wanted it with you."

"Don't do that," he says.

I try to clear my throat, but I'm shaking too badly.

"Don't act like I changed you. Don't act like you care about me," he says. "I can't trust anything you've said. I can't even trust how I feel about you." These last words sting the worst, and I grimace. He thinks I made him love me, that I seduced him just like Olivia did. "You lied to me about everything."

"Not everything," I try to say, but he doesn't want to hear it.

He drops the knife from my throat. "I don't want to hear anything else." His eyes are like stone, rimmed with hatred for what I am. Mine are pleading for forgiveness. But it's too late for that. I killed his brother. There is nothing more to say.

I have made myself his enemy. And now he recoils from me.

And just as the beam of light from the lighthouse passes over his face, he turns away, the rain slamming against his back, and ducks through the door into the lighthouse.

His shadow moves through the lantern room and disappears down the stairway. "He doesn't love you, Hazel," Olivia says, as if to console me. "He loved what he thought you were. But you've been lying to him."

"This is your fault. You did this."

"No. *You* did this. You thought you could be one of them—human—but we've been dead for two hundred years—nothing will change that. Not even a boy you think you love."

"How the hell would you know? You've never really loved anyone in your whole life. Only yourself. I don't want to be miserable like you, stuck in that harbor for eternity."

"You can't change what we are."

"Watch me," I say, and I push away from the wall and dart back into the lighthouse.

"Where are you going?" she shouts after me.

"I'm going after him."

TWENTY-TWO

The bonfire outside the greenhouse is a smoldering heap of coals, unable to survive in this downpour. And everyone who had come to the island for the summer solstice is now gone. A party cut short by the return of Gigi Kline.

The shadow of Bo is already headed down the path to the dock, and the wind and rain between us makes it seem like he's miles away, a mirage on a desert highway. I open my mouth to yell down to him but then clamp my lips closed. He won't stop anyway. He's determined to leave this island . . . and me. For good.

So I start to run.

At the dock, the cluster of boats and dinghies that had been clotted together only a few hours earlier are now all gone. Only the skiff and the sailboat remain, thumping against the sides of the dock, the wind battering down on them like an angry fist.

Out on the water, several lights sweep through the dark, still searching for Gigi, unable to locate her, while the others must have given up and returned to the marina. She might still be out there somewhere, hidden. Midnight inching closer. Or maybe she's already gone beneath the waves, Aurora dissolving back into the deepest dark

283

of the harbor. But if I know my sister, she will find a way back to shore so she can wait out the last few minutes until midnight. Savor these fleeting moments until she has to return to the brutal sea. And Marguerite will do the same. Maybe she will stay atop the lighthouse, staring out over the island, watching the storm push inland over the Pacific, until she's forced down to the water's edge in the final seconds.

Bo is not in the skiff, so I scan the sailboat. He appears near the front starboard side, throwing the moor lines.

"Where are you going?" I shout up at him, just as he tosses the last bowline. But he doesn't answer me. "Don't leave like this," I plead. "I want to tell you the truth—tell you everything."

"It's too late," he replies. The auxiliary motor rumbles softly, and he walks to the steering wheel at the stern of the sailboat. It sounds just like I remember from three years ago—a gentle sputter, the wind aching to push against the sails once the boat reaches the open ocean and can grasp the Pacific winds.

"Please," I beg, but the boat begins to drift forward from the dock.

I follow it until there is no more dock, and then I don't have a choice. Two feet separate me from the stern of the sailboat where the blue script letters painted on the back read WINGSONG. Three feet. Four. I jump, my legs catapulting me forward, but I fall just short. My chest slams against the side, pain lancing across my ribs, and my hands scramble for something to keep from falling into the water. I find a metal cleat and wrap my fingers around it. But it's slick, and my fingers start to give way. Seawater splashes up against the backs of my legs.

Then Bo's hands tighten around my arms and pull me upward

onto the boat. I gasp, touching my left side with my palm, pain shooting through my ribs with each deep breath. Bo is only inches away, still holding on to my right arm. And I look up into his eyes, hoping he sees me, the girl inside. The girl he's known these last few weeks. But then he releases my arm and turns away, back to the helm of the sailboat. "You shouldn't have done that," he says.

"I just need to talk to you."

"There's nothing else you can say."

He steers the boat not toward the marina, but out to sea, straight into the storm.

"You're not going to town?"

"No."

"You're stealing a sailboat?"

"Borrowing it. Just until I get to the next harbor up the coast. I don't want to see that cursed fucking town ever again."

I press my fingers to my ribs again and wince. They're bruised. Maybe cracked.

The sailboat heaves to the side, the wind fighting us, but I shuffle to where Bo is holding tight to the steering wheel, maneuvering us right out into the heart of the storm. The tide swells; waves crash over the bow then spill out the sides. We shouldn't be out in this.

"Bo," I say, and he actually looks at me. "I need you to know. . . ." My body shakes from the cold, from the knowing that I'm about to lose everything I thought I had. "I didn't force you to care about me. I didn't trick you into loving me. Whatever you felt for me was real." I say it in the past tense, knowing that whatever he felt is probably now gone. "I'm not the monster you think I am."

"You killed my brother." His gaze peels me open, severs me in half, crushes me down to nothing. "You fucking killed him. And you lied to me."

This I can't make right. There's nothing that can change it. It's unforgivable.

"I know."

Another wave slams into us, and I grab on to Bo instinctively then let him go just as quickly. "Why did you do it?" he asks. I'm not sure if he's asking about his brother or asking why I lied about who I am. Probably both.

And the answers are tied up in each other. "This town took everything from me," I say, blinking away the water on my lashes. "My life. The person I once loved. I was angry . . . no, I was more than angry, and I wanted them to pay for what they did to me. I took your brother into the harbor like I've taken so many boys over the years. I was numb. I didn't care whose life I stole. Or how many people suffered."

I grip the wood helm beside the steering wheel to keep from being thrown sideways by another wave. This storm is going to kill us both. But I keep talking—this might be the last chance I get to make Bo understand. "This summer, when I took Penny's body for the third time, I awoke in her bed just like the last two years, but this time a new memory rested in her mind: a memory of you from the night before. She was already falling for you. She saw something that made her trust you. But I was in her body now. And you were on the island—the boy she brought across the harbor and let stay in the cottage. And for some reason I trusted you too. It was the first time I've trusted anyone in two hundred years." I brush away a stream of tears with the back of my hand. "I could have killed you. I could have drowned you that first day. But for some reason I wanted to protect you. Keep you safe. I wanted to feel something again for someone—for you. I needed to know that my heart wasn't completely dead, that a part of me was still human . . . could still fall in love."

Rain and seawater spill over the hard features of his face. He's listening, even if he doesn't want to.

"No one should exist for as long as I have," I say. "Only getting small glimpses of a real life each summer, tormented by dark waking dreams the rest of the time. I've spent most of my two hundred years down there, at the bottom of the sea, a spook . . . an apparition moving with the tide, waiting to breathe air again. I can't go back there."

Not alive—not dead. A phantom trapped as the months tick by, every hour, every second.

"So you'd keep this body forever?" he asks, squinting into the storm as we near the end of the cape and chug out into open water.

"I'm not sure what I want now."

"But you stole it," he answers sharply. "It's not yours."

"I know." There is no justification for wanting to keep this body. It's selfish, and it's murder. I would be killing the real Penny Talbot, tamping her down as if she never existed at all. I wanted to believe I was a different person because of Bo, because I haven't killed this summer. But I'm no different from who I've been for the last two hundred years. I want something I can't have. I am a thief of souls and bodies. But when will I stop? When will my torment on this town be enough? My revenge satiated?

Penny deserves a full life—doesn't she? The life I never got to have. And in a burst of realization, I know: I can't take it from her.

All my thoughts surface at once. A deluge of memories.

They snap like little firecrackers in my mind. Explosions along every nerve ending. I can fix this. Remedy the injustices. Give Bo what he wants.

"I've only been on this sailboat once before," I tell him. He frowns at me, not sure what I'm talking about. "The first summer that I took Penny's body, her father was suspicious of me. He figured out what I was. I think that's why he collected all those books in your cottage: He was trying to find a way to get rid of me without killing his daughter—the same thing you were searching for. Except he found a way." Bo turns the boat south down the coastline, and the wind shifts direction too, hitting us from the starboard side. "That summer," I continue, "he left the house one night after dinner and walked down to the dock. I followed him. He said he was taking the sailboat out and asked if I wanted to go along. Something didn't seem right. He seemed off—anxious—but I went because that's what Penny would have done. And I was pretending to be her for the first time. We didn't get very far out, just past the cape, when he told me the truth. He said that he knew what I was—a Swan sister—and that he was giving me a choice. He had found a way to kill me without destroying the body I inhabited—Penny's body. He had discovered it in one of his books. But it involved sacrifice. I draw in a shallow breath, locating the words lodged at the base of my throat. If I jumped into the sea," I say, trying to steady my voice, "and drowned again, like I did two hundred years ago, I would die, but Penny would not. I had to repeat my death. And he believed it would also kill my sisters, effectively breaking our curse. We would never return to the town of Sparrow again."

Bo tilts his head to look at me, his hands white-knuckled and braced around the steering wheel, fighting to keep us from being blown to shore or capsized completely. "But you didn't do it?"

I shake my head.

And then he asks what I knew was coming. "What happened to Penny's father?"

"I thought he was going to push me overboard, force me to do it. He came toward me, so I grabbed the mooring hook and I . . . I struck him with it. He wobbled for a minute. Off balance as the boat rolled with each wave." I choke back the memory. I still wish I could go back and undo what happened that night. Because Penny lost her father, and her mom lost her husband. "He went over the side. And he never came back up to the surface again." I look out at the sea, midnight blue, churning and pockmarked with rain, and I picture him sucking in water, drowning just like I did so many years ago. "There was a book sitting on the deck of the boat, the one where he had read how to break our curse, so I threw it overboard. I didn't want anyone else finding out how to kill us." I had watched it sink into the dark, having no idea that there was an entire cottage filled with books he had collected. "The boat had slowly been drifting toward shore," I explain. "The sails were down, thankfully, and the motor still running. So I steered it away from the rocks and somehow made it back to the island. I tied it to the dock and crept back up to the house. And there it has sat, until now."

"Why are you telling me this?" Bo asks.

"Because I know what I need to do now. I should have done it that night. I should have changed the course of everything. Then your brother would still be alive, and you never would have come here. I was selfish then, and a coward. But I'm not anymore."

"What are you talking about?" He releases one hand from the steering wheel.

"I'm going to give you what you want—your revenge."

I turn away from him and walk to the starboard side of the sail-boat, facing out to sea. My grave—the place where I belong. Lives have been lost. Deaths counted. It started with my sisters and me when we were drowned in the harbor all those years ago, but we have caused more suffering than can ever be measured.

"What are you doing?" Bo's voice is still hard, but I sense a hint of uncertainty in it.

"I wanted to stay in this body and live this life . . . with you. But now I know that I can't . . . for so many reasons. You will never be able to love me knowing what I've done, who I am. I'm sorry for your brother. I wish I could take it back. I wish I could take back most of the things I've done. But at least now I can end it. Make right this wrong." I close my eyes briefly, drawing gulps of air into my lungs.

"Penny," he says, a name that isn't mine. He steps away from the wheel, the motor still rumbling, the sailboat crashing through the waves without a captain to pilot it. He doesn't touch me. But he stands in front of me, rocking side to side with the heaving sailboat. "Hazel," he tries instead, but there is still the burning of anger in his voice. "You ruined my life; you took my brother from me. And then I fell in love with you—I fell in love with the person who killed him. How am I supposed to deal with that? What do you want me to say? That I forgive you? Because I can't." His eyes waver away from me. *He can't forgive.* He never will. I can see the struggle in him. He feels like he should try to stop me, but a part of him, a bitter, vengeful part of him, also wants me dead.

"I know you can't forgive me," I say. "I know I hurt you—I ruined everything. I wish it were different. I wish *I* were different. But . . ." I choke down on the words I need to say. "But I did love you. That was real; everything between us was real. I love you still."

I hope to see a glimmer of something in his eyes, recognition that a part of him still loves me too. But he can't see through what he now knows I am. I am only the girl who drowned his brother—that's all.

When he doesn't speak, I glance over to the steering wheel, where a small clock is mounted to the dash. Eleven forty-eight. Only twelve minutes left until midnight, and then it'll be too late. I can't stay in this body, not now. I can't steal another life. But if I plunge into the icy sea, if I don't allow my soul to escape but instead let this body drown with me inside, I will be the one to die. Not Penny. I will drown just like I did two centuries ago. And hopefully, if Penny's father was right, she will survive.

"In years past, when we've returned to the sea," I explain, the wind blowing my hair straight out behind me, "we leave the bodies we've stolen before the clock reaches midnight. But I think, for this to work, Penny's body has to drown with me inside it. I will die, but she can be brought back. You will have to save her. I will be gone, but she can live."

He looks through me, like he doesn't want to believe what I'm saying.

I turn toward the railing. The sea spraying my face, the dark sky like a funeral. This will be my last breath. My last glimpse of the life I could have had. I close my eyes, knowing I can't turn back.

But then Bo's hands grab me, spinning me around to face him. "No," he says. His eyebrows are tugged together, lips cut flat. There is torment in him. He doesn't know what to feel, what to do. And this is why I'm taking the decision away from him. I'm ending this once and for all so he doesn't have to. He speaks anyway, says what he thinks he should: "It doesn't have to end like this."

I smile a little, shaking my head. "You know there's no other way. My sisters will just keep on killing. And I don't want to go back into the sea for another two hundred years. I can't. It's not a life. And I'm tired."

He slides his hands up to my cheeks and into my soaking-wet hair. And even though there is love in his eyes, a pain that I recognize, there is also hate. Deep, undeniable, entrenched hate. I took his brother from him. And there's no going back from that.

But even with loathing in his dark green eyes—which still remind me of the place where the sea meets the sky after a storm—he pulls me to him, pressing his warm lips to mine as the rain continues to fall between us. He kisses me like he won't let me go, even though I know he will. Desperate and angry. Loving me and hating me. And his fingers pull against my hair, drawing me even closer. My fingernails dig into his chest, trying to hold tight to this moment. This feeling. I could take him with me, like both Olivia and Aurora suggested. I could drown him now, and he would be trapped in the sea with me for eternity. But I don't want him like that—confined to a watery prison. It isn't real. And he doesn't deserve it.

His lips lift only an inch away from mine, and I draw in a tight breath of air.

"Thank you for giving me these days with you," I say. Tears push forward, and I don't try to stop them.

I close my eyes and rest my forehead against his chest, breathing him in, wanting to remember his scent forever. But right now he just smells like the sea. A boy drifted in on the tide. Like a dream, like a memory I hope I'll never forget.

I drop my hands from his chest, turning to look out at the ocean. Wild and turbulent. The bottomless black Pacific beckoning me into its cold interior. It's nearly midnight, and lightning spiders against the clouds in the distance, drawing closer. "When I jump in," I say to Bo over the crashing waves and wind, "after I've drowned, you need to pull her body back out."

He doesn't nod. No response. He can't comprehend what's happening. But he knows he has to let me go.

I meet his forest-green eyes for the last time, seeing myself reflected back in them. "Don't tell her what happened to her father," I say. "Don't tell her about me. I think it's better if she doesn't know."

Thunder snaps down from the sky. He nods.

I will leave the good memories inside Penny's mind, and I will take the bad ones with me. She will remember images of Bo, of his warmth beside her in the cottage, of his hands on her skin, his lips on hers. She will remember days when her heart felt about to burst with love for him. She won't recall going to the cemetery to say good-bye to Owen; she won't remember speaking to Marguerite in front of the old perfumery. She won't remember talking to Gigi Kline as if she were her sister. She will only recall that she provided sanctuary for Gigi from the boys who had been hunting her. She will live the life I wish I could have. She will miss her father, but sometimes missing is better than knowing. I will give her the gift of good memories. The gift of Bo—the last boy I loved.

The boy I love still.

I step over the wire railing. The deck is slippery, and I almost lose my footing. My heart begins to pound, fear and doubt seizing me. My fingers grip so tightly to the railing that they begin to throb.

I don't take my gaze off him. "I told you that love is like falling, like drowning. This will be the same. I just have to let go." My lips quiver. "Don't forget me."

"Never," he answers. And his face is the last thing I see before I jump over the side and hit the water. And everything turns black.

The world is instantly made silent. The storm churns and crashes above the waterline, but down here, everything is calm and quiet.

I swim hard. I pull myself into the deep, closer to the bottom of the sea. The cold turns my hands and feet numb almost immediately—the cold that will slow my heart and preserve Penny's body. The darkness is absolute, blotting out the surface of the ocean so that I can't tell which way is up. But I don't want to change my mind—I don't want any chance of swimming back up and sucking in a breath of air.

I plummet like a coin sinking down to the pirate wreckage in the harbor. I think about the penny I tossed into the water the night with Bo and Rose and Heath. We each made wishes. Some tangible. Some likely not. My wish was to be human again. To live a normal life. But it didn't come true. I fall deeper, darker, colder. But maybe this, what I'm doing right now, is the most human I've ever been. To die. To sacrifice yourself so others don't have to. To make a choice.

And I fell in love. What's more human than that?

The cold seizes my extremities so that I can no longer move my fingers and toes, arms and legs. And the dark makes shapes that I know aren't really there. Death plays tricks on me.

I think I see my reflection in the water, which is impossible. But there are two images: Penny's face and mine, masked deep beneath her skin, the real reflection of me—Hazel Swan. Dark hair, wide green eyes, lost. Alone. But not really alone. I've known love—deep, foolish love. And that has made it all worth it.

I squeeze my eyes closed.

I open my mouth, gulping down the sea. It tastes like salt and absolution. Like letting go. And then, drawing inward from the cold, is massive warmth. My body is no longer numb. It feels like I'm lying in a hollow of beach grass under an afternoon sun, watching clouds bounce lazily across the sky. The warmth is so real that I open my eyes again, and then I'm swallowed by it.

PENNY TALBOT

I have forgotten the day. The hour. But I feel bitterly cold and I draw in a breath like it's the last and the first. My ribs ache.

Arms around me, tugging me onto a boat. The wind racks my ears, the rain makes me shiver. I'm huddled at the stern, a blanket over my shoulders. "Where am I?" I ask, and a faint voice shouts over at me, words I can't seem to understand. The dark sky spins above me.

The dock beneath my feet.

The long march up the walkway.

And then the cottage I haven't been inside of in years. A fire starting low and then growing warm and bright. I sit on the floor. Books everywhere. Again a voice and a face I don't recognize brings me hot tea, and I drink it carefully, warming my insides. *How did I get here?* Everything is a dream I'm not sure I want to remember.

But then I do remember. The boy crouched beside me, his face. I do know him. From the marina, looking for work. And then the party on the beach. He saved me from Lon Whittamer, who tried to pull me into the water. And then we sat beside the bonfire and talked. His name is Bo. He's cute. And the singing from the harbor chased us all the way back to the island. I told him he could stay here in the cottage, that I'd give him work for the summer. And here he is. Drenched, worry lines punctuating his face.

"Did the singing stop?" I ask.

"The what?" he says.

"The Swan sisters. The singing. Have they all returned yet?"

He pauses a moment, his expression pulling at the edges of the scar by his left eye. *Where did he come from?* I wonder. There is kindness in his eyes. But he shouldn't be here in Sparrow. It's too risky. "Yeah," he finally answers. "The singing stopped. And I don't think we'll ever hear it again."

I fall asleep on his couch. A blanket tucked over my shoulders. And each time I open my eyes, he's still awake, staring into the fire like he's looking for something, or waiting for someone.

"What happened to me?" I ask as dawn inches through the windows.

He turns around, sorrow scribed into the features of his face. The coolness of morning slips through the cracks in the doorway, making me shiver even with the fire roaring behind him.

He squints at me, like it pains him just to look at me. A deep, wretched heartache. But I'm not sure why. "You've been asleep for a while," he tells me. "Now you're awake."

I look down at my hands, curled together in front of me. On my left index finger is a pink scar, nearly healed. At least a week or two old. But I don't recall how I got it. I can't seem to find the memory in the trenches of my mind. So I tuck my hands back inside the blanket and push the thought away.

I know there is more meaning in his answer than what he's willing to reveal. But my head still feels foggy, my body wanting to drag me back into my dreams. So I ask one more question before I drift off. "What happened to you?"

"I lost someone I loved."

THE HARBOR

S ome places are bound in by magic. Ensnared by it.

The town of Sparrow may have possessed slivers of magic long before the Swan sisters arrived in 1822. Or maybe the three sisters brought it with them across the Pacific. No one would ever know for sure. Their beauty and unluckiness may have been its own kind of spell, spun together in a rugged place like Sparrow, Oregon, where gold washed down from the mountains and the sea pulled ships under when the moon was full and the tide vengeful.

Magic is a tricky thing. Not easily measured or metered or weighed.

Even though the Swan sisters will never again return to torment the small town, their enchantment still resides in the sodden streets and the angry winter winds.

The morning after the summer solstice, a local fisherman steered his boat out into the harbor in search of crabs rolling along the seafloor. The tourists had begun their exodus from the bed-and-breakfasts, loading into cars and boarding buses. Returning home.

The Swan season had ended. But what the tourists and locals didn't yet know was that there would never again be another drowning in the town of Sparrow.

Olivia Greene would wake the following morning atop the light-house on Lumiere Island. She would recall only fragments of the party the night before and assume she drank too much and passed out on the cold stone floor, her friends having abandoned her.

Gigi Kline, who had been missing for several weeks but reappeared unexpectedly at the summer solstice party, would wake up on the rocky shore of Lumiere Island, her feet halfway submerged in the water and three toes swollen and frostbitten, unable to be saved. After having fled into the harbor the night before, Aurora circled back around to the shore, easily evading capture from the mob of mostly drunk Sparrow High students. She was watching the boats drift farther away, her arms hugging her chest, soaking wet, about to slip back into the water and relinquish the body she had stolen, when she collapsed right there on the rocks.

Neither Aurora nor Marguerite Swan ever made it back into the water. Because at eleven fifty-four, their sister Hazel Swan dove into the sea and drowned herself, severing the two-centuries-long curse in a single act of sacrifice.

Aurora and Marguerite vanished from their stolen bodies like a wisp of sea air, a rivulet of smoke finally extinguished for good.

But still, unknowingly, the following morning a local fisherman navigated his boat among the wreckage of sunken ships, drifting over the very spot where the three Swan sisters had been drowned two hundred years ago. And in that place, bubbles rose up to the surface. Usually caused by crabs knotted together, moving among the silty bottom. But not this time, not on this morning.

What he saw was something else.

Three bodies, dressed in gossamer-white gowns that clung to

their ashen skin, drifted together with the current. He pulled them aboard his boat, unaware of what he had just discovered. They were not skeletons, not chewed apart by fish and salt water; it was as if they had been drowned that very morning.

The Swan sisters' bodies had finally been recovered.

And when they were carried ashore and laid on the dock in Sparrow, people gasped. Children cried and women cut off locks of the sisters' hair for good luck. They were beautiful. More stunning than anyone had ever imagined. More angelic than any portrait or story had ever described.

The curse of the Swan sisters had been broken.

It took several days for the locals to decide what should be done with the perfectly preserved bodies. But eventually they were buried in Sparrow Cemetery atop Alder Hill, overlooking the bay. It was only fitting.

People still come to take pictures beside their gravestones, even though the Swan season has never returned. No songs whispered from the deep waters of the harbor. No bodies stolen for a brief few weeks in June.

But there is one who comes to the cemetery every week, a boy who lost a brother, who fell in love and then let her slip into the sea. Bo Carter kneels down beside the grave of Hazel Swan, he brings flowers, he tells her stories about the island and the tide and the life they never had. He waits for the sun to set before he stands and walks back down Ocean Avenue to the docks.

He still lives in the cottage on Lumiere Island. He is the keeper of the lighthouse. In the summer, he harvests apples and pears, bringing crates into town to sell. And during a storm, he takes the sailboat out alone past the cape to the open sea, battling the wind and the waves until the morning sunlight breaks over the horizon.

But he is not alone on the island. Penny Talbot wanders the orchard rows with him, her memories slowly returned in the days after the summer solstice—memories that were plucked just for her, only the good ones. On calm, sunny days, Bo teaches her how to sail. She eats forgetful cakes in the afternoons—gooseberry and cinnamon spice—brought to the island by Rose, who worries about her more than Penny can understand.

Her mom bakes apple pies and fresh pear tarts; she hums while she works; she makes cups of tea and invites locals out to the island to foretell their futures. She watches her daughter—who is herself once again—and she knows she's lost many things, but she didn't lose Penny. Her mind settles; her grief eases. She stacks smooth rocks beside the cliff overlooking the sea. A marker, a grave for the husband she lost. He belongs to the Pacific now—like so many others.

In the evenings, Penny reads tea leaves at the kitchen table, blinking down at her future and her past, recalling something she once saw in their smudged remains: a boy blowing in from the sea. And she thinks that maybe her life has been predestined from the start.

But even when they kiss between the apple trees, Bo seems caught in a memory, carried away to another time she can't see. And late at night when he folds her in his arms beside the crackling fire and kisses the space just behind her ear, she knows he's falling in love with her. And maybe he's loved her long before this, long before he pulled her from the water on the night of the summer solstice—the night that is a blur in her memory. But she doesn't ask. She doesn't want to know about the before.

Because she loves him now, with the wind seeping through the cracks in the cottage windows, Otis and Olga curled up at their feet, the world stretched out before them.

They have eternity. Or even if it's just one life, one long, singular life—that's enough.

LAND AND SEA

Graveyard of the Pacific: That's what locals call the waters off the coast of Sparrow. Not only because of the hundred or so shipwrecks dotting the seafloor, but because of all the lost souls drowned in the ocean over the last two centuries.

Some days the sea is calm, lapping gently against the shores of Sparrow, seagulls diving among the rocks and tide pools in search of trapped fish. On these days it's easy to forget the history of what happened here.

But on stormy days, when the wind whips violently against the town and the tide rises over the seawalls, you can almost hear the song of the sisters blowing in from the deep—an echo of years past, the ocean unwilling to forget.

When the sky is gray and mournful and the fishermen push out beyond the cape through the fog, they will look up to the island and say a prayer—for good winds and full nets. They say a prayer to her, the girl they often see standing on the cliff's edge, the girl who was drowned long ago but returned again and again, white gown catching in the wind.

And during harvest in early spring, when the island smells sweet

307

and bursting with sunlight, a figure can be seen wandering the rows, examining the trees. *She* is still there. An apparition caught in time, the ghost of a girl who lived longer than she ever should have, who dared to fall in love. Who lingers still.

Not because of revenge. Not because she's looking for atonement in the seams and shadows of the town.

But because this is where she belongs, rooted where she first came ashore two centuries ago. This land is hers. Damp and moss green and salt winds. She is made of these things. And they are made of her—the same sinew and string. Death cannot strip her of this place.

She belongs where the land meets the sea.

She belongs with him.

In those quiet moments when she stirs the new spring leaves on the apple trees, when she watches Bo moving down the rows, his eyes bent away from the afternoon sun, his hands rough with the soil, she leans in close—so close she can recall the warmth of his skin, his hands against her flesh—and she whispers against his ear, *I love you still.*

And when he feels the wind flutter against his neck, the scent of rosewater and myrrh in the air, a hush sailing over him like a memory he can't shake . . .

He knows. And he smiles.

ACKNOWLEDGMENTS

Magic resides in many things, and most certainly in humans. Without the following magical people, this book would still just be a few scribbles on tea-stained paper.

For her tireless work, encouragement, and badassery, I thank the inimitable Jess Regel. You have been my ally, my agent, and now you are a friend.

To my extraordinary editor, Nicole Ellul—you see hidden meaning in the margins, spells in the spaces between words, and I adore you for it. I couldn't have asked for anyone more skilled or clever or magnificent to shepherd this book into the world.

Thank you Jane Griffiths at Simon & Schuster UK for your enthusiasm and belief in the book. And for seeing exactly where the forgetful cakes belonged.

Everyone at Simon Pulse, you have given this book a home and championed it in so many ways. Mara Anastas, Mary Marotta, Liesa Abrams, Jennifer Ung, Sarah McCabe, Elizabeth Mims, Katherine Devendorf—how you ladies juggle it all, astounds and impresses me! Jessica Handelman for designing a perfectly spooky cover and Lisa Perrin for the bewitching artwork. Jessi Smith—thank you for reading the book numerous times! To the crusaders who stand on apple boxes and shout about all the books that need to be read: Catherine Hayden, Matt Pantoliano, Janine Perez, Lauren Hoffman, and Jodie Hockensmith. You all deserve daily cake and tea.

Acknowledgments

To my inspiring, fearless, unbelievably talented writer friends—you know who you are—who have been on the other end of my phone calls when my characters wouldn't behave or I wanted to burn it all. I thank you for being rocks and also warm blankets.

To Sky, I think I'll keep you forever. Your support and belief in me are more than I deserve. Someday we'll write the Lightkeeper's Apprentice story. I heart you.

My parents, you filled our home with books, and you let me believe I could write them someday too. I thank you for it all. More than I can measure.

Praise for *Winterwood*

"A spellbinding tale of witchery, deadly secrets, and woods that hold grudges. *Winterwood* is immersive, atmospheric, and bewitching. I could feel the cold in my toes and the Walker magic swirling around me as I read."

—STEPHANIE GARBER,
#1 *NEW YORK TIMES* AND INTERNATIONAL BESTSELLING AUTHOR
OF THE CARAVAL SERIES

"*Winterwood* casts a deliciously dark spell with a rich lineage of witches, secretive boys, and a sinister forest that will pull in any reader and never let them go."

—MEGAN SHEPHERD,
NEW YORK TIMES BESTSELLING AUTHOR OF *GRIM LOVELIES*

"The beauty and mystery of the natural world infuse every moment in this lush, spellbinding story that weaves romance with witchcraft—a seductive, lyrical tale of lost boys, old legends and haunted woods."

—LEXA HILLYER,
AUTHOR OF *SPINDLE FIRE*

"Mystery unwinds at an accelerating pace for the undersupervised teens, and the malicious, haunting Wicker Woods are lovingly characterized and as compelling as the formidable heroine. . . . A delectably immersive, eerie experience."

—*KIRKUS REVIEWS*

To all those with wild hearts

PROLOGUE

A boy went missing the night of the storm.

The night snow sailed down from the mountains and howled against the eaves of the old house as if through gritted teeth—cruel and baleful and full of bad omens not to be ignored.

The electricity flickered like Morse code. The temperature dropped so fast that trees cracked down their centers, sweet-smelling sap oozing to the surface like honey, before it too crystalized and froze. Snow spiraled down the chimney and gathered on the roof, until it was so deep it buried the mailbox at the end of the driveway, until I could no longer see Jackjaw Lake beyond my bedroom window.

Winter arrived in a single night.

By morning, Barrel Creek Road—the only road down the mountain—was snowed in. Blocked by an impassable wall of white.

The few of us who lived this deep in the woods, and those who were housed at the Jackjaw Camp for Wayward Boys on the far side of the lake, were trapped. Stuck in the rugged heart of the wilderness.

We just didn't know for how long.

Or that we wouldn't all make it out alive.

NORA

N*ever waste a full moon, Nora, even in winter*, my grandmother used to say.

We'd wander up the Black River under a midnight sky, following the constellations above us like a map I could trace with my fingertips—imprints of stardust on my skin. She would hum a melody from deep within her belly, gliding sure-footed across the frozen river to the other side.

Can you hear it? she'd ask. *The moon is whispering your secrets. It knows your darkest thoughts.* My grandmother was like that—strange and beautiful, with stories resting just behind her eyelids. Stories about moonlight and riddles and catastrophes. Dreadful tales. But bright, cheery ones too. Walking beside her, I mirrored each step she took into the wilderness, in awe of how swiftly she avoided stinging nettles and poison buckthorns. How her hands traced the bark of every tree we passed, knowing its age just by touch. She was a wonder—her chin always tilted to the sky, craving the anemic glow of moonlight against her olive skin, a storm always brewing along her edges.

But tonight, I walk without her, chasing that same moon up

the same dark, frozen river—hunting for lost things inside the cold, mournful forest.

Tree limbs sag and drip overhead. An owl hoots from a nearby spruce. And Fin and I slog deeper into the mountains, his wolf tail slashing above him, nose to the air, tracking some unknown scent to the far side of the riverbank.

Two weeks have passed since the storm blew over Jackjaw Lake. Two weeks since the snow fell and blocked the only road out of the mountains. Two weeks since the electricity popped and died.

And two weeks since a boy from the camp across the lake went missing.

A boy whose name I don't even know.

A boy who ran away or got lost or simply vanished like the low morning fog that rises up from the lake during autumn rainstorms. Who crept from his bunk inside one of the camp cabins and never returned. A victim of the winter cold. Of madness or desperation. Of these mountains that have a way of getting inside your head— playing tricks on those who dare to walk among the pines long after the sun has set.

These woods are wild and rugged and unkind.

They cannot be trusted.

Yet, this is where I walk: deep into the mountains. Where no others dare to go.

Because I am more darkness than girl. More winter shadows than August sunlight. *We are the daughters of the wood*, my grandmother would whisper.

So I push farther up the shore of the Black River, following the map made by the stars, just like she taught me. Just like all Walkers before me.

Until I reach *the place*.

The place where the line of trees breaks open to my right, where two steep ridges come together to form a narrow passage into a strange, dark forest to the east—a forest that is much older than the pines along the Black River. Trees that are bound in and closed off and separate from the rest.

The Wicker Woods.

A mound of rocks stands guard ahead of me: flat stones pulled up from the riverbed and stacked four feet high beside the entrance to the wood. It's a warning. A sign to turn back. *Only the foolish enter here.* Miners who panned for gold along the riverbank built the cairn to steer away those who would come later, those who might wander into this swath of land, unaware of the cruel dark that awaited them.

The rocks that mark the entrance have never toppled, never collapsed under the weight of snow or rain or autumn winds.

This is the border.

Only enter under a full moon, Grandma cautioned, eyes like watery pools dewing at the edges. Inside this hallowed wood, I will find lost items, but only beneath a full moon—when the forest sleeps, when the pale glow of moonlight lulls it into slumber—can I slip through unnoticed. Unharmed. *A sleeping forest will allow safe passage. But if it wakes, be prepared to run.*

Each month, when the swollen moon rises in the sky, I enter the Wicker Woods in search of lost things hidden among the greening branches and tucked at the base of trees. Lost sunglasses, rubber flip-flops, cheap plastic earrings in the shape of watermelons and unicorns and crescent moons. Toe rings and promise rings given to girls by lovesick boys. The things that are lost at Jackjaw Lake in summers past are once again found in the woods. Appearing as if the forest is giving them back.

But sometimes, under a particularly lucky full moon, I find items much older—long forgotten things, whose owners fled these mountains a century ago. Silver lockets and silver buttons and silver sewing notions. Toothbrushes made of bone, medicine bottles with labels long since worn away, cowboy boots and tin cans once filled with powdered milk and black coffee grounds. Watch fobs and doorknobs. And from time to time, I even find gold itself: crude coins hammered into a disc, gold nuggets tangled in moss, flakes that catch in my hair.

Lost things found.

By magic or maleficence, these things appear in the woods. Returned.

Fin sniffs the air, hesitant. And I draw in a breath, spinning the thin gold ring around my index finger. A habit. A way to summon the courage of my grandmother, who gave me the ring the night she died.

"I am Nora Walker," I whisper.

Let the forest know your name. It had seemed stupid once—to speak aloud to the trees. But after you step into the dark and feel the cold pass through you—the trees swallowing all memory of light— you'll tell the Wicker Woods all manner of secrets. Stories you've kept hidden inside the cage of your chest. Anything to lull the forest—to keep it in slumber.

I pinch my eyes closed and step over the threshold, through the line of tall soldier trees standing guard, into the dark of the forest.

Into the Wicker Woods.

Nothing good lives here.

The air is cold and damp, and the dark makes it hard to see anything beyond your toes. But it always feels this way—each time colder and darker than the last. I breathe slowly and move forward, stepping carefully, deliberately, over fallen logs and dewdrop flowers frozen in place. In winter, these woods feel like a fairy tale suspended in time—the princess forgotten, the hero eaten whole by a noble fir goblin. The story ended, but no one remembered to burn the haunted forest to the ground.

I duck beneath an archway of thorny twigs and dead cypress vines. Keeping my gaze at my feet, I'm careful to never linger long on a single shadow, a thing skittering just beyond my vision—my mind will only make it worse. Twist it into something with horns and fangs and copper eyes.

The dead stir inside this ancient wood.

They claw their fingernails along the bark of hemlock trees, they wail up through the limbs, searching for the moonlight—for any sliver of the sky. But there is no light in this place. The Wicker Woods are where old, vengeful things lurk—things much older than time itself. Things you don't want to meet in the dark. *Get in. Get the hell out.*

Fin follows close at my heels, no longer leading the way—so close his footsteps match mine. Human shadow. Dog shadow.

I am a Walker, I remind myself when the thorn of fear begins to wedge itself along my spine, twisting between flesh and bone, prodding me to run. *I belong in these trees.* Even if I'm not as formidable as my grandmother or as fearless as my mom, the same blood swells through my veins. Black as tar. The blood that gives all Walkers our nightshade, our "shadow side." The part of us that is different—odd, uncommon. Grandma could slip into other people's dreams, and Mom can lull wild honeybees into sleep. But on nights like this, venturing into the cruelest part of the forest, I often feel terrifyingly ordinary and I wonder if the trees can sense it too: I am a girl barely able to call herself descended from witches.

Barely able to call myself a Walker.

Yet, I press forward, squinting through the dark and scanning the exposed roots poking up through the snow, searching for hidden things wedged among the lichen and rocks. Something shiny or sharp-cornered or rusted with time. Something man-made—something that's value is measured by weight.

We pass over a dried creek bed, and the wind changes direction from east to north. The temperature dips. An owl cries in the distance, and Fin stops beside me—nose twitching in the air. I touch his head gently, feeling the quick pace of his breathing.

He senses something.

I pause and listen for the snapping of branches underfoot, for the sounds of a wolf stalking through the trees, watching us. Hunting.

But a moth skims past my shoulder—white wings beating against the cold, flitting toward a sad, spiny-looking hemlock tree, leaving imprints of dust wherever it lands. It looks as if it's just come through a storm, wings torn at the edges. Shredded.

A moth who's faced death. Who's seen it up close.

My heartbeat sinks into my toes and my eyelashes twitch, certain I'm not seeing it right. Just another trick of the woods.

But I know what it is—I've seen sketches of them before. I've even seen one pressed against the window while my grandmother coughed from her room down the hall, hands clasping the bedsheets. Blood in her throat.

A bone moth.

The worst kind. The bringer of portents and warnings, of omens that should never be ignored. *Of death.*

My fingers again touch the gold moonstone ring weighted heavy on my finger.

Every part of me that had felt brave, had felt the courage of my grandmother pulsing through me, vanishes. I squeeze my eyes closed, then open them again, but the moth is still there. Zigzagging among the trees. "We shouldn't be here," I whisper to Fin. *We need to run.*

I release my hand from Fin's head, and my heart scrapes against my ribs. I glance over my shoulder, down the narrow path we followed in. *Run, run, run!* my heart screams. I take a careful step back, away from the moth, not wanting to make a sound. But the moth circles overhead, bobbing quickly out over the trees—called forth by something. Back into the dark.

Relief settles through me—my heart sinking back into my chest—but then Fin breaks away from my side. He darts around a dead tree stump and into the brush, chasing after the moth. "No!" I shout—*too loud,* my voice echoing over the layer of snow and bouncing through the treetops. But Fin doesn't stop. He tears around a cluster of spiny aspens and vanishes into the dark. Gone.

Shit, shit, shit.

If it were anything else, a different kind of moth, or another wolf he will chase deep into the snowy mountains only to return home in a day or two, I'd let him go.

But a bone moth means something else—something cruel and wicked and bad—so I run after him.

I sprint around the clot of trees and follow him into the deepest part of the forest, past elms that grow at odd angles, down steep, jagged terrain I don't recognize—where my boots slip beneath me, where my hands press against tree trunks to propel me forward, and where each footstep sounds like thunder against the frozen ground. *I'm making too much noise. Too loud.* The woods will wake. But I don't slow down; I don't stop.

I lose sight of him beyond two fallen trees, and little stabs of pain cut through me. "Fin, please!" I call in a near hush, trying to keep my voice low while the sting of tears presses against my eyes, blurring my vision. Panic leaps into my throat and I want to scream, shout Fin's name louder, but I bite back the urge. No matter what, I can't wake the woods, or neither Fin nor I will make it out of here.

And then I see him: tail wagging, stopped a few yards away between a grove of hemlocks. My heart presses against my ribs.

He's led us farther into the Wicker Woods than I've ever been before. And the moth—frayed body, white wings with holes torn along the edges—flutters among the falling snowflakes, slow and mercurial, as if it were in no great hurry. It moves upward toward the sky, a speck of white among the black canopy of trees, and then vanishes into the dark forest to the north.

I step carefully toward Fin and touch his ear to keep him from running after it again. But he bares his teeth, growling. "Shhh," I say softly.

His ears shift forward, his breathing quick as he sucks in bursts of air, and a low guttural growl rises up from deep within his chest.

Something's out there.

A beast or shadow with hooked claws and grim pinhole eyes. A thing the forest keeps, a thing it hides—something I don't want to see.

My fingers twitch, and dread rises up at the base of my throat. It tastes like ash. I hate this feeling building inside me. This awful fear. *I am a Walker.* I am the thing whispered about, the thing that conjures goose bumps and nightmares.

I swallow and stiffen my jaw into place, taking a step forward. The moth led us here. To something just beyond my vision. I scan the dark, looking for eyes—something blinking out from the trees.

But there's nothing.

I shake my head and let out a breath, about to turn back to Fin, when my left foot thuds against something on the ground. Something hard.

I squint down at my feet, trying to focus in the dark.

A mound of snow. A coat sleeve, I think. The tip of a boot. A thing that doesn't belong.

And then I see. *See.*

Hands.

There, lying beneath a dusting of snowfall, in the middle of the Wicker Woods, is a body.

Snowflakes have gathered on stiff eyelashes.

Eyes shuttered closed like two crescent moons. Pale lips parted open, waiting for the crows.

Even the air between the trees has gone still, a tomb, as if the body is an offering that shouldn't be disturbed.

I blink down at the corpse and a second passes, followed by another, my heart clawing silently upward into my windpipe. But no sound escapes my lips, no cry for help. I stare in stupefied inaction. My mind slows, my ears buzz—an odd *crackle crack* crack, as if a radio were pressed to my skull. I inch closer and the trees quiver overhead. For a second I wonder if the entire forest might snap at the roots and upend itself—trunks to the sky and treetops to the ground.

I've seen dead birds in the woods before, even a dead deer with the antlers still attached to the hollowed-out skull. But never anything like this. Never a human body.

Fin makes a low whine behind me. But I don't look back. I don't take my eyes off the corpse, like it might vanish if I look away.

I swallow and crouch down, my knees pressing into the snow. Eyes watering from the cold. But I need to know.

Is it him? The boy who went missing from the camp?

His face is covered by a dusting of snow, dark hair frozen in place. There are no injuries that I can see. No trauma, no blood. And he hasn't been here long, or he wouldn't be here at all. The dead don't last in the mountains, especially in winter. Birds pick apart what they can before the wolves close in, scattering the bones across miles of terrain, leaving barely an imprint of what once had been. The forest is efficient at death, a swift wiping away. No remains to bury or burn or mourn.

A soft wind stirs through the trees, blowing away the snow from his forehead, his cheekbones, his pale lips. And the hairs along the base of my neck prick on end.

I lift my hand from the snow, my fingers hovering over his open palm, trembling, curious. *I shouldn't touch him*—but I lower my hand anyway. I want to feel the icy skin, the heaviness of death in his limbs.

My skin meets his.

But his hand isn't rigid or still. It twitches against my fingertips.

Not dead.

Still alive.

The boy's eyes flinch open—forest green, gray green, alive-green. He coughs at the same moment his fingers close around mine, gripping tightly.

I scream—a strangled sound, swallowed by the trees—but Fin immediately springs up next to me, tail raised, nose absorbing the boy's newly alive scent. I yank my arm away and try to stand, to scramble back, but my legs stumble beneath me and I fall backward onto the snow. *Run!* my spiking heartbeat yells. But before I can push myself up, the boy is rolling onto his side, coughing again, touching his face with his hands. Trying to breathe.

Alive. Not dead. Gasping for air, warm skin, grabbing my hand, kind-of-alive. My throat goes dry and my eyes refuse to blink. I'm certain he's not real. But he draws in deep, measured breaths between each cough, as if his lungs were full of water.

I sling my backpack off one shoulder and reach inside for the canteen of hot juniper tea. *It will save your life if you ever get lost*, my grandmother would say. *You can live off juniper tea for weeks.*

I hold the canteen out to him, and he lowers his hand from his face, his eyes meeting mine. Dark sleepy eyes, deep heavy inhales making his chest rise and fall as if it's never known air before this moment.

He doesn't take the canteen, and I lean forward, drawing in a breath. "What's your name?" I ask, my voice broken.

His gaze roves the ground, then moves up to the sky, like he's searching for the answer—his name lost somewhere in the woods. Taken from him. Snatched while he slept.

His eyes settle back on me. "Oliver Huntsman."

"Are you from the boys' camp?"

An icy wind sails over us, kicking up a layer of snow. His mouth opens, searching for the words, and then he nods.

I found him.

The Jackjaw Camp for Wayward Boys is not an elite facility, not a place where the wealthy send their sons. It's a meager collection of cabins, a mess hall, and several neglected administration buildings—most of which were once the homes of early miners who panned the Black River for gold. Now it's a place where desperate parents send their headstrong boys to have their minds and hearts reshaped, to turn them into docile, obedient sons. The worst come here, the ones who have used up their last chances, their last *I'm sorrys*, their last detentions or visits to the principal's office. They come and they go. Each season a new batch—except for the few who spend their entire high school years at the camp. They learn how to survive in the woods, to make fire from flint, to sleep in the cold under the stars, to behave.

Two weeks earlier, the morning after the snowstorm had rolled down from the mountains, I woke to find my house draped in snow. Ice coated the windows, the roof moaned from the weight, and the walls bowed inward as if nails were being pushed free from the wood. The radio had said we'd get twelve to eighteen inches of snow. We got nearly four feet—in a single night. I crawled from bed, the cold leeching up from the floorboards, and went outside into the snow.

The landscape had changed overnight.

I walked down to the lake's edge and found the forest dripping in white marshmallow fluff. But it wasn't quiet and still like most winter mornings. Voices echoed across the frozen lake, coming from the boys' camp. They shouted up into the trees. They stomped around in their heavy snow boots and sent birds screeching unhappily into the bleak morning sky.

"Morning!" Old Floyd Perkins called, waving a hand in the air as he trudged up the shore, head bowed away from the blowing wind, shoulders bent and stooped with time and age and gravity. When he reached me, he squinted as if he couldn't see me clearly—cataracts clouding his already failing vision. "A bad winter," he said, tilting his gaze upward, soft flakes falling over us. "But not as bad as some." Mr. Perkins has lived at Jackjaw Lake most of his life. He knew my grandmother when she was still alive, and he lives at the far south end of the lake in a small cabin beside the boathouse store that he runs during the summer months—renting out canoes and paddleboats and selling ice cream sandwiches to the tourists under the hot, wavy sun. And every morning, he walks the shore of the lake, his gait slow and labored, long arms swinging at his sides, arthritis creaking in his joints. Even in the snow, he makes his morning rounds.

"What's happening over at the camp?" I asked.

"A boy went missing last night." He rubbed a knuckled hand across the back of his neck, gray hair poking out from his wool cap. "Vanished from his bunk during the storm."

I looked past him up the shore to the camp. A few boys were shoveling snow away from their cabin doorways, while most of the others moved up into the forest, calling out a name I couldn't make out.

"Talked to one of the counselors," Mr. Perkins continued, nodding grimly, considering the gravity of the situation. "Boy might've just run away, made it down the mountain before the snow fell last night."

The wind roiled up from the surface of the frozen lake, and it made me shiver. "But they're looking for him up in the woods." I crossed my arms over my chest and nodded to the trees beyond the camp.

"They have to be sure he didn't get lost, I suppose." He raised one thick gray eyebrow, his gaze solemn. "But if that boy went up into those woods last night, there's a good chance he won't make it back out. And they'll never find him."

I understood what he meant. The snow was deep it continued to fall—any tracks would be long buried by now. And the boy himself might be buried as well. Even Fin would have a hard time tracking his scent in this.

"I hope he did run away," I said. "I hope he made it down the road." Because I knew the outcome if he hadn't. Even though the boys at camp learn wilderness skills and how to build snow shelters in tree wells, I doubted any of them could really survive a night out in the cold. During a blizzard. On their own.

The lake creaked and snapped along the shore as the ice settled.

And Mr. Perkins asked, "You lose power last night?" He glanced behind me up into the trees, where my home sat hidden in the pines.

I nodded. "You?"

"Yep," he answered, then cleared his throat. "It's going to be a while before that road clears. Before the power's back on again." He looked back at me, and the soft squint of his eyes and the wrinkles lining his brow made me think of my grandmother. "We're on our own," he said finally.

The only road down the mountain was blocked. And the nearest town of Fir Haven—a forty-five-minute drive—was too far away to walk. We were stuck.

Mr. Perkins tipped his head at me, a grave gesture, a certainty that this was going to be another tough winter, before continuing up the edge of the lake toward the marina. Toward the boathouse and his home.

I stood listening to the shouts of boys fanning out into the trees, the sky growing dark again, another storm settling over the lake. I knew how ruthless the forest could be, how unforgiving.

If a boy was lost out there, he likely wouldn't survive the night.

It's still dark—the deepest kind of dark. Winter dark.

The boy, Oliver Huntsman, follows me through the trees, stumbling over roots, coughing—gasping for air. He might not make it out of the Wicker Woods; he might drop dead in the snow behind me. He stops to lean against a tree, his body trembling, and I walk back to his side and wrap an arm around him. He is taller than I am and broad in the shoulders, but together we continue through the dark. He smells like the forest, like green. And when we reach the border of the Wicker Woods, we step over the threshold and back out into the open.

I release my hold on him, and he bends forward, gripping his knees and gasping for air. His lungs make a strange *rasp* sound with each breath. He's spent too many nights alone out here, in the forest, in the cold. Where the creeping, crawling sounds of unknowable things rest just out of sight, and fear becomes a voice in the back of his mind—nagging and threading along sleepless thoughts. A person can go mad in these trees. Hatter mad.

Beside us, the sound of rushing water beneath the frozen surface of the Black River is both palliative and eerie. Oliver glances up at the night sky, his expression slack, in awe, as if he hasn't seen the stars in weeks.

"We need to keep moving," I say.

His body shakes, skin pale and muted. I need to get him inside, out of this snow and wind. Or the cold could still kill him.

I fold my arm around him again, hand against his ribs where I can feel the rise and fall of each breath, and we march downriver until Jackjaw Lake yawns open ahead of us—frozen solid out to its center.

"Where are we?" he asks, his voice thin, a crisp edge to each word.

"We're almost to my house," I tell him. And then because I think maybe he means something more—his memory blotted over—I add, "We're back at Jackjaw Lake."

He doesn't nod and his eyes don't shimmer with recognition. He has no memory of this place, no idea where he is.

"My house is close," I add. "I'll take you back to camp in the morning. Right now, we just need to get you warm." I'm not sure he'd make it another mile around the lake to the boys' camp. And the nearest hospital is an hour down a road that's snowed in. I have no other option but to take him home.

His hands tremble, his eyes skipping warily through the trees—as if he sees something in the dark. A trick of shadow and moonlight. But the woods surrounding Jackjaw Lake are safe and docile, not nearly as ancient as the Wicker Woods where I found him. These trees are young, harvested over the years for lumber, and the pines that loom over my home were saplings not long ago—still soft and green at their core. They have limbs that sway with the wind instead of moan and crack; they aren't old enough to hold grudges or memories. To grow hexes at their roots. Not like inside the Wicker Woods.

We reach the row of log cabins that dot the shore, and Fin trots ahead through the snow. "My house is just there," I say, nodding up through the trees. Most of the cabins along the shore are summer homes, owned by people who only visit Jackjaw Lake when the weather warms and the lake thaws. But Mom and I have always been year-rounders, just like our ancestors before us. We remain at the lake through all the seasons, even the brutal ones—*especially* the brutal ones. Mom dislikes the tourists who come in summer, with their thumping music and fishing poles and beach towels. It grates on her. But the quiet of winter pacifies her—calms her racing, fidgety mind.

Our house is at the end of the row, closest to the mountains and the wilds of the forest beyond—tucked back in the woods. Hidden. And tonight, it sits dark, no lights humming inside, no sputtering of electricity through the walls—the power still out since the storm.

I stomp the snow from my boots and push open the heavy log door, letting the cold air rush inside. Fin brushes past my legs into the living room, where he plops down on the rug beside the stove and begins chewing the snow from his paws. I drop my pack onto the faded olive-green sofa, its cushions sagging and slumped as if it were sinking into the wood floor.

"I'll start a fire," I say to Oliver, who still stands shivering in the entryway. Looking like a boy who's near death. Whose eyes have the hollow stare of someone who can already see the other side, only inches away.

My grandmother would know the right herbs, the right words to whisper against his skin to warm the chill deep in his bones. To keep him rooted to this world before he slips into the next. But she's not here, and I only know the tiniest of remedies, the barest of spells. Not enough to conjure real magic. I clench my jaw, feeling an old familiar ache: the burden of uselessness I carry inside my chest. I can't help him, and I wish I could. I am a Walker whose grandmother died too soon and whose mother would rather forget what we really are.

I am as helpless as a girl by any other name.

I stoke the few embers that still glow among the ash, coaxing the fire back to life inside the old stove, while Oliver's jade-green eyes sweep slowly over the house: the log walls, the rotted wood beams that sag overhead, the faded floral curtains that have the rich scent of sage that's been burned thousands of times within the house to clear out the old stubborn spirits.

But Oliver's eyes aren't caught on the curtains or the thick walls. Instead, they flicker over the odd collection of items crowding every shelf and cobwebbed corner of the aged house. Old pocket watches and wire-rimmed glasses, hundreds of silver buttons in glass jars, delicately carved silver spoons, and silver candlesticks with wax still hardened at the base. An ornate gold-rimmed jewelry box with only dust kept safely inside.

All the things that we've found inside the Wicker Woods over the years, the things we didn't sell down in Fir Haven to a man named Leon who owns a rare antique shop. These are the things that mean something—that I can't part with. The ones that hide memories inside them, the stories they tell when you hold them in your palm.

Just like most of the Walker women before me, I am a finder of lost things.

And standing in the entryway is a boy named Oliver Huntsman.

My latest found item.

OLIVER

Her hair is long and dark and braided down her back, like a river woven into knots.

I've heard about her, *the girl who lives across the lake*. The boys at camp say she can't be trusted. They say her shadow can be seen on the roof of her house during a full moon, casting dark magic into the ice-flecked sky. They say she is descended from these woods—that she is a Walker. And all Walkers are witches.

Her home sits hidden in the trees, a small gingerbread structure that smells of earth and sod and wood. A place that could easily lure Hansel and Gretel in with the promise of sweets, where they would likely meet their end inside these walls. *Just like I might.*

She moves through the living room with the ease of a bird, her footsteps hardly making a sound on the old wood floor, little puffs of dust rising up around her feet.

I'm standing inside the home of a witch.

"What happened?" I ask, trying to bend my fingers, but they're frozen in place—the cold running through me like tap water from a winter faucet, ice crystals forming at every joint. My thoughts keep skipping back and forth, rattled loose. Every memory is the color of snow, too icy-white, too blinding and painful to see.

"I found you in the snow," she answers, kneeling beside the woodstove. She moves swiftly, deftly, using her bare hands to add more logs to the flames. Never wincing away from the sparks that lick at her skin.

I move partway into the living room, my boots sliding across the floor, closer to the heat of the fire, and my eyes sway to the window, where snow is eddying against the glass, willing my mind to remember. *I woke in the woods. The shadow of a girl knelt over me. Her soft fingers touching my skin.* But it feels like days ago, the hours slow and dripping, thawing like the snow settled in my bones.

"What day is it?" I ask.

Flames ignite suddenly over the dry logs, sending out a burst of heat, and she gestures for me to sit on a small chair facing the fire. I do as she says, removing my hands from my coat pockets and holding them out toward the stove.

"Wednesday," she answers, brown eyes flicking to mine only briefly. Like she's afraid of what she'll see in my gaze. Or she's afraid of what I'll see in hers.

My hands ache when I close them into fists, circulation returning to my skin in painful jolts. *Wednesday*, I think. But it means nothing. I should have asked the week, the month, the year even. My thoughts sputter slowly across synapses. I can't recall the moments that led me here, that led me into that forest, lying on my back, snow falling in a slow, endless rhythm—burying me alive.

The girl walks into the kitchen and hums something under her breath, like she doesn't think I can hear: a soft melody—a lullaby maybe, slow and tragic. But then her eyes snap up to mine and she stops.

I drop my gaze to the floor, heat pricking my cheeks, and I hear her footsteps move across the room. "Drink this," she says, holding out a red porcelain mug filled to the brim with hot tea. "It'll warm you." She nods at me and I take it, hands shaking, the scent of something sharp and pungent rising up from the steam.

Drink this. Eat that. Alice down the rabbit hole. *Is that where I've returned from?* Wonderland or Neverland? Or a place much worse? Filled with more monsters than sweet lemon cake and song-filled happy endings?

"You're still at risk of hypothermia," she adds, her lips pressed flat. "But you're in better shape than I thought you'd be."

I don't feel like I'm in good shape. I feel like I'll never be warm again. Like I can feel tree roots growing up the inside of my bones, and soon they'll break me apart. Tear through my skin and push thorns from my eyes.

I feel cavernous. A husk of who I used to be.

I hold the mug of fragrant tea in my hands—craving something stronger. A stiff cup of black coffee, something with grit in it, thick like tar. But I take a sip of the tea without protest, wincing against the bitter taste. She watches me finish it, little freckles pinching together along the bridge of her nose—they aren't year-round freckles, they're scattered reminders of warmer seasons and days spent in the sun. She takes the empty mug from me, her gaze still cautious, rueful even, her fingers grazing mine. *Pale white fingertips.*

There is something stark about her, a wildness. That look you sometimes see when you're driving down a back road at night and an animal crosses your path, its startled eyes caught in your headlights. That unbroken look, a creature who is more free than you could ever truly understand.

Again, a knot of fear begins to tighten inside me. *She is the girl who lives across the lake.* A girl to steer clear of, to avoid. She will hex you, charm you, toss you into the fire just to watch the skin peel away from your bones. But she doesn't look at me with wickedness in her eyes, with a feral need to kill. She saved me and brought me back.

She holds the empty cup in her hand, and her mouth falls open, her gaze fixed on the floor beneath me.

I hear the odd *splat* of water hitting wood.

One after another.

She touches the sleeve of my coat and feels that it's soaked through, as if I were made of ice and am now melting, making a puddle at my feet.

"We need to get you out of these wet clothes," she tells me, a hint of urgency in her eyes. In her breathing.

I nod, my brain clicking forward on autopilot, the cold sapping any ability to protest.

I shrug out of my coat, my long-sleeve-shirt, and my jeans, right beside the fire. If it were any other day, if my mind were clear and sharp, I might feel strange standing bare chested in only my boxers, my body shivering, jaw clenching, in front of a girl I don't know. But the cold is all I feel. All that's left.

Her eyes sway over me, catching for a half second before she turns away. Pretending she wasn't staring. Pretending her cheeks aren't flushed.

I sit back on the chair and she drapes a heavy wool blanket from the couch over my shoulders, then hangs my wet clothes above the woodstove to dry. They have the scent of pine and wind and wilderness, a scent that's hard to describe—unless you've trekked into the forest and returned with it clinging to your hair and the fibers of your clothes. It's as if the woods followed me back, trailing me like campfire smoke.

"In the morning, I'll take you back to the camp," she says, facing the fire now, rubbing her own palms together. "They've been searching for you."

"How long have I been gone?" I ask bluntly.

She chews on her lower lip, revealing a row of white teeth, and it feels like I'm seeing too much of her. Like I'm staring too closely, watching every shiver and shift of her dark eyes. "Since the storm," she says at last, lowering her hands from the fire. "Two weeks."

The room slips out of focus, wobbles briefly, then snaps back into place. *Two weeks, two whole weeks.* I shake my head. "That can't be right," I mutter, blinking to keep from tipping out of the chair. "I would have died out there if I'd been gone that long."

"But you didn't," she answers, and she moves to the window, her reflection staring back: dark hair and dark moonless eyes. "Maybe the woods kept you safe." I don't understand what she means, and a gust of wind rattles the house, sending dust down from the overhead beams. "Everyone at camp thinks you tried to run away."

I didn't run away. But I don't say this, because I can't explain how I ended up in that dark forest. Where only bursts of light reached me through the never-ending dark, where trees swayed like long skeleton arms moving to some macabre ballet, the wind the only music that filled my ears. *Always the wind. Cold and biting and cruel.*

I blink away the memory, sharp as a nail, and let my eyes stray across the living room again—the woodstove is the only light flicking up the walls, illuminating a small kitchen, a narrow hallway, and a set of stairs near the back.

"The power's out?" I ask.

She nods. "Landlines too. Cell phones have never worked this high in the mountains. Our only contacts with the outside world— with the nearest town—are landlines and the road. Both of which were knocked out in the storm."

"So, we're trapped?" I ask.

She shrugs. "The road will clear eventually. We've had bad winters like this before." Her gaze slips away from mine, as if remembering. "Three years back, it was two months before the road thawed and the power flickered back on. We're used to being on our own." She pulls in her lower lip, like maybe she's said too much, revealed a weak spot. "We're used to the solitude," she clarifies, her voice dissolving away, vanishing up into the high ceiling. "You'll get used to it too," she says, as if I'll never leave these mountains. As if I'm one of the residents now, stuck here until they bury me in the ground.

A shiver rises up along my arms and I wonder: Maybe what they say about her is true—maybe I shouldn't be here, in her home. A place of darkness and rot.

"You found all these things?" I ask, swallowing hard and diverting my attention to the magnifying glasses, the old perfume bottles, and the belt buckles lining the windowsill. My mind is pulled back to the stories I've heard, the stories the boys tell about how she goes into the dark woods—*a place no one else will enter*—where she finds lost things. How she is the only one who can, that she is made of the forest, that if you cut her open she will bleed sap just like a tree. How her family is cursed and damned and more dangerous than a winter storm. That her hair is made of stinging nettle and she grows talons through her fingernails.

"Yes," she answers cautiously. "Just like I found you."

A strange winding silence ropes itself around us, and it feels like we might choke on it. She steps closer to me and lifts her arm, brushing her palm across my forehead, her warm fingers against my skin—gauging my temperature. I feel myself draw in a breath and hold it there, trapped inside my lungs. "You need to sleep," she says. "You might have a fever."

Her dark brown eyes blink back at me, as dark as the woods, but she seems as if she's looking into the past, a soft slant to her mouth that I can't read. She smells like the wind, like rain on grass, and she can't possibly be all the terrible things the boys say about her.

She can't possibly steal boys from their bunks and bury them beneath the floorboards. She can't possibly turn herself into a fanged beast and crash through the forest, knocking down trees. She can't possibly be a witch who boils toads for breakfast and ties knots in her hair to bind curses that can't be broken. *She is just a girl.*

With raven hair and crush-your-heart-in-half eyes.

"You can sleep on the couch," she says softly, lowering her hand and stepping away from me, and I know I've stared at her too long. "It'll be close to the fire."

Outside, the sky is dark, not even a hint of light, and I can't be sure of the time. Or how long it will be until the sunrise. Perhaps my memories will slip back into focus once I feel the morning sun on my face. Once the shadows are scared back into their dusty corners.

"Thank you," I say, sleep tugging at me.

She places a pillow and two more blankets on the couch, smiling once, before she turns for the stairs, the wolf trailing after her. She pauses on the bottom step, like she's forgotten something. *Tomorrow you'll feel right as rain. Tomorrow you won't remember the woods at all. Tomorrow you won't even remember me.*

But she doesn't speak, her hair falling over her eyes just before she starts up the stairs. I listen to the sound of her footsteps, small depressions in the wood, the creak of the ceiling overhead. And I feel unsettled, alone, a spike of uncertainty wedging itself into my thoughts.

I am in the home of the girl who lives across the lake. The girl who should never be trusted. Her name rises up into my chest, the name whispered by the other boys at camp when they tell stories about her late at night in our bunks. Stories meant to scare and frighten.

The name that rings between my ears: Nora Walker.

The girl with moonlight in her veins.

NORA

I lie in bed in the loft and think of the boy.

Oliver Huntsman.

The way his eyes twitched to mine when I spoke, and hung there, a ripe green that reminded me of the grass that pushes up from the soil in spring. A kindness in them. The way his wet hair dried in soft little waves around his ears. The way he held his breath just before he spoke, considering each word—each syllable. The way my heart swung up into my throat and made me dizzy. A feeling I tried to tamp down, to ignore. But couldn't.

I think of the woods, the moment I found him in the snow: how his eyes snapped open, the whites like cracked eggshells. Fear trembling across his lips. *What did he see in those woods?* Why did the forest let him live? I wish I could peel him open, cut away his hard exterior, and see what he hides inside.

Now he sleeps downstairs, and I know that even the heat from the woodstove won't warm the chill from his flesh, won't cure what haunts him.

He needs medicine. Not the kind from a white room in a sterile white building prescribed by people in white coats. He needs forest medicine.

The only way to cure a chill caused by the forest is to use a remedy grown inside it. My grandmother's words are always buzzing along my skull, always close.

I tiptoe back down the stairs, past the kitchen, to the rear of the house. Quiet as a winter mouse. Quiet as the seeds that fall to the ground in late spring.

I push open the door to my mother's room and step inside. It smells like her: vanilla bean and honey. *Always the scent of honey.* It sticks to her, in her wavy auburn hair, honeycomb under her fingernails. It can never be properly washed off. Not completely. Three weeks ago, she left on a delivery to the coastal town of Sparrow with four crates of her wild clover honey placed safely in the back of her truck. During a full moon, she collects the sticky comb from the wild hives inside the Wicker Woods, then funnels it into glass jars and delivers them to small boutiques and organic food markets along the west coast. Stores pay a premium for her Wicker Wood Honey, said to be sweeter than real cane sugar and able to cure all manner of skin ailments—including hives and poison oak and sunburns.

I haven't spoken to her since she left, since the phones have been down and the road blocked. But we're used to winter storms. To being cut off. And although maybe I should feel alone, isolated and afraid without her, I don't. She and I have always been more opposite than alike. I am the daughter who wants to be a Walker, and she is the mother who pretends she isn't: a Walker or a mother.

349

She feels betrayed by my curiosity, my need to know our past—to know who I am.

To understand the darkness that lives in my veins.

And I feel betrayed by her: her silence when she's home, her refusal to talk about Grandma or about the Walkers who came before us.

I prefer it when she's away, when I can be alone in the old house.

Mom has never been one to worry about me anyway—she knows I can take care of myself until the road thaws. I could take care of myself even if she never came back.

Inside her room, I kneel down on the floor and reach my arms beneath the bed, past a discarded, half-burnt candle; past dust bunnies that skitter away; and past a pale-yellow sock missing its mate, until I find the wooden box she keeps hidden.

I slide it out, resting the box on the floor in front of me, then quietly open the lid.

Inside rest an assortment of keepsakes: old photographs and family letters kept safely inside their envelopes, my grandmother's pearl necklace, an old music box once owned by Henrietta Walker. Family heirlooms tucked away beneath a bed where they will eventually be forgotten. Things that remind me of who I am—that make me feel less alone.

And under it all, I find the book.

I touch the faded words handwritten on the front: *Spellbook of Moonlight & Forest Medicine*. And sketched below it is a compass with the four cardinal directions: north, south, east, west.

But I don't open the book—not here in my mother's room, where I fear she might sense it once she returns, sense that I sat on her floor with the book fanned open in front of me. So I tuck it under my arm, the weight of my family history inside its pages, and leave the honey-scented room before I leave too many clues that I was here.

With the fire roaring downstairs, my own room is sweltering when I return, and I push open one of the windows—letting the snow spiral inside and settle on the floor. I grew up in this room, in this loft overlooking the lake. I was born here too, seventeen years ago under a watery full moon while a rainstorm flooded the banks of the lake and turned the shore to mud. All Walkers are coaxed into the world when the moon is brightest. As if our birthright were calling to us.

I place the book on the bed, feeling like a thief.

The spellbook will belong to me one day, passed down from one Walker woman to the next. But for now, it belongs to my mother, and she never opens it, never pulls it out to sift through its pages. It's a burden to her. Our family history like a disease she can't be rid of.

When I was younger, when my grandmother was still alive, she'd bring the book into my room when my mother was away on a delivery. *Your mom wants to forget the old ways*, she'd say. *Who we really are.* Grandma Ida would settle onto my bed and turn through the pages of the book like she was sifting through dust, revealing artifacts from the past. Her wrinkled, unsteady fingers knew the pages by heart.

The memory causes an ache in my chest, recalling the kindness in her graying eyes. The soft, knowing tenor of her words.

She'd read me passages in a hush, as if the walls might tell on us. Pages and pages of notations and recipes and hand-drawn sketches. There were instructions on how to decipher the spiderwebs built by peppercorn spiders to predict the weather. How to locate the precious thimbleberries that were used during pregnancy to know if it was a boy or girl stirring inside the belly. Grandma would read to me old recipes written down by Scarlett Walker and Florence Walker and Henrietta Walker, women who seemed more like characters from folklore than real women who lived in this house and strode through the forest gathering primrose and hemlock. Who had more power, I fear, than I may ever have.

Some recipes were innocuous enough: instructions for baking spiced prickly pear pie or a particularly tricky recipe for rutabaga-and-parsley stew. The best method for steeping juniper berry tea, and how to harvest yarrow root in the fall. But others were for conjuring up things that were more witchcraft than forest medicine. How to trick a bat into hunting a common house mouse. How to grow wild strawberries and sword ferns and wax myrtle for protection and divination. How to see the dead wandering among gravestones.

There was no index in the back of the book, no rhyme or reason to the order of recipes and spells. Things were merely written down in succession, from one Walker to another. The book is tea-stained and chocolate-smeared, and the first few pages are completely unreadable, the ink having faded to nothing with time. And every few pages, a brief history has been written down—the story of a Walker who once lived, and how she died—recorded like a family ledger, so each tale, each woman, would never be forgotten.

But after my grandmother passed away, only a week before my fifteenth birthday, my mother took the book and shoved it inside the wooden box beneath her bed. Like she didn't trust me with it, like she was trying to blot out the memory of my grandmother and all the Walkers along with it. But she can't erase our past, can't scrub clean the moonlight in our veins. Mom only ever wanted to be normal. To leave the past where it belonged. To no longer be called witches or weird or be forced to avoid sidelong glances when we went into town, catching the last of a muttered word about how spiders lived in our hair and beetles under our toenails.

We are Walkers. And our ancestors have lived in these woods since long before the first miners set up camp along the Black River. We came from this forest. From the roots and brine and weather-worn stones.

We are the daughters of the wood.

One cannot survive without the other.

I sit cross-legged on the white bedspread. Snow floats into the room, catching in my hair, landing on Fin where he's curled up on the floor, nose tucked beneath his tail.

I flip open the front cover of the book and am met with the musty scent of burnt amber and jasmine. Just like the nights with my grandmother. A thrumming begins in my chest—a peculiar sort of ache. The thrill and also the fear leaping through me. If Mom found out I took it from beneath her bed, she would be angry. She'd hide it where I wouldn't be able to find it ever again. Maybe she'd even destroy it.

Still, I bend over the pages and my hair falls loose from its braid—fine and inky-black, just like my grandmother's. Even the sturdy slope of my nose, the dark storm resting behind my eyes, the melancholy curve of my lips—it's all her. The reminder of my grandma always hidden in my own face.

The weight of the moonstone slides the gold ring around my finger as I skim over recipes and drawings outlined in charcoal, until

I find what I'm looking for. A simple concoction—a crease folded down the page where the book has been fanned open countless times. The recipe isn't true witchery. But Grandma used to make it during the cold months of January, to warm chilled bones, to calm a cough, to bring circulation back into numb fingers and toes.

Silently, I descend the stairs to the kitchen.

The ingredients are easy to find. One whole cupboard is lined with glass jars filled with dried herbs and powdered roots and fragrant liquids with descriptions handwritten on the lids. There is even a jar labeled *lake water*, in case a recipe needed to be made in haste and there was no time to walk the few yards down to the lake itself.

Mom has kept the cupboard stocked, never throwing anything out, even though she doesn't use the herbs—not like Grandma did.

I pour the few ingredients into the same copper bowl my grandmother once used: ground cloves and powdered cardamom, a dash of fawn lily and burdock root, and a pinch of a reddish-rose tincture labeled *bero*.

I sift the mixture into a small cotton pouch, then cross the living room to Oliver. His hair is now dry, dark and wavy, and he doesn't stir when I slide the cotton pouch beneath the blankets beside his bare ribs. His chest rises, the slow measured weight of his lungs expanding. A shudder runs through him and his eyelids flicker, his body tensing briefly—spurred by some dream I can't see. He reminds me of an animal near death. Fighting it, struggling. I could crawl beneath the blankets and wrap my arms over his chest, I could feel the beat of his heart against my palm, I could wait for the heat to return to his skin before I went back to my own bed.

But he is a boy I don't know. A boy who smells of the forest now. Who reminds me of the winter trees, tall and lean with bark that is rough and raw and could tear open flesh. No soft edges.

I catch my own breath and turn away. *He is a boy I don't know*, I repeat to myself again. He is a boy with his own secrets. A boy unlike all the others—in ways I don't understand. I can't pinpoint.

The recipe instructs that the herbs should be kept close to the body while you sleep for three nights in a row, and then the chill will be banished from the bones.

It's all I can offer him, all I know how to do—I am a Walker without real magic. Without a nightshade. It will have to be enough.

Back in the loft, I close the book and bury myself beneath the sheets, trying not to think of the boy. A stranger asleep downstairs.

The sunrise is close, the light through my bedroom window turning a carmine shade of pink.

I pull the blankets up to my chin, begging sleep to find me. To draw me down and give me at least an hour's rest. But my heart drums against my ribs, a nagging that won't go away. It's not just the boy downstairs. It's something else.

The moth I saw in the woods. White shredded wings and black pebble eyes. The moth is a warning.

And I know what it means. I know what's coming.

My eyes flick to the wall above my bed, where a collection of items gathered from the forest are tacked to the wood. Bits of moss and dried maple leaves, a raven feather and a broken magpie egg, Juneberry seeds and other things found along the forest floor. A dozen dried wildflowers hang with stems to the ceiling, dusty pollen drifting down to my pillow. It's good luck to bring the forest indoors, to let it watch over you while you sleep. These things protect me. They bring me good dreams.

But not tonight.

Even with the open window, with the snow gathering on the floor in drifts, I sweat through the sheets, my cheek sticking to the pillow.

And in my fever dreams, I have the strange sense that by morning, Oliver will be gone. Melted into the floor like a boy made of snow.

A trick of the woods.

As if he were never here at all.

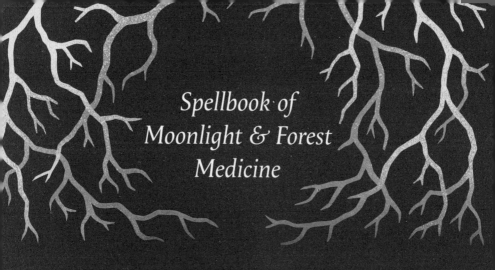

Spellbook of Moonlight & Forest Medicine

FLORENCE WALKER was born in 1871 under a green Litha moon.

Crows gathered on the windowsill when she drew in her first infant breath, and they kept watch at her crib, wings folded, every night as she slept.

On Florence's wedding day, a white-crowned sparrow in a nearby birch tree sang a tune that sent chills down the spines of those in attendance. *She's a bird witch*, they said. *They do her bidding.*

But it was merely her nightshade that drew the birds to her.

She kept sunflower seeds in her pockets, and she left piles of them on rocks and along the shore of the lake. And when she wore her yellow-apricot dress, seeds spilled out through the hole in her pocket and made little trails wherever she went. She whispered omens to the birds, and in return, they told her the secrets of her enemies.

Later in Florence's life, the Walker home built in the trees was always filled with the chitter-chatter of house finches and spotted towhees. They flew among the rafters and slept crowded around the bathroom sink.

Florence died at age eighty-seven. A nasty bout of tuberculosis.

An owl cried from the footboard of her bed frame all night, until Florence finally let out a little *chirp* and went still.

In the garden, a crow can still be seen hopping between rows of garlic and geraniums, searching for earthworms. Its eyes are that of a girl.

How to Lure the Crow from the Garden:
One handful birdseed
A wisp of sapphire smoke
Two clovers picked beside the garden gate
Click your tongue and speak Florence Walker's name
    three times. Wear a sun hat.

NORA

Sweat beads from my forehead and I kick back the blankets. Hot and disoriented.

The morning sun is a diffused orb of light through my bedroom window, and Fin is panting beside the stairs, tongue lolling in the heat of the loft. A tiny pulsing spurs at my temples from not enough sleep, and then I remember the boy. Full lips and too-deep eyes.

I climb free from the bed, light-headed, on edge, and Fin follows me down the stairs—both of us needing the cool relief of fresh air. Something to wipe away the fevered dreams still clacking through me. The ones I can't shake.

But when I reach the bottom step, I stop short.

In the living room, the fire burns low, barely a flicker from inside the stove.

On the couch is a heap of blankets, a pillow rumpled and wrinkled and slept on.

But no Oliver Huntsman.

I yank open the front door and hurry out into the snow—the cold air pouring into my lungs, stinging the tips of my ears. A thin edge of panic worms itself between my shoulder blades. Not because I'm worried about him—but because I can't be certain he was ever here at all. That I didn't imagine him: a boy made of snow and dark stars. And once the sun rose in the sky, he turned back into dust and disappeared.

I stand on the deck and scan the trees, looking for footprints in the snow, for some hint that he snuck away in the night. Returned to the Wicker Woods.

And then I see.

An outline appears among the trees, between the house and the frozen lake, and the breath catches in my lungs—a defiant itch crawling up the back of my neck.

It's him.

He's wearing his clothes from yesterday, now dry, and perhaps it's just the morning light—all swimmy and strange and beautiful— but he looks oddly valiant, like a boy about to set off on a journey. Some perilous adventure he surely won't return from.

Snow skitters down from the charcoal sky, and he spins around, sensing me watching him. His lean emerald eyes stare back at me—a starkness in them I can't decipher. And in his hand I see the cotton sack of herbs I placed beside him while he slept.

"Are you okay?" I ask, moving to the edge of the deck, but the words feel useless, sucked dry by the cold air as soon as they leave my lips.

"I needed the fresh air," he says, shifting his weight in the snow. "I was hoping the sun might be out." His gaze skips up to the sky, where the dark clouds have snuffed out the blue beyond. And I won- der if he thought the sunlight would warm him, heal him—a balm on his weary mind. That it might return his memories to him in one swift inhale.

His knuckles close around the pouch of herbs and he glances down at it, eyebrows drawn together, like he doesn't remember holding it.

"I made it for you last night," I explain, a twinge of embarrassment slicing through me. *Witchy herbs gathered by a witchy girl.* I am a Walker who has never wanted to be anything else, but I also don't want him to look at me like the kids at school do, like the other boys at the camp do. Like I am a monster, strange and eerie with wickedness in my heart. I want him to see only a girl. "It will help to warm you," I add, as if this makes it less odd. As if a sack of herbs were as common as a spoonful of strawberry cold syrup before bed.

But his eyes soften, unafraid, unfettered.

"You need to sleep with it for the next two nights," I say, although I don't expect him to really keep it—a strange bag of sharp-smelling herbs.

He nods, and when he speaks, his voice is raw and shredded by the cold. "Thank you."

Fin plods down the steps and pushes his nose into the snow, trailing some scent through the low morning fog, past Oliver's legs. "Another storm is coming," I say just as an icy wind churns up off the lake, nasty and mean. It blows through the trees, stinging my face, and a feeling of déjà vu ripples through me so quickly I almost miss it. As if I've been here before, looking out at Oliver standing in the trees, his mouth pinched flat. Or maybe I will again—time slipping just barely forward and then back. I count the seconds, I blink, and when I open my eyes, the feeling is gone.

Oliver lowers his gaze, and I wish I could pull words from his throat—I wish I knew what he was thinking. But he's as mute as the jackrabbits who sit on the porch in autumn, peering in through the windows, thinking their docile, unknowable thoughts.

When he still doesn't reply, I clear my throat, preparing myself for the question I need to ask. The one that has simmered inside me all night, burning holes of doubt through my skin. "How did you end up in the Wicker Woods?"

How did you survive in that dark, awful forest for two weeks?

In the cold?

His eyes slide back over me, but this time his mouth is turned down, a puzzled expression forming along his brow. "The Wicker Woods?" he asks.

"That's where I found you."

He shakes his head. "I didn't know," he answers first, and then, "I don't remember what happened."

The prick of something tiptoes up my spine—mistrust maybe.

"It's dangerous in there," I say. "You could have died. Or gotten lost and never found your way out again."

"But you went into the Wicker Woods," he points out.

His expression is calm. While my thoughts turn in circles, round and round without end.

"It was a full moon last night," I say quickly. "And I'm a Walker." *Everything you've heard about me is true*, I think but don't say. All the stories. The rumors passed through the boys' camp, the word whispered in a hush: *witch*.

If he had grown up here, he would know the lore of my family. All the tales told about Walkers: of Scarlett Walker, who found her pet pig in the Wicker Woods, where it had turned an ashen shade of white after eating a patch of rare white huckleberries. Of Oona Walker, who could boil water by tapping a spoon against a pan. Or Madeline Walker, who would catch toads in jars to silence people from telling her secrets.

But Oliver doesn't know these tales: the legends I know to be true. He only knows what the boys have said—and most of their stories are lies. Born from fear and spite, not from history.

He doesn't know that Walkers can enter the Wicker Woods because our family is as old as the trees. That we are made of the same fiber and dust, of roots and dandelion seeds.

Yet somehow, this boy entered the dark of the Wicker Woods and came out unharmed. He came out alive. As if some strange form of magic were at work.

"How did you survive in there?" I urge him again, watching his face for any flicker of a lie. For something he's trying to hide.

He chews on the question, mashes it around in his skull, and when he shakes his head, I wonder if he truly doesn't know. Perhaps his mind has scrubbed away what needs to be forgotten. The unpleasant things. Better to not remember the woods. Or how dark the dark can be.

I swallow hard: frustrated, tired. Something happened to him out there—but he won't say. Or he honestly doesn't remember. And my mind skips strangely back to the moth, its white wings in the dark air. The memory of it *flit flit flitting* through the trees, leading me to Oliver, where he lay slumped in the snow. I wince and cross my arms, willing the memory away. *Maybe I was wrong.* Maybe it wasn't a bone moth but only a common forest moth, oversized and snowy white. A moth that wasn't a warning at all.

Maybe.

Maybe.

"We should get you back to the camp," I say, letting out a breath.

His shoulders sink and his jaw sets in place. I can tell he doesn't want to go back there, to the camp, but I also can't keep him. *Finders keepers.* He is a lost item that belongs at the Jackjaw Camp for Wayward Boys. Not mine to keep—to place on a windowsill, to dust and admire.

Even if I want to.

He nods—a solemn gesture.

"And we should go before this storm gets worse," I add. The sky has turned the color of a broken bruise before it's begun to heal, and the wind lashes through the trees, blowing snow up off the lake.

Oliver's eyes lift, and there is a disquiet in them that betrays something else. Fear perhaps. Restlessness. Or just lack of sleep. "Okay," he relents.

Fin whimpers from the front porch, eyes big and watery.

He doesn't want to be left behind—but it's safer if he stays. In summer, the tourists often think Fin is a full-blooded wolf. Dangerous and wild—and they might be right. When he appeared on our doorstep two years ago, scratching at the wood to be let in, he looked to be part wolf, part collie, part savage glint in his eyes. Like he might bolt back into the woods at any moment, returning to where he belongs.

Even the boys at camp who've seen him from afar will shout that a wolf is stalking through the woods. Or throw stones at him.

They fear him—and fear can make people do stupid things.

"Stay," I say, patting Fin on the head, and Oliver and I cut a path through the trees, following the shoreline. To our left, the frozen surface of the lake is a web of fractures crisscrossing out toward the center. In warmer months, the water is a soft blue, glittery and mild. But now, the lake has fallen dormant. Black and grim and bone cold.

"The others at camp say it's bottomless," Oliver says behind me, our feet punching through the snow, our breath forming little white clouds with each exhale.

"No one's ever seen the bottom," I answer. "Or touched it." Sometimes I will stand at the shore and imagine falling *down down down* into that dark pool, and I feel both terrified and the strange thrill of curiosity. *What waits down there, where no sunlight has ever shone? What lurks at the deepest point?* What monsters hide where no one can see?

"So you think it's true?" he asks, stopping to face the lake. His voice sounds strong, a deepness to it that wasn't there last night. Maybe the herbs are working.

I bite the side of my lip and lift a shoulder. "You live here long enough, you start to believe in things you might not in the outside world," I tell him, certain he won't understand what I mean.

I feel him looking at me, his green eyes too green, and then his hand lifts, reaching toward me. His fingers just barely graze my hair, tickling the soft place behind my ear. "A leaf," he says, pulling it away and holding it out for me to see. A yellow three-pointed leaf with golden edges rests in his hand. "It was tangled in your hair."

The closeness of him makes me uneasy, and I brush my fingers quickly through the strands of my hair. "It happens a lot," I answer softly, looking away from him and feeling the heat rise in my cheeks. "The forest sticks to me."

His smile is full and wide, and it's the first time I've seen it—the slight curve of his lips, the crooked slant to one side, the wink of his eyes like he might laugh.

I don't let him see my own smile trying to break across my lips. I know he thinks me strange. A girl who makes potions and whose hair is tangled with leaves. *Surely a witch.* Couldn't possibly be anything else.

I turn away from him and we continue on. A half mile around the north end of the lake, we reach the camp.

The first outpost ever built in these mountains.

The first structures to rise up among the trees.

The Jackjaw Camp for Wayward Boys was founded fifty years ago, built from the remains of the early gold-mining settlement. In the early 1900s, rugged men and woman made their fortunes in these mountains, panning gold along the banks of the Black River. And even the lake itself gave up grains of gold dust in the early years.

But not anymore—the gold is long gone.

Now two dozen cabins sit nestled back in the snow-covered trees, with several smaller, odd-shaped buildings scattered along the shoreline, including a maintenance shed and a pump house that were all once part of the deserted gold-mining town.

The snow at the camp is worn with tracks: the boots of four dozen boys meandering this way and that, from cabin to cabin and back again. In summer, the beach is a chaos of boys playing Frisbee and soccer and wading out into the water with canoes and sailboats they built themselves—most barely seaworthy.

Icicles hang from the eaves of the mess hall, and we clomp up the steps to the two massive wooden doors. From the other side, we can hear the low cacophony of voices—breakfast at the camp is underway.

I glance back at Oliver, his shoulders raised against the cold. I have the distinct thought that maybe I should take him back to my house, hide him in the loft, keep him safe. But again, I know: He's not mine to keep.

"You coming?" I ask, a waver in my voice, crackling along each word.

Maybe he's preparing himself for whatever punishment he will face once the camp counselors see that he's returned. Maybe he wishes he was still out in the woods, flat on his back in the snow. Lost.

But I can't take him back to the woods.

A thing found cannot be unfound.

He nods, so I push open one of the heavy wooden doors, and we step inside.

The strange clamor of voices and the thick, smoky air barrel into us as soon as we enter. Like stepping from a quiet, snow-muted dream world into a loud, buzzing, awake one. And it takes a moment for my eyes and ears to adjust.

The room is expansive, stately, and looks like it could withstand a thousand years of heavy snow and wind before it ever started to decay. A fire roars from a huge stone fireplace against the far left wall, and the air smells of blackened toast and has a dusky, dim quality, as if the mournful winter air were trying to creep inside.

Two long wooden tables are set with candles that illuminate the faces of the boys seated along either side, and the racket of their voices echoes off the high timber ceiling. Most are eating breakfast, forks scraping against plates and orange juice sloshing onto the tables, but a few are at the far end of the room playing Ping-Pong near the fireplace.

I've been in here before, a handful of times.

The boys' camp hosts a gathering every summer and winter where they invite locals from Fir Haven to a potluck party with music and tours of the old mining outpost. Mostly girls come up from Fir Haven—to see the boys, to kiss them behind nearby trees. Mom insisted I go the last two years, said it was good to meet new people. Make friends. As if my life is somehow lacking without a coven of girls to invite over for sleepovers on the deck in summer, sleeping bags fanned out beneath the stars. As if I couldn't be perfectly happy without these things. As if these woods and Fin and a loft filled with books and found things weren't enough.

Oliver and I stand for a moment, waiting for someone to look our way, to notice: Oliver Huntsman has returned.

But they continue shoving forkfuls of waffle dripping with syrup into their mouths, slurping orange juice, and laughing so heartily that I'm surprised they don't choke.

Oliver stares across the landscape of boys like he's trying to pinpoint the names and faces of the people he knew before he vanished, but it's now just a muddled blur. He uncrosses his arms and turns to face me, a severe line of tension cutting from his temples down to his chin. "Thanks," he says. "For letting me stay at your place last night." There is no warmth in his gaze. And a cold stone of doubt settles into my chest. I may have saved him from the woods, but bringing him back here feels wrong—worse than the dark of the forest and the promise of death.

I force my lips to smile, but all I say, all that rises up from my chest, is "You're welcome."

This is where he belongs. Among a sea of boys.

He turns away without another word, without even a *goodbye*, and moves toward the row of tables—blending in with the other boys. I wait for someone to recognize him, to shout his name. But no one does. The room is too draped in shadow, too hard to discern one boy from all the rest. *A boy they've already forgotten.* Although I'm certain that once the camp counselors discover he's returned, they will want answers. They will want to know where he's been and what happened. Will he tell them the truth—that he's been in the Wicker Woods all this time? Does he even know the truth? Does he even remember how he ended up way out there?

I stare after him, knowing this might be the last time I see him.

Even if he stays a whole year at the camp, he'll be just another boy among a crowd of nameless boys. They come and they go. And soon he'll be gone too, shuttled back to wherever he came from. One of the flat states, or the humid states, back home to his parents and his friends. He'll soon forget this place and the night a girl found him inside the woods and let him sleep in her home beside the fire. An old memory replaced with new ones.

He vanishes among the mass of boys—my first found item that was made of flesh and a thumping heart, and now he's gone.

My own heart betrays my head, sinking in on itself. Concaving. As though a deep, unknowable pain is squeezing it into a tiny kernel. A feeling I don't want to feel. I refuse to feel.

I turn back for the double doors, pushing the feeling away, when from the corner of my eye I see someone approaching. Tall and slight and moving not with the hulking stride of a boy, but with the ease of a girl who is at home in her own skin.

The willowy Suzy Torrez—acorn-brown hair tied in a ponytail at the back of her head, eyelashes so long they're like hummingbird wings—saunters toward me, lips drawn into a grin. "Nora!" she calls.

I feel my mouth dip open and my smile fade. "What are you doing here?" I ask once she reaches me.

Suzy lives in Fir Haven and goes to Fir Haven High. I only know her vaguely—our lockers were next to each other last year, but we've never been friends. She has a crowd of besties who do everything together and a crowd of boys who fawn over her, and I don't have either of those things. But I also don't want those things.

Still, I see Suzy from time to time at the lake, mostly in summer, sunbathing down by the shore, stretched out on a beach towel with all her friends—lathered in coconut oil and laughing so loudly their voices carry across the lake. She usually has a summer fling with one of the boys at camp, a seasonal crush who she swaps out when the next selection of boys arrive. I've always envied the ease with which her heart can flutter from one to the next. A buoyant, pliable thing.

"Been stuck up here since the storm," she says. Her eyes slide across the room. "I snuck up to see Rhett Wilkes. Didn't realize I was never going to leave these mountains again. Camp counselors weren't happy when they found me hiding in Rhett's cabin, but what were they gonna do?" She shrugs. "They couldn't send me home." Her gaze flicks away then back again, eyebrow raised. "I've never hated boys more in my whole life than I do right now." Her nose twitches like she can't shake the stench of all these boys, crowded together, smelling of wood smoke and sweat, stuck in the woods. Then her eyes narrow. "You live across the lake, right?" she asks.

I nod. Of course she knows—everyone knows where the Walkers live: the house where witches are rumored to practice the foulest of magic, where Walkers cast spells and drink the blood of our enemies. The house most locals avoid.

"What're you doing at the camp?" she asks, white teeth gleaming, voice all drippy and cool. As if I were any other girl from school. As if we were friends. The kind of friends who stay up late talking on the phone, giggling, bedsheets pulled over our heads to muffle the sound. A thing I've never known. Maybe never will. A feeling that aches, that kerplunks into my stomach like a stone tossed into a deep pond. Sinking, *sinking* until it's a gone.

"I found that boy who went missing," I tell her. "I brought him back."

She scowls, like the memory of a boy going missing sends odd spikes of pain through her chest. "I assumed he was dead," she answers, her voice tight. "Frozen somewhere out there in the snow, and they'd find him in the spring." At this she shudders, yet her description seems oddly callous, as if to die in the woods were commonplace up here. *One dead boy, easily replaced by any of the others.*

I raise an eyebrow, and she coils her long, dark hair over one shoulder, tapping a foot against the floor as if she were feeling impatient. Our conversation beginning to bore her.

The candles along the two long tables flicker briefly, sending shadows dancing up the walls, and Suzy crosses her arms, moving closer to me. Her chin dips down like she doesn't want anyone to hear what she's about to say. "This place gives me the creeps."

"It gives everyone the creeps," I answer, eyeing the strange shapes the candlelight makes on the high ceiling. Hands and faces and bones that twist at wrong angles. Boys have always complained that the camp is haunted, that the ghosts of miners rattle the halls and sway through the trees at night. The boys aren't used to living in the woods, to the constant scratch of branches on windows and the wind against your bare neck while you sleep.

"Yeah," she agrees softly. But I can see her mind turning it over, the itching of something along her skin. She rubs her palms down her arms and looks away from me, biting her lip. "I can't stay here anymore," she murmurs, more to herself. Her chin dips to her chest and she breathes slowly, like she's trying to pretend she's somewhere else—*three clicks of her heels and* poof, *she'll be back home*—instead of trapped in these mountains, living with all these awful boys.

The candlelight vibrates again, and the wind shakes the sturdy walls. Another bad storm blowing in. I hear the whoosh of air just before the two double doors behind us tear open, pushed in by the wind, and bang back against the wall with a loud crash.

In an instant, the entire mess hall is dipped into darkness—all the candles extinguished, the fire at the far end reduced to embers. Chairs scrape back across the wood floor, plates are pushed aside, silverware dropped. Faint, gray daylight filters through the open doorway, but it's hardly enough to illuminate the shadowy mess hall.

"All right, everyone, settle down," a voice booms from somewhere in the dark—one of the camp counselors. "Take a seat and we'll do a head count." A flashlight is flicked on across the room, and then a couple more, the eerie beams of light slicing across faces and the towering walls.

"Please," Suzy says furtively, as if each word were a secret. "Can I stay with you, just until the road clears?"

I feel both my eyebrows raise. Suzy Torrez has never stepped foot inside my house. Suzy Torrez wouldn't be caught dead talking to me in the halls of Fir Haven High. She's never asked me to sit with her in the cafeteria during lunch or invited me to one of her birthday parties, and now she wants to spend the night. At my home.

"I've been sleeping on a cot in a little room off the kitchen. It's the only place that isn't bunking with the boys. I can't take it anymore," she urges, she insists. The whites of her eyes too white.

A lantern is lit and it throws more light across the room as boys make their way back to the long wood tables. "I—" I start to open my mouth to speak, but Suzy cuts me off.

"At least until the phones come back on, then I can call my parents, they'll find a way to come get me." Her eyes bore into me now, pleading. Her hair falling about her face. Her fingers twitching like there's an itch somewhere along her skin she can't reach.

I feel sorry for her, the desperate curve of her mouth, the watery rims of her eyes. I wouldn't want to sleep here either, in this damp, cold place. And a part of me—a part I don't want to admit to— thinks it might be nice to have someone else at the house. To fill the silence. Last night, sleeping in my room with Oliver downstairs on the couch, felt oddly comforting. Another warm body and beating heart within the walls. "Okay," I say at last.

A smile breaks across her face, revealing her perfectly straight teeth. "I'll go grab my bag. Meet you outside?"

I nod and she spins around, crossing the immense room and vanishing into a dark doorway that must lead back to the kitchen.

Candles are relit across the thick wood tables, flames becoming little points of light in the dark, shining up the walls. But before I can slip out through the open doorway, I notice something flitting down from the ceiling—something I couldn't see before in the dark.

A moth.

It must have been hovering up in the rafters, and now it quivers through the air, drawn toward the candlelight. Its white-gray body is paler than it should be. Its antennae too long and bleached white. *Not a common moth.*

It's the same kind I saw in the Wicker Woods.

A bone moth.

Seeing it again is like a spark against my eyelids—cold as January frost. Wild as February wind. Like a premonition. But I've never been able to foresee what's to come. Not like Georgette Walker, my great-great-aunt whose nightshade let her see the future in dewdrops suspended on blades of grass. *This* feeling is something else. A certainty resting at the base of my throat. A dull, stagnant ache. A ringing in my ears.

I turn away, a chill rolling down my spine, and dart back outside—before the camp instructors decide I need to be tallied and counted along with the others—and brace myself against the cold wintry air.

My hands shake at my sides, and my heart slams against the delicate rungs of my ribs. I lean my shoulder against one of the large posts holding up the deck, gasping for air, blinking away the snow. Blinking away the afterimage of wings stained against my eyelids. I told myself the moth I saw in the woods was only a common night moth, *a winter moth the color of snow*, nothing more. But I was wrong. It's the kind I should fear. The kind that are mentioned inside the spellbook countless times. Charcoal sketches of wings torn

374

into ribbons at the edges, woolly legs, black orb eyes that seek only one thing: death.

My eyes water from the cold, and my head thuds.

A fog sinks over the lake, the gloom as thick as wet alder smoke, and it reminds me of the day we buried my grandmother in the small cemetery at the west end of the lake—a place where old miners are laid beneath the ground, the headstones worn and crumbled, and sinking into the dark earth.

Funeral fog, Mom called it that day. The kind of weather only suitable during a burial: for grief, for masking tears that stream down cheeks, for numbing hearts that have split in two. But now the funeral fog has descended over the lake, rolling down from the mountains in endless waves. A reminder—or maybe a warning.

It's a good day to bury the dead.

OLIVER

When I was ten, my dad took me camping deep in the Blue Mile Mountains. We spent the night sleeping in a tent while the rain beat down outside and dripped through a hole in the thin nylon fabric. The rain made a puddle around our sleeping bags, and I shivered all night.

I had never been so cold in my whole life.

Until now.

These woods are a ruthless kind of cold. The kind that gets inside you, beneath clothes and socks and skin, and down to the marrow of your bones. I escape the mess hall through a back door, before any of the counselors can see me—before *anyone* does. The candlelight is dim and I am just another shadow passing through.

Fog lies heavy over the trees, and I weave my way through the snow, past cabins tucked back in the pines. The cabin numbers are out of order. Cabin four, then twenty-six, then eleven. It makes no sense. But I reach cabin fourteen—the place where I was assigned to sleep when I first arrived, weeks ago now—and I push open the small door, ducking inside.

Most people have never heard of Jackjaw Lake, or a boys' camp hidden deep in the mountains. Even the nearest town is an hour's drive down a steep, winding road. It's a place not marked on most maps. An easy place to get lost, to be forgotten.

But I never intended to go missing.

Inside the cabin, there's a bunk bed against each of the two walls—four boys to a cabin—and the air smells of damp wood and campfire smoke. It's a smell that has settled into the bedsheets and starched-white pillows and the frayed green rug in the center of the room, into everything.

I crouch down beside the potbellied stove set in the corner.

The counselors tell us not to let the fires go out in our stoves— to keep them burning day and night, to keep the cabins warm. But most of the boys forget. And our stove has gone dark.

I place dry logs on the embers, coaxing the fire back to life, but the room is still cold, wind howling at the windows, rattling the thin glass. I kick off my boots and walk to the wood dresser on the right-hand wall. I kneel down and pull open the bottom drawer—the drawer that was mine. But it's empty. My clothes, the backpack I brought with me, the handful of books, the dead cell phone—they're all gone.

The counselors must have taken everything out. Boxed up my few belongings when I went missing, ready to ship it all back to my uncle once the road cleared. *We're sorry to inform you that your nephew, Oliver Huntsman, has gone missing from the Jackjaw Camp for Wayward Boys. If he turns up, we'll let you know. In the meantime, here's all his stuff.*

I push the drawer closed, a strange hollowness sinking into my gut. My few things are gone—hardly enough to represent a life any-way. But it was all I had. All I had left that meant anything at all. Of my life before. My parents. And I hold back the threat of tears. The wretched twisting in my chest. Perhaps the counselors were already clearing away space for another boy. My single drawer, my bunk—wiped clean of any memory of the boy who vanished.

Oliver Huntsman, swept into nonexistence.

I climb the ladder to the top bunk—my old bunk—and the sad, sagging mattress settles beneath me. I stare up at the low ceiling, an arm's length away, the wood carved with boys' names and symbols and crude drawings. Nights when boys couldn't sleep or were bored or didn't want to be forgotten, they dug the blade of a knife into the wood. Proof that they were here.

Inside my coat pocket, I find the cotton pouch filled with herbs *she* gave me. It smells like my mother's garden, where she used to grow thyme and potatoes and carrots we would eat straight from the soil. I press the pouch against my chest, my ribs, trying to push away the cold. Push away the memory of my mom that is a raw blade against my throat. That makes me feel alone. Awfully, desperately alone.

The boys call Nora a witch. *A moon witch who is full of weird thoughts and strange words. Who lives inside a strange house, filled with strange things.*

Maybe they're right. Or maybe they only tell stories to pass the time. They tell stories about her so that no one will tell stories about them.

Maybe she feels alone too. Misunderstood. A vacant gap inside her that will never be filled.

Just like me.

The fire crackles and I close my eyes, pulling the blanket up over my head to keep out the cold. I try to sleep. To let the day melt away around me. And for a while I do sleep, but my dreams are black and bleak and I'm running through trees, eyes flashing upward, searching for the starry night sky but I'm lost and I sink into the snow and the cold until she touches my hand and I snap awake.

My eyes flutter open and I'm still in my bunk, peering up at the ceiling.

But I'm not alone.

Voices carry through the cabin. The shuffling of boots across the floor.

The others have returned.

I stay still, listening to their lumbering movements, the door shutting behind them. The cabin is dark, the sun long set, and they don't know I'm here, hidden in the top bunk. *They don't know I'm back.*

"Told you the fire wouldn't go out," one of them says. I recognize the voice—the voices of the boys who I shared a cabin with before my mind went blank. Before I went missing. It sounds like Jasper, his words more pitched than the others.

I hear someone add more wood to the stove, the kicking off of boots, the opening and closing of dresser drawers. The bunk below me creaks as Lin flops onto his mattress and starts tapping a foot against the wood frame.

Jasper, whose bunk is directly across from mine, says, "I don't know why I need to learn this shit. When will I need to use a compass? After I leave here, I'm never going into the woods again."

"You'll probably get a job as one of the counselors," Lin suggests below me, and laughs in a quick burst.

"Hell no," Jasper answers.

379

A long pause settles between them, and the wind grows louder outside, making the fire in the stove pop and crack. Drops of rain begin to drum against the roof.

I think they've fallen asleep, but then Jasper says, "It's been two weeks."

Below him, in the bottom bunk, Rhett snaps, "Shut up, man."

"I just wonder where he is," Jasper adds quickly.

"He'll turn up," Rhett answers, his voice biting. Sharp as tacks. Maybe I should say something, tell them I'm here—but I stay quiet, a knot twisted in my stomach.

"Can you blame him for not wanting to come back?" Lin asks below me. The room falls quiet. "I'd hide too."

Jasper makes a sound. "No shit."

Someone grumbles, someone else coughs, but no one speaks. And soon the cabin is filled with the sounds of sleep. Of mutters and snores, feet kicking at their footboards, blankets tugged up beneath chins to keep out the cold.

Wind squeals through cracks between the thick log walls. A never-ending scream. Long and hollow. A desperate sound.

The rain turns to sleet and then snow, collecting on the windowsills. The dark outside becomes darker.

But I lie perfectly still, listening to their breathing. They don't know I'm back. That I've returned from the woods. *I'd hide too*, Lin said.

What happened that night, when the storm rattled the walls of the cabin, when my memory blots out?

I push back the blanket and move silently down the narrow ladder, then across the room. None of them stir. I could wake them, tell them I'm back, ask them what happened that night—ask them to fill in the parts I can't remember. But the gnawing in my throat won't let me. The sliver of pain thrumming inside my chest tells me I shouldn't trust them.

Something happened that my mind won't let me remember.

Something that is more darkness than light.

I can't stay here, with them. There are only bad memories in this place.

I yank on my boots and open the door just wide enough to slip through. I glance back and see someone stirring, Rhett I think, his head lifted. But I pull the door shut before he can focus through the dark.

Before he can see me sneaking out.

NORA

N ight comes swiftly in the mountains.

The sinking sun devoured by the snowy peaks. Eaten whole.

I carry in freshly cut logs from the woodshed and drop them beside the woodstove—enough to keep Suzy and me warm through the night. If they'll actually light.

"You found all these things in the woods?" Suzy asks, standing at the darkened window, running a finger over the items that fascinate her placed along the windowsill: silver candlesticks and a small, palm-sized figurine in the shape of a boy and girl dancing, the freckle-faced girl's head inclined like she's facing an imaginary sky. These found things I know by heart. The stories they tell.

Suzy spent most of the day holding her cell phone in the air, near windows, trying to find a signal—even after I told her she'd never get reception out here. Then she'd walk into the kitchen and pick up the landline, listening for a dial tone. But there was always nothing. Just the flat silence. Finally, she turned off her cell phone again to save the battery.

Now, with evening upon us, she seems defeated, her voice low and disheartened.

"Yeah," I tell her. "During a full moon."

She watches the snow eddy against the window. "People at school talk about you," she says absently, like I'm not really listening. "They say you talk to the trees. And to the dead." She says it in a way that makes me think she wants to believe it, so she can return to school when this is all over and say: *I stayed in the house of Nora Walker and it's all true.*

And maybe I should feel hurt, wounded by her statement, but I know what people say about me, about my family, and their words fall like dull raindrops on my skin, never soaking in. I know what I am—and what I'm not. And I don't blame them for their curiosity. Sometimes I think it might only be envy they feel—a desire to be more than what they are. To escape the blandness of their ordinary lives.

I walk into the kitchen and light two candles with a match—one for Suzy and one for me. "I've never talked to the dead," I admit. The truth. Although Walkers have often been able to see shadows, glimpses of ghosts wandering through the old graveyard on the far side of lake. We see flickers of the in-between, phantoms moving from one corner of the house to the other. Our eyes see what others can't. But I don't tell Suzy this. Proof that I might really be what they say I am.

Suzy's eyelids flutter and she taps her fingers against her opposite forearm, narrowing her gaze like she doesn't believe me, like she's certain I must be hiding something—a dozen black cats in the attic, a broomstick tucked behind winter coats in the hall closet, jars filled with my victims' hearts beneath the floorboards. But nothing so gruesome exists within this house. Only herbs and chimney soot and stories that rest inside the walls. "I'll make you a bed on the couch," I tell her.

The blankets and pillow from when Oliver slept here last night are still rumpled at the end.

But Suzy glances to the couch, with its sagging cushions and frayed armrests and stuffing bursting out, and she frowns. She drops her arms, and her mouth makes a little pout. "Is there a bed where I can sleep?"

"Sorry."

Her eyes cut away and she surveys the living room. She had probably hoped I lived in one of the larger homes on the lake—the log villas with five bedrooms, game rooms in the basement, and spa bathrooms where she could take a bubble bath to soothe the constant chill. "Could I maybe . . . ?" Her words trail away. "Could I sleep with you, in your room?"

Another twinge of sympathy shudders through me.

I don't want to say yes, I don't want to share my bed with a girl who surely talks about me at school, who will only stare at all the strange things in my room and then spread more stories about me back at Fir Haven High. But a part of me also wants to feel normal— an ordinary girl who can have friends over and stay up late and not worry about what Suzy will say about me back at school.

The word slips out before I can catch it. "Fine."

I lock both doors and we climb the stairs to the loft, Fin close behind.

Suzy strides over to the wall of windows, and I divide the pillows on my bed: one for Suzy, one for me. The snow is heavier now, falling in thick waves against the glass. I wonder if the moth is out there, stalking me, waiting in the trees. The week before my grandmother passed away, a bone moth had been pinging against the windows of the house all morning, *tap tap tapping*; *flit, flit, flitting*. I thought it was going to break the glass, its delicate wings beating so frantically, its tiny head thumping against the windows. It was the first time I'd ever seen one—the kind of moth my grandmother warned about—and I watched my mom pace through the house, ringing her hands together, braiding and unbraiding her hair methodically, as if the solution to the moth were in the folds of her dark hair.

She knew death was coming—the bone moth was a sign.

And when we woke to find that Grandma had wandered down to the lake in the middle of the night, taken her last breath on the shore, autumn leaves scattered around her—sad shades of orange and golden-yellows—we knew the moth had been right. Death was coming. Just as we'd feared.

And now, one follows me.

"Why do you stay here in the winter?" Suzy asks, touching her fingertips to the window.

I pinch my eyes closed, shoving away the memory of the moth and my grandmother. "It's my home."

"I know, but you could leave in winter, like everyone else."

"I like the winters," I say. *I like the quiet. The cold, unending silence.* But it's more than that. *I belong here.* Every Walker for generations has lived in these woods. Between these ancient pines. It's just how it's always been.

We don't know how to live anywhere else.

"Your house is older than the others," Suzy notes, still peering out the window where she can just barely see the outline of other homes along the lake.

"My great-great-grandfather built it," I tell her. "Long before any other houses lined the shore." Her gaze is soft, and the light from the candle she holds flickers across her cheekbones and tawny hair. "He was a gold miner," I continue. "He made his fortune in the Black River." But like most of the men in my family, he came and went just as swiftly as the hours fell into night. It wasn't their fault— Walker women were known to be fickle, uncertain when it came to love. And men were only ever a passing fascination. Much like the man who was my father. Whether by bad luck or our choosing, men never stayed long in our lives.

I walk to the closet and change into black sweatpants and a thick, knobby sweater. But Suzy stays at the window, pressing her palm to the glass. "You said you found that missing boy?" she asks.

I close the closet door, catching my reflection in the closet mirror briefly—sleepy eyes and hair that needs to be brushed. "Up in the woods," I say cautiously.

Locals know of the Wicker Woods. They speak about it in a hush, in tones never above a whisper. As if saying it aloud will draw the darkness out. *Never speak of the Wicker Woods behind its back*, a notation inside the spellbook warns.

"He survived out there all this time?" she asks, dropping her hand from the window.

"He got lucky," I say. Or maybe it's opposite of luck. To find yourself lost inside the Wicker Woods is catastrophically unlucky.

One of the ill-fated, my grandmother would say if she were here. *Doomed. A boy to steer clear of.*

An itch trickles down my vertebrae, cold as ice, lodging itself like concrete in my chest.

"He could have ended up like that other boy," Suzy says.

My gaze snaps to hers, her silhouette outlined against the huge windows, snow swirling against the glass. "What other boy?"

She lifts one shoulder. "The one who died." She swivels around to face me. "The same night your boy went missing."

He's not my boy, I want to say. But instead I ask, "A boy died?"

Her mouth pinches flat and severe. "Yeah, the night of the storm."

"What happened?"

"Don't know. Just overheard the other boys talking about it. They wanted to call the police, but the phones have been down."

I step closer to her. "Who was he?"

"Not sure." She weaves a bit of hair through her fingers. Not nervously, just out of habit. "They kept it pretty quiet, no one wanted to talk about it. But I overheard their whispers in the hall, when they thought I couldn't hear."

"Did they say how he died?" I ask. My lungs have tightened in my chest, the breath held still at the back of my throat.

She shakes her head, her eyebrows drawn close—wincing at the thought of someone meeting their demise way out here, in these woods, in the bitter cold. "I only heard them say that a boy was missing and another was dead."

I sink onto the edge of the bed, looking past Suzy to the window. "Someone died," I say softly, mostly to my myself, and I run my finger over my grandmother's ring, feeling the oval shape of the gray moonstone. As if I could summon her, hear the soothing tenor of her words whenever she told me one of her stories. But she doesn't appear.

Suzy and I are silent for some time, the cold slipping through the walls as the fire downstairs begins to die. The room feels strangely hollow, a ringing starts in my ears, and when I blink, I think I see the walls vibrate before snapping back into place.

I must be tired. It must be from lack of sleep.

Suzy finally blows out a breath. "I don't want to talk about it," she says. "It's too awful." And she shuffles across the room to the other side of the bed, crawling swiftly between the sheets, still in her sweatshirt and jeans. As if she could hide from it—the death of a boy. A thing easily wiped away with a shroud of warm wool blankets.

Her eyelids sink closed, and her soft, oceany hair fans out over the pillow. She smells of rose water, like an old French fragrance no longer used except by ladies in nursing homes who smoke thin cigarettes and still paint their nails cherry-blossom red.

And for a moment, I could almost trick myself into believing we're having a sleepover, two best friends who stayed up late eating buttered popcorn and watching horror movies, curling each other's hair, and giggling about the boys we've kissed at school. A different night entirely. A different life.

Others look at me and see a witch. A girl who is dangerous and fearless and full of dark thoughts. But they don't see the parts of me I keep hidden. The loss, the feeling of being alone, now that the only person who ever really understood me, my grandmother, is gone. That I carry around a feeling of being not quite good enough. A hollow brick lodged in my rib cage.

No one sees that I have just as many wounds as everyone else.

That I too am a little broken.

Reluctantly, I slide into bed.

Suzy's knees bump mine, an elbow to the head, and when she finally falls asleep, she snores against her pillow, a soft muttering that is almost soothing.

But I lie awake. My mind crackling.

A boy is dead. And I feel sick. *A boy is dead.* And we're trapped in these mountains. *A boy is dead.* And I don't know how to feel. If it were summer and the road were clear, the police would come. They'd ask questions. They'd determine cause. But none of this will happen until the road opens, and I don't know if I should be afraid or not. *How did he die? Accident or something else?* Suzy skimmed over it like a footnote, something she would barely recall a year from now. *Oh right, that winter a boy died, how did that happen again?*

But I've never known anyone who has died, aside from my grandmother. And perhaps if it wasn't for the moth, or the boy I found in the woods, I'd feel less fidgety. My mind less clacking and clicking like the grasshoppers who twitch in the tall beach grass under autumn moons. Perhaps.

But instead my thoughts writhe in circles: Does Oliver know what happened to the boy who died? Was he there when it happened? Does he remember?

An hour passes and snow collides against the windows, a storm tumbles down from the mountains. Fin scratches against the wood floor, his paws twitching—dreaming of chasing rabbits or mice.

I force my eyelids closed. I beg sleep to fall over me.

But I stare at the ceiling instead.

Until, when the night seems darkest and my mind the most rest-less, there is a *thump* against the house. Then a *tap tap tap* on glass.

Someone's here. Outside.

* ✳ *

"What is it?" Suzy mumbles, eyes still closed. She might only be talking in her sleep—not really awake at all.

"I heard something downstairs," I hiss softly, pushing up from the bed. "At the door." My eyes skip to the stairs, listening.

"Mm," she answers, wriggling herself deeper and burying her head in the pillow.

The wind claps against the house, and my heart claps inside my chest. I move down the steps, one at a time, careful and quiet. *A boy is dead*, my mind repeats with each thud of my heartbeat.

I hear the knock again, distinct and quick, coming from the other side of the front door. It might only be Mr. Perkins or one of the counselors from camp—come to warn me that a murderer is among us. Come to tell me to lock my doors and stay inside. I used to be the one to fear in these woods, but maybe not anymore.

I walk to the front window, breathing slowly, trying to calm the adrenaline pressing at my temples, and pull back the curtain. Some-one stands on the porch, hands in pockets, shoulders bent away from the cold.

My fingers slide the dead bolt free and pull open the door. Snow coils in around me, wind whipping into the living room, and he lifts his head.

Oliver.

"I didn't know where else to go," he says, a line puckering between his brows.

The breath returns to my lungs and I take a step back, letting him move swiftly inside. "What are you doing here?"

He pushes back the hood of his sweatshirt, and his eyes sweep up to mine. Dark pupils, made even darker in the unlit house. "I need a place to stay."

I cross my arms over my midsection, my thoughts still cycling over the words I can't shake, a tune on repeat: *A boy is dead.* "Why can't you stay at the camp?" I ask.

I watch him, trying to pinpoint all the reasons why I shouldn't allow this boy I hardly know to stand inside my home, why I should tell him to leave, but I only see the boy I found inside the Wicker Woods: cold and shivering and alone. His bare chest facing the fire when I brought him back. How his hands felt like ice, how his jaw clenched, how his muscles only relaxed when I touched him.

"I don't trust anyone there," he answers.

"Why not?"

His eyes hook on mine before slipping away. And after a long, muted pause, he says simply, "I don't have anywhere else to go."

I think I hear movement upstairs, Suzy waking up, or maybe just turning over in bed. The sound fades. *A boy died*, I think again. The words on loop, echo, echo, *echo*. I swallow and look back at Oliver, saying aloud the thing I can't escape. "A boy died the night you went missing," I say, words tumbling out, causing a strange pain inside my ribs—like being snagged by a fishing hook.

Oliver's brow stiffens. "What?"

I feel my jaw contract, my eyes afraid to look away from him, afraid I'll miss a flutter of an eyelash that might mean something. Reveal some clue Oliver is trying to hide. "A boy is dead," I say, firmer this time.

But Oliver's expression tightens, like he doesn't understand.

"You didn't know?" I ask.

"No. I don't . . ." He trails off, swaying a little on his feet, and I see how pale he is—the cold hasn't left him completely yet. "I don't remember anything. I can't . . ." Again his voice breaks.

I want to touch him, to steady him, but I keep my hands at my sides, examining every line of his face, the slope of his cheekbones. I'm looking for a lie, for something he's hiding. But there is only muted confusion.

"I can't go back to the camp," he says finally. "If the road wasn't snowed in, I'd leave, but"—he exhales deeply—"I'm stuck here."

Oliver breathes and I swear the wind calms, he closes his eyes and the forest trembles against the house.

My lost item found in the woods. Who is now more forest than boy.

I say the next thing before I can stop myself, before I can tell myself it's a bad idea. "Okay." A prick of unease cuts through me. "You can stay here tonight."

One night, I tell myself. One more night, I'll let him sleep here, this boy who speaks as if a soft wind stirs inside him, who can't remember what happened to him the night another boy died. Whose eyes make me feel slightly unmoored in ways that make me want to scream. Walkers cannot trust our own hearts—our slippy, sloppy bleeding hearts. They are reckless, stupid things. Muscles that beat too fast, that cave inward when they break. Too fragile to be trusted. Yet, I let him stay.

I lock the front door and add more logs to the stove. And when Oliver settles onto the couch, I see he still has the bag of herbs I gave him, clutched in his hand. I was certain he wouldn't keep it—but he did.

"Thank you," he says to me, and I stall at the bottom of the stairs, chewing on the side of my lip, twirling the moonstone ring around my finger.

"Can I trust you?" I ask. *Too late now*, I think. I've already let him stay. I've already let my heart slip two degrees off-center, let myself believe he might be different. That he isn't like the others. That he might have the same hole inside him that I do. And if he says no, will I force him to leave? *Probably not.*

He watches me with his moon-deep eyes, and my head feels fizzy and light, filled with feathers and dust, no rational thoughts skipping around up there. Only seasick thoughts. No compass or stars to steer me back to shore.

"I don't know," he answers finally, and my throat feels too dry.

A boy is dead. Dead, dead, dead. The words have now lodged themselves stiffly in my skull—planted there, where they will grow roots and thorns and venomous flowers, burrowing into my thoughts, becoming true.

There is a storm growing inside me, inside this house, and it darkens the doorways—the dark spreading out from corners and from beneath old, creaky bed frames.

Back in my room, I feel alone, out of place in my own bedsheets. The loft ceiling too steep and jagged, like brittle bones that might snap at the knees and shatter. I force my eyes closed, but I see only the moth, the memory of ash-white wings moving toward me in the dark. Hunting me.

Oliver has returned from the woods.

And something happened the night of the storm. *Something bad.*

When you see a pale moth, my grandmother told me time and again, her eyes like black moons, *death isn't far behind.*

Spellbook of
Moonlight & Forest
Medicine

WILLA WALKER wailed and wailed and wailed.

She was born in 1894 during the winter of an ox moon. A restless baby, she cried even when the summer stars reconfigured themselves in the sky, dancing across her hand-carved crib. Her mother, Adaline Walker, believed something to be wrong with the small child—an omen of illness or bad luck.

When Willa was sixteen, she stood on the shore of Jackjaw Lake and wept into the shallow water. Her tears filled the lake until it overflowed—muddying the banks and turning the lake bottomless.

Willa's nightshade was more dangerous than most. Her tears could fill oceans if she let them. They could drown men and overflow rivers and turn the forest to water.

The depth of Jackjaw Lake was forever unknown after that day, and Willa's mother made her carry a handkerchief wherever she went, the thin cotton meant to catch every teardrop that fell from her cheeks. To prevent the world from drowning.

Willa fell in love twice, and twice suffered a broken heart.

She died on the second night of Beltane, after her twenty-third birthday. Cause unknown.

Cure for Heartache & Unexplainable Weeping Fits:
Two pinches skullcap
Powder of lemon balm and Saint-John's-wort
Nectar from a milk thistle bee
One horsehair, burnt at both ends
Combine in wooden mortar. Drink or place beneath
    tongue.

NORA

I shouldn't care.

It shouldn't matter that Oliver was gone from the couch when I woke and came downstairs—just like the morning after I found him inside the woods.

But still, I stand on the porch looking out at a trail of deep footprints cut through the fresh layer of snow, veering around the twin pines that stand guard beside my house, then wandering down toward the lake. A ripple of déjà vu passes through me, just like before—the snow falling in familiar waves, every blink of my eyelashes is a second I've felt *once, twice* before. Time swivels and then lurches back into place.

Tick, tick, thud.

I steady myself against the porch railing, hands gripping the cold wood, and focus back on the footprints leading through the snow.

This is the second time he's slipped out of the house while I slept, and maybe I should feel angry. But something nags at me instead, a disquiet that won't go away—a pulsing curiosity just behind my eyes that wants to follow his path, see where it leads. I can't be sure what time he left the house, but when I touched his pillow, the scent of woods and earth still lingered against the cotton. Yet the warmth from his skin was long gone.

Fin trots down the porch steps and out into the snow, sniffing at the ground.

The sunrise is a sickly pale glow on the horizon, and maybe I shouldn't follow his footprints, maybe I don't want to know where he's gone. Yet, I push my hands into my coat pockets and clomp down the steps into the snow anyway.

A boy is dead. And maybe Oliver decided to leave in the middle of the night, tried to hike down the road to town. He'll never make it if he did. Or maybe he's gone somewhere else. Perhaps he has other secrets he's trying to hide—a deep well of them.

Fin leaps through the snow happily, trailing Oliver's tracks, and when we reach the lake, the footprints turn left, toward the southern shore.

The air whirls with flecks of ice; the morning sky is velvet—like fabric that was handwoven, marred by deep clouds and imperfections. Not machine made. And Oliver's path around the lake takes me to the small marina, where docks sit frozen in the ice, waiting for spring. Canoes rest with their bellies to the sky.

In summer, tourists converge on this side of the lake, children sprinting down the docks to fling themselves into the water, orange and cherry and watermelon Popsicles dripping onto toes and down sunburnt arms. Normal kids with normal lives—a thing I never knew. The air always smelling of sunblock and campfire smoke, the afternoons burning so brightly that nothing dark and shadowy can possibly survive.

But now, the boathouse store sits boarded up for the winter, a ▒▒▒▒ sign hanging crooked above the turquoise-blue door—the wind thumping it against the wood, a *thwap thwap thwap* that reminds me of a woodpecker searching for bugs in the trunks of spruce trees.

"Hello!" someone calls, and I whip around to face the lake.

Old Mr. Perkins is out on one of the docks, his green rain boots kicking through a layer of snow, the hood of his yellow slicker pulled up over his head—as if it were spring, as if the air were mild and drizzling.

"Morning," I call back to him.

When Grandma was still alive, she and Mr. Perkins would often sit on the docks at sunset, chatting about the years that lay behind them—back before the tourists came, when you'd find gold on the bottom of your boots just walking around the shore, and fish swam in the lake as thick as mud. Now, from time to time, Mom and I will make the walk down to the marina to check on Mr. Perkins, especially in winter. We'll bring along a thermos of hot cinnamon-apple tea, a sweet pumpkin cobbler straight from the oven, and jars of freshly sealed honey.

But this time, I haven't brought pie.

Mr. Perkins tips his head to me, and in front of him is a broom he had been sweeping side to side, brushing the dock clean of the snow. An odd thing to be doing in winter. But Floyd Perkins has never been ordinary.

"Docks were starting to sink," he says, as explanation. "And my snow shovel broke." He waves a hand at the broom, as if the solution were obvious, then squints up at the sky. "This damn snow won't let up. It's nearly as bad as the year your great-aunt Helena started tossing ice cubes out her window." Mr. Perkins knows most of the Walker tales. He was here the winter Helena Walker lobbed ice cubes out the loft window each morning—a peculiar spell for conjuring snow. A spell only Helena could perform. Winter lasted eight months that year, and after that, Helena's mother, Isolde, forbade her from summoning the snow again—placing a lock on the icebox. The thought of it still makes me smile: Helena's wild red hair spiraling up around her as flakes seethed down from the sky.

"The forest seems angry," I say, nodding up at the mountains, where clouds gather against the jagged slopes to the north. It isn't Helena Walker who's responsible for this winter's storms; it's something else. A darkness over the lake—a forecast of something to come. I shiver and tamp my feet in the snow to keep the circulation moving through my limbs.

"These woods have a temper," he agrees, the corner of his mouth lifting. "Best not to anger it."

A tree all alone may grow hatred in its bark and moth-eaten leaves, a note handwritten in the margins of the spellbook reads. *But an entire forest can weave malice so deep and well-rooted that no safe passage can be made through such a place.* The entry was written as if it was an afterthought, but it's always stuck with me. The severity of it. The warning that a forest cannot be trusted. The trees conspire. They watch. They're *awake.*

I turn away from the mountains and ask, "Did you see someone walk around the lake this morning?"

Mr. Perkins wipes at his forehead, then holds his hand over his eyes, as though he is looking out across an endless blue sea, in search of land. "Who you out looking for?"

I'm not sure I want to say, to explain about Oliver. About all of it. So I just say, "A boy from camp."

Mr. Perkins leans heavily against the handle of the old wiry broom, like a crutch or a cane. "Are those boys bothering you?" he asks. His face hardens into a protective look. The worried arch of his gray eyebrows, the downturn of his upper lip. He's the closet thing I've ever had to a grandfather, and sometimes I think he worries about me more than my own mom does. "If those boys ever say anything to you that is less than chivalrous, you let me know."

He worries they'll call me a witch to my face. That they'll throw stones at me like locals used to when they saw a Walker roaming around the lake. He worries I might be as fragile as ice—easily shattered with a harsh word.

But I have more of my grandma in me than he thinks. "The boys haven't done anything," I assure him, offering a tiny smile.

He sticks out his chin and says, "Good, good," before shifting his shoulders back, fighting a tired, crooked spine. His left hand begins to tremble—as it often has in recent years—and he grips it with his right, to stop the shaking. "Haven't seen anyone out walking this morning, boy or deer or lost soul."

"It could have been earlier." My lips come together, feeling foolish for even asking. For following Oliver's tracks in the snow. "Maybe before the sun was up." I try to imagine Oliver sneaking out from the house in the dark, without saying goodbye, and wandering down through the trees as if he were hiding something. As if he didn't want to be followed.

He left, and a thin edge of hurt works its way under my skin. A feeling I don't want to feel. A pain I won't allow to dig any deeper into my flesh. I won't let this boy unsettle every part of me.

Mr. Perkins shakes his head. "Sorry, not so much as a jackrabbit came by this way." His eyes skip out over the lake, like he's remembering something, and he scratches at his wool cap revealing the tufts of gray hair underneath. "It can be hard to find someone in these woods," he adds, his jaw clenching, shifting side to side, "if they don't want to be found."

Fin trots off ahead through the snow past the dock—back on Oliver's trail again.

Maybe Mr. Perkins is right. If Oliver doesn't want to be found, maybe I should leave it alone. Go back to the house. I glance to the mountains where a dark wall of clouds is descending over the lake. "Another storm will probably hit within the hour," I tell Mr. Perkins. "Maybe you should head back inside."

A chuckle escapes his throat—as if the sound began in his toes and had time to gain momentum. "Just like your grandmother," he says, clucking his tongue. "Always worrying over me." He waves me off and begins shuffling back down the dock. "At my age, an hour feels like an eternity." He sweeps the snow from the edge of the dock onto the frozen ice. "Plenty of time." Instead of saying goodbye, he hums a familiar tune under his breath, a tune my grandma used to sing. Something about lost finches flying too far east, poison berries held in their talons, seeking the weary and brokenhearted. A fable song— about time being cut short, slipping through fingertips. Hearing it makes my chest ache. A strange sadness that I will never be rid of.

It makes me feel impossibly alone.

Fin heads around the shore, and I think again that maybe I shouldn't follow. But curiosity is a nagging thump inside my skull. Urging me on.

I push through the deep snow, beneath the stormy sky, until we reach a place where Oliver's tracks veer away from the lake. Where they lead up into the trees—to a place I rarely visit.

A place where the gloom of darkness never lifts. Where I've often seen human shadows wandering at twilight—specters who don't yet know they're dead. Where Walkers prefer to avoid.

The Jackjaw Cemetery.

The graveyard sits between the rocky shore and the forest—visible from all sides of the lake. A hundred years ago when the first settler died, the mourners walked a few yards down the shore and decided this was as good a place as any. They dug a hole where they stood, and this became the spot where the dead were lowered into the earth.

Fin trots into the graveyard, then stops at a row of old stones, digging his nose into the snow, pawing at the ground briefly. I don't want to be here, among the dead, but I follow Oliver's tracks to where they end.

My skin shivers. My temples itch like bugs crawling across my flesh. I kneel down beside the grave where Oliver's prints came to a stop and run my palm over the face of it, wiping away the layer of snow. I know this grave—I know most of the ones that belong to my family.

Willa Walker lies here, beneath several feet of hard-packed earth and clay.

Boys from camp often come here to the graves of Walkers. They drink beers and howl at the moon and rub their palms over the stones, making wishes. It's a place to gather, to try to frighten one another. On Halloween night, kids drive up from Fir Haven and camp out among the graves, telling stories about Walkers, casting their own made-up spells, and hexing one another.

But why did Oliver come here now, to Willa Walker's resting place—a Walker who wept into the lake and made it bottomless? Who cried more than any Walker who ever lived. Whose tears were said to be as salty as the sea. Whose nightshade could drown the world.

I hold my palm against the gravestone, as if I could feel the past within the worn surface. As if I could see Oliver standing over the grave and recall what he felt, conjure up the thoughts that clattered around inside his skull. If only that was my nightshade, to draw forth memories from objects. Then I'd always know the truth.

But no memories skip through me, and I release my hand, lowering it to my side. If I were any other Walker, I might be able to glean some hint of the past, conjure some speck of moonlight to show me what I cannot see. But instead, I feel only the cold air against my neck. The snow beneath my feet. Nothing of worth.

Still I wonder, why did Oliver come here? What was he looking for?

What does he remember?

My hands tremble, and I feel an odd swaying sensation in my chest, like the trees and the charcoal sky are wobbling, rolling like a ship about to capsize. It happened last night in my room, this morning on the porch. And now again. Like the world is teetering along the edges of my vision, about to slip out of alignment.

I blink and force the sensation away.

Beside me, Fin's nose twitches in the air and he skims past my legs, back out through the cemetery gate—trailing the footprints that circle back around to the lake. Oliver didn't wander any deeper into the cemetery; he didn't linger. He came to Willa's grave and then left.

Maybe he hated it here as much as I do.

The sad-looking graves and the bones resting beneath the soil. The constant wind coiling along my neck. The fear that I might see one of the dead, loping among the dying trees, unaware of what they are. Gray, rotted fingers reaching out for me. Pleading. Trying to draw me farther into the cemetery. *Don't be afraid*, my grandma would tell me whenever we passed by here. *All Walkers can see the dead.*

But I don't want to see one tonight, so I stand and walk to the cemetery gate.

Fin starts up the shore again, toward the boys' camp, but I call him back.

Oliver didn't try to walk down the mountain to town. He came to the cemetery, then went back to camp. And maybe it was all part of some stupid trick. Some prank. Maybe he only pretended he needed somewhere to stay last night; maybe the other boys dared him to *stay in the house of the witch girl*. To see if he'd survive another night. Usually the boys at camp leave me alone—they're just wary enough to avoid the Walker house. But maybe they thought Oliver could talk his way back in. That I'd be foolish enough to let him. And I did.

The thought makes me angry.

That perhaps none of what he's told me is true. That he remembers more from that night than he'll admit.

I leave the cemetery before I see any shadows, any figures between gravestones. Ghosts trapped in the in-between.

But Oliver was here. He was here, at Willa Walker's grave, and I don't understand why.

OLIVER

I round the lake, past the marina.

Smoke rises from the chimney of a small cabin set back from the lake, and there is movement at one of the windows—a man peering out from inside. For a moment I think he sees me, but then he steps away and the curtain falls back into place.

The shoreline cuts sharply to the right, the banks grow steep, and large rocks rise up from the edge of the frozen lake. It's deceiving, the calm surface, the layer of ice that seems solid and safe. *Nothing to fear here.* And I wonder what the lake looks like in spring, thawed and glistening under the lemon-yellow sun.

Docile and inviting. A place to cool the sweat from your skin.

I arrived at Jackjaw Camp for Wayward Boys just as autumn settled over the mountains, as the temperature began to drop and the lake started to freeze. I came later than most of the boys, who had been here for the whole summer—or longer. I was the new kid.

I was the one who didn't belong.

But in truth, I don't belong anywhere. There is no bedroom waiting for me when I leave these mountains. No one to write letters home to. No front porch or garden gate with the smell of mint and laundry drying on the line.

And without a place to call home—to call my own—I don't have anything to lose. No one to disappoint. No reason to fear what might come next. I'm on my own. And in books, those with nothing to lose often become the villain. This is how their story begins—with loss and sadness that quickly turns into anger and spite and no turning back.

I wish I could see the memories lost somewhere inside me. I wish I didn't feel bitter and frustrated. Alone. I wish this buzzing would stop grating against my skull.

I never wanted to be the villain, I never wanted to wake in the woods with the cold weaving its way along my bones, and a certainty that something bad has happened *click, click, clicking* against my eardrums. Something I can't take back.

But it's not always a path you choose—becoming the villain—it's a thing that happens *to* you.

A series of circumstances that lead you to a fate you can't escape.

Ahead of me, set back in the trees, sits the cemetery with its crumbling headstones and overgrown greenery and dying trees. It's an old graveyard, and I wonder if it's even still used. If locals still bury their loved ones here.

I step through the small metal gate, which sits bent at the hinges, into the plot of land—and I know I've been here before. The memory doesn't wash over me clear and sharp. Instead, it's a knot that binds inside my stomach—the feeling of the hard, hollow ground beneath my footsteps. The shock of air, like stepping into a cooler. Stepping into a tomb. I've felt it all before.

I walk a few paces, listening to the morning birds caw from the nearby pines, and then my feet stop. My legs refusing to go any farther. I've stood beside this row of graves before, where the ground is uneven, the headstones decaying in the winter wind. My ears begin to ring, a memory wanting to push to the surface, and I recall the name on the grave at my feet, without even needing to read it: Willa Walker.

I stood here in the dark, snow under my feet, stars smeared out by a low layer of clouds, and peered down at this same grave.

Voices rise up in the back of my mind, back of my throat. Memories scratch and claw at me, drawing blood, violent bursts like a punch to the chest.

I press my hands over my eyes and try to blot them out.

But I hear them anyway. And I know I wasn't alone that night.

The others were here too—the boys from my cabin. Rhett and Jasper and Lin. They were all here. Snow fell around us, a storm blowing in. I can taste the whiskey at the back of my throat, feel the warmth in my stomach, hear the stiff, sharp laughter.

We were here that night. *I was here.* My heart thumped too fast, my legs ached to run—I didn't want to be in this cemetery with a storm drawing close.

But it wasn't just the four of us.

There was someone else. *Another boy.*

Their laughter echoes against my ribs and I take a step back. Then another. I don't want to be here—the memories beginning to slice me open. Raw and serrated.

I reach the gate, my heels bumping into it, my boots getting stuck in the snow.

I stagger through the opening and press my hands to my temples. *A boy died that night*, Nora told me. A boy died and I vanished into the woods.

The wind howls against my ears, a scream that sounds like a warning, like the trees remember, they know who I am. I stumble toward the lake, away from the cemetery—I let my legs carry me toward camp. Anywhere that isn't here.

A boy is dead, my head repeats, the wind screeches.

And one of us who stood in this cemetery that night is to blame.

NORA

The old house facing the lake has sheltered nearly every Walker who has ever lived. Aside from the earliest few who I know little about—the ones who were said to emerge from the forest, hair woven with juniper berries and foxglove, feet covered in moss, eyes as watchful as the night birds.

Legend says we appeared as if from a dream.

Early settlers claimed they saw Walkers weaving spells into the fibers of their dresses: moonscapes and five-pointed stars and white rabbits for protection. They said Josephine Walker stitched the pattern of a severed heart into the fabric of her navy-blue dress, with a dagger splitting it in two, blood dripping down the folds of her skirt to where it met her shoes. And two days later, the boy who she loved—but who loved another—fell from his porch steps onto the hunting knife he kept sheathed at his side. They say it tore straight through his rib bone to his beating heart, slicing it clean through.

And the blood on Josephine's dress trickled down the fabric and made perfect round drops on the floor of the old house. The spell had worked.

After that, locals knew with certainty that we were witches.

Whether the story is true, whether Josephine Walker really did stitch a spell into the folds of her dress or not, it didn't matter. The Walker women would forever be known as sorceresses who should never be trusted.

And in this town, we would never be anything else.

It can be a burden to know your family history—to belong in a place so completely that you understand every hiss from the trees, the familiar pattern of spiraling ferns, the sound of the lake crackling in winter. The certainty that something isn't right, even if you can't quite see what it is.

"It's so fucking cold in here," Suzy says when I step through the front door.

She's sitting on the edge of the couch, a blanket draped over her shoulders, legs twitching.

"Fire went out last night," I say, shedding my coat and boots to bend down beside the stove.

"Where were you?" she asks.

I bite my lip, not looking at her. I don't want to tell her the truth, but I can't seem to think of a lie fast enough.

"Looking for Oliver."

"The boy you found in the woods?" Her eyebrows lift and so does her upper lip—smirking.

"He was gone when I woke up. I just—I didn't know what happened. I thought something was wrong."

"You were worried about him?" she says, her grin spreading wider.

"No." I shake my head. "I just thought it was weird that he left before the sun was up."

Suzy stops shaking and she leans forward. Her curiosity has cured the cold inside her.

I scrape a match against the edge of the stove, and it sparks to life—the brightest thing in the house—then I wait for the flame to catch on the small twigs scattered across the bottom of the stove. The glow of the fire soon spreads over the larger logs and I close the door, letting the heat build inside.

"He stayed here last night?" she asks.

I stand up and cross into the kitchen, feeling on edge—I don't want to talk about this, about him. "He didn't have anywhere else to go," I say. *Or it was all just a game*, I think. A stupid prank, and I fell for it. A dare from the other boys, who have never seen the inside of my house. Maybe they dared him to steal one of the lost items while I slept, but when I do a quick survey of the living room, nothing seems to be missing.

Something else is going on that I don't understand.

But Suzy's grin is so wide that even her ears raise up slightly. "Why doesn't he want to stay at the camp?" she asks.

"I'm not sure." *Of anything.*

"He probably just wants to stay here with you," she suggests through the broad row of her grinning teeth.

I shake my head—"I doubt it"— and pull down the box of oatmeal from the cupboard.

"Wait." Suzy sits up straighter. "Does he know what happened to the kid who died?"

My fingers touch the edge of the counter, feeling the cold tile, the divot where I once dropped a glass honey jar and chipped the surface. Glass shattered and honey dripped everywhere. Mom was

413

furious, but Grandma only cooed and sang a song about honey making the house smell sugary sweet. I think she made it up on the spot to make me feel better.

"He said he doesn't," I answer, remembering the stunned look that spread across Oliver's face when I told him. But maybe I misread everything in his cool-green eyes. Maybe I'm foolish to think anything he's told me is the truth.

"It was probably just an accident anyway," Suzy adds, sinking back into the couch cushions, suddenly bored again.

I release my fingers from the counter. "What do you mean?"

She draws her lips to one side, thinking. "That kid who died, he probably just fell from a tree or froze to death during some wilderness exercise."

"Maybe," I answer. "But if it was an accident, why is it such a secret? Why didn't the camp counselors tell everyone what happened?"

"Who knows. Maybe they wanted to call the boy's parents first. Or they didn't want to scare anyone until the police came. I don't know how this stuff works." Again, her tone seems callous. As if she doesn't want to be bothered with my questions.

But her expression drops and I realize it's not that. It unsettles her to talk about it. She's pretending it's no big deal so that it won't be. So she doesn't have to think about being trapped up here, in these unforgiving mountains, with someone who may have killed that boy.

"Can we not talk about it?" she adds, and I know that I'm right. *She's afraid.* And maybe she should be—maybe we should both be terrified.

"Sure," I agree.

But it doesn't mean I'll stop thinking about it. That the thin, acrid feeling isn't carving a gaping hole inside me. That I don't feel restless and edgy, and that I won't double-check the locks tonight before we go to sleep.

"I'm not even supposed to be here," Suzy murmurs, her voice almost a whimper. Like she's holding back tears.

The cabin roof creaks and moans as the wind outside picks up.

"The road will thaw eventually," I say, a tiny offering of hope. But with winter now settled firmly over the mountains, it could take another month, maybe more. Storms have been rolling in over the lake daily, snow piling up on roofs and driveways and the only road down the mountain. We're trapped. Hemmed in. Captive.

Suzy runs her fingers through her long, wavy hair, pulling against her scalp, and tucks her forehead against her knees, like she's a little girl playing hide-and-seek. If she can't see the darkness, then it can't see her.

She doesn't belong here.

"I can't wait to leave this place," she says, lifting her head to look out the window. I wonder if she means Jackjaw Lake, or Fir Haven—where she lives. If she wants to leave completely, escape this wild part of the country. "I hate the cold, these mountains, all of it. As soon as I graduate, I'm gone. I've been saving up." She flashes me a look, like she's divulging her deepest secret. "My parents don't know. But I refuse to end up like everyone else who gets stuck here."

I've heard it before, the desperation, the plotting to escape— it's common at Fir Haven High, especially from the seniors as the months tick down to graduation. They talk of moving out east, or down to California where it never snows, or overseas, as far away as they can get. Yet, the truth is, most will stay. They get jobs working at the lumberyard or one of the nearby Christmas tree farms that dot the valley. They get stuck. They forget about the dreams they had to travel far, far away from here.

I should tell her that I believe her, but I'm not sure that I do.

Instead, I place a pot of water on the woodstove and wait for it to boil. I add more logs to the fire.

"Will you leave after high school?" Suzy asks, and the question actually startles me—as if she cares about me, even just a little—and I swallow stiffly, unsure how to feel. No one's ever asked me this. Not even my mother, or grandmother. Because Walkers never leave Jackjaw Lake. At least not for long. We find it hard to breathe beyond this forest. The farther we go, the more it throbs inside us, our lungs gasping for air. My mother left for a whole year when she was nineteen. Traveled around Alaska, met my nameless father, got pregnant, then returned home with regret in her eyes—at least that's how my grandmother told it. Mom thought she could escape who she was by leaving these woods. But Walkers always come back. I think that's why she travels to the ocean to sell her jars of wild honey; it's a way for her to escape, to stand facing the open sea and to feel momentarily free—before returning to Jackjaw Lake.

Returning to me: the daughter who has kept her trapped here. Her burden. And a knife digs deeper into my heart every time she leaves, every time she promises to be back but I'm not entirely sure that she will. If this time she'll leave for good and never return. And I feel guilty for wanting it sometimes, for wishing she would stay away.

Perhaps it's easier: being alone. Building walls. A solitary life with no one to lose. No one to break your heart.

"No," I tell Suzy finally. "I won't leave." I don't need to escape—I'm not like her, my mom. I don't need to run away from here, I don't need to see palm trees or vast parched deserts or glittering cities at night to know this is where I belong. To know I wouldn't survive out there. I am a forest creature. I can't dwell anywhere else.

"But you could," she says. "You could get out of here. You could come visit me wherever I am. Paris maybe." Her eyes widen at the thought of it, as if she were already halfway there just by thinking it—the taste of a buttery croissant already on her lips.

I smile in spite of myself. And shake my head. "I don't think I'd know what to do with myself in Paris."

"Why not? We could eat pastries for breakfast and gelato for dinner and fall in love with whoever we want. We wouldn't even have to learn French, we could just let the boys whisper their foreign words in our ears and lose track of the year. Lose track of who we used to be."

I laugh and sink onto the couch next to her. Suzy snorts, her cheeks rosy red. I like her dream, her imaginary world where we can go anywhere and be whoever we want.

"Okay," I say, because I like this moment too much. Because I want to believe she's right and we can do these things.

For this moment, I am a girl who leaves the forest behind. A girl with a friend who convinces her to sneak out her bedroom window late one night and run far, far away from here. A true, *forever* kind of friend. One you'd go anywhere with. A friend you'll never lose—no matter what.

"We should pack tonight," Suzy says with a wink, continuing

our impossible little dream. "Make sure we have the right hats, we can't go to Paris without the perfect Parisian hats."

"Agreed," I say. "And shoes."

"And sunglasses."

I nod and laugh again.

"We'll also need new names," she says, swiveling her head to face me. "To match our disguises. We can't have anyone knowing we're two small-town girls."

"Obviously."

"Agatha Valentine," Suzy says, her eyes beginning to water with laughter. "That's my name."

I shake my head. "It sounds like a private investigator's fake name," I say.

"Or the heiress to a greeting card company."

I break into laughter.

"You'll be Penelope Buttercup," she tells me, raising an eyebrow. "The daughter of a racehorse tycoon, whose champion thorough-bred, Buttercup, won the Kentucky Derby. But not the Belmont Stakes, which was his greatest embarrassment."

"My backstory seems slightly more elaborate than yours," I point out, still chuckling.

Suzy's eyes are weeping now, and I think we have a touch of cabin fever. That feeling that once you start laughing, you can't stop—when everything becomes funny. Even though it shouldn't be. "A greeting-card heiress and racehorse royalty," she continues. "We'll be invited to all the best Paris parties." She snorts again.

We sit this way, wiping away tears, giggling the last of our pent-up laughter. And when silence finally sinks over us, the house feels too quiet. The air too still. I realize how absurd it is to be laughing, to find anything funny when we're snowed in and trapped and Oliver is missing and a boy is dead. I feel embarrassed and stand up from the couch, rubbing my hands down my pant legs.

We forgot where we were, we forgot there are still things to fear.

The pot of water on the stove begins to boil, and I carry it into the kitchen to make us oatmeal and a cup of tea. Suzy lowers her chin on her knees, and I see that her smile is gone—her thoughts have strayed back to this room, this house in the woods, the cold always looking for a way in. This place where a boy has died. It all floods back through her, and I think I see the fear that blinks out at me behind her fawn-colored eyes, Paris now impossibly far away.

We are quiet the rest of the day. Afraid to speak—afraid we'll lose ourselves to foolish, imaginary daydreams. Instead, I sit beside the front window and watch for a figure moving through the trees outside, for any sign of Oliver. But he never appears. Only a deer that picks its way through the snow just as evening sets over the forest. It walks down to the shore and paws at the surface of the frozen lake, trying to break through the ice, but something startles it—a bird maybe—and it darts back into the forest.

I look to Suzy, curled up beside the fire like a child's doll, carefully placed with her hands in her lap, and for a moment I can't be sure how much time has passed, how many hours—how many days and months—since she first came to stay with me. Since the storm hit and the road became blocked. I feel like I'm losing track of the minutes. Time playing tricks on me ever since I found Oliver in the woods, ever since my eyes met his.

Tick, tick, thud.

I stand up from the chair to shake away the feeling, to root my feet against the floor. The clock above the kitchen sink ticks, *ticks*, weaving itself along the fibers of my mind, pushing the seconds forward, *too fast*.

Tick, tick, thud.

I squeeze my eyes closed and hear the clock waver, like time is stuck between seconds. A trembling sound leaves my lips. A wheezing gasp of air.

"You okay?" Suzy asks.

My eyelids peel open and I nod. "Fine," I breathe.

"You were shaking."

I clench my hands together so she won't see, and I pull them into my sleeves. "I'm just cold," I lie.

But I know it's something else. Déjà vu or slipping time— something is happening that I've never felt before. Grandma would tell me I need rest, she'd place her hands on my forehead and make me drink tea with chamomile root and vanilla leaf. Then, while I slept, she'd creep into my dreams to see what was really wrong with me. She'd use her nightshade to fix me.

I walk to the stove and hold my hands over the heat. "Maybe we should sleep down here tonight," I say. "It'll be warmer beside the fire."

She nods, but her skin has gone pale, like she's barely listening to me. Her eyes no longer glimmer with laughter, and she chews on the side of a fingernail, staring down at the floor.

We are safe in here, I want to tell her. But that would imply we aren't safe out there, in the forest, in the mountains, in the dark.

But the truth is:

I don't know anymore.

A bone moth is following me. A boy is dead. And my mind is clattering between my ears—threatening to crack.

And maybe . . . the worst hasn't even happened yet.

"Nora! Nora!" a voice is repeating. "Wake up."

"What?"

"Get up."

My eyes whip open, white spots flashing across my vision. I'm lying at one end of the couch, facing the fire, knees pulled up to my chest—Suzy had taken up the rest of the couch.

But now she's standing over me, eyes like saucers.

"What's wrong?" I push myself up to my elbows. "What time is it?"

"Almost midnight," she answers.

I clear my throat and rub at my eyes, glancing around the dark living room where everything looks just as it did when we fell asleep.

"There's a fire," she says, lifting an eyebrow. "Down by the lake."

"What?" I stand up from the couch, letting the blanket that had been draped over me fall to the floor.

"I couldn't sleep," she adds, like she needs to explain herself. "I was standing beside the stove, trying to get warm, when I saw the light outside."

At the windows, I press my palm to the glass, where ice has formed on the thin pane. Intricate and spiny. Beyond the wall of pine trees, down near the lakeshore, a bonfire tosses sparks up into the night sky like confetti. And I can just make out the silhouette of boys backlit by the flames.

"It might be Rhett and the others," she says. "They probably snuck out of their cabin." She smirks a little and walks to my side. "We should go down there," she adds, nodding to herself, looking at me like she hopes I'll agree.

But I shake my head, the buzzing inside my ears growing louder. "They can't have a bonfire that close to the trees," I say.

Her expression drops. "Why not?"

But I'm already moving past her to the door, my pulse thudding down every vein, a drum in my chest pulled tight. Fin lifts his head from his place beside the woodstove, ears forward, gaze expectant. "Stay," I tell him and he lowers his head.

"Where are you going?" Suzy asks, trailing me with her eyes.

"Trees don't like fire," I say. "I'm going to put it out."

✴ ✴ ✴

Their shrill laughter bounces among tree limbs and echoes over the lake, sharp and grating.

I move quickly through the forest, my feet punching through the snow, fury growing in my belly with each step. I don't even have time to think this might be a bad idea when I reach the circle of trees and step into the ring of firelight. My arms are stiff at my sides, fingernails against my palms. But the boys don't notice me, not at first—I am a blur against the backdrop of pines, no different from the shadows—but then one of them glances my way, his mouth falling open. "Shit," he says, startled.

The boys all flinch in unison.

Eyes going wide.

Brains slow to react.

I can almost hear the *clunk clank* of gears grinding forward. The shock of seeing a girl appear from the forest.

I don't recognize any of them—but I rarely do. They come and go so frequently to the camp. *Temporary boys.* I look for Oliver, his too-green eyes and wavy hair, but I don't see him and my stomach tightens.

"Who the hell are you?" one of them asks—a boy wearing a thick winter hat, the kind with fuzzy flaps over the ears. Red plaid and lined with fake fur. He looks ridiculous—the hat too small, perched atop his head. And I wonder if he brought it with him or if he dug it out of the camp's lost and found.

"You can't have a fire this close to the trees," I say, ignoring his question. I can hear the pines shivering strangely around us, the fire's flames licking at the lower limbs, tasting the dull sap that has gone cold for the winter. "You have to put it out."

I wait for the boys to react, to say something, but they stand like mute dolls. Eyes shuttering open. Eyes shuttering closed.

I think of my mother, how she will march down to our neighbors' homes in summer when they have barbecues too close to sagging limbs, or when they set off fireworks in July near a cluster of dead aspens. *You'll burn the whole damn forest down*, she'll snap. She's never cared about making enemies of our neighbors. *This is our forest*, she often tells me when she returns to the house, still fuming, her cheeks flushed with anger. *They're only summer tourists.*

"You're going to piss off the trees," I continue, louder this time. In winter, a fire is less dangerous, the limbs and underbrush less flammable. But I can still hear the restlessness in the trees. The murmur of creaking branches. Fury roiling in the roots beneath our feet. I draw my shoulders back as if I might be able to make myself bigger, a beast from the forest—like the darkling crows rumored to roost at the farthest edge of the Wicker Woods—someone to fear.

But two of the boys laugh. Deep, obnoxious belly laughs, cheeks bright red like smeared thimbleberries.

I shake my head, irritated. *They don't believe me.* "Trees have a long memory," I warn, my voice like gravel. The forest remembers who carved names into their trunks, with little hearts dug in the wood; who dropped a cigarette into a clump of dry leaves and scorched their raw bark. They know who broke a limb and tore off leaves and pine needles by the handful just to start a bonfire.

They remember. And they hold grudges. Sharp branches can draw blood. Briars can snag a foot, causing a person to tumble forward and crack their head wide open.

"You a Girl Scout or something?" one of the boys asks, eyebrows raised severely, mockingly. I can tell he's holding in another burst of laughter. Reddish-blond hair crowns his head, and a slight gap between his two front teeth stares back at me. He's not even wearing a coat—only an ugly sweater with a giant reindeer's face stitched onto the front. Although I suspect the bottle of dark booze he's holding in his hand—the liquid nearly gone—is keeping him warm.

"She's Nora Walker," a voice answers behind me, and Suzy saunters into the circle of light cast by the bonfire.

Her cheeks are rosy from the cold. Her mouth curled up at one side, as if she's just revealed a perfectly timed secret.

The boys' faces turn sallow, mouths open, cheekbones slack. But they aren't staring at Suzy. They're looking at me.

I am a Walker.

A *winter witch*, a *forest witch*, a girl with madness in her veins who belongs in an institution, and all the other things the boys from camp have called me. Names that sting and hurt, but only a little.

"You're the moon girl," the boy wearing the ear-flap hat finally says.

But Suzy shoots him a look. "Don't be an idiot, Rhett."

He frowns at her—*Rhett*—the reason she snuck up to the camp in the first place. He's why she's here, why she's trapped like the rest of us. And I eye him, trying to understand why he's the boy she chose. He's cute, obviously, with a roundish face and a dimple in one cheek, but his eyes are not soft and warm like the rest of him seems. There is something callous in them. Cruel even. A boy who usually gets what he wants.

"Ignore them," Suzy says, flicking her hand in the air and brushing a bit of her long wavy hair over one shoulder. "They're just pissed they have to live way out here in these miserable mountains."

But that's not why they call me the moon girl, why they look at me with unease etched into the slopes of their brows. It's because they're afraid of me. They believe my blood is the color of the blackest night and my heart is woven with spikeweeds and vinegar. I should be feared. And most importantly, avoided.

They don't know that unlike my ancestors, unlike the Walkers of the past, there is no nightshade brimming along my edges.

Suzy clears her throat and lifts her chin. "That's Rhett." She nods to dimple-boy, and he looks at me but doesn't smile—a cool, calculating gaze. Like he's trying to see if the rumors are true. If I could turn his blood cold with a flick of my outstretched finger. And right now, I wish I could.

"That's Lin," she continues, glancing to the boy on my left, who nods but doesn't speak. The oversized navy-blue puffy coat he's wearing is like a cocoon—hood pulled up, his hands stuffed deep into the pockets. Like he doesn't plan on taking it off until spring, like he's never been so cold in his entire life. He must have been sent here from somewhere warm, like California or Florida. Somewhere where the sky is usually aqua blue and the air smells like coconut.

"I'm Jasper," reindeer-sweater boy interjects, smiling across the fire at me and holding out the bottle of dark liquid, wagging an eyebrow. "Whiskey," he says, nodding for me to take it. But I ignore the bottle.

I don't care what their names are; I didn't come down here to hang out. To drink booze, torch marshmallows, and tell childish ghost stories. "You have to put the fire out," I say again, sharper this time, my thumb fidgeting with the moonstone ring on my finger, twirling it in a circle.

Rhett sneers and picks up a stick, poking at the fire, sending more sparks up into the overhead limbs. Taunting the trees.

"Maybe we should listen to her," Lin says, lifting his shoulders in his too-big coat. "After everything that's happened—"

Rhett raises the stick in the air, a thin coil of smoke spiraling from the blackened tip. "Shut up, Lin," he says, wrapping his free arm around Suzy, who has inched closer to him. "We're not talking about that."

"Who's she going to tell?" Lin fires back, eyes cutting over to me.

Jasper waves the bottle in the air. "Anyone she wants."

"This is fucked," Lin mutters, kicking at a mound of snow at his feet, digging a small trench down to the ruddy soil, mud sticking to his shoe.

Things he wants to say, but can't, stir behind his eyes.

"The whole thing is fucked," Rhett agrees, jabbing the smoldering stick into the snow at his feet. And his eyebrows spike upward beneath his fuzzy hat, like he's giving Lin a warning to stop talking. "But it's already done."

I realize now that this isn't just a few boys who stole a bottle of booze and came down to the lake to get drunk. This is a meeting. They came to talk in secret, in private. *About what happened.*

"The road will open eventually, and then we'll have to deal with this," says Lin, lifting his gaze.

"The Brutes don't know what happened," Rhett answers coldly. I've heard this name before, *the Brutes*. It's what they sometimes call the camp counselors.

"The Brutes are idiots. It's going to be a lot worse when a detective starts asking questions," says Jasper, his jaw tensed, the bottle in his hand swaying at his side, spilling little drops onto the snow. "This was my last shot, getting sent here to this camp." His eyebrows dip together, a weakness there—a flicker of doubt and fear and uncertainty. As if he's truly afraid of what might happen to him. "If I screw it up," he continues, "my parents probably won't let me come home."

They all fall silent and the trees quiver, wind curling up off the lake and sailing into the surrounding forest, knocking snow from limbs. The wilds of this place dislike our midnight chatter, our rising voices, the flickering flame and the sparks wheeling up through the trees. We have woken it.

"You're talking about the boy who died?" I dare to ask.

They all seem to wince in unison, recoiling from my words. I swallow hard—feeling too many eyes on me. Feeling suddenly outnumbered. *This was a bad idea, coming down here.* Even the trees lean in close, listening, stirring awake from their snowy slumber.

My heart clatters. My stomach knots.

But then Rhett looks to Suzy, anger in his eyes. "What did you tell her?"

"Nothing," Suzy answers quickly, lifting her shoulders, lifting her hands, lifting both eyebrows in a show of innocence. "You never told me anything anyway. It's only what I've overheard."

"Perfect," Jasper remarks, his upper lip tugging into a sneer as he sways back slightly from the fire, his balance teetering, no longer sober. "We're all so fucked."

I shake my head. "I only know that a boy is dead."

And that Oliver went into the woods that night. That I found him in the trees. And that he walked around the lake to the cemetery yesterday and stood over Willa Walker's grave. *That something bad happened the night of the storm.*

One boy survived. One boy died.

"It was an accident," Jasper insists, looking at me from across the fire, both eyebrows raised, but his head lolling a couple degrees to the left, like he wants me to believe him. Like he's trying to convince me. *Only an accident. Nothing to see here. Nothing to report. Go about your business.*

But I don't let it go. "How did he die?"

Rhett tosses the half-burnt stick into the fire, letting it be devoured. "We said it was an accident," he growls, releasing his arm from around Suzy. Fed up. Pissed. He doesn't want me here, standing around their bonfire, asking questions.

A hush cuts over the group, and I know I've pressed it too far. Rhett stares at me like he might step past Suzy and fold his hands around my throat to shut me up. To keep me quiet. For good. A wedge of unease folds itself beneath my skin, willing me to turn and leave. But I don't move.

Jasper clears his throat, staggering to the left, like he's struggling to keep himself upright. "I vote we just keep drinking until the road clears, then we get the hell out of here." He tilts his head back and takes another gulp of the booze, eyes swaying back into his skull. "I barely notice any of it when I'm drunk."

I catch Suzy rolling her eyes. It's obvious Jasper has had too much to drink, and it's irritating even her.

Another brief quiet falls over the group, and I try to stop myself, to hold it in, but the question falls out anyway. "Notice what?"

"The voices," Lin answers quickly, in a near whisper, before Rhett can stop him. And the whites of Lin's eyes peer at me like I should know what he's talking about. Like the moon witch can surely read his thoughts. Understand the hint of something hidden behind his pursed lips.

And maybe I do know what he means.

I think about the howls I used to hear when I was little, echoing from the cemetery—weeping howls, madness howls, the howls of the dead. Just like all Walkers before me, we hear what others can't. We see.

My heart vibrates too quickly and a chill rolls down my back, one vertebra at a time. "What kinds of voices?" I ask. I need to know.

Lin's eyes blink in slow motion, chewing over the words in his mouth before he spits them out. "At night, in our cabin. We hear things."

Jasper flicks something in his free hand, and it catches my eye. It looks like a lighter, silver and shiny-sided. He stares down at the tiny flame before he flicks it closed and pushes it back into his pocket. Like he doesn't want anyone else to see it, to admire it for too long. "It's not just at night," Jasper says, coughing once. "I've heard it during the day, too. In the trees, like it's following me."

I step forward, closer to the fire. "What's following you?"

Lin shrugs and Jasper takes another drink of the whiskey. Rhett stares down at the flames—his round face a sharp contrast of light and dark shadows. But no one answers.

Maybe because they don't know. Or maybe because they're afraid of something.

Something they can't see.

Or perhaps it's all in their heads. *Snow madness*, my grandma called it. The cold can solidify itself in the mind, tendrils of ice scattering all sane thoughts. A buzzing fear that makes the eyes see things that aren't there. Hear things that don't exist. The forest playing tricks on you.

Jasper sways back from the flames, his face bright red. "It's Max's fault this happened," he declares now, each word mashed together, a slurred jumble of sounds.

"Don't blame it on Max." Rhett's jaw constricts. And this time his dagger eyes are focused on Jasper.

But my thoughts are stuck on one thing: Max.

Is he the boy who died?

"So you think we should blame Oliver?" Lin asks defensively, removing his hands from his oversized coat pockets, like he's preparing for a fight.

"It's someone's fault," Jasper counters, puffing out his chest.

But Suzy steps forward, lifting both hands in the air. "Stop it," she interjects.

430

They all stand with rigid shoulders, like strings that were pulled too tight, about to snap. They eye one another, unblinking, the air tensed in their throats.

And I wonder: Do they know *I* found Oliver, that I'm the one who brought him back from the forest? Do they know that he's been staying in my house, that he says he doesn't trust them? A part of me starts to doubt that Oliver appeared on my doorstep as a dare. A silly prank. If he was friends with these boys, wouldn't he be here with them now? At the bonfire?

"What did Oliver do?" I ask swiftly, my eyes ping-ponging between Jasper and Lin, hoping someone will tell me.

The strain in the air seems to soften, even if only just a little.

Suzy lowers her arms and even her gaze, sinking back beside Rhett.

The air between them has changed.

They refuse to answer my question, to tell me the truth. Maybe they're protecting Oliver—they don't want me to know what he did. And I can feel everyone holding their breath. The seconds stalling around us, waiting for someone to speak, to admit some truth I can't yet see. *What happened that night?* I want to scream. *What did Oliver do?*

The fire writhes and spits up more smoke, chewing apart the damp wood.

Jasper rolls his head back, looking up at the trees. "I hate these woods," he murmurs, staggering to one side, the bottle in his hand sloshing amber liquid onto his reindeer sweater. "Shit," he cries out suddenly, lidded eyes going wide as he starts to wheel backward, off-balance. He trips on something—maybe his own feet—and he careens back away from the campfire, arms waving in the air, and crashes hard against the base of a broad fir tree.

Suzy clasps a hand over her mouth, stunned.

Jasper lets out a small gasp of air and a wheezing moan. Blood trickles from his cheek—where a branch sliced his flesh as he fell— and I watch the drops fall, painting the snow red. My heart stutters in my chest.

"Fuck!" Jasper exclaims, rubbing a hand over the gash, blood smearing his palm, as pinecones tumble down from the tree, plop-ping onto the snow around him.

"You're so fucking wasted," Lin remarks, shaking his head.

Rhett laughs at this, but the trees closest to us bristle, roots turn-ing in the soil. They don't want us here.

I take a swift step forward and kick snow onto the fire, dousing it in one quick motion. Gray, ashy smoke spirals up into the sky.

"Why the hell did you do that?" Rhett barks.

"Told you that you'd anger the trees. You can't build a fire this close to the forest."

Rhett takes a step toward me, his hands clenching and unclench-ing at his sides. "Stupid witch," he spits under his breath.

But Suzy reaches out and grabs his arm, and he looks back at her. "Leave her alone," she says.

Rhett's eyebrows pull together, but his arm relaxes—as though just her touch is enough to calm his temper.

"I don't like it out here anyway," Lin admits, stepping back from the group and moving toward the trees, toward the lake.

Jasper glances down at the empty liquor bottle lying in the snow. "And I need more booze," he slurs, before crawling to his feet.

"Fine," Rhett says, his tone blunt-edged and irritated, eyes watching me a second more before turning back to Suzy. "We can go back to the cabin." He slings an arm over Suzy's shoulder. "You coming?"

She tilts her head up at him, giving up a coy little shrug, like she's considering her other options for the night. Other plans. She glances at me and slips free of Rhett's arm, saying softly so only I can hear, "You should come too."

I shake my head. "No thanks." I have zero interest in spending a single minute more with these boys.

Rhett slaps Jasper on the shoulder as he stumbles to his feet, laughing, but Jasper shrugs him off. Like he's embarrassed.

"Maybe you shouldn't go with them either," I whisper to Suzy, keeping my voice low.

Her eyes sag a little, like she's tired, or maybe it's pity I see—she feels bad for me. *Nora Walker who has no real friends.* "I'll be back before the sun comes up," she says, like she wants to reassure me.

But I don't nod; I feel only a twinge of unease. "I don't think you should trust them." Maybe I'm being paranoid, or maybe it's only because Oliver said he doesn't trust them. But I don't want her to go with Rhett, with any of them.

She smiles, lifting an eyebrow conspiratorially. "They're idiots, I know. But they're fun and I'm bored." She gives me a wink and reaches forward to squeeze my hand.

I open my mouth to tell her not to go, but I snap it shut again. She won't listen to me anyway. And she can do what she wants. She can leave and sleep in Rhett's cabin and she doesn't owe me a thing. But it doesn't stop the gnawing worry that presses at my temples. The hurt at the back of my skull.

I watch them all march off through the snow, down toward the lake, Jasper staggering behind with the empty bottle in his hand. The fire pit smolders—the air tinged with the scent of ash—and I listen carefully to the trees settling back into slumber. Their roots sinking beneath the soil, limbs swaying softly.

And I wonder if maybe it's only the sounds of the trees that have frightened the boys. If that's what they hear at night when everything is too quiet—the voices they think haunt them at camp. Or if it's something else. Something worse.

Something they won't talk about.

I feel the sinking weight of the cold, of too many questions, and I suddenly don't want to be out here in the dark—alone. I turn and start for the house, snow blowing in drifts of white.

I'm only a few yards into the tree line when I feel the shiver of someone watching.

My pulse crackles in my ears—like little pops of warning. *Someone is out there.* I stop short and peer up the slope, through the pines, ready to run. Back toward the lake. To the boys' camp if I have to.

But then I see.

Oliver.

Spellbook of Moonlight & Forest Medicine

CEECEE WALKER was born during the winter of a pale alpine moon.

Maybe it was the soft layer of snowfall muting all sound; maybe it was that her mother never wailed or wept during delivery. Maybe it was that the midwife was deaf in one ear.

But when CeeCee opened her infant eyes for the first time, she never let out a single cry. Not a whimper or a coo.

Not once did CeeCee wail for a bottle or for a diaper to be changed. It would be seven years before she spoke her first word: *abacus*. Much to her mother's confusion.

She never uttered another word of English again. When she was nine, she spoke only German, muttering things her mother and sisters could not decipher or understand. When she was eleven, she switched to French and then Russian. By twelve, she spoke Arabic and Spanish and Hindi. From age thirteen to the winter of her seventeenth birthday, she uttered only Portuguese.

Her mother once refused to hem a dress for CeeCee unless she asked for it in English. The girl would not, and she spent the remainder of that year in dresses that were too long, the skirts tearing wherever she walked.

CeeCee fell in love with a hero in a book instead of a real boy, and she dreamed of sailing the globe with him in his ship made of glass and pearls. Her nightshade allowed her to speak any language she liked, yet she remained in the forest, surrounded by those who spoke only one language. The one she disliked the most.

Later in life, she preferred the way Chinese vowels curled off her tongue, and she spoke it while walking through the autumn aspen trees reading from her favorite book.

But in her final moments, she stared up at the loft ceiling, her younger sister at her side, and whispered one last word: *abacus*. For reasons, still, no one understood.

How to Conjure a Language:

Cut a wild onion into thirds, then hold below the eyes
until they water.

Shake tulip pollen onto a white cotton cloth, then place
beneath your pillow on the last night of Lammas.

Before you sleep, speak three words in the language you
wish to know while holding your tongue with your
index finger and thumb.

Eat only oats and radishes for one week.

By the next quarter moon, the language will reside beneath
your tongue.

OLIVER

"You scared me," Nora says, striding into the house, then turning on her heels to face me. Her hair is coming away from its braid, black strands trailing over her neck, and her skin is flushed from the cold—strawberry cheeks and bone-white eyes.

"I'm sorry," I say.

She raises her eyebrows at me, like she needs more of an explanation, like the softness she felt for me the night she first found me is now gone. Replaced by something else: doubt. And maybe even fear.

Perhaps I am becoming the villain after all.

"What were you doing out there?" she asks.

My hands shiver, and I curl them into fists so she won't see. "I saw Rhett and the others sneak away from camp," I tell her. *The truth. Only the truth.* "I followed them."

"Why?" she asks, the space between her eyes punctuated by tiny lines.

"I don't trust them." I repeat what I told her last night. A puddle of melted snow collects at my feet, but I don't remove my boots. I don't know if she'll let me stay. If she wants me here at all. If *she* trusts *me.* "I saw the bonfire, and you, and I wanted to make sure you were okay," I admit.

Her eyes narrow, and she looks stricken by something, a pain I can't quite see. "You don't need to follow me," she says. "Or protect me."

"I know." And I do know. She's not weak, she's not frail or breakable or scared of much. She is the storm that tears away roofs and knocks over trees. Yet, I needed to be sure she was safe. I needed to be nearer to her. She is the only thing that dampens the feeling of the cold, the memory of the forest always at the nape of my neck. She mutes the darkness always looking for a way in.

Nora blows out a breath and crosses her arms. "Where did you go this morning?" she asks, eyebrows slanted down at the edges.

"I couldn't sleep."

Her mouth comes together in the shape of a bow, like she doesn't believe me. "I followed your footprints around the lake," she confesses. The wolf lifts its head from the floor and sniffs the air, like he smells something unfamiliar, before resting his chin back on his paws. "Why did you go to the cemetery?"

I divert my eyes away from her for the first time, away from what she wants to know. I don't know how to explain what I remember, what I felt. They are only shards of memory that slice and sting when I try to focus on them. "I think I was there that night," I say—the only thing I can be sure of.

"And you stood over Willa Walker's grave?"

A white-hot pain begins to pulse behind my eyes. "Yeah."

"Why hers?"

"I don't know." The pulse turns into a thud, slamming between my ears, an ocean spilling out from the cracks in my skull. "But I don't think I was alone."

"Were the others there, the boys who were at the bonfire tonight?" she asks.

I nod.

"And Max?" she asks, the question like the sharpened tip of a blade.

Max.

I feel myself wincing at the sound of his name.

"Do you remember him?" she prods.

I shake my head, and the heat from the fireplace is suddenly too hot, the air too thick, my lungs tightening in my chest. "No," I say aloud. A lie. *Quick and easy.*

"He died, Oliver," she says, shaking her head, and I want to tell her that I wasn't there, that I had nothing to do with it. But I can't because I don't know for sure, and the cold look in her eyes hurts worse than anything else. It hurts because I might be the villain. Heartless stare and wicked laugh and secrets to hide—stuffed deep, *deep* down inside.

She's scared of me—of who I really am, of what I might've done. And maybe she should be.

"I wish—" My voice feels like a razor in my throat, the line between truth and lie slicing me into halves. "I wish I could remember," I say at last.

But Nora presses her palms to her temples, her ring shivering in the firelight—she doesn't know what to believe.

I shouldn't be here. In her house. She shouldn't trust me.

I reach for the door and pull it open, letting the wind lash

439

against the walls, the curtains, Nora's long, whispery hair. I don't say goodbye.

But from behind me, I hear her say, "Wait."

When I look back, she's moved across the room, only a couple of paces away. "Where are you going?" she asks.

"I don't know."

She bites her lip and looks to the floor. I don't want her to tell me to leave, but I know that she should. She should push me outside and lock the door and ask me to never come back.

Her eyes lift, hazel dark, and even though they give away a rim of uncertainty, she says, "You can stay here. You can stay as long as you want."

I shake my head. But she cuts me off before I can protest.

"It's my house." She swallows. "And I want you to stay."

The thud of my heart is too loud—loud enough to break my chest open, loud enough for her to hear.

And when I look at her, an ache forms inside me, a nagging itch I try to ignore. I should tell her the truth: that I remember just enough from that night to know that she's right to be afraid. That nothing good happened that night, in the cemetery, beside the lake. That there are lost memories buried inside me that frighten me— that I never want to see.

I should tell her these things, but I also want to stay—more than anything—I want to stay here with her. I don't want to be alone. I don't want the crack inside me to widen, for the ocean of loneliness to creep in. I don't want to drown.

And I don't want her to drown either. To suffocate on the same thing: the hurt we both keep stuffed deep inside.

So I keep my mouth shut.

I close the door, and the curtains settle back against the wall; her hair falls back to her shoulders. My hands tremble just a little, and I step toward her. My breathing *hitches, claws, scrapes* against my ribs. My fingers want to reach out for her, touch the palm of her hand, the long line of her forearm, the curve of her collarbone, where her skin is pink and flushed. I want to disobey the beating of my own heart, telling me to leave.

I want to let myself feel this thing I don't understand. The wings in my throat and the itch at my fingertips.

I don't want to be the villain.

But then the front door swings open and someone brushes past me into the house, smelling of booze and rose perfume.

NORA

Suzy strides into the living room, coat zipped up to her chin, snowflakes dusting her shoulders and hair.

"It's so damn cold," she proclaims, slamming the door shut and brushing past Oliver to the woodstove. Her cheeks and nose are red, and she holds out her hands, warming them over the fire.

I look to Oliver, but his expression is slack.

"What happened?" I ask Suzy. "I thought you were staying at the camp?"

"Rhett's a jerk," she says, brushing the hair from her forehead with a flick of her hand, and I can tell she's been drinking. Maybe they found another bottle of alcohol in the camp kitchen, and they've been taking shots back at the boys' cabin. "He said I shouldn't trust you." Her eyes tick to mine, bloodshot and watery. "He said we'll get in trouble because of you, because you know too much."

The room feels suddenly airless, vibrating along my periphery. I glance at Oliver again, but he's taken a step back. He barely even looks my way—like his own thoughts are clouding his vision.

"I don't know anything," I tell Suzy, facing her again.

But she continues talking, like she doesn't even hear me. "I told

442

him he's an asshole and he can sleep alone tonight." She waves a hand dismissively in the air, her head rolling to one side, like she can barely keep herself upright. I'm surprised she stood up for me—surprised and grateful. Maybe she does think we're friends. And for a moment I want to reach out and hug her.

"Men are jerks," she blurts out, and her eyes swivel around the room, blinking on Oliver. I wonder if she's going to say something to him—call him a jerk too, say that he's just like all the rest. But then her gaze wheels back to the woodstove, like she's going to be sick.

"Maybe you should sit down," I say, touching her shoulder.

She flinches away and swivels herself toward the couch, plops onto the cushions, and pulls the blankets up to her throat in one swift motion. She closes her eyes and mutters, "Sing me a song, Nora." Like she's a little kid who wants a bedtime story. Tea and cookies and a kiss to the forehead.

"Suzy?" I ask softly, but a soft snore escapes her mouth. She's already asleep.

Her hair lies draped across her cheekbone, her mouth slack, and I wonder if she'll remember any of this by morning. If she'll remember what the boys said.

"I'm sorry," Oliver says behind me. He moves closer, and just his proximity makes my stomach ache. Deep and strange. Sailor's knots inside my belly.

"For what?"

His voice is low when he speaks, like he doesn't want to wake Suzy—but I doubt she'll be stirring anytime soon. "For what those guys said."

"I'm used to people talking about me," I tell him, shaking my head and letting the side of my mouth tug into a smirk. I want him to see that it doesn't bother me, that I'm stronger than he might think. But still, I touch my grandmother's ring and let my mind click over everything the boys said at the bonfire, how they talked about voices in their cabin, how they weren't sure who to blame: Oliver or Max.

They're just paranoid, I think.

They're hearing things that aren't really there.

"I don't need to stay here," Oliver says, his voice cautious, as if he doesn't really mean the words he says. His eyes stray to Suzy, now occupying the couch—the place where he's slept the last two nights. "I can find somewhere else."

It's odd how easily you can fool yourself into believing there is nothing to fear. How easily you can look at a boy you hardly know and trust every word that leaves his lips. Maybe I am a fool. Or maybe the buzzing, tenuous feeling in the center of my chest, the fragile stutter of my heartbeat, means something. Maybe there is truth in that feeling.

A feeling I shouldn't ignore.

A feeling I don't want to.

"No," I say at last, his gaze on me a moment too long, making it hard to breathe. "You can sleep in the loft."

His eyes soften and the room starts to quiver, walls melting from the edge of my vision, the clock in the kitchen clicking too loud. Oliver blurs out of focus, and I think about him standing in the trees, watching me at the bonfire. He followed the boys from camp because he was worried about me. And I'm not sure how to feel or what to say, but my heart is spurring against my ribs, causing little fits of pain.

I look away from him, afraid the house is going to splinter around us, afraid the clock on the wall will cease to tick.

"You all right?" he asks, touching my arm, my hand.

But when his eyes meet mine, all the words dissolve on my tongue, catch inside my teeth, so I only nod. *Fine, fine, fine.* Everything is fine. My head doesn't feel like it's going to cleave in half and let all my thoughts spill out onto the floor. The house doesn't feel like it's going to cave in. Time doesn't feel like it's going to shatter.

I'm fine.

He releases my hand and I walk to the front door to lock it—sensing a storm building outside. Not from the mountains, but from something else.

A storm made of fury and spite woven inside reckless boys' hearts.

I light a candle—a ritual now—and walk to the stairs. The house no longer swaying. The clock no longer a drum against my ears.

Without a word, Oliver follows.

Maybe he belongs here now, with me, inside this house.

No one has ever belonged to me before—not really.

In the loft, my bed is still unmade, pillows slumped and wrinkled from the previous night. And Oliver stands at the top of the stairs, scanning my room, the stacks of books on the floor, while Fin plods past him—making a low *huff* sound as he settles onto the rug at the foot of the bed. "I'll sleep on the floor," Oliver says, eyeing the place where Fin has curled into a ball, nose tucked under his tail.

"No, there's plenty of room," I say, hastily straightening the quilt and pillows. But Oliver still doesn't move any farther into my bedroom, like he might turn and retreat down the stairs. "It doesn't have to be weird," I say, lifting an eyebrow. "It's a bed, that's all. A place to sleep."

He smiles a little, then walks across the room and looks out the window at the snow-covered lake while I shed out of my coat and sweater. I wonder what Mom would say if she knew a boy was in my room. I've never even come close to having a boyfriend, or even a friend who slept over. She would likely smile—pleased that she was raising a normal daughter after all, and not the girl my grandmother wanted me to be.

"Why do they call you a witch?" he asks, still facing away.

I sit on the edge of the bed, a little caught off guard by the question, and begin plaiting my hair into a braid—a woven pattern my grandmother would teach me each night, until I got it right. "Because they don't know what else to call me."

The dull glow of the moonlight barely touches his skin, his silhouette draped in shadow. "Are you?" he asks, looking back at me. "A witch?"

I release my hair and touch the edge of the bedspread, playing with the hem. No one has ever asked me this—not to my face. But there is no malice in his tone, not even curiosity, it's something else. A calmness, like he is only asking me my favorite color. My middle name. My favorite book.

"My family is older than witches," I tell him, crossing my hands in my lap, knowing I'm revealing more than I've ever said to anyone. "Older than the word itself."

"But you can do things," he says, his voice slightly strained, like this is the root of what he's asking—what he's been trying to get at all along. "You made that bag of herbs for me."

"That wasn't real magic," I say, shifting my eyes away, feeling strange talking about this—*about magic, about what I really am.* Things I've never talked about with anyone who wasn't a Walker. "That was only medicine."

Grandma often talked about the *old way.* How our ancestors spoke to the moon and slept under the trees and didn't fear anything. How they used magic from their fingertips as if it were as common as whipping butter for toast.

But the *old way* was lost. Spells forgotten—the ones not written down in the book. The heartiest kind of magic slipped away. Not for any single reason, merely because time dilutes what once had been strong. Only our nightshades remain now, that glimpse of magic inside each of us that recalls what we are. The parts of us that are still witches.

Walkers began using herbs and small blessings, instead of con-juring dark spells to hex those who had done us wrong. *We merely will the moon to bend in our favor*, Grandma would say. *We no longer command it.*

Oliver steps out of the moonlight and moves closer to the bed. "So you can't undo something that's already been done?"

"Like what?"

"Like someone who's dead."

I swallow and my fingers grip the edge of the bed, nails digging into fabric. *I know what he's asking.* "Like Max?" I ask. And I wait for him to answer, but the words are lodged like little thorns in his throat. "I can't bring anyone back from the dead," I tell him. "No one can."

That kind of magic was used by a different kind of witch, an old form of witchery that's been lost almost entirely. And for good reason.

The dead should never return from where they've been.

What they've seen.

Oliver walks across the room, his footsteps stirring up lavender-scented dust, and he sits at the end of the bed, pressing his hands against the bones around his eyes, and my heart sinks in a way I didn't expect it to. He thought maybe I could fix this, bring back the boy who died. And I suddenly feel worthless that I can't—that I can't undo what's been done. That I'm not *that* kind of witch. The kind he wants me to be.

A familiar feeling of dread rises up inside me, the feeling that I'm hardly a Walker at all. Only in name. But lacking any true magic—lacking a nightshade.

"How did he die?" I ask, I try. Maybe he knows, maybe he remembers. Maybe he will finally say. *And maybe I don't want to hear the answer.*

"I don't know," he says. And when his chin lifts and his eyes sink into mine, I see the forest reflected back in them. I see the dark, clouded sky and the slow slippage of time. "I want to remember," he says, a hint of unease running through him. "But it's like the memories have been replaced by something cold, like I'm back in the forest and I can't see a thing." Emotion catches in his voice, and I know he's telling the truth. He might be lying about other things, but not about this.

"Sometimes our minds want us to forget," I say, my own voice sounding raw, like gravel along the banks of the lake. And there is a hurt growing inside me, expanding. *My own things I'd like to forget.* Like the day my grandma died and left me alone. Left me with a mom who doesn't want me to be what I am. "It's less painful that way."

He stares at me, and there is sorrow in him—a feeling I understand. *I know.* I want to reach out and touch him, place my hand on his. On his cheek, on his chest. I want to tell him it's going to be okay. But the moment slips past. Gone.

"My grandmother used to say that our dreams washed away the day," I tell him, words that often soothed me. "That sleep was the best remedy for most things."

I pull back the blankets and slip into bed. Oliver walks around to the other side, then hesitates before lying down beside me, and I wonder what he's thinking, his breath rising heavy in his lungs, his eyes lidded like he's trying not to look directly at me. As if I were a distraction—one he couldn't trust.

I blow out the single candle on the bedside table, and in a blink, the room feels impossibly dark. Even the moonlight fades beyond thick clouds. The mattress shifts when Oliver lowers his head onto the pillow, and he stares up at the ceiling, at the odd assortment of things—ferns and bits of tree bark and green, tacked and draped above my bed. I feel embarrassed: They are childish things. Things collected by a little girl who believes in luck and mossy dreams.

It occurs to me that my house is filled with strangers: with a boy who I found in the forest and a girl who up until a few days ago would have probably laughed at me if I'd asked to borrow a pencil in history class. And I like the feeling: a house brimming, bursting. Filled with so many beating hearts.

For the first time in a long time, I don't feel alone.

The loft fills with the rise and fall of our breathing, and the stillness in between. And I feel wholly at ease, like Oliver belongs in my bed, like he's slept here a hundred times before and it's just how it's always been.

But then the silence starts to itch at me, my mind unable to sleep, and I feel Oliver shift beside me—still awake.

"Why did you get sent to the camp?" I ask, a question I've wondered about since I first found him in the woods. But I've been too afraid to ask. Too afraid to hear the answer.

His breathing changes, turns shallow, and I can just barely make out the line of tension along his jaw. "My uncle sent me here, didn't want to deal with me anymore. . . ."

There is a pause at the end of his statement—the hollow place where more words should be. Where his thoughts broke in half.

"You've always lived with your uncle?" I ask carefully, afraid maybe I'm asking things he won't want to answer.

He waits so long before he speaks I'm afraid he never will. But then he clears his throat. "No. My parents died a year ago—" His voice catches, then re-forms. "It was a car accident. Two miles from our house."

A sharp pain pings through my chest. *I never should have asked.* "I'm so sorry," I say, but my words sound useless—itty-bitty things that slide right off the skin like oil on water. Never being absorbed.

"I hardly knew my uncle; he never wanted me to live with him," he continues. "So he sent me here." He scrubs a hand through his hair, then drops his hand to his side. "Even if I escape this place, I have nowhere to go."

I almost say *sorry* again but catch myself. He doesn't want to hear *sorry*. I hated the way it sounded when people said it to me after Grandma died, the pity dripping off their tongues. The awful, mournful look in their eyes. The *sorry*s didn't change anything.

Oliver wants to hear that wrongs can be made right. That moments in our past can be undone. That I am a Walker and I can bring back the dead.

But I can't fix anything. The past is already decided.

I close my eyes, and I feel painfully hollow. My own emptiness engulfed by his, becoming the same. We are both alone. Both on our own. I squeeze my eyes tighter and pretend everything is different. I pretend Oliver never went missing the night of the storm. I pretend I never found him inside the Wicker Woods. I pretend he belongs at Jackjaw Lake, just like me, that his parents never died and he grew up a few houses down the shore and we've known each other our whole lives. I pretend we used to wade out into the shallow water in summer, me in my yellow ruffle swimsuit, he with his long boyish arms tanned by the sun, and he'd try to pull me under the water, laughing until our lungs ached. Refusing to go inside even once the watermelon-tinted sun had set. I pretend he was my first kiss.

I pretend I can keep him forever, my found thing.

I reach out and touch Oliver's hand, winding my fingers through his. And his hand flexes softly against mine—he doesn't pull away.

Don't let go, I think. Or we both might drift away. We both might forget what's real. We'll forget how slippery time can be—how ruthless and mean. If you blink, you might miss everything.

His breathing grows heavy, sleep drawing him under, and my wretched, traitorous heart burns a hole in my chest. I close my eyes and see only the moth—wings against the window, searching for a way in. I close my eyes and see Oliver lying in the trees, snow falling over him, burying him alive.

I slide across the floral-printed sheets, only inches away from him, our fingers still woven together. And I wish I could slip into his dreams—just like my grandmother could. I wish I could see what he sees.

Then I'd know for sure, the secrets he keeps.

Spellbook of Moonlight & Forest Medicine

IDA WALKER was born at the last hour, on the last night of the wolf moon, with chalky-blue eyes and a ribbon of blond hair that later turned black.

She sucked her thumb until she was nine and she often fell asleep in unusual places: the crook of a dogtooth elm tree, a patch of stinging nettle, between the paws of a mother wolf, on the roof of the old house during a rainstorm. Ida could sleep anywhere, even while floating on her back in Jackjaw Lake.

When she was eleven, she saw her first dream that was not her own.

She never intended to spy, but every dream she saw from then on didn't belong to her. When Ida closed her eyes, she fell headfirst into the dreams of others while they slept. She learned to decipher those dreams with startling accuracy, but she knew that most people would not understand, or grasp, the true meaning of their dreams, so she told them fanciful fairytales instead.

Every full moon she brewed crowberry tea with spinster lemon, and she wove stories together as tightly as the braid down her back.

She fell in love only once—to the man who gave her a moonstone ring that reflected the slate-blue color of her eyes, the same man who gave her a daughter who could charm wild honeybees.

Ida Walker died on a warm autumn night, the bone moth at her window.

And no regrets in her heart.

To Brew Crowberry Tea:

One handful crowberries—picked during the coldest night

One pinch poppy flowers, star anise, licorice, clover

Steep all night during a full moon. Drink before sunrise

    in a teacup held away from the nearest clock.

NORA

I want to trust him.

I don't want to do what I'm about to do.

But there are things—*at least one thing*—he's not telling me.

I watch the swell of his chest, the shiver of his skin while he sleeps as if he were recalling the forest, the snow, the night I found him inside the Wicker Woods. It haunts him still.

And when I'm certain he's really asleep, I slip from bed, pressing my feet silently to the wood floor. I creep across the loft, through shadows and long patches of moonlight, avoiding the places where I know the floorboards give way an inch or two and would let out a soft shudder. Fin breathes softly from the floor. The whole house is sunken into dreams—except me.

I kneel down by the small chair beside the window, where Oliver stripped out of his coat, and feel along the thick fabric until I find a pocket. I slip my hand inside. And find nothing. My fingers trail along the collar, finding the other pocket filled with a few small twigs and broken bits of pinecone—not uncommon after tromping through the wilderness. I settle back on my heels. *Maybe there is nothing to find.*

Maybe I shouldn't look through his things. I would be furious if I found him snooping through my closet, my bedside table. A soft prick of guilt nags at me. But I touch the coat again, the heavy canvas, finding the main zipper and then sliding my hand along the interior of the coat. Sure enough, there is a hidden pocket, smaller than the others, but tucked high along the chest. I feel for the opening and reach inside. Something small and soft meets my fingertips. I pull it out and hold it in my palm: the pouch of herbs I gave him. I squeeze it in my hand, the scent of cloves and cardamom and lily now long gone.

He's kept it all this time—inside his coat, close to his chest.

I hear him breathing in the bed, and I sink back onto my heels, feeling stupid for looking. For thinking I would find some clue, some small thing to prove him guilty or not. A liar or not. Instead, all I've found is the pouch of herbs I gave him—as if he couldn't part with it, even when its potency wore off.

Wishing I had never snooped in the first place, I slide the pouch back into the pocket. But I feel something else.

Smooth and cold.

I pull my hand back out and watch a small chain unravel, something bulky and shiny at one end.

It makes a soft *clink* sound, and I quickly cup my palms over it, to keep from waking Oliver. My knees ache on the hardwood floor, but I shift closer to the window, opening my palms like a clam unveiling a single pearl inside, and there, resting in my hand, is a silver pocket watch. The chain is broken—one of the links bent, the rest of the chain missing. But a soft ticking sound emanates from inside, the hidden gears clicking forward, tiny mechanisms fluttering in soft unison. It still works. I run my thumb over the glass, peering in at the white face of the watch, the gold hands keeping time.

It's a simple pocket watch, skillfully crafted. And I wonder if it belonged to Oliver's father or his grandfather. A memento maybe. Or perhaps he found it in the Wicker Woods—a lost item he plucked from the forest floor.

I turn the watch over, feeling the weight of the metal in my palm, gauging its worth, its value. It's not particularly old, but it's well made. Crafted by someone who knew what they were doing. I tilt the watch so I can see it more clearly in the moonlight. Lacelike designs are etched across the back, careful and delicate. But that's not all. There are letters, too. A name. This was made for someone. A gift—a birthday present maybe.

It reads: *For Max.*

I drop the watch from my hand and it hits the floor with a blunt *thud*.

Shit, shit, shit.

My eyes cut over to the bed where Oliver has stirred, shifted onto his side, but he doesn't wake. Doesn't sit up and see me at the window—picking up something from the floor that doesn't belong to me.

Something that doesn't belong to him, either.

He didn't find this watch in the woods.

It belonged to Max. The boy who is dead.

Lies sift along the floorboards like mice searching for a place to nest.

I touch Fin gently behind the ear, so I won't startle him. His eyes open in one swift motion and I whisper, "Come on." He rises and stretches on the rug before plodding after me to the stairs. His paws make soft *clip clip clip* sounds down each step, and I cringe at the noise, hoping no one will wake.

In the living room, I pause beside the door and look to Suzy, one arm draped off the edge of the couch, her face pressed into a cushion, snoring. She won't be waking anytime soon.

But looking at the soft slope of her nose, the gentle flutter of her russet eyelashes, I wonder suddenly if she knows more than she's saying. If little secrets bounce along behind her eyelids. Was she there that night, when the storm blew over the lake and they gathered in the cemetery? Was she there with the others?

A hard wedge of mistrust slams through me. *Two strangers in my house.* And maybe I can't trust either of them.

I don't take a breath, I don't swallow the feeling of dread expanding in my chest. I turn for the door and run out into the pale dawn light.

For the first time since the storm, for the first time in a very long time, I actually wish my mom were here. Someone I can trust, who can see things clearly.

But I know this is a stupid thought. Mom would never believe me, never believe all the things that have happened. She would look at me with numbness in her eyes. Indifference. She wouldn't be able to make anything right.

So I sprint down to the lake, ducking through the trees—heading toward the only place that feels safe.

I veer up along the shore, deep inhales and ragged exhales burning my lungs, and I glance back over my shoulder to see if Oliver has woken and come to look for me. If Suzy is standing among the pines. But I'm still alone, crashing through the snow. Gasping for air. Legs burning.

The light changes around me—becomes pale and milky. Night transforming to day. Yet, the morning birds don't wake and chatter from the limbs. It's too cold. The world too silent. Or maybe they're too afraid. *A Walker girl stirs among the trees with fury in her eyes—safer to stay quiet. Safer to stay hidden.*

Thin ribbons of smoke rise up from the chimney of the small cabin beside the boathouse, and a candle gleams from one of the windows. Mr. Perkins is awake.

I hurry up the shallow steps to the porch, my breathing still sandpaper. And I knock on the door.

Breathe in, breathe out.

I flash a look over my shoulder, but the lake is still silent, a few soft flakes swaying down from the sky, remnants of last night's storm. Late to arrive.

There is no sound from the other side of the door, and my body begins to shake, the cold settling beneath my skin. And inside my coat pocket is the silver watch—I can feel it ticking, the tiniest of vibrations against my palm, becoming a part of my own heartbeat. I stole it. And when Oliver wakes . . . how long until he realizes it's gone?

I knock again at the door, and this time I hear the shuffling steps of old Mr. Perkins inside. Making his way slowly across the creaking wood floor—*too slowly*. A moment later the door swings inward, and Floyd Perkins peers out at me with the keenness of a bird, sharp eyed and watchful. "Morning," he says, blinking as a winter wind blows through the open doorway.

"Can I come in?" I ask. My voice sounds broken, worse than I expected it to.

The wrinkles around his eyes draw together and he grumbles—

not out of irritation, but rather the stiffness of old joints as he pushes the door wide. "The wolf stays on the porch," he says, giving Fin a quick glance. Mr. Perkins has always thought Fin was too much wolf and not enough dog. *He's a wild animal,* he said to me once. *I don't trust anything that could kill me in my sleep.*

Fin obeys and lowers himself down to the porch—he prefers to be outside in the cold anyway, instead of in the cramped oven of Mr. Perkins's cabin.

I step through the doorway and the roaring wave of heat is almost unbearable, the scent of smoke filling my nostrils, beads of sweat already rising across my forehead.

"Awful early to be out in the cold," Mr. Perkins says, ambling across the living room and settling into one of the old rocking chairs beside the fireplace. "Only those looking for trouble or trying to escape it are out this early."

I glance around his cabin, a perfect square. Barely enough space to fit a kitchen, a living room, and a bedroom at the back. There is no light glowing from the tall metal floor lamps in the corners; only the fireplace casts an eerie flicking glow across the walls and ceiling. Mr. Perkins built the home when he was still young and had a strong back, after he found gold in the Black River. Unlike most miners who fled the mountains when the gold ran out or their fear of the woods grew too deep—the cold whisper of the trees always against their necks—Floyd Perkins stayed. I suppose he belongs here just as much as Walkers do.

"Is your phone working?" I ask hastily, even though I'm certain that if mine isn't working, neither is his.

He eyes me and I know I must look panicked, my jaw clenched

so tightly that a headache stabs at my temples. "Still nothing," he answers.

I scratch my fingers up my arms and watch the flames chew apart the logs inside the stove. A soothing sight. Familiar. *If you have a fire, then you have something*, Grandma would say.

"Why do you need a phone? Did something happen?" Mr. Perkins's gray eyebrows flatten.

I've come because I don't know where else to go. But with Mr. Perkins looking at me with concern in his eyes, waiting for me to explain why I'm here, the reasons feel too jumbled up. My thoughts too scattered.

"I found a boy in the woods," I say, rubbing my palms together over the flames even though sweat gathers along my spine.

His gaze narrows and he leans forward in his chair. "Which wood?"

The air feels too thick, the scent of woodsmoke sticking to the walls and in my hair. I let my gaze sway around the room, to a row of handmade picture frames along one wall—each filled with a different species of fern or wildflower or insect, the scientific name for each handwritten at the bottom. "The Wicker Woods," I tell him.

"You found him alive?" he asks, tapping his slippered foot against the floor. Mr. Perkins has never been inside the Wicker Woods—he knows better.

"He was hypothermic," I say, "but alive."

He stops tapping his foot. "How long was he out there?"

"A couple weeks, I think."

"Ah." He nods with the slow cadence of a man with all the time in the world—to sit and ponder, to assess the strangeness of my discovery. "Perhaps the woods grew fond of him. Decided not to devour him after all." His eyes shimmer like he's making a joke. But I don't laugh.

"And there's something else," I say, pushing my hands back into my coat pockets, watching the fire toss sparks out onto the rug, expecting one of them to ignite—to catch on the curtains and torch the whole tinderbox in seconds. "I think a boy has died."

His jaw makes a circular motion, but he doesn't speak.

"I found his pocket watch," I continue, pulling out the watch and holding it by the broken chain, letting it hang in the air for Mr. Perkins to see. He squints but doesn't make a move to touch it, to reach out for it. "Maybe he went into the woods," I suggest. "Maybe both boys did, and only one returned." Maybe Oliver and Max went into the Wicker Woods that night and something happened, something Oliver would like to forget. "Maybe—" I begin again, "one of them is to blame for the other's death."

My fingers tremble, and I worry I might drop the watch, so I place it back in my pocket. My head thuds and my vision darkens, making it hard to focus, to see anything clearly—to be sure of what I know from what I don't.

"You found the watch in the woods?" Mr. Perkins asks. I can tell he's starting to worry, the creases deepening along his jaw, around his weary, tired eyes.

"I found a boy," I clarify. "And he had the watch hidden in his pocket."

"And you think he did something to the boy who died?"

I pull my lips in, not wanting to answer.

Mr. Perkins leans forward, his hands quivering in his lap, arthritis in the joints. "Many miners died in these mountains over the years," he says, facing the flames. "A felled tree once crushed a miner's tent, flattened him where he slept. Some miners broke through the ice on the river and drowned, some got lost in those woods and froze to death, their bodies recovered in spring. But mostly, the men killed one another over gold claims and theft. Those woods up there are dangerous," he says, nodding up at me, knowing that I understand, "but not as dangerous as the men themselves."

I know what he's saying: There is more to fear in men's hearts than in those trees.

He leans back in the chair, his eyes clouding over, like he's drifting into a dream or a memory. "Some say they still wander the lake and the forest, lost, not realizing they're dead."

I feel cold suddenly, even though sweat drips from my temples. I think of the boys at the bonfire, how they said they heard voices, something in their cabin, in the trees. Not the voices of miners, but maybe something else. *Someone else.*

Max.

"Those early settlers were superstitious," he adds, circling around a point he's trying to make but not quite getting there. "They would make offerings to the trees, to the mountains." He taps a finger against the chair, his expression turned serious. "They thought it would appease the darkness that lived in the Wicker Woods. They dropped their most precious items into the lake, letting the water swallow them up. They believed the lake was the center of everything, the beating heart of the wilderness."

"Did it work?" I ask, feeling like a little girl asking about a bedtime story, a fairytale that was never real. "Did it calm the woods?"

His eyes squint nearly closed, mulling over the question. "Perhaps.

Who's to say where a bottomless lake might end." He pushes up from the rocking chair and walks to one of the front windows, looking out at the frozen lake, a cluster of empty summer homes, and a boys' camp across the way. "But you can't always blame the Wicker Woods," he adds, "for the bad things that happen."

I push my hands into my pockets and look past him through the window, at an ocean of spiky green trees for as far as I can see. And beyond, the snow capped mountains poking up into the dark clouds. A place that is rugged and wild. Where bad things happen.

A boy goes missing.

A boy dies.

Who's to blame?

The morning sun breaks through the clouds, and for a brief moment it passes through every window in Mr. Perkins's home—illuminating every dark corner, every dust mote tumbling across the wood floor, the stacks of books lining the walls, the old picture frames hanging from bent nails, the cobwebs sagging between the rafters like silky ribbons.

I had hoped for something in coming here, but I'm not sure what. Answers to the wrong questions, answers that Mr. Perkins doesn't have. If my grandmother was alive, I would go to her and she would draw me into her broad arms and hum a melody only she knew until I drifted off to sleep. And in my dreams, she would whisper answers to all the things I needed to know. When I woke, my heart would feel clear and raw and new, a feeling like being untethered. A dizziness that made you want to laugh.

But she is gone and my mom is not here and all I have is Mr. Perkins.

I am alone.

"Thanks," I tell him, my voice solemn. I walk through clouds of heat to the front door and pull it open. I feel weighted and worthless and adrift. A Walker who doesn't know what she should do next. Who to trust.

Before I can escape out into the cold, Mr. Perkins clears his throat, now standing behind me. "A moth follows you," he says.

My eyes lift to see a white bone moth skimming along the porch roof.

My heart stills in my chest—afraid to move.

"I've seen it many times now," I say softly, the cold cutting through me. The truth I can't avoid.

"And you know what it means?" he asks from the doorway.

My jaw clenches, and when I open my mouth to speak, I feel the stiff edge along each word. "Death is coming."

Mr. Perkins's hands begin to tremble again. "It means you don't have much time."

I swallow and look back at him, his expression grim, as if I were the one who was closer to death, not him. A sharp chill settled in the air between us.

"Be careful," he says at last, turning his gaze to the fireplace—nothing else to be said. That could be said. My fate already decided.

Death is coming for me.

I watch the moth wheel away into the forest beyond Mr. Perkins's home, vanishing into the rays of sunlight peeking through the dense trees. "Leave me alone," I hiss up at it, but it's already gone.

Death lingers. Death is already here.

OLIVER

The pocket watch is gone from my coat.

Nora found it. She knows.

I stand at the window, my heart caving in, and I know nothing will be the same now. She fled the house. Escaped into the dull morning light. And I lied to her. Told her I didn't know how Max died, didn't remember. But I had his watch in my pocket.

And she'll never trust me again.

The wolf is gone too, and when I walk downstairs, Suzy is still passed out on the couch, snoring softly, muttering to herself. I leave through the front door, because I don't belong here. Not now. Maybe I never did—only fooled myself into believing it. Fooled myself into thinking I could sleep in her home, in the loft, the scent of her pillows like jasmine and rainwater, the feeling of her hand in mine. That I could stay and my memories wouldn't find me. I could stay and the dark would be kept at bay. *Always the dark. Knocking at my skull, finding a way in.*

Nora's footprints pass through the trees, a trail in the snow. But I don't follow.

I walk around the lake, every step heavy, each inhale a pain in my chest. I should have told her the truth—but the truth is gray and pockmarked, no clear lines separating it from the lies, gaps still marring my memory of that night. My mind an untrustworthy thing.

But the watch was in my coat when I woke in the woods.

And it can only mean one thing.

I reach the boys' camp and pass the mess hall—everyone already inside for breakfast. They won't return to their cabins until after dinner, when they will sneak cigarettes and eat the candy bars they keep hidden under their mattresses, where the counselors won't find them. But the counselors are lazy. They've barely taken notice of my return and then immediate disappearance again. I've spent only one day in my bunk since I returned from the woods, and not once did a counselor come to speak to me, to haul me off to the main office where the camp director could ask me questions about where I've been. About where I was the night a boy died. They've stopped caring.

Or maybe the other boys told them a story, a lie. Said I ran away again. Said I made it down the mountain.

The fresh layer of snowfall from last night dusts the landscape, and I make tracks through the trees until I come to cabin number fourteen, and slip inside.

The room is as unremarkable as it was the last time I was here. But this time I've come looking for something: a memory maybe, something to explain the black spots in my mind.

Something to make all the pieces fit together.

The cabin smells of damp earth, and I walk to the bunks, willing my mind to remember the rest, to remember what happened that night. The cemetery. Jasper and Rhett and Lin. And Max was there too—he was there and we were all drinking. We were laughing about something, our laughter ringing in my ears. A bell that won't stop.

I climb the wood ladder and lie on my bunk. Lin's bunk below mine. And on the opposite wall, Jasper's and Rhett's. *Four boys to a cabin.*

But where did Max sleep? Not here with us—somewhere else.

In a different cabin?

I roll onto my back and squeeze my eyes closed. *Why does my brain refuse to remember? What is it blotting out?* The truth about what happened. About what I did.

A hole is widening in my chest: the place where I have ruined everything. Where I lied to her. Where I have nothing left to lose.

Nothing to go back to.

No one to trust. *No one who trusts me.*

I open my eyes and peer up at the low ceiling—at all the little knife marks, the divots and slashes that form words and images and meaningless symbols. The face of a rabbit etched into the wood stares back at me. Several trees carved along the lowest, sloping part of the ceiling, crude lines for every branch, create a tiny forest. Every cussword you can think of has been slashed into the boards. Permanently preserved. Boys' names crisscross the wood beams, a way to mark their time here—a reminder that a hundred boys have slept in this bunk before me.

But a name catches my eye, carved where the ceiling meets the wall, nearly hidden. Each letter is cut deeply, as if in anger. A night when he couldn't sleep. When the trees felt too close. The air too cold. His home too far away.

The letters spell: MAX CAULFIELD.

Max slept here. In this cabin. In this bunk.

I sit up and touch the wood grain, my finger sliding along the indentation of each letter. *Max slept here.*

Bursts of filtered moonlight cut across my vision, the memory of snow against my skin. I think of Nora, her hand pressed to mine last night, but I push the memory away. My mind plays tricks on me—always drifting back to her. I try to recall the cemetery, laughter rising from the others' throats. But I wasn't laughing with them. *They were never my friends,* my mind repeats. They were laughing at *me.*

Taunting me.

I sit up and scramble down the ladder, away from the bunk—from the place where I once slept. *But it wasn't always my bunk.*

I arrived at camp late in the season, when the air had already turned sharp and the boys had already been assigned their cabins. I was the new kid. The outsider.

I never belonged.

Max had gotten in trouble before I arrived. I remember it in waves now, breaking against the shore of my mind. Salt and foam, crashing over me. He had been caught sneaking into the counselors' cabins and rooting through their stuff, caught spiking his morning coffee with whiskey. Offenses that were worse than most of the boys'.

So the counselors moved him to a cabin beside the mess hall, a single room with no other boys. A cabin flanked by the counselors' cabins, where he couldn't easily sneak out without being heard. *I remember it now,* when I arrived at camp and the boys told me that I had been assigned to Max's old bunk.

He hated me for it—like it was my fault.

I move back away from the bunks, my heels hitting the heavy wood door.

They made me go to the cemetery that night; they laughed and passed around a bottle of booze and I stood rigid, ready for a fight. Ready for them to attack me.

We were never friends.

And Max—he hated me the most.

NORA

H ello?" I call into my own home.

As if I were the stranger. The intruder picking locks and slinking through shimmied window frames.

Fin sniffs the air, quick inhales through his nostrils.

I tiptoe into the living room, trailing snow across the floor. *Tink, tink, tink* go the droplets of water.

And then someone appears at the bottom of the stairs. "Shit, you scared me," Suzy says.

My shoulders drop. "I thought the house was empty." But my tone betrays something—the uncertainty I feel, looking for cracks along her edges, for something she's hiding.

"Just me." She moves into the kitchen and leans against the white tile counter, as if she's still a little unsteady on her feet, a little hungover after last night. Dark circles rim her eyes.

"Oliver's gone?" I ask.

Her mouth puckers to one side. "Guess so. No one's in your room." She rubs at her temples, then lifts her bloodshot eyes to mine. "I only went up there to see if you were still asleep. I wasn't snooping."

"It's fine," I say. I walk to the stove, the fire burning brightly—

she must have added more logs. My head has started to pulse, little pricks of light fanning across my vision.

"Where were you?" Suzy asks.

"Just needed to get out of the house," I say. I don't know why I lie, why I don't tell her that I went to see Mr. Perkins. That I found a watch that belonged to Max in Oliver's coat. That I think he did something he can't take back.

But I *do* know why I don't say any of this: because I'm not sure I can trust her.

I'm not sure she doesn't know more about Max. About everything.

She blinks several times, like she needs more sleep. "What's wrong?" she asks. She senses something is off.

But there are too many things wrong. A bone moth is following me, a dead boy's watch was in Oliver's pocket. Something bad is happening and I can't tell who's the villain and who's just as scared as me.

Nervously, I twirl the moonstone ring around my finger. "Were you there with them that night?" I ask, the timbre of my voice cracking.

"When?" Her eyebrows crush together.

"The night Max died. And Oliver went missing."

She frowns even deeper, little lines creasing the sides of her mouth, confused. "No," she answers, straightening up from the kitchen counter. "I was asleep in Rhett's bunk when they all left."

"Did you know they were going to the cemetery?"

She crosses her bony arms, her sweatshirt twisted around her torso, a defensive posture. "No, what are you talking about?" A strand of hair slips free from the tanged bun atop her head.

472

"But when they came back," I urge. "You must have known something happened? That Max and Oliver weren't with them."

She chews on the side of her cheek like she's trying to remember, to sift through the drowsy fog of her mind. A little black smudge is just visible by her right eye, her mascara rubbed away while she slept—the only makeup she must have brought with her. "Why are you asking me this?" Her tone is suddenly acrid, flint scraping together. Sparks catching on her teeth.

Because a bone moth is following me, I want to say. *Because the throb at my temples won't go away.*

Because death is coming for me. Tiny black spots of doom—just like her smeared mascara—always just beyond my vision.

Suzy and I stare at each other, neither of us breathing, looking for the truth in the other's face. In the lines around our eyes that often reveal when someone's lying.

Never trust anyone who blinks too often: a note—a warning— within the spellbook.

"I didn't know anyone was missing that night," she says flatly when I don't answer her. "I don't keep track of who sleeps in which cabins."

Anger boils up inside me now, wings thwapping against my ribs—the certainty that she knows something she won't say—and I take a step closer to her. "But you heard them talking about it—that someone had died?"

She lifts both shoulders in an exaggerated shrug, her perfect dark eyebrows raised like little tents. "I guess," she answers. "I wasn't really paying attention. I was more worried about being stuck up here."

"A boy died, and all you cared about was being stuck?"

She sets her jaw into place and uncrosses her arms, looking suddenly rigid. "You think I had something to do with it?"

"I just want to know what happened."

"And you assume I'm lying?"

"I don't have any reason to believe you aren't." The words should probably sting, but I'm beyond that now. Beyond caring what she thinks. I feel like I'm losing control. Like I can't see what's right in front of me—everyone is hiding something and I want to scream. This is my forest, the place where I've always felt safe, yet I have no idea what's happening.

I am a Walker who can't see the truth.

Suzy moves her hand too quickly, and she knocks one of my mother's honey jars off the counter onto the floor. It lands with a loud shatter, the glass breaking on impact, and the sticky amber liquid spills into the cracks. She stares at it, like she might apologize, but then she lifts her eyes and says, "Why would I lie?"

The honey pools along the wood floor, following the divots and lines, filling in the scrapes like mud. Slow and mercurial. "To trick me," I say at last, my ears ringing louder now. "To make me look like an idiot. Because that's what people like you do—find ways to torment the Walker witch."

People like you, I think. People who only pretend to be nice but say awful things about me behind my back. People who form circles that no outsiders can enter. Who like to watch others squirm while rumors are passed ear to ear.

Her mouth hangs open for a second, and then her eyebrows dip back down. "I thought you were my friend," she says, her voice thin as paper, tearing slowly along a crease. Like she might sink into a crack and disappear. Just like the honey.

But I refuse to feel bad for her. "We were never friends before this," I point out, my voice bitter and quick. I don't belong in her world, among her circle of friends. I am lost in that gray in-between. Not quite normal enough to have friends, not quite powerful enough to summon real magic like the Walkers before me. "You've never talked to me at school, you've never even smiled at me in the hall." The words are tumbling out. "I'm just a convenience for you. Because I'm all you have right now—because you have nowhere else to go. You're just using me." The words have left my mouth before I can even regret them. Before I can feel their full weight slam down inside my skull.

Suzy's round lips snap shut.

And the anger I felt dissolves on my tongue just as quickly, turns to nothing. And I'm left feeling empty—as hollow as an acorn husk.

Suzy crosses the room to the couch without even looking at me, grabs her bag from the floor, and walks to the front door. As she passes, the air has the hint of stale rose perfume—the last of whatever she dabbed onto her skin days ago. She pauses and flicks her gaze back to me. And for a moment I think I should say something, a string of words to undo what's been said—a balm for the wounds I've just caused. But she speaks before I can. "I always thought everyone was mean to you at school for no reason. I defended you to Rhett and the others, I told them you were nice and that all the rumors weren't true." She pulls her jaw back into place. "But maybe I was wrong."

She yanks open the door and ducks out into the snow, slamming it shut behind her before I can say anything else.

Gone.

The honey sinks and settles.

I pick up the shards of glass one by one and toss them into the trash. Feeling just as broken. Just as worthless as honey smeared onto the floor.

Upstairs, the loft is empty—no sign of Oliver—just like Suzy said. And I sit on the edge of the bed.

The house feels oddly vacant now, only echoes and exhales and settling floorboards. I'm all alone. And the guilt folds over me like an old blanket—torn fibers and threads unraveling and stinking of mothballs. I never should have said those things to Suzy. Even if I don't believe her, even if she knows what happened that night but isn't saying, I never meant to be so mean.

I pull out the pocket watch and hold it in my hand, running my thumb over the engraving of Max's name. The broken chain falls between my fingers—a clue I don't understand. There is no blood on the watch. No tiny spots of red scattered across the glass. And there was no blood on Oliver when I found him in the woods. *Blood can be wiped off*, I think. But not easily. Not when you're lost in the forest, freezing to death.

Something else happened. I just can't see it. Can't make the pieces fit.

A moth follows you, Mr. Perkins said when I left his house, the bone moth fluttering up into the trees. Always close.

Death is coming for me.

But I don't want to end up like Max. A corpse—lies buzzing around like flies.

I pick up the spellbook from the bedside table and set it in my lap, flipping through the pages. I don't know what I'm looking for: an explanation, a remedy, a way to make the bone moth stop following me. To destroy it, maybe. *To keep death at bay.*

I read the stories of my ancestors, the strange accounts of years past: the autumn a palomino horse went missing inside the Wicker Woods, and Dodie Walker found it using a water-witching stick. She rode the horse out of the woods bareback, and locals said her eyes had turned the same mustard brown as the horse's. The summer a plague of prairie locusts descended over Jackjaw Lake, covering porch lights and spilling down chimneys. It wasn't until Colette Walker caught one of the locusts inside a glass jar and muttered a tiny spell into its ear that the air finally cleared and the prairie locusts left the mountains.

Near the bottom of the page there is a notation about the best way to lure an insect into the loft:

Open window after sunrise.
Burn a blue-lavender candle to its nub, to lure insect.
Catch insect in a glass jar and whisper desired spell into its ear.
*spell not advisable for those who fear creatures of a winged
    or creepy-crawly sort*

The spell seems simple enough. No blood or sacrifice or special pagan holiday needed to perform it. And if I can catch the moth, maybe I can compel it to go away. To leave me alone and take *death* with it.

I have to try.

I find one of my mother's empty honey jars in the kitchen and bring it upstairs. I dig out a lavender candle from my dresser drawer, the one that's nearly burnt down to the base, and I light it, placing it on the floor.

When I open the window in the loft, snow drifts into the room. Little dancing flakes that slide across the sill, in no particular hurry.

I look for any signs of Oliver or Suzy out among the trees. But nothing stirs—the forest is silent and humanless.

I'm truly alone. Last night, two people slept in my house, swelling lungs and tired eyelids. But now a well of sadness rises up inside me, salty tears wanting to stream down pale cheeks—but I don't let them. *I'm a Walker.* We're used to being on our own. Surviving. Calloused hands and sharp eyes and sturdy hearts.

And I don't want Suzy or Oliver to return—not really. I fear what Oliver may have done, and I fear what Suzy might've seen. *I'm safer without them.* Locked doors are better than friends you can't trust.

Still, the quiet of the house is a burden inside my chest.

I walk back across the floor and sit beside the flickering candle. I hold the glass jar in my hand, and I wait for the moth to flutter through the open window, to be beckoned by the light. But it never comes and the room grows cold.

The daylight fades to evening.

The shadows turn to full darkness.

And I lay my head on the hardwood floor.

Fin stretches out beside me. His paws touching my shoulder, his breathing quick in his lungs. And again my eyes want to sting with tears.

I know the bone moth will never come into the loft.

I know it won't be so easily fooled by a lavender candle on a bedroom floor. A bone moth is not the same as catching a locust or a bee or a buckthorn firefly.

And even if I had caught it, I'm certain I wouldn't have been able to whisper a spell powerful enough to compel it to leave me alone. A spell to banish it from these woods. And what good is a Walker who can't even charm an insect? A witch who doesn't know the simplest of spells? Whose grandmother died before she could teach me how to summon the moonlight inside me, whose mother would prefer I never utter a spell within the walls of this house again.

I'm a Walker who is barely a witch at all.

I thought I wanted to be alone, that I was brave and strong and didn't need a single thing from anyone. But now I'm not so sure. Now my heart crumbles inside the cave of my chest, and I wish I was the size of a gnat, so small I could fold myself into a crack in the floor and disappear. Tiny and forgettable.

I let the candle burn down to nothing, wax dripping onto the wood floor beside my feet until the flame fizzes and blinks out. I let the glass jar roll away from my fingertips and thud against the bedpost. I draw my knees to my chest and curl my toes under the rug. But I leave the window open—I want to feel the cold—and I listen to the wind bite against the eaves of the house.

A soft pain forms inside my ribs, a hurt that won't go away. Empty and hollow, like my gooey insides have been carved out with a blade. Jack-o'-lantern slop.

Eventually my eyelids sink closed and I drift into an awful sort of sleep.

My dreams are strange and green, and I feel myself being pulled under by moss and golden leaves. Rich, dark soil blots out my vision, it clots my ears and mouth, it suffocates, it buries me alive. I can taste the earth, the cold frozen ground caving in on top of me.

But then there is music, metallic and thin and far away, vibrating through the soil of my dreams. I wake, choking and grabbing at my face as if to pull the roots away, to claw my way back aboveground. But I'm still on the floor of the loft. Not buried—not dead.

The night sky fills my room, the sun long set. *How long have I been asleep?*

Snow blows in through the open window, along with something else.

A noise from somewhere outside, in the trees, in the snowy dark.

The music was not in my dreams.

It was real.

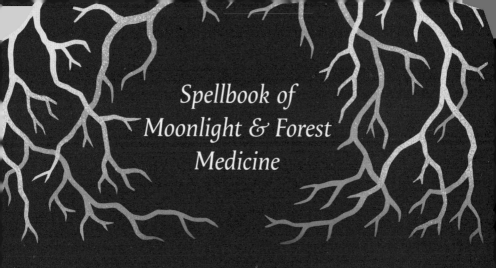

Spellbook of Moonlight & Forest Medicine

EMELINE WALKER was born a month late under a ghost moon—instead of the dwarf clover moon, as was intended. Her eyes were alabaster white, and when she opened her mouth to cry, only air slipped out.

She was a quiet child, who spoke to herself and played cat's cradle alone in her room and dug her toes into the mud to feel the worms wriggling beneath.

But at seventeen, during an unusually windy autumn when wild dandelion fluff blew over the lake like tiny parasols, Emeline went into the Wicker Woods and lost her mind.

Yet, it was not her fault.

She had lost the silver locket her true love had given to her, so she went into the woods where all lost things are found. She roamed the forest, kicking away rotted leaves and smooth black stones, in search of it. She slept in the trunks of trees. She wove stonecrop flowers around her wrists. A year later, when she finally emerged, strands of her long raven hair had turned bone white and dirt was clotted under her nails, but there was no locket clutched in her hand.

For the remainder of her life, Emeline continued to search the old house—inside teacups, behind books, and under the floor-boards. Each night she shook out her bedsheets, in case the locket had slipped between the cotton.

She lived to be an old woman, long white hair to her ankles, trail-ing her through the garden where she dug up marigolds and vanilla leaf and wild ginger, certain the locket would be found among the roots. Emeline never knew her shadow side, her Walker magic, her nightshade—it eluded her, just like the locket.

On her deathbed, Emeline Walker clasped the hand of her little sister, Lilly, and said, "Ah, there it is." And went still.

How to Unravel a Knotted Mind:
Toss heated salt water out an upstairs window.
Clasp hands around a circle of freshly tilled spring soil
    and spit over your left shoulder.
Don't bathe for three nights in a row. On the fourth
    night, drink a glass of golden turmeric milk, braid
    your hair tightly down your back, and sleep with
    no socks.

NORA

Music vibrates through the trees—tinny and muffled.

I follow the sound, the bass thumping through the hard, frozen ground, voices rising in laughter. I'm nearly halfway down the string of boarded-up summer homes, almost to the marina, when I reach the origin: the old Wilkinson place, with its large wraparound porch, thick log walls, and two peaked bay windows overlooking the lake. It's one of nicest log homes on Jackjaw Lake, and the Wilkinsons only visit twice every summer. They bring their three dogs and five kids and too-loud friends. They have barbecues and parties late into the night, and the adults get drunk on dark red wine and laugh at the same jokes they tell year after year.

Now, under a cocoon of snow, the house is buzzing again.

My feet carry me up to the front porch—as if still in a dream— my hands push open the front door that's been left slightly ajar, and my eyes absorb the sway of boys crowded inside. *I shouldn't be here.* But my heart betrays my mind.

Oliver might be inside.

And if he is, I don't know what I'll say. Maybe I'll scream and thump my fists against his chest. I'll tell him he lied; I'll tell him he killed someone that night and kept a pocket watch hidden in his coat. Or maybe I'll turn and leave, unable to find the right words. But I need to see his face, the gentle curve of each eye, the kindness I once saw in them, and maybe I'll know. I'll *really* see. A monster. A villain. Or the boy I remember from the trees.

I clench my hands at my sides and step through the doorway.

Nearly the whole camp is here. Boys hold wineglasses and champagne flutes filled with dark liquor. To my right, several boys play a game of flip-cup on the dining room table, shouting loudly. Drunk. A fire burns brightly from the massive fireplace to my left, logs haphazardly tossed onto the flames, too close to the salmon-colored living room rug—the edges already singed.

I slip past a group of boys, and no one seems to notice me. Already too intoxicated. Standing atop the coffee table is a boy wearing a green wool blanket as a cape, shouting about how his dad swore he'd only have to stay at the camp for two months but it's been six. His eyes glaze over me, but he doesn't seem to register the girl among an ocean of boys. My feet knock into empty beer cans littered across the floor, and a portable stereo sits on a long table beneath a window, blaring country music from some distant radio station—powered by batteries or maybe a windup crank at the back.

The boys have broken into the Wilkinsons' summer home.

And they're going to destroy this place.

The air buzzes against my ears with heat and laughter, and the scent of spilled beer is nauseating. The flickering candlelight throughout the room creates the illusion of human ghosts climbing up the walls. Long spiny arms and legs. Insect people.

I scan the faces but don't see Oliver. And maybe he wouldn't come here, with all these boys from camp, if they really aren't his friends. Unless he lied about that, too. About everything. A lump lodges itself in my throat and I feel sick, standing among all these strange faces. Boys I don't know.

One of them eyes me, a boy in a green shirt with blond hair and a nose ring. He's standing only a couple feet away, his mouth sagging open, and he looks like he's trying to speak but his soupy mind can't form words.

I shouldn't have come, I think suddenly. This was a bad idea.

I start to turn away, to weave back through the crowd, when I see her: Suzy. And my stomach sinks.

She staggers toward a set of stairs and grips the railing, leaning against it, smiling. She's drunk. And the same rush of guilt pours through me.

I bite down on the urge to flee, and instead cross the room toward her, threading through the crush of boys. The boy in the green shirt and nose ring winks at me but still doesn't speak—his voice lost to the booze. Another boy with freckles, smoking a cigar he surely pilfered from the house, arches his eyebrow at me and says, "Hey, moon girl." A few others glance my way but don't say anything. Maybe they're afraid of what I might really be. That the rumors might be true.

Suzy's cheeks are flushed pink when I reach her, and in her hand is a silver beer can. She sloshes a little onto the floor when she sees me, pushing away from the stair railing. "You came," she says flatly, as if I received an invitation—foil-embossed card stock delivered in the mail, covered in glitter. *Please join us for a winter bash at the Wilkinsons' home. Just let yourself in, because we sure will.*

"You guys shouldn't be here," I say. "This is someone else's house."
It's not what I intended to say, not at first. I meant to apologize. Or say
something about not knowing who to trust, about sleepless nights and
finding the watch and that I didn't mean to say she wasn't my friend.

Still, Suzy grins widely—already forgetting our earlier fight.
"Who cares," she answers.

"The camp counselors are going to find out," I add. "They'll
realize most of the boys are missing from their cabins."

Suzy's loose, mushy smile doesn't break, her eyes watering with
drunken happiness, and she laughs. "The counselors don't care what
the boys do," she says, tossing a hand in the air. "It's not like they can
kick them out of camp—we're all stuck here."

Her eyes drift closed and whip open again. She frowns at me,
like she just remembered how mad she is, that I'm the last person she
wants to talk to.

"I'm sorry about earlier," I say quickly. "I shouldn't have said all
those things. I'm just—"

A boy bumps into me, spilling dark liquid from a red cup onto
my shoe. "Sorry," he mutters, glaring at me like it was my fault.

He staggers away, toward the kitchen, and I turn back to face
Suzy. "I'm just trying to figure out what happened," I say.

She raises one sharp, pointed eyebrow, and I realize how tired she
still looks, lids wanting to slip closed. "You mean, you're just trying
to figure out if your boyfriend is responsible?"

I breathe and look away from her, out over the crowd of boys.
Someone is singing along to the music and his voice isn't half bad, if
it weren't for the hiccups punctuating every few lines. "A boy is dead,
Suzy," I say, swiveling back to her. "And someone is responsible."

Her mouth goes slack and she leans against the railing again. "Accidents happen," she says, and she takes a long swig of her beer.

"What do you mean?" I step closer to her, breathing her alcohol-tinged breath, which is masked only slightly by her floral perfume. But she shakes her head and turns away, using the railing for balance as she wobbles up the stairs. "Suzy!" I call, but she's already reached the top and disappeared down a hall.

Accidents happen. It's similar to what Rhett said at the bonfire.

I glance back to the front door, still open from when I came inside. I should leave, go back home, lock the door, and wait for the snow to thaw—for the road to open and for everything to go back to normal.

But I don't. I climb the stairs after Suzy. I go deeper into the house.

Maybe she does know what happened.

I pass two open doorways, bunk beds lining both rooms. A place for kids to pile into on balmy summer nights.

Muffled voices carry down the hall. The low chatter of boys talking.

I pause beside the last door, pressing myself up against the wall, listening.

"Your girlfriend's drunk," someone says from inside the room. Jasper, I think. *The boys from the bonfire are here.* He sounds far away from the doorway, though, across the room.

"Shut up, man," Rhett answers. And I hear Suzy make a sound from her throat, like she's offended.

"She shouldn't be here," Jasper adds.

"I'm not his girlfriend," Suzy snaps finally. "And I can go wherever

I want." She sounds wasted and I can imagine the boys' faces, sneering at her, rolling their eyes.

"You've told her too much," Jasper continues. I can hear footsteps and I wonder if he's moving toward Rhett. A warning or a threat, perhaps. "She just runs and tells everything to that witch friend of hers."

"I haven't told her shit," Rhett barks.

There's more movement from inside. It sounds like someone shoves someone else. *They don't even trust one another*, I think. They're starting to crack, lines being drawn. Secrets wedged among them. They can't stop talking about it—the fear rooted inside them now.

"Stop!" Suzy shouts, and she must step between them because everything falls quiet.

"You guys are only making it worse," another voice interjects. Lin, probably.

Someone lets out a deep exhale and then there's the sound of someone sitting, the depression of springs—probably a bed.

"We just need to wait it out," Rhett says, but his voice sounds tight, strangled in his throat. Like maybe he doesn't believe his own words.

A lull falls over the room, and I press myself closer to the wall, straining, unsure what's happening.

But then someone finally speaks—Lin, the timbre of his voice like strings on a violin stretched too tight. "They're going to find him eventually."

Another long pause, as though everyone is too afraid to break the silence.

Suzy clears her throat, but it still sounds cracked when she speaks. "You guys know where Max is?"

There is a low, desperate undertone of grumbles. One of the boys says something I can't make out, a hush of words like he's afraid the walls will hear. *Or a girl hiding in the hall.*

"It's only a matter of time until the counselors find him," Lin continues, maybe in response to what I couldn't hear. "He's not hidden that well."

This is the thing they're keeping secret. The thing they've avoided. But now Lin has said it out loud.

My heart begins beating like a drum, *thwap thwap thwap*, and I press my nails into the wall behind me.

"They're not going to find Max," Rhett answers, his footsteps crossing the room, like he's moving away from the others, toward a far wall. Maybe he's looking out a window.

Max. His body, his corpse, tucked away somewhere.

Hidden.

"I can't get in trouble for this," Jasper says, his tone an equal measure of fear and threat.

"None of us can," Rhett answers.

Jasper makes a balking sound. "It's different for me. My dad will kill me if he finds out. This was my last shot, coming here. I can't . . ." His words break off.

"It's the last shot for all of us," Lin offers up. The boys who are sent here to the Jackjaw Camp for Wayward Boys aren't away on a winter holiday. They aren't here because it's a reward or a brief escape from public school and curfews. They're here because they've already screwed up. They've already made a mess of their other lives. This is supposed to be the place where they get righted, set back on course. Fixed. But not if a boy winds up dead. And not if they're to blame.

"There's nothing we can do about it now," Rhett answers, his footsteps crossing the room again. Pacing maybe. "It already happened."

Another voice mumbles something so low I can't make it out. I wish they would talk louder, I wish I could just step into the room without being seen.

And then their tone changes.

"I still hear things at night," Lin says softly, as if he were facing the floor when he says it.

"That's what happens when someone drowns," Jasper snaps, his voice so high it sounds like it might break, as if his mind were fraying along seams. "They fucking haunt you because they're pissed."

Drowned.

Drowned.

Drowned.

Haunt, haunt, haunt.

My heart is now in my nose, and I can barely breathe. I have to tell my lungs to inhale, to exhale, to not make a sound.

Max drowned. *In the lake?* Broke through the ice? My head throbs and the blood pumping through my veins feels too loud, a crush inside my ears. I should leave, slink down the hall before they hear me, find me, discover me spying.

"Shut up," Rhett says, and I hold a hand over my mouth, to silence my own breath.

"I can't sleep," Lin argues. "I can't take it."

More unheard words, and then Suzy's voice rises above the others, her inflection strange—covert. "Nora says she found Oliver in the woods."

I feel my eyebrows pinch together—unsure why she's saying this. Why it matters.

"She said he was there for the last two weeks, hiding or something."

"What?" one of them says, Rhett maybe.

The music downstairs pauses suddenly, then starts up a second later with a new song. There are shouts from below, someone arguing. A drunken disagreement.

One of the boys on the other side of the wall says something else I can't make out, and then I hear the shuffle of feet, the lazy tread of three boys and a girl walking toward the door.

I waited too long.

Rhett steps through the doorway, and for a second I think that if I don't move, maybe they'll walk right by me, they'll think I am only a shadow pressed against the wall. Only a ghost. But Rhett jerks and his eyes bore into me.

"What the fuck!" he exclaims.

And in the next second, Jasper is shouldering past Rhett and grabbing my arm. "She fucking heard everything we said." Across Jasper's left cheek is a bright-red gash, the place where the tree limb sliced him open at the bonfire.

Rhett squeezes his temples with his hands. "Shit."

I yank my arm back, but Jasper grabs me again, harder this time. Fingers pinching my skin. "Don't touch me!" I shout, my body stiffening, resisting, but he's too strong and he forces me into the room.

Moonlight glints through the window onto a bed neatly made with an embroidered patchwork quilt. The room is cold, as if there were a draft, but the window is closed.

"Shit, shit, shit," Rhett repeats, pacing across the dark room, his voice like shards of glass, slicing me open each time he speaks.

Suzy stands in the doorway, and I flash my eyes to hers but she won't look up, her arms crossed over her chest, like a bird with its wings folded in on itself, shielding her eyes from mine.

But Rhett glares at me like I'm an animal caught in a trap—which is exactly what I am. *Trapped.* I hold my arms at my sides, rigid as a girl who will bite and claw her way out of here if she has to. A girl with teeth to tear away flesh.

"What did you hear, moon girl?" Rhett asks, taking a half step closer to me, his eyes concealed in shadow, as if he's deciding my fate.

"Nothing," I say, my voice defiant.

"She's lying," Jasper snarls, still holding my arm, his tall frame towering over me. "She heard us talking about Max. She'll tell the cops when the road clears."

I squint up at him, a thorn pricking at my temples.

Rhett rakes a hand through his dusty-blond hair, looking for answers in the dark corners of the room. He shakes his head at me and takes a step back, toward the door.

"We can't trust her," Jasper adds, his gaze now on Rhett.

My eyes sweep to Suzy again and then to Lin—wearing his big puffy coat with the hood pulled up, even inside—and I wait for one of them to say something, to interject, to tell Jasper to let me go. But neither of them will look my way. They're afraid of Jasper and Rhett, their eyes sunk to the floor.

"You're staying in here," Rhett says, his pupils like black bottomless holes, "until we figure out what to do with you."

I move toward him, but Jasper still has a hold of my arm. "You can't lock me in here!" I shout.

Rhett's shoulders draw back. A cold pallor washed over his face.

"Rhett," Suzy says finally, stepping farther into the room. "She doesn't know anything."

But Rhett turns on her, only a few inches from her face. "Do you want to stay in here too?"

"No," she answers. "But you can't do this."

"Watch me," he replies.

For a moment, Suzy blinks up at him like she might say something else, like she might shove him in the chest and yell for me to run. But then her gaze falls away, not meekly, but in understanding—she knows there's nothing she can do. She's outnumbered. My heart sinks. And when Rhett steps back through the doorway, he grabs her by the hand and pulls her with him.

He's already made up his mind. And he's going to leave me in here.

Jasper releases my arm and slips quickly out into the hall with the others, just before Rhett pulls the door shut with a hard thud.

The room dips into darkness.

I run to the door, fumbling for the knob, nails scratching against the grain of the wood. But it's too late. I pound on the door, I try to yank it open, but the door only bends slightly. They've locked it somehow, secured it shut to keep the witch in her cage.

"No!" I shout, pulling again on the knob. But it won't budge. *Shit.*

I press my ear to the wood of the door, listening to see if they're still there. But then I hear the clomping of footsteps moving away, back down the hall.

"Wait!" I scream against the door. "Please!" But there's only silence.

And the dark of the room.

I turn and lean against the door, pressing my head back. I think of what Mr. Perkins told me, how more miners died at the hands of one another than in the cruel dark of the forest.

It's the hearts of men we should fear most.

But they can't keep me in here. Not for long.

The camp counselors will discover the boys have snuck out from their cabins. They will hear the music thudding from across the lake. They will come to investigate. Search the house. *They will let me out.*

But what if the counselors don't come? What if Suzy was right and they no longer care what the boys do, no longer care if they sneak away, as long as they're back in their bunks by sunrise?

If I'm left here, locked inside, how long until they come back to let me out?

"Hey!" I call, feeling desperate again. I pound my fists against the door. *Bang. Bang. Bang.* Maybe one of the other boys will hear me, come let me out. Though I doubt they can even hear my shouts over the music. Or that they'd even care.

Drowned, I think again.

Max drowned in the lake, sank to the bottomless bottom, maybe froze to death before the water even had time to fill his lungs.

Then where is his body? Where is it hidden?

I'm missing something.

Some great big part of it doesn't make sense.

I breathe in slowly. I stay calm. *Calm, calm, calm.*

I think I hear a voice.

"Nora."

I whip around to face the door. "Hello?" I ask against the crack in the doorframe.

"Are you okay?" It's Suzy.

"No," I say back. "You have to let me out."

I think I can hear her breathing. The soft inhale of her throat, the wobbly exhale against the grain of the wood. "I can't," she says after a moment.

"Why not?" I feel the pinch in my heart growing tighter.

"They'll lock me up too, if I help you. . . ." Her voice trails away, like she's looking down the hallway, listening for anyone approaching. "They're really paranoid. Rhett thinks they're all going to jail."

They're so paranoid they're willing to lock me inside a room. They're so paranoid they're hearing voices in their cabin—they think they're being haunted by something. *By Max.* They're not thinking clearly, about anything, and I feel my heart clawing at my rib cage. Beginning to panic. "Just let me out, Suzy," I plead. "If they catch me, I won't tell them you helped me. But I can't stay in here." The dark feels like it's swallowing me up. A gulf of black.

Another long pause. I think maybe she's gone, left me here.

"Please, Suzy."

But then I hear her breathing again. She's still there. "I'm sorry," she says. "I have to go back downstairs before they realize I'm gone."

I slap my palm against the door. "No!"

"They're just drunk," she adds quickly. "I'm sure they'll let you out in the morning." Another pause. "I'll talk to Rhett. I'll tell him you don't know anything. I'll try."

"Suzy," I beg. "Just open the door. Don't leave."

But I can hear the quick pace of her footsteps down the hall, moving away. She's already gone.

"Shit," I mutter again, dropping my hand from the doorframe. I press my palms to my eyes, hard, like I could press myself right out of this room. When I open my eyes again, the room is too dark, and it's hard to tell one wall from the other, the ceiling from the floor. My head spins and the same feeling I've felt before sinks over me, the shiver and tremble of air, the buzz and crack of it. Seconds becoming minutes, then wavering back again.

Tick, tick . . .

"No," I breathe. I don't want to feel this now.

I push away from the door and move across the room until my shin hits the corner of the bed. I wince at the sharp pain, buckling over, before continuing forward, hands out in front of me to feel for other obstacles. I reach a wall and a window, and I push aside the curtain. Muted light spills into the room from the half-moon. I touch the glass and peer out into the snow. But the drop to the ground is too far down, far enough to break bones. There has to be another way out. The thrumming noise of music pumps louder through the floors, and the walls vibrate, but I hear something else. Something distinct. *Something I've heard before.*

The whisper of an insect on glass. Of wings.

A sound so faint I'm surprised I can hear it at all. It grows louder, thudding against the window. Black eyes and swollen belly.

I drop my hand from the window and take a step back, fear clawing up the rungs of my ribs. *No, no, no.*

The moth found me, even here, even locked in this room. And the certainty burrows deep beneath my skin.

"Go away," I whisper, my words desperate and thin.

It spins and thumps against the window—*thump, thump, thump*—searching for a way inside. To reach me. So it can brush its wings against my skin, mark me, so death can find me more easily.

Death is coming.

My body pulses and I slide against the wall, dropping to the floor, tucking my knees to my chin. Anything to block out the sound. *Thump-thump-thump.* "Stop it!" I scream, I plead.

My heartbeat is a percussion in my chest, the same rhythm as its wings.

"Go away. Go away. Go away," I whisper into my hands. Until it's all I hear.

All that fills my ears.

OLIVER

I have to find her.

The lake is impossibly dark; it swallows up the stars as I circle around the shore. Certain this place, these mountains, are watching every move I make.

I remember enough now—enough to know I can't trust the others. The past is a blurred wreck in my mind: the cemetery, the taste of booze in my throat, the laughter. The feeling of my fists clenched at my sides, ready for a fight. Still, I recall enough to know that they are capable of awful things.

And I think only of her, of Nora.

They don't trust her. The witch in the woods.

I need to find her, make sure she's okay, and keep her safe.

Turning away from the lake, I hike up through the pines toward her house. I know she won't want to see me. I know that whatever I say, she won't want to hear it, she won't let me in—and this hurts worse than anything. But I have to try. I don't need her to trust me, I just need her to stay away from Rhett and Jasper and Lin.

I knock on the door and hold my breath until my lungs start to burn and ache.

Memories flit through me. I remember the way Max tipped his head back in the cemetery, taking a long gulp of whiskey. How he eyed me like he was daring me to make the first move, to say something that would piss him off. But I wasn't afraid. I felt something else: anger.

I bring my fist to the door again and knock harder, waiting for Nora to come, to peek through the curtains. But she never does. *Something's wrong.* The house is too dark, no candlelight through the windows. And I can hear Fin—the wolf—whining from the other side, a sad whimper. I try the knob and the door swings open.

Night swallows the place whole. No candles. No fire in the woodstove.

The wolf darts out past my legs, down into the snow, and cuts through the trees. "Fin!" I call, but he doesn't listen. He doesn't even slow his pace.

I run before I lose him, before he slips into the trees and is gone. *Maybe he knows where she is, maybe he's found her scent.* I chase his narrow path through the snow, along the row of summer homes, until he finally stops several houses down, his tail dipped low, ears forward.

Music wheezes out from inside the house, and through the lower windows I can see several boys from camp. They've broken in—they're having a party.

Fin whimpers again, nose sniffing the air, and I touch his head—unsure why he's come here, to a house that isn't his. I follow his gaze up to the second floor of the home.

Someone is at the window.

A girl, face barely visible from the other side of the glass.

Her.

Something's wrong, some hint of panic in her eyes. I don't go to the front door—I don't want the others to see me. So I leave the wolf in the snow and use the lowest window to hoist myself up to the edge of the overhanging roof. My fingers grip the gutter, and I swing a leg onto the upper ledge, just like when I used to climb onto the roof of my neighbor Nate Lynch's house, when we'd drink beers he'd swipe from his dad's garage. It feels like a hundred years ago now—a whole different life, far away from these mountains. But scaling up the corner of this house is no different. Aside from the wet, slick snow.

I reach the window on the second floor, crouching low away from the wind, and tap against the glass.

Nora lifts her head to face me. She scratches her hands through her hair, her eyes cautious and dark in the shadow of the room.

"Nora," I say against the glass, pointing at the window for her to unlock it. But she doesn't move toward me. She takes a step back. And maybe I don't blame her. Maybe I'm the villain. My feet slip an inch on the snow, but I right myself before sliding toward the edge of the roof. "Please," I say, unsure if she can hear me.

She closes her eyes, as if she doesn't think I'm real. As if I might vanish if she wishes for it hard enough. But when she opens them, I'm still here. Her mouth sets in place and she takes two swift steps toward the window, reaches out for the lock, and slides it free.

I place my palms against the sides of the window and push it up in the frame, then duck into the room, bringing the cold air and snow with me.

"Are you okay?" I ask, afraid to move too close to her, afraid I'll scare her.

Her mouth pulls into a line. "What are you doing?" she asks. "How did you know I was here?"

"I followed Fin."

She glances at the closed door behind her.

"What happened?" I ask. "Why are you in here?"

She backs away from me again, her fingers tugging at the hems of her sleeves.

"They locked me in," she says, her voice turned sour, and she rubs her hands up her arms, making herself small, closed off. I hate that she's afraid of me; I hate that she looks at me with darkness in her eyes; I hate that every move I make causes her to shiver, to twitch away from me.

"Who?" I ask.

"Rhett and the others."

Anger boils up into my chest, red-hot. Fury that makes me want to break down the door and go find them. Make them pay for doing this to her.

My eyes flash to the locked door, and another part of me thinks maybe I shouldn't have come at all, seeing the fear in her eyes, the mistrust—but I also can't leave her here. Caged like this. Awaiting some fate that's yet to be decided.

"I think they're hiding Max's body," she says cautiously, like she regrets the words as soon as they leave her mouth.

Max's body. The words feel wrong. *A body hidden, concealed.* The idea doesn't fit with my memory, so I push it away. I swallow and hold out a hand to Nora, but I don't move any closer to her. "We need to get out of here," I say.

Her fingers release the sleeves of her coat, but they curl into fists instead of reaching for me. "I'm not going anywhere with you," she says, her voice rising.

Footsteps pass by outside, probably just one of the boys looking for the bathroom, then they vanish down the hall.

"I found the watch," Nora blurts out, her voice lower this time. "Max's watch." In the dim light I can see her features change, the soft roundness of her cheeks turns hollow, her eyes crease at the corners, like she is trying to see something at a distance, just out of focus. "In your coat pocket," she adds. "You had a dead boy's watch in your pocket."

My chin dips to the floor, then back up to her. I knew this moment would come, that she would ask about the watch. And a cold thread of ice trickles down my spine, down my fingertips, settling into my toes. "I know," I say.

"Did you kill him?" she asks, the thing she really wants to know the root of her fear. I don't blame her for it. Still, the words hang in the air, dissolving there, like broken pieces of glass—sharp edged—ready to tear me open.

"No," I answer, but my voice sounds tight, the word forced out. A little white lie so tiny it's easily forgotten, glanced over. Hardly there at all.

She shakes her head. "I don't believe you." And her voice rises too loud again, eyes watering at the edges, holding back tears. Yet, I see doubt in her, uncertainty shifting just behind her pupils—she's trying to see if I could really be a murderer. If I could take someone else's life and lie about it. If I'm a killer.

She steps back, slinking into the dark, farther away from me.

"Why are they protecting you?" she asks, she shouts. "Rhett and Jasper and the others? Why are they covering up what happened?"

I shake my head. "I don't think they're protecting me."

A second passes and snow collects on the carpeted floor at my feet, music screeches from downstairs, rising up through the floorboards. It feels like we're stuck in an odd-shaped dream. In a room, in a house, where neither of us belong.

"Then what's going on?" Her voice sounds frightened and small again. Like a tiny shell cracking open, revealing the fragile thing inside. And I want so bad to reach forward and touch her, tell her that it's okay, that I'm not what she thinks I am. But I can't. Because I'm not sure. *I might be the monster.*

I might have done something bad.

Nora clears her throat. "I don't know what to believe," she says, a tiny whimper against her lips. Her eyes lift and she's about to speak again, but I move forward, pressing her up against the wall, and place my hand over her mouth—silencing her.

She tries to push against my chest, to push me back, but I put a finger to my lips—a sign to be quiet. Someone has stopped outside the bedroom door, the floorboards creaking beneath their weight. They grab the knob, like they're checking to be sure it's still secure. They pause and listen. *Maybe they heard us talking.*

If they find me in here, I don't know what they'll do.

My exhale stirs against her dark raven hair. We're so close I can hear her heartbeat against her throat, the rising rhythm of her lungs with each breath. I don't want to move away from her—I want to move closer. But I know we're not safe in here.

The footsteps plod away, back down the hall to the stairs, and I lower my hand from her mouth. "Sorry," I whisper, still only a few inches from her face.

She doesn't push me back, she doesn't yell at me, she just blinks and breathes and peers up into my eyes.

"Nora," I say, barely above a whisper, blood rushing into my ears. "We have to leave this room."

She chews on her lower lip, *breathing, breathing*, and I think my heart might rise up into my throat. And then she nods.

NORA

Oliver is so close—too close—I can smell the wintergreen scent of his skin. See the soft waves of dark hair along his temples, snow melting in the strands. I could touch a single snowflake and let it rest at the tip of my finger; I could graze his cheek, his collarbone. I could press my hand to his chest and feel the cadence of his heart, listen for the thrum of someone capable of murder. Someone who has pushed another boy beneath the surface of the lake and watched him drown.

But I don't.

I don't because I'm afraid of what I will feel. I'm afraid of letting myself sink closer, *closer*, into him.

So I let him take my hand in his—the hands he may have used to press the life from Max's lungs—and he pulls me to the open window.

In one swift, effortless motion, he hoists me through the window and onto the roof.

The wind is at our backs and Oliver goes first, scaling down the corner of the house. I should be terrified, knowing we could fall, but with his hands on me, bracing footholds, I feel safe.

My fingers start to go numb where they grip the rain gutter, my feet barely touching the top of a first-floor window, and the final drop is another six feet below me. I hesitate and Oliver whispers, "Let go." I squeeze my eyes closed and release my hands, feeling only a half second of weightlessness before Oliver catches me. His hands tighten around my torso, my ribs, and he lowers me to the ground.

Fin licks my palm. "I'm okay," I whisper, running a hand down his coat. He must have sensed something was wrong, heard my cries echoing through the trees. He found me.

Oliver gives me a look, and I know we need to get away from the house. We move up into the trees, into the dark where we won't be seen, weaving along the backside of summer homes until we reach my house.

I let Oliver follow me inside and I lock the door behind us, sliding the dead bolt into place. I close the curtains over the front windows.

I keep out the things I fear. But I lock Oliver inside with me, who perhaps I should fear the most.

"Maybe we shouldn't stay here," he says, drawing back a curtain to look out into the dark. He thinks the boys will come for me. That once they discover I'm gone from that room, they will come beat their fists against the door and drag me out into the snow.

"Where would we go?" I ask.

"We could hide in one of the other homes?"

"If they really want to find me, they'll check all the homes anyway."

Oliver's hand taps at his side, and he walks to the back door to make sure it's locked, then scans the trees. But no one is there. The boys probably haven't even realized I'm gone yet.

"Let's go up to the loft," I say. "We can see farther into the woods—if anyone does come." I don't know why I want him to stay. *But I do know.* It's the knocking around inside my rib cage, the soft ache I can't trust. He's familiar—not like the others. He's the only one who makes me feel not so alone.

Oliver nods. But I can't meet his eyes.

He saved me, that must mean something.

The loft is warm, the heat trapped by the ceiling, and Fin takes up a post at the top of the stairs. Like he senses there is danger out there somewhere.

I sit at the edge of the bed and look down at my hands. I want to trust Oliver, I want to believe him. *He says he didn't kill Max.* But a thousand lies rest beneath the surface. A thousand little cuts filled with salt.

"Did you see the moth?" I ask. "At the window, before you found me?"

"No." He shakes his head.

I exhale and press my hands together.

"It's a bone moth," I explain. If he won't tell me his secrets, I'll tell him mine. "It's been following me."

"What do you mean?"

"It was there the day my grandmother died. And now it's back." Tears well against my eyelids, and they break down my cheeks before I can stop them—the weight of everything slamming through me. They fall to the floor and soak into the wood—becoming a part of the house. A sadness that will live in the grain of the wood forever.

Oliver moves across the room to only a foot from the bed, and the gravity of him so close makes it hard to breathe. But he doesn't sit beside me, he doesn't touch me—*he doesn't want to hurt me*. To split me in two, to make me shudder away from him in fear. "A moth?" he asks.

"It's a death omen," I say, my voice on the verge of breaking. "It means death is close, it means it's coming—" I wipe away the tears from my cheeks, and I wish he would reach out for me; I wish he would pull me into his arms and I could sink into his chest. I wish I could close my eyes and make everything dark and listen only to the sound of his breathing in my ears. But he doesn't and my eyes dip to the floor, feeling like I might be sick. Like the room is tilting off axis and I don't know how much longer I can keep from tipping over. From shattering completely. *A glass girl made of glass shards. Who cries glass tears.*

I stand up from the bed to feel the hard floor beneath my feet, to ground myself to something, and I walk to the window.

Oliver moves slowly, standing beside me, and I try to see what's really there: I try to see all the things he's buried deep, kept just out of reach. "Tell me the truth," I say, I plead, each word a knife. "Tell me what happened at the cemetery, at the lake. Tell me if you killed him."

The question is so sharp in the air that I can see the whites of his eyes expand and my heart wants to cave in. Little bursts of fear exploding in my mind.

He opens his mouth—about to speak—and suddenly I'm terrified of what he's going to say. What he will admit. I shake my head and move closer to him. I want to take the words back. I want to stuff them down into my throat. *I don't want to know what he did.* I don't want the room to tip upside down when the truth leaves his lips—

when his confession drops to the floor and shatters like too-thin glass.

"Wait," I say, holding a hand up to stop him from speaking. I breathe and he breathes, the seconds swelling like a balloon about to pop. "Don't say anything."

He looks hurt, like he doesn't understand.

"If you tell me," I say, the words breathless on my lips, "I know it will change everything." My teeth clamp down. "If you tell me, you can't take it back."

He steps toward me, his dangerous, perfect, awful green eyes melting in with the dark room.

"And I don't want to be afraid of you," I say. The worst kind of afraid. The kind that won't let you sleep, that burrows in so deep that even bone moths steer clear of such things. Such memories. Such awful deeds. Max is dead and Oliver went into the woods and all the boys were at the lake that night. All of them were there and maybe it wasn't an accident, maybe they all played some part, maybe they're all to blame.

And there's no way to make it right.

"You're not afraid of me now?" he asks, inhaling deeply.

"No."

He watches me in a way that makes my heart swim, loosened in my chest—my lungs caught mid-exhale. He looks like someone stuck in a place he doesn't belong, a spike of fear running through his center—he looks as wild as the wilderness beyond the window.

Maybe it's the look in his eyes: of desperation, of restlessness. Like every second is a clock counting down. *Tick, tick, tick.* Something stirs inside him, something neither of us can escape.

He shifts forward and presses his lips to mine.

His fingers find my collarbone, gentle like snowflakes caught in hair, and I kiss him back. I kiss him before my heart swells up into my throat. Before I crack open and become a puddle who used to be a girl. I kiss a boy who's been to the farthest, deepest edge of the Wicker Woods and returned, who tastes like the violent winds that settle over the lake in winter. A boy who is more forest than flesh.

I press my fingers against his shoulder, his chest, searching for his heartbeat. Touching all the places I've wanted to a hundred times before. *I need to know if he's real.* Or if the woods have made him something else, soil and stones. He kisses me softly at first, and then with an ache inside him, his hands against my ribs—*pressing, pressing*, as if he were leaving little bruises where his fingertips rest. Maybe for all the same reasons. To be certain I'm real. To see if I taste like memories, like winter, like the forest that nearly killed him.

We're both looking for something to hold on to—gravity or fingertips or lips to make us real. To make us last. Before the truth wedges itself firmly between us.

His lips are warm on mine and his hands slip around my back, around my neck, around and up into my hair. His dark, sleepy eyes close and I sink into him, pressing my lips harder. His touch feels like moonlight beneath my skin.

Beating hearts and swollen rib cages.

He is familiar when he shouldn't be. He is not mine to keep, but I found him and brought him back.

The walls bow outward away from us, the ceiling bends and drifts away, the snow outside the window and my small wooden bed are watercolor blurs at the edge of my vision. I feel my heart slow, as time stalls like a single drop at the tip of a leaf, waiting to fall, to shatter apart on the ground below. My room expands and I'm certain I've been here before, felt Oliver's lips on mine, kissed him just like this.

I draw my mouth away from his.

My lungs burn.

I press my palms to his chest, for balance, to keep from sinking to the floor. To keep time from wheeling away from me.

Something is happening that I don't understand.

His eyes shiver open—as if waking—emerald eyes and full lips and I know I could drown in him if I let myself. I could vanish. And it feels like a tale from a book. Rosy cheeks and forever kisses and sunsets that last and last and last. Where there is no heartache and no death. No tears making rivers at your feet.

But this is not that tale.

His throat shivers before he speaks, his fingers falling away from my hair, careful and slow. "It's late," he says gently. "You should sleep." But he's peering into me, his gaze refusing to let go.

Words bloom in my throat and press against my lips. But I don't let them out because they are the wrong words. Dangerous words. Frail, breakable things that I won't be able to take back. And sleep tugs at me, exhaustion like a black hole.

He looks just as weary—a darkness in him that needs rest. "So should you," I say.

"I'll stay awake," he answers, eyes still soft and lidded. "I'll keep watch."

Little sparks rise across my skin—a feeling I can't trust. But one I don't know how to ignore. *We see heartache coming from a mile away,* Grandma would say. *But we don't know how to step out of the way.*

The snow softens outside, only a few flakes whirling against the glass, and I crawl into bed—sinking gratefully into my pillow. I'm still wearing all my clothes—just in case. In case I have to wake suddenly, kick back the blankets, and run from the house.

In case the boys come for me.

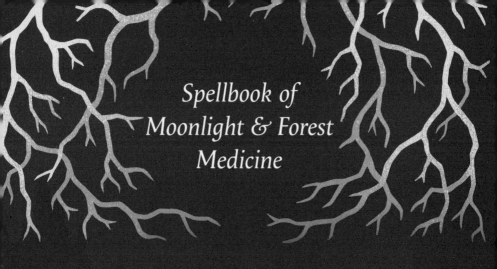

Spellbook of Moonlight & Forest Medicine

HENRIETTA WALKER came into the world on a hot summer night during a strawberry moon. She was the youngest of four girls. And she was the loudest.

She stomped down the halls and down the stairs and down to the lake. She yelled into the trees to scare away the birds and splashed out into the water wearing all her clothes. She ate carrots and radishes straight from the garden and wore her muddy boots into the house. She slept with knots in her hair and dirt under her fingernails and some said she was more raccoon than girl.

But when she walked beneath the oak tree near the old cemetery, acorns fell at her feet, an offering from the tree. When she waded in the shallows of the lake, tadpoles swam around her legs and wriggled beneath her toes. She was a marvel—to her sisters and everything she met. She was also misunderstood.

On the eve of midwinter, when the snows came and the night was the longest, she would sing from the shore of the lake and the woods would go quiet. Even the birds stopped their chatter to listen. The men at the tavern across the lake, after a long day panning for gold in the Black River, would walk down to the lake's edge to hear Henrietta's song.

When her nightshade rose up within her, she could tame the wilds of the forest, silence any man.

She was noisy, so no one else had to be.

She died on the calmest night of the year, when not a breeze or a bird stirred against the walls of the house. She walked into the garden and lay down beside the rosemary and went to sleep.

<u>Midwinter Night Blessing:</u>

Frankincense for burning

Chestnuts for eating

Lavender for bathing

Bells to warn the night crows back into hiding

NORA

I stand at the edge of the lake.

The wind pulls my hair free from its braid, dark strands blowing about my face, the air green and dark—well after midnight.

I tried to sleep but couldn't.

When Grandma was alive, she often slipped into my dreams then recounted them for me in the morning—deciphering their true meaning over pancakes with lavender honey and bits of sugar amethyst on top.

A raven in flight means misfortune.

A dream about castles means you should light a candle in your south-facing window to keep your enemies at bay.

A farewell or long goodbye in a dream means you should bury a lock of your hair under the front porch.

But tonight, in my dreams, I saw only the lake. A calm frozen eye—the center of everything. Deep and black and bottomless, where nothing good can live. So I left the loft and walked through the snow and came to see for myself. Is this where Max died? Where he drowned—out beneath that ice?

Is this the place where it all makes sense?

The lake remembers, my grandmother used to say. *It's been here as long as the forest. Longer maybe.* Her words hiss through my ears, stirring the dust inside my skull, and I take a slow, deliberate step out onto the frozen lake.

Doubt skips through me. Hesitation.

I swallow and twirl my grandmother's ring on my finger and think of how I've always compared myself to the women in my family, even the women I've never met. Who lived long before I was born. Women whose stories ink the pages of the spellbook—who stare out at me from the past, leering, bewitching, unafraid. But without a nightshade, I can't help but wonder if I'm really like any of them at all. If my name deserves to be listed in the spellbook among them.

I take another step forward.

The lake remembers. Each word a drop of water against my skull.

The lake remembers. Each word a midnight spell.

The ice is solid along the shore, frozen down to the rocky bottom, but as I inch farther out onto the lake, the sound of the ice changes, little tiny cracks opening up beneath me—tension skipping out toward the center.

I know this is a bad idea—I know creeping out over the lake in the middle of the night is how people go missing, how they slip through the ice and are never seen again. Not even a trace. But my grandmother's words make loops along my skin, they singsong and fill my ears until it's the only thing I feel. *The lake remembers.*

And maybe Max was here that night, out on the ice. Oliver, too. They were here and something happened. Death and cries for help and breaking ice and water in lungs.

I shuffle forward, and the lake flexes beneath me—water bubbles rising up, looking for a way out. I glance over my shoulder. I'm only a third of the way from the shore, not anywhere near the center of the lake, but it feels like I'm fathoms away. Too far to turn back now. Or maybe I'm too far to keep going.

But I don't want to be afraid—not of the lake. Not of anything. I want to be like the women who came before me, brave and clever with the shimmer of dark moonlight in their veins. I need to do this, to prove something—to know what happened that night. Because if I can't see the truth, if I can't see what's right in front of me, then I'm not a Walker at all.

Keep moving, I tell myself. If I stop, I might break through the ice—the water flat and black beneath my feet.

Miners dropped things into the lake to appease the wilderness, Mr. Perkins said. A place to make offerings. To quell the forest. But I have not brought an offering. Only myself.

I'm nearly to the center when I see it: the change in the surface of the ice, the reflection of stars on water. A hole has been broken away in front of me.

A hole in the ice.

I inch closer to the edge of the jagged opening—spiderweb cracks fanning out around it, turning the black ice white along the veins. *A hole in the ice. Large enough for a person to fall through.*

Is this where Max broke through the ice and fell into the deep, hands pawing at the surface? His eyes wide while his limbs went numb—becoming useless—and the others only looked on? I try to imagine Oliver standing over him, watching as Max drew in his last breath—his chin, his eyes, dipping beneath the surface. Did Oliver stare in shock with the others? Or did they laugh side-splitting laughs? Did they want him to die?

Did *Oliver* want him to die?

They aren't my friends, he said. So why was he here that night? Why was he with them?

And how did he end up in the forest?

I shuffle an inch closer, wanting to see the dark water, to imagine a person *sinking, sinking, sinking*, falling into a bottomless chasm, never to come back up. Never to return. Did he stare up at the pinhole of light through the broken ice, the last thing he saw before he was swallowed by the black? I shudder and take a quick step back. But my boot slides over something—something thin and shiny.

I bend down and pick it up, hold it in my hand. It's a tiny thing, silver and glimmering. A chain. And it's broken at one end, with a silver ring at the other.

I know what it is—and I wish I didn't. I almost drop it, a shiver slicing up my spine, my pulse pounding against my throat.

It's the missing chain from the pocket watch I found in Oliver's coat.

The watch with Max's name engraved on the back.

I close my hand around the chain, squeezing tight. The link broken and bent.

All this time, it has sat here in the center of the lake, where a boy fell into the dark water and sank.

And now I know for sure they were here. Max and the others. This is the place where he drowned. Where the chain broke and Oliver clutched the watch as if it were a prize. The one who survived.

I don't need him to admit it, I'm already certain.

He killed Max.

My heart unspools in my chest and I tilt my head up to the sky, feeling like I might faint.

Everything is wrong.

My knees start to buckle and I want to cry, but the air is too cold and the tears evaporate against my eyelids. I want to yell into the trees. I want to blame someone—anyone—other than Oliver. But my head clatters and my grandmother's words keep repeating: *The lake remembers.* But I don't want to know the truth. I want to go back to the loft, to earlier tonight with his lips on mine and his hands in my hair and my palms against his rising chest. I want to forget. I want to undo everything that's been done. I want to go back to the night of the storm and tell Oliver to not go to the cemetery. To not go out onto the lake. To avoid this place and those boys. Because once death has wrapped its cool hooked claws around you, it cannot be undone. And only regret remains.

Sorrow and guilt and regret.

And now the lies cannot be put back together. Not when you hold the truth in your hand.

I slide the chain into my pocket, my breath flat and fettered. *All this time.* Maybe this is why he went into the Wicker Woods— to hide, to wait until the road thawed so he could flee. Escape the punishment he would face.

But he got lost, went too deep into the forest—a forest that is ancient and cruel and doesn't so easily let people back out. I found him and brought him back, and now he is asleep in my room, in my house. And I am split in two.

I shuffle away from the icy hole, my whole body trembling,

my mind wheeling forward and back, remembering my lips sinking against Oliver's. Remembering his hands in my hair, the same hands that surely struggled with Max, that forced him into the icy water, that broke the chain of the watch. The same hands that refused to pull Max back up—to save his life. The hands that touched my skin, my collarbone, so close to my throat.

I blink down at the hole one last time, branding it to memory, when I hear the sound of hairline cracks spreading out beneath my feet.

I've stood here too long, the hole widening in front of me, pieces of ice bobbing at the surface, some sinking into the dark, dark water below. Shit. *I waited too long.*

Cold mountain air blows through my hair, and I take several slow, careful steps back—the ice a sheet of glass beneath my feet. Bending, breaking, giving way.

In the distance, I hear my name, carried up and away by the wind—almost not there at all. My head turns slowly, afraid to move, afraid to blink, and I see Oliver standing on the shore, snow whirling around him. He calls my name again, his voice swallowed by the cold.

Fractures spread outward from the hole, little white veins, criss-crossing and separating. I lift one foot and place it behind me, careful and slow. The ice bends away, water bubbling up through the cracks. *It's too thin*, my head screams. *It's too late.*

I suck in a deep breath, then let it slip out through my nose. My eyes feel huge, unblinking, and I glance at Oliver, a word resting beneath my tongue: *Help.* But I never get a chance to say it.

In one violent crack, the ice breaks beneath me.

Shatters into a hundred tiny fragments.

And I plummet into the lake.

Black *black* water. A million knives stabbing my skin, slicing me open. My lungs shrink in on themselves, my hands claw for the surface, already going numb, and I feel my grandmother's ring—the moonstone she gave me—drift to the end of my finger. I reach for it, almost catch it, but it slips off—sinking, sinking, sinking. *No*, I want to yell. My eyes shiver open, staring through the dark water, the shock of cold.

I watch the tiny gold band flit down beneath me, into the deep.

My ribs crush my heart, my whole body caving in on itself. *I'm in the lake. The cold too cold. My mind slowing . . .*

Above me, the surface of the lake and the moonless sky split open, revealing a palette of stars. *So beautiful*, I think. A stupid thought—my body, my mind, already going into shock. Heart rate battering against my chest.

I need air, my body screams. *Air.*

OLIVER

N ora is gone.

Daisy-printed sheets tossed back from her bed, pillow crinkled where her head lay, bits of yellow pollen scattered across the cotton—fallen from the dried flowers hanging over the headboard.

They say she's a witch, and maybe they're right.

She thinks I'm a murderer, and maybe she's not wrong.

I fell asleep when I promised I'd stay awake. And now, the wolf follows me down the stairs, my mind skipping back to earlier—to Nora's rose-shaped lips pressed to mine, the smell of her hair on my neck, like jasmine and vanilla. I don't think she knows how much she upends me. How for the briefest moment, the dark of the forest felt very far away. How her fingertips blotted out the cold of the trees that's always writhing along my joints, twisting around my kneecaps and shoulder blades and down my spine. When she's close, my memory of that place falls away.

She keeps it at bay.

She's the only thing that makes me believe maybe I'm not the villain after all. But the hero. Or the one to be saved, rescued from the dark wood.

My part in this tale may not be what I think. A character whose role has not yet been determined.

Downstairs, I find the kitchen dark with no sign of Nora. The fire is out in the woodstove. And then I see it: the dead bolt on the front door slid open.

I yank the door wide and spot the tracks in the snow, leading down to the lake. I run down to the shore and the trees moan and stir, as if sensing the urgency in my steps, the thunder of my lungs sucking in air.

I know something's wrong before I've even reached the lake, before I see Nora standing out on the ice. I call out to her and she looks back, her hair a firestorm—the wind churning up around her, making her look as if she is made of magic. *A real witch.* A girl with fury at her fingertips—who could command mountains and rivers and time itself.

She turns, glancing over her shoulder, and I can see the look in her eyes—something isn't right. She seems afraid—*really* afraid for the first time.

And then the ice gives way beneath her. A shudder and a crack and she disappears into the lake.

I run, my heart flattening against my ribs, my feet slipping on the ice.

I drop to my knees at the edge of a vast hole, black water peering back. And beneath the surface, her hair swirls and eddies like reeds, like kelp in an ocean. A gentle, almost tranquil sight. She's staring past me—eyes blurred over—as if she is looking lazily up at the midnight sky and the stars beyond. A quiet evening swim. But I plunge my arms into the ice-cold water, grabbing for her hand floating just above her head.

And I pull her up, dragging her onto the ice and into my arms.

NORA

I feel weightless, drifting among dark stars.

Arms fold around me, and I press my face against the hard warmth of a shoulder. His neck smells like the forest, like a winter that goes on and on and on. Endless like the bottom of the lake.

I hear the water dripping from my hair, or maybe I only imagine it. Drops that turn to ice before they hit the ground.

The trees bob and shiver above me, and I peer up at deep-green limbs—at stars that look like silver coins dropped into a black pool. My head spins, the circulation gone from my skin, but I don't mind. I like the weightlessness and the scent of Oliver and the forest revolving above me. We reach the house, and Oliver kicks the door closed behind us, then releases me gently onto the couch.

He's saying something, words that slip and slide together. Maybe he's saying my name. *Nora, Nora, Nora.* But I can't be sure. I like the way his voice sounds, bouncing along the walls of the house.

Fin pushes his nose against my palm, warm and wet, a lick to the ear. I try to speak, to open my eyes, but they are too heavy. I squint and at the end of the couch, Oliver is shoving more logs into the woodstove, filling it quickly. He cusses, slams his hand in the door maybe, then stands up and crosses the room again. Waves of heat surge into the cabin. But I don't sweat—I shiver.

"Nora!" he says again, I'm certain of it this time. "Stay awake," he tells me. I nod, or I think I do. My mouth opens to tell him I'm fine, but I feel my jaw hang there, no words escaping past my lips. My mouth too numb, my tongue worthless.

He drapes blankets over me—heavy, heavy blankets made of wool—so heavy they push me into sleep. They push me down into the fibers of the old dusty couch, between the cushions. Where lost paper clips and rose petals and M&M's hide.

But I'm convulsing now, the cold shot through my lungs, severing my skin down to bone, and everything starts to blur over. Water pressing against my eyes, *sinking*, everything turning not black but white. Bone white. Moon white. Ash white.

"Why did you go out there?" Oliver's voice says from somewhere far away, from up in the rafters of the house. I feel his hands against my feet, rubbing them, sending spikes of pain up my calves. *It hurts!* I want to tell him, to scream. But my mouth still won't move, or he just doesn't listen. My blood is too hot, scalding, as it surges back through cold veins.

I kick my legs but they don't move. I close my eyes and chase the moth down through the trees, I run after it, and when I catch it I will pluck its wings clean from its body. But it spins high up toward a strange purple sky where three moons sit on the horizon, and it laughs at me. *Foolish girl*, it hisses. *Hiss hiss hiss.*

I flash my eyes open and look up at the ceiling, at cobwebs draped woefully from the beams down toward the corner of a window. "I saw the hole," I say, but it sounds like nonsense. "I saw where he drowned," I try, but my lips are too frozen, and Oliver presses his hand to my forehead. He rubs a warm cloth across my skin.

"Nora," he says again. Always my name, like there is nothing else to say. He wants me to wake, to open my eyes, *to prove I'm not a witch*. I shake my head. I'm hearing things that aren't real. Imagining words that never leave his lips.

I try to bend my fingers into fists, but they won't move. So I give up.

My eyelids lower, a velvet curtain at the end of the show—a macabre ballet about witches and cruel boys and lakes that swallow people up—and I fall asleep listening to the roar of the fire and Oliver saying my name and the crackling pain of warmth returning to my bones.

Men never stay long in our lives, Grandma would say.

We drive them away. We sneak potions into their coffee to make them crave the smell of the sea, so they will leave these mountains and never come back. We refuse proposals and leave love letters unopened and don't come to windows when boys toss pebbles against the glass at sunrise. We prefer to be alone.

But it doesn't mean our hearts don't unravel. It doesn't mean we can't love deeply and painfully and chase after boys who refuse to love us back. But in the end, always in the end, we find a way to shatter whatever hint of love had grown inside us.

I wake on the couch thinking of this.

I wake recalling Oliver pulling me from the lake and carrying me home. I recall his hands on my skin, wiping the sweat from my brow. And I think that maybe, possibly, he cares about me. But I'm also certain I'll find a way to ruin it.

Just give me time.

I press my palms into the couch, my arms shaking as I prop myself up. Outside, the sky is dark. But I have a memory of the sun shining through the windows, reflecting off the walls, a hollow orb that felt too bright. *How many days have passed? How many nights?*

I flex my fingers and the numbness is gone—a dull warmth returned to my skin.

I untangle myself from the blankets, grip the edge of the couch for balance, and pull myself up to my feet. My joints crack and my head sways a little, as though water is still trapped in the hollows of my ears.

Fin is lying at my feet, and I reach down to run my fingers through his thick fur, his tail swishing once against the floor. "I'm all right," I assure him, and he blows out a soft breath of air and lowers his head, like he can finally sleep now that he knows I'm awake.

On wobbly feet, I walk into the kitchen and drink a glass of water, then two more—my body desperate for it. Sandpaper in my throat. I hold on to the edge of the counter and listen for Oliver. "Hello?" I call into the house, but my voice comes out as a croak. Barely audible.

Maybe he's gone back to the camp. Or is out gathering more firewood. Or maybe he grew desperate when I didn't wake, and he went to get one of the counselors who is trained in basic first aid. Wherever he is, I'm alone in the house.

I consider shuffling back across the living room and collapsing onto the couch, letting sleep tug me under once again. But I'm wearing the same T-shirt as when I went out onto the lake. The sweatshirt and jeans I had on are now gone—Oliver must have removed them when he brought me back to the house. All of my clothes soaked through.

I walk to the stairs, knuckles tightening around the railing, and I drag myself slowly up each step to the loft.

But once inside the loft, the room feels different, and it takes a moment for my eyes to adjust. The bed is crisscrossed in shadows, no candles lit, and a cold breeze slides over my skin. The window is open, pushed up in the frame, and the thin embroidered curtains sway out from the wall then settle back again, like they're underwater.

On the floor, a dusting of snow has gathered.

And through the window I see him standing out on the roof.

He didn't go back to the camp—he's still here.

I pull on my heaviest sweater from the closet, thick wool socks, my slippers with the rubber soles, and step out onto the roof—into the snow.

My muscles are weak, and the cold almost knocks me over. I feel hollow boned like a bird—a soft wind could surely carry me away.

Oliver hears me and turns. "What are you doing?" he asks urgently, crossing the space that separates us. "You shouldn't be out here. It's too cold."

"The air feels good," I say, my eyes blinking closed, then open again. But he shakes his head. "Just for a little while," I tell him. "I just want to stand outside." I need to feel my legs beneath me, the air in my lungs. *Alive.*

He folds my hand through his arm and helps me to the edge of the roof, where the view of the lake is the clearest, where a few stars even prick out from the dark, clouded skyline.

"I used to come out here when I was little," I say, my voice still shaky. "My mom hated it, said I would slip off the edge and break my neck. But I did it anyway." I smile in spite of the cold. "It's quiet up here," I add. "The sky feels closer."

Oliver tilts his head up at the sky, but his mouth turns down, like he doesn't see what I see. Like he sees only shadows. Only the grim, spiny outline of trees. "I was worried you might never wake up," he says, his voice thinner than I've ever heard it. Like he can still see the image of me in the lake, hair like seaweed, my body limp as he drew me up from the water—and the memory haunts him still.

Perhaps I am now *his* found thing. The girl he hauled up from the lake and brought home.

"Walkers are hard to kill," I answer, laughing a little, then instantly regret it—*a strange thing to say*. The wrong thing to say. I dig a toe into the snow, kicking some off the edge of the roof onto the ground below. "Why are you out here?" I ask, to divert my thoughts away from death. *From drowning*. So easily I could have sunk and never been found. If Oliver hadn't woken when he did and pulled me from the lake, the bone moth's omen would have come true. And I would be just another tale inside the Spellbook of Moonlight & Forest Medicine—a brief notation. Another Walker who met her end in these mountains. *Died too young*, it might say. *Died before she ever fell in love*. Or just as she was starting to.

Oliver's gaze lifts, eye level with the branches—with the tangled nests made by birds who have flown south for the winter. Abandoned their homes. And when they return in spring, they will construct new nests, new lives—the old ones not worth hanging on to. "To watch for the others," he says. "I've come up here every night."

He seems distracted, his shoulders rigid, his eyes straining out into the distance, watching for figures marching up through the pines, coming to take the witch and hang her from a tree, make sure she never talks. *Just like locals once did to my ancestors.* He's up here to protect me.

I draw my hands into the sleeves of my sweater to keep out the cold. I count the thuds of my heart. *One, two, ten . . .* I lose track. *Time is not a measure of seconds, but of breaths in the lungs.* "I dropped my grandmother's ring in the lake when I fell in," I finally say, my voice small. A thing that doesn't belong to me anymore—the cold stripped it away.

"I know," he says, and he looks at me for the first time. "You were talking about it in your sleep."

What else did I say? What other feverish murmurings that I didn't want him to hear?

I clear my throat. "How long was I asleep?"

"Three days." He exhales deeply, as if recalling the hours, the nights that passed when he sat beside me, waiting for me to stir. "You woke up a few times, but you were pretty out of it."

"I was probably hypothermic," I say, then chew on the corner of my lip, imagining him feeding me soup while I mumbled nonsensically. When I found him in the woods, he was near death, chilled to the bone, and I made him strip out of his clothes and sit beside the fire. Now we're even. "Thank you," I say. "For pulling me from the lake. For taking care of me."

His sleepy eyes settle on me, and his jaw contracts. "You could have died in that water." I understand now why he looks at me like this, why the muscles in his arm tense when I speak.

"I know," I say flatly, feeling my heart rise and then fall, recalling the cold depth of the lake trying to swallow me up. "I'm sorry."

"Why did you go out there?" he asks pointedly, swiveling to face me, but still keeping my arm looped in his. So I won't collapse.

I shake my head because I don't know what to say. *Because my grandmother slipped into my dreams and whispered about the lake, about remembering. Because I thought I was brave. Because I thought the lake would give up its secrets to me. Because I'm a Walker.* "I found a broken chain on the ice," I say at last, as explanation. "The chain from the watch I found in your coat."

Oliver's expression goes cold, as if his heart darkens in his chest, turns as black as magpie wings. "You still think I killed him?"

I don't answer, and I pull my arm away from him—afraid to tell him what I think. Afraid to say that even if he doesn't remember it, he might have killed a boy. And that this single thing might destroy everything.

"I didn't want to be there that night," he tells me, his voice tiptoeing around each word.

"But you were," I say.

He shakes his head and looks back at the sky, a waning moon peeking out from clouds, blurring the stars around it. Devouring them.

Oliver bites down on the words before he says them, and they come out bitter and clenched. "And what happened can't be taken back," he says. The wind kicks up over the lake, sending spires of white rising into the air.

"If it was an accident, like the others said, then it was no one's fault," I offer, trying to make everything okay. Not as bad as it seems.

"You don't understand, Nora," he says, swallowing hard and turning to look at me. "It wasn't an accident. They knew what they were doing."

A river of cold spikes down my center. "Who?" I ask.

"All of them."

"They wanted Max dead?"

Oliver is quiet—midnight quiet, tiptoe quiet—and I ask, "Do you remember what happened now?" Is this why he's standing out here on the roof, watching for the boys? Because his memories have returned? Because he recalls each moment out on that lake, with Max and the others?

He uncrosses his arms, slow and deliberate. "It's too late now anyway. We can't undo what's been done." His chest rises with each breath, his flat green eyes so wretchedly deep and dark that I feel drawn to him again. And even though there is disquiet in him— doubt and fear and fury, for the things he won't say—I could also reach up on my tiptoes and press my lips against his. I could blot out his thoughts, the worry set deep in his eyes. I could blot out everything, take it from him and swallow it down and make it untrue. I am a Walker, and I should be able to do this one thing. A simple, singular thing: take a memory, take a death—and make it right.

But I can't undo it. And I don't lean forward and kiss him under the weight of the sallow moon. I stare at him and wait for him to speak. And when he does, it's like vinegar and salt, a wound that will never heal. "I don't want to hurt you," he says, his eyes sloped down at the edges.

"You won't," I say. As if I can be sure.

He looks back into the trees, and dread burrows into the marrow of my bones, writhing inside me like shipworms making tunnels in my flesh.

He shakes his head—he doesn't believe me. "I don't want you to be afraid."

"I'm not afraid," I tell him. But I know that I am, a wretched knot of fear growing in my gut. I'm scared to trust him, to let this flutter inside my chest become a hammer that will smash me apart. *We love painfully,* Mom always says. *With our whole hearts.* But *we bruise easily too.* She has always been afraid of her own careless heart, of past mistakes, of what she really is. And I don't want to be like her: cynical and fearful and full of more doubt than anything else.

Oliver steps closer to me, and I think he's going to kiss me, but his hand touches mine instead. "You're shaking," he says.

My body trembles, the cold sapping what little warmth is left inside me. But I say, "I'm fine."

He squeezes my hand and pulls me to him, my head against his chest, his breath in my hair. He holds me to him and I want to cry—as if this will be the last time. "We need to get you inside," he says. But I don't want to, I want to stay out here with him and let the cold turn me to stone.

Still he pulls me back to the window, my muscles too weak to resist, and he lifts me up, placing me back through the open window into the loft.

My legs shake, and I crawl into bed, pulling the blankets up to my chin, while he shuts the window with a thud and locks it in place. As if to keep out the things we fear the most.

"Will you stay here with me?" I ask when he starts to move toward the stairs—my voice shaking. "Please."

I don't want to be alone, in this awful dark. With my skin like ice. I touch the place on my finger where my grandmother's ring used to sit, feeling stripped bare without it. *My accidental offering to the lake—just like the miners who used to drop things into the water to calm the trees.*

Oliver looks back, his eyes coursing with something I don't understand. A battle inside him. He wants to stay here with me, but he's also afraid of what he might do. Or what he might say. He's constructed an armor around himself, stone and metal and painful memories. Before, there was only confusion in his eyes—the void of what he had forgotten. Now, there is a wall of shadows. Tall and wide.

Still, he nods and crosses the room to lie beside me.

Maybe he doesn't want to be alone either.

He smells like snow, and I fold myself into him—tiny like a shell. His arm drapes over my ribs, and his breath is at my neck. He could place his lips at the soft place behind my ear, he could run his fingers through my hair, but instead he only lies still. Warming my skin with his. *Please*, I want to say. *Tell me what you did that night. Tell me what you saw out on that ice; tell me what you regret.*

Tell me so I can build my own armor. A fortress in this tiny loft, a battlefield you cannot cross.

But I also know it's too late for that now.

I turn, coiled in his arms, to face him. I take his hand and place it against my chest, over my heart. "I don't know if I can trust this," I say, I confess. "This thing inside my own heart." I let myself bleed for him to see.

His mouth softens but he doesn't speak, his eyes shivering.

"The women in my family always fall in love then find a way to ruin it." I smirk, lips drawn up to one side. "I know you think I should be afraid of you. But you should be afraid of me."

"Why?" he asks softly, carefully.

"Because I will end up hurting you."

A smile forms in his eyes, and the space between us feels impossibly small. Only an exhale separating us. I don't wait for him to speak—I don't want to hear any more words—I cross the fathom between us and I lay my lips on his. And it's not like before, not like when we kissed in my room to be certain we were both real. Now it's a kiss to prove that we're not. A certainty that this won't last. That perhaps all we have left is here in this bed, lavender pollen against the pillows, air spilling from his lungs into mine. All we have left is this one, singular, fragile night. Snow on the roof and snow in our hearts and snow to bury us alive.

I kiss him and he kisses me back. And all at once, there is heat inside my veins, heat in the palm of his hand as he slides his fingers up inside my sweater, up along my spine. He wipes away the cold. And I feel my body shudder, pressing myself closer to him, touching his neck, his throat, his shoulders where they brace around me, drawing me to him. I exhale and kiss him harder. There is nothing but his hands on my bare skin. The weight of his kiss, of his chest breathing so deeply I can almost hear his lungs aching against his ribs.

Nothing but these slow seconds of time. Nothing but fingertips and swollen lips and hearts that will surely break when morning comes.

His kiss against my ribs, my fingers in his hair.

I close my eyes and pretend Oliver is just a boy from camp who never went missing. A boy I met on the shore of the lake. A boy with clear green eyes and no lost memories.

I pretend I never saw a bone moth in the trees the day I found him.

I pretend this room, with mountain moss and bleeding-heart acorns hung by string above my bed, is the only place there will ever be.

I pretend Oliver and I are in love. I pretend he will never leave—I pretend to make it true.

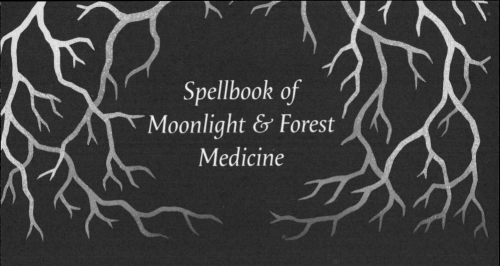

Spellbook of Moonlight & Forest Medicine

RUTH WALKER was born in late July of 1922 under a white deer moon. Her lips were the color of snow with eyes as green as the river in spring. But Ruth Walker never spoke.

Not once in her whole life.

Her mother, Vena, swore she heard Ruth whispering to the mice that lived in the attic and humming lullabies to the bees outside her window. But no one else ever heard such mutterings.

Ruth was short and beautiful with wavy crimson hair that never grew past her shoulders, and she clucked her tongue when she walked through the woods. When she was twelve, she began deciphering messages in the webs made by the peppercorn spiders.

The webs foretold the following year's weather, and Ruth knew the dates of rainstorms and dry summer weeks and when the winds would blow away the laundry hanging on the line.

In return, Ruth fed the spiders bits of maidenhair mushrooms that she grew in a clay pot in the back of the loft closet. Much to her mother's displeasure.

When Ruth was ninety-nine, she became tangled in a web while walking through the Wicker Woods. She died under the stars, as silent as the day she was born.

How to Read Peppercorn Spiderwebs:

Harvest maidenhair mushrooms (grown for nine months before picking).

O☒er less than an ounce, more than a teaspoon, to peppercorn spider.

Sleep in soil beneath web for one night. Wait for dew to settle on silk strands.

Remain silent, careful not to tear web. Decipher forecast for following season.

OLIVER

It was different before. Before I remembered.

They weren't lies then, but now they are.

Sprinting across the frozen lake, pulling her up from the water, I felt the sting of *that* other awful night. Like a brick sinking into my stomach, I remembered what happened.

The cemetery was only the beginning. What came later was the end. The lake and my hands around Max's throat. The others shouting from shore.

I never should have been there.

It's not a thousand little lies that amount to nothing. It's one large lie, so big it will swallow me up. And it will destroy her.

Tonight, with my hands against her skin and my face in her hair, I know I will hurt her. If not by sunrise, eventually. Soon enough she will look at me with sharp, serrated fear in her eyes. She will look and know what I am.

So I hold it inside for as long as I can. I lie beside her, our fingers knitted together, and I pretend it will stay this way forever. Because she is all that roots me here. The only thing that blots out the feeling of the cold forest inside me. The only cure for the dark I can't escape.

She is long auburn eyelashes and little white half-moons on her fingernails and a voice that always sounds like an incantation.

And she just might be a witch.

So I kiss her temple where she sleeps, her breath a tiny sputter of air. Because I know this won't last.

There is no escaping what comes next.

But for now I let her sleep.

I let her rest without knowing who lies beside her. I let her breathe and think that everything will be fine and there is nothing to fear in this house.

I lie.

I lie.

I lie.

But by morning, I will be gone.

NORA

Walkers are born with a nightshade.

Our shadow side, Grandma called it. The part of us that isn't like anyone else. The part of us that *sees*. That *compels*. And sometimes *commands*. Our shadow side allows us to slip into the Wicker Woods unharmed. It's the ancient part of us that remembers.

The quality of moonlight in our veins—the gift we each possess.

For my grandma, her shadow side let her slink into other people's dreams. My mom can soothe the wild honeybees when she gathers their comb. Dottie Walker, my great-great-grandmother, could whistle up a fire. Alice Walker, my great-aunt, could change her hair color by dipping her toes into mud.

Walker women are lit from within, Grandma said.

But I have never possessed nightshade. A thing I can do that other Walkers cannot.

It will come, Grandma would say. *Some Walkers wait their whole lives for it to rise up inside them.* But maybe not all of us are born with it. Maybe my shadow side is only a thin sliver, hardly there at all.

Maybe there will not be a story to tell about me when I die—a story to be written down inside the spellbook.

For I am a Walker who was never granted her shade.

Fin is barking. In my dreams. In my sleeping ears.

In my room.

My eyes snap open.

His bark echoes off the walls, and I try to focus, but the room is still dark and my eyes blink, unable to see what's wrong.

"Shut that thing up!" someone yells.

I sit up quickly, shadows moving across my room, panic ringing in my ears. Fin lunges forward, toward someone standing near the stairs. His teeth sink into their flesh, and they yell in pain. Someone else grabs Fin and pulls him off. "Fucking wolf!" the boy beside the stairs shouts, holding his arm where Fin bit into him. *A voice I've heard before.* Jasper.

My eyes finally focus—finally see the boys in my room.

Rhett is standing over my bed, wearing the same red-plaid hat he had on at the bonfire. "Get up," he demands. I scan the loft quickly and Oliver is gone. No longer in the bed beside me. *He left me alone.* "I said get up!" I can hear in Rhett's voice that he's drunk. Wasted drunk. Slurring drunk. They've probably been up all night—his eyes are bloodshot, skin saturated with the stench of booze.

"No," I answer defiantly. "You get the hell out of my house."

Jasper laughs, quick and blunt. He's wearing the reindeer sweater again, but it's dirty, slept in, spilled on, frayed along the neckline.

"You're going to take us into those woods," Rhett says, a strange smile peeling across his upper lip, like he's enjoying this. "You're taking us to Oliver."

I frown. "Oliver isn't in the woods."

He lowers himself closer to me, eyes wide, nostrils flared. "No? Then where is he?"

"I don't know."

"You told Suzy that you found him in the woods, that he's been hiding there, and now you're going to take us. You're going to show us where he's been all this time."

"No," I tell him again.

Jasper moves across the room and grabs me by the arm, pulling me up from bed. The cut on his cheek has healed slightly since I saw him last, white along the edges, but red in the center where the border of the scar will never heal completely. "Yes, you are," Jasper declares through clenched teeth.

Fin is growling from the corner where Lin is holding him tightly by the scruff at the back of his neck. And in an instant, I'm on my feet and they're forcing me down the stairs.

Oliver left me. A pain cuts through me, knowing he fled while I slept. And he didn't say why. *He just left.*

Jasper tells me to pull on my boots and coat, and I do, then they push me out the front doorway. I see that the door's been kicked open—the hinges bent, the lock broken. I didn't even wake at the sound. Only Fin heard them enter.

"You're wasting your time," I say. They manage to close the broken door enough to keep Fin from following us. But I can hear his whine from the other side—at least they didn't hurt him. "Oliver's not in the woods."

In the moonlight, standing on the deck, Rhett looks wild eyed and bored and edgy all at once. The boys remind me of a pack of wolves out searching for something to tear apart. They're fidgety and drunk. Reckless.

"Then where is he?" Rhett asks, leaning so close I can feel the heat of his breath.

"He was here," I say, glowering up at him. "He's been staying with me, but now I don't know where he is."

"She's lying," Jasper says, his voice like a braying cow.

"You've been hiding him here this whole time?" Rhett asks.

I set my jaw in place and my eyes flash to Lin, who stands with his hands in his jean pockets, looking not entirely comfortable with what's happening, but not trying to stop them either. "He wasn't hiding," I say. "He just didn't want to stay with you assholes."

Rhett sneers. "If Oliver was staying with you, then why isn't he in your house?"

"I don't know."

"We can't trust anything she says," Jasper interjects. "She's just trying to protect him." He winces, and I see that his sweatshirt is bloody where Fin bit into him.

"You're taking us up to those woods," Rhett announces, the decision made.

Jasper grabs onto my arm again, but I yank it back. "We can't," I tell them, my thumb itching at the finger where my grandmother's ring used to sit, wishing I still had it, wishing she was here now. "It's not a full moon."

"So what?" Jasper says.

"The forest will be awake. It will see us."

Jasper laughs—an unpleasant sound—and Rhett moves to only a few inches from my face. "I don't care if it's Saint Patrick's Day and you're worried about leprechauns stealing your gold, you're taking us to where he's hiding. And no more of your witchy bullshit."

Jasper pushes a palm against my back, and I move forward just to keep him from touching me again. We march down the steps, little tin soldiers all in a row. They're drunk and desperate. Whatever happened that night, out on that lake, whatever they've been hearing in their cabins, they can't escape it—and it's starting to make cracks along their minds.

But then I see someone else standing in the trees, chin lowered, waiting for us.

Suzy.

She came with them—*she's part of this*. And a raw, acrid pit sinks into my stomach. Rotting me from the inside out. This must be what betrayal feels like.

But none of them realize, none of them understand: If we go into the Wicker Woods now, under a half waning moon—when the trees are awake—we won't come back out.

"You guys don't have to do it like this," Suzy says, running toward us when she sees me, a deep set of lines across her forehead. "You could have just asked her to take us into the woods."

"She never would have done it," Rhett argues, barely glancing her way.

Suzy falls into step beside me, chewing on the edge of her fingernail. "Nora, I'm so sorry," she whispers nervously, shooting me a helpless look. But I don't want to hear it. "I told them about Oliver, how you found him in the woods. They just want to see him and—"

She stops before finishing and starts chewing on her fingernail again.

And hurt him, I think. They want to find him and hurt him, because when bad things happen, you have to blame someone. *And maybe Oliver really is to blame.*

"Just show them where you found Oliver," she says now, eyebrows sloped together, pleading with me. "It'll make it easier."

She looks like a broken porcelain doll, missing all her insides, like she's been gutted clean. But I refuse to let myself feel sorry for her—like I have before.

"Yeah, don't make it any harder on yourself," Jasper chimes in, walking behind me, his tall, gaunt frame looming over me.

We march along the lake's edge, then turn north, toward the mountains, toward the mouth of the Black River. Rhett leads the way and I follow, the other boys close behind me—in case I decide to run. And Suzy is last, dragging her feet, probably wishing she hadn't come—parading behind three drunk boys who are forcing me up the mountainside in the dark.

Maybe I should feel afraid, of what might happen, of what they might do to me.

But I'm only afraid of the woods.

The clouds move farther south, the moon winks out from the black sky, and an owl calls from somewhere in the trees to our left—it doesn't want us here, we'll scare away the rodents it hunts at night.

Our troop of drunken boys, staggering through the snow, is not passing through the wilds unnoticed. And we haven't even reached the Wicker Woods yet.

We trudge higher up into the mountains, until we reach the two steep slopes, the ravine, the cairn of rocks standing guard. *The entrance.*

The boys fall silent for the first time, each staring into the dark, opening through the trees—the boundary of the Wicker Woods.

"I don't like it," Lin says, standing back, away from the border. "It's fucking creepy. Doesn't feel right."

A cold wind slides out from the entrance, smelling like the darkest *dark*, like wet rocks and soil that have never felt sunlight, like the place where monsters sleep. Not imaginary ones, but ones that hunt and slink and creep. Ones that stare out at us, hoping we'll step inside. Hoping we're dumb enough. "That's because we shouldn't be here," I say, a shudder sliding along my voice. "This is the only way in," I tell them, "and it's the only way out."

Suzy swallows, an audible gulp. "Maybe we should wait until it's light," she suggests. "When we can see." The fear is evident in her voice. Gone is the girl I remember from school, who buzzed down the halls of Fir Haven High laughing loudly so everyone could hear, kissing as many boys as she could on Valentine's Day. Keeping count. Now she looks deflated, a girl who's lost all her air.

Rhett ignores her. "You go in first," he says to me, pushing a hand against my shoulder. I bite back the urge to turn around and shove him in the chest, to scratch and claw at his face, to make him bleed. But I still feel weak, my muscles tensing against the cold, and so far they haven't hurt me—I'm not going to give them a reason to.

"It's not a full moon," I repeat. "We can't go in there."

"I don't give a shit," Rhett replies. He shoves me again and I stagger forward, one foot at the very edge of the entrance into the woods. I glance back at Suzy, who is biting her lower lip, watching me like I'm about to be swallowed up by the trees. Like she has never felt more terrified in her life. And in her eyes, I think I see her urging me to run—to turn and dart back down the mountain. But she doesn't know how weak I am, that I'm having a hard time even standing.

"You don't have to hurt her," Suzy pleads, but Rhett has stopped listening to her.

Knots bind together inside my stomach, and I crane my head up to the night sky—clouds sailing away, the moon a deflated half circle. *Not full.* Not safe to venture into these dark, vengeful woods.

I blow out a breath and whisper the words I've said so many times before, hoping they will protect me, hoping the woods will remember me and let me pass unharmed. "I am Nora Walker," I say softly so the boys won't hear. And then I repeat it twice more, for good measure, for luck.

But I sense it might be too late for that.

Walker or not, perhaps none us will survive the night.

So I stiffen my arms at my sides and take a step past the threshold, into the Wicker Woods.

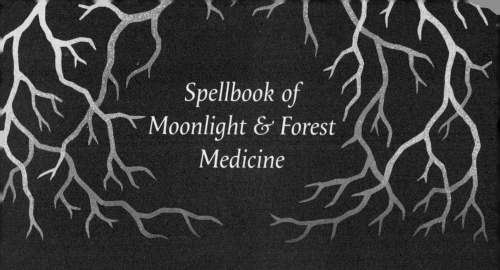

Spellbook of Moonlight & Forest Medicine

IONA WALKER was born under a black harvest moon—the darkest night of the year.

Even as a baby, she cast no shadow across the ground. Even on the brightest afternoon, even when the sun burned at her neck.

But a girl without a shadow can see in the dark. A rather useful nightshade for sneaking and spying.

Iona often wandered through the house while her mother slept, never flicking on a single light, never stubbing her toe on a rocking chair she couldn't see. Her vision was even better than that of her cat, Oyster, who learned to follow Iona through the dark.

When she was twenty-three, she met a boy who gathered night phlox and coal berries and ninebark leaves after the sun had set. On a cool October night, she kissed him under a full moon, and he swore he'd never leave her side.

Until the night Iona lost sight of him somewhere among the shadowed trees. He wandered too near the Wicker Woods, slipped beyond the forest boundary, where no one but a Walker should enter, and he was never seen again.

Iona banished the dark after that, and never again went into the woods once the sun had dipped below the treeline. She died on a late August morning, sitting on the front porch of the old house overlooking the lake. And as her eyes slipped closed, her shadow stretched out long in front of her.

It had been there all along, coiled up inside her, too afraid to step into the light.

How to Find Your Shadow:

○ Hang foxglove from the back door by a black, knotted rope.

Only step outside during moonlight (no direct sun) for five nights in a row. Your shadow will reveal itself on the sixth.

NORA

I feel the weight of the trees as soon as I enter, the bony edges of the forest lunging out at strange angles.

We shouldn't be here.

"Keep going," Rhett urges from behind me, and I wave a hand out in front of me, feeling my way. My senses dulled, cotton in my ears. Usually I can traverse these woods with some sense of direction. But now the forest is too dark and colorless.

Thorns cut sharply across my hands, moss catches in my hair, and I can feel the trees inching closer, death creaking along each limb, the wind cold and severe.

The trees are awake.

"I can't see shit," Jasper remarks behind me. A line of us stumbling through the woods. And then I hear the click of something. A light sparking sudden and bright from Jasper's hand.

He's holding a lighter out in front of him, and the trees react instantly.

The woods hiss—like air escaping a basement that's never known daylight—limbs moan and weave together, suffocating the moon above.

"Put the fire out!" I bark back at him.

The trees respond to my voice, the ground swelling and turning beneath us, roots seething. *The forest is awake. It knows we're here.*

In the last bit of light before the small flame blinks out, I see the faces of the boys, of Suzy, and the strange panic in their eyes. The whites too white. Their teeth clenched. Mouths zippered shut. They weren't expecting this—for the forest to move around us. For their hearts to tighten so quickly in their chests.

"Maybe we should head back?" I hear Lin say.

"We just got here," Jasper says, the lighter gone dark in his hand.

"We're not going until we find Oliver," Rhett declares, but his voice is hoarse, like he's trying to hide the nagging unease he feels. The cold that's found him and won't let go.

"Rhett, please," Suzy tries. "I don't like it in here. It feels like the trees are moving."

The trees *are* moving, uprooting themselves to shift closer. *Awake, awake, awake.*

"If we find him, then he'll prove we didn't do anything wrong," Rhett says, his voice sounding desperate now. They need this. As if he thinks Oliver will somehow make it right, that Oliver is the key. "He can tell the counselors, and we won't be in trouble."

"He's not here," I insist, keeping my voice low, trying not to anger the woods. "We need to leave." But when I swivel around, I have no idea where we are. *We've gone too far*, I think. But it's not that—we've only been walking for a few minutes. The forest has changed around us, blocked the path back out.

The trees are awake. And they are moving.

"Look!" Jasper says too loudly, and I hear the quick shuffle of his feet. His silhouette drops to the ground, kneeling over something. I think maybe he's hurt, but then he holds up his hand. "Gold," he says.

I take a step closer, barely able to make out the object in his hand.

"What is it?" Rhett asks, moving toward Jasper.

"A belt buckle, I think." He brushes away the dirt and snow from the thing in his palm. "And there's more." He fans his hands across the ground then picks up something else. Suzy and Lin step closer, trying to see what he's found. "Buttons," he says. "Made of bone." He holds one up for us to see, but it's too tiny. "And some look like silver."

Lin drops to the ground as well, digging through the snow at the base of a tree, down to the soil. "There's a spoon over here," he says.

Rhett wheels around to face me. "This is where she finds all that stuff in her house." He's close enough that I can see him raise an eyebrow. "And this is why she didn't want us coming in here—she thinks it all belongs to her."

Even Suzy crouches down and starts searching the ground with her outstretched palms.

"You can't keep any of these things," I say, meeting Rhett's gaze, my jaw grinding against my back teeth. "You can't leave the woods with any of it."

"Yeah, right." Rhett says with an upturned smirk—no longer afraid. He doesn't believe me. And suddenly, none of them seem to care about finding Oliver, about the trees inching closer. They only care about the items scattered across the forest floor.

"If you leave with any of these things tonight, the woods will see. They will know what you've stolen."

"So what?" Rhett says, his eyes swaying away from me and then back, still intoxicated.

"You have a whole house filled with this stuff," Jasper interjects, sitting forward on his knees. "And nothing's happened to you."

"I took those things when it was a full moon," I say, trying to keep my voice low, trying to make them understand: This isn't an ordinary forest. "I took them when the forest was asleep." But none of them are listening. Even Rhett begins to scan the ground too, searching.

Misfortune will follow you. Words from the spellbook scroll across my mind. *If you take something from the Wicker Woods when it isn't a full moon, misery and catastrophe will trail you home.*

The trees moan around us, and I turn in a circle, trying to orient myself—to see which direction will lead us back to the entrance of the woods. But none of it's familiar. The landscape has changed, the woods playing tricks. The path we took from the edge of the forest is no longer there. It's been wiped away or hidden, or a tree has re-rooted in its place.

If Fin were here, he would know the way out, sense it, his nose to the soil would lead us home. My head begins to thrum and the forest grows darker—any speck of light through the treetops squeezed out.

A low, wailing hiss sails through the lower limbs, like the forest is baring its teeth, snarling.

Suzy hears it too, and she stops scanning the ground. She looks at me, then stands. "What's happening?" she asks, inching closer to me.

"We have to get out of here," I say softly. "Or we might not get out at all."

Lin makes a sudden noise to our left. "Shit!" he says, scrambling toward us, dropping a collection of silver trinkets that hit the ground with a *clank*. "Something grabbed me." He jumps up and down and wipes at his foot, like he's still trying to shake it off. "A fucking tree root or something." He moves into the center of the group, twitching, slapping at his legs.

"Maybe we should head back," Jasper suggests finally—the first smart thing he's said.

Rhett nods. "We can come back during the day, when we can see. Oliver won't be able to hide as easily."

"I told you we should wait until morning," Suzy mutters, shifting closer to me, the hiss around us growing louder. Trees lumbering near, crowding over us—closer, closer, *closer*. We're running out of time. "I don't like it in here," Suzy whispers, and she reaches out and takes my hand. Squeezing. A branch brushes against her hair and she swats it away. "We need to go!" she shouts to the boys, to Rhett.

"Lead the way, witch girl," Rhett says, waving a hand at me.

But I stare back at him blankly. *I don't know the way.*

For the first time, I don't know how to get out of here. "I don't—" My voice breaks off. "I don't know where we are," I admit.

Jasper pushes a handful of found things into his coat pocket. "This place can't be that big," he says. "Just pick a direction." And without waiting for anyone to answer, he starts off into the trees, shoving limbs aside.

"We don't know if that's the right way," Suzy points out, eyebrows sloped down, worry etched into every line of her face.

"You don't have a choice," Rhett says, stepping behind Suzy and me, waving a hand forward. "Can't let you go off to warn Oliver that we're looking for him. So you're coming with us."

Suzy squeezes my hand tighter, and we fall into step behind Lin. Rhett behind us.

"We should stay together, anyway," Suzy whispers.

But I'm not sure that will help. We're louder as a group—the boys crash through the forest, snapping limbs beneath their feet, easily tracked. The forest doesn't want us here. And the boys make it impossible to pass through unnoticed.

We might be forging deeper into the dark woods: a place I've never been, farther than I've ever trekked. Or maybe we will get lucky and find our way back out, emerging at the entrance. *But luck doesn't live inside these woods.*

Whichever path we take, the forest knows we're here.

Claws open wide, ready to pull us in.

"We're lost," Rhett barks at Jasper.

"I never said I knew the way out," Jasper bemoans, swiveling to face Rhett.

We stop where a shallow channel carves through the terrain, a creek bed long ago dried up. There is hardly any snow here, the woods too dense.

"We never should have come in here," Lin says, his voice sounding far off, as if the words came from the trees themselves, not his throat.

Suzy leans in close to me. Suddenly she wants nothing to do with Rhett. He led us out here, and now we're deeper into the Wicker Woods than I've ever been, surrounded by land I've never seen, trees so wide they are like the swaying pillars of a catacomb. *The Wicker*

Woods cultivate fear, the spellbook warns. *They are architects of misfortune and mischief.*

And now we're moving deeper into the belly of the woods, a place we won't return from. *This is how people vanish.* How five teenagers slip into a forest at night and are never seen again.

"Maybe we should stop here and wait until morning," Jasper suggests, resting his shoulder against the broad trunk of a tree. "Then we'll be able to see."

"It's too cold," Suzy answers, voice breaking like she might cry. "We won't make it that long."

I should know the way out, I should sense the path that will lead us to the edge of the woods. But I can't tell north from south or light from dark, the stars and the sky smeared out by the trees. If I was as clever as my grandmother, as sharp as most of the Walkers in my family, I could squeeze my eyes closed and feel the direction of the wind, the hiss of the river in the distance. But instead I feel dull and muted. The forest is hiding the way free, shifting around us—it doesn't want us to leave.

Lin starts pacing along the old creek bed, his shadow bent at the shoulders. "We never should have come in here," he repeats. "It was a dumb idea."

"If Oliver was really hiding in here, we had to find him," Rhett reminds the others. "We had to be sure." I can tell they've all sobered up. Whatever stupid plan they made back at camp when they were drinking, whatever they thought they'd find by trekking into the Wicker Woods, is all starting to fall apart.

"She probably never found Oliver in these woods anyway," Jasper says. "She made it all up."

I shoot Jasper a look but he doesn't notice. "I didn't make it up."

"Did you ever see him?" Rhett asks, peering at Suzy.

But Suzy shakes her head. "No."

I turn to her, standing only a foot away from me, and I feel the corners of my mouth turn down. "When you came back to my house, drunk, after the bonfire, he was there in the living room with me."

She lifts one shoulder. "I don't really remember that night," she admits. "I don't remember coming back to your house, just waking up on the couch."

I shake my head at her. *I didn't make him up!* I want to scream.

"Walkers can't be trusted," Jasper points out. "You're all liars."

I lift my gaze to him and take a step closer. I'm going to wrap my hands around his throat. I'm going to push all the air from his lungs to make him shut up. I can't stand the sound of his voice. I can't stand any of them.

But Suzy touches my arm, and when I look at her, she shakes her head. "Leave it," she whispers.

I pull my arm away from her. She's lying about Oliver—about not seeing him. To protect herself maybe. But I don't know why.

Lin has stopped pacing, but he knits his hands together nervously, his skin gone pale. "We're going to die out here."

Rhett barks at Lin. "Don't be an idiot. We're not going to die."

Lin says something back, but I've stopped listening. I'm walking away from them, toward the trees, where I can see movement in the shadows—limbs writhing, coiling. *Something isn't right.*

"We have to get out of here," I say aloud. But no one is listening.

Rhett and Jasper and Lin are arguing. About the woods, about being lost, about whose idea it was to come in here in the first place.

"I'm not going to fucking die in here!" Jasper shouts.

"Maybe if you weren't so wasted, you wouldn't have led us deeper into this screwed-up forest," Rhett says.

"It was your idea to come looking for Oliver," Jasper barks back, shoving Rhett in the chest.

"Stop it!" Suzy yells.

But Rhett shoves Jasper back and their faces are twisted in anger, hands curled into fists.

"Cut it out," Lin says, and he ducks between them, pushing them apart. "You guys can bloody yourselves up when we get out of here."

"If we ever get out here," Rhett snaps.

Jasper's face twists into an odd shape—eyebrows peaked sharply into his forehead—like he's thinking something wicked and dark. Something we couldn't possibly imagine. "I'll fucking get us out of here," he says suddenly, lip curling upward.

The next few motions happen quickly.

Jasper pushes his hand into his pocket, reaching for something—the lighter. "We'll burn our way out," he says defiantly, chin raised, eyes so huge he looks half-crazed. "We'll burn this whole fucking forest to the ground."

He holds the silver lighter out in front of him, and Lin exclaims, "What the hell are you doing!" But Jasper flicks the lighter and it sparks to life in his hands.

I can feel the trees inching closer; the ground shudders, roots pushing upward. "What's happening?" Suzy asks, glancing back at me. A tendril of spiky roots has begun to circle around her ankles, slithering up her calves.

I've never seen the forest like this—violent and angry. Awake.

559

Suzy hasn't yet noticed the root rising up from the soil—she's staring at me, pleading for me to do something. And in the next second, Jasper drops the lighter onto a nest of leaves and pine needles near the base of a tree.

"No!" I shriek, stepping toward Jasper, as if I could stop him. But it's too late.

"You idiot," Lin cries out. "You'll burn us alive with it!"

I don't expect the flame to catch, to ignite. The woods are too damp, too cold—but the fire licks through the pine needles quickly and expands to a nearby bearberry bush, the sudden burst of light illuminating the forest for the first time. And I see what I couldn't before. The Wicker Woods have lowered over us, forming a cage of branches and limbs and roots. A web to ensnare us.

This is how it kills. It traps and suffocates. It smothers the life from living things who have intruded where they shouldn't have. This is why no deer pass through the Wicker Woods. No rabbits or mice or birds. They fear this length of forest. They know what hides inside it: death.

The forest shivers with the rupture of firelight. The trees howl—a sound unlike anything I've ever heard.

The flames move swiftly now, spiraling up a dead tree into the night sky. The roots that had entwined themselves around Suzy's ankle slither back down beneath the soil, retreating. "Nora?" Suzy asks, looking like a small child, terrified.

"We have to run," I say. Fire leaps from one tree to the next, roaring, creating its own wind, sparks catching on limbs and scattering across the forest floor. Fury igniting them, malice and anger more flammable than any fuel.

"Which direction?" Suzy asks.

I don't know. I don't know.

Rhett is squeezing his hands against his hat, Jasper's eyes are too wide, and Lin is looking back at me, waiting for me to tell them what to do.

Ash already begins to flit down from above, burnt remains of pine needles, some still lit and smoldering. And then, between the particles that fill the air, I see the subtle flicker of wings.

White wings beating.

White wings that won't leave me alone.

White wings zigzagging through the strange air—sparks and burning trees and the night sky opening up above us.

My moth. A bone moth.

It hovers a few feet ahead of me, then quivers away in the direction of the old creek bed. Death wants me to follow.

So I do—what choice do I have? Any of us?

I start down the shallow creek and Suzy follows. The moth moves quickly, fleeing the smoke and the growing flames—white shredded wings thumping nervously. It wants free of these woods just like we do. *It wants out.*

I break into a run, and I can feel the trail of boys behind me—everyone sprinting now. No one worried about finding Oliver or gathering lost things, we just need to get out. *Now.*

The air turns hot and ashy, smothered by smoke, and my eyes water—stinging with each blink. I try to see the terrain in front of me, but I trip on rocks and clumps of snow and roots woven above the earth. I blink and I run. *I run.* I had felt chilled only moments ago, but now sweat beads from my skin, slips down my spine, and trickles into my eyes, making things worse.

I lose sight of the moth. It gets lost in the growing smoke, in the thick brush, but then it reappears again. The dry creek bed fades to nothing. I can't be sure we're going the right way—deeper into the mountains or back toward the lake. The ground slopes down, but at times we climb up. Higher, farther into the wilderness.

The fire expands, groaning and popping and wailing, like a beast chasing us, spurred on by its own cyclone of wind. The heat is unbearable, the smoke suffocating.

"We should be out by now," Rhett calls from behind me. But I ignore him.

Every breath grates against my throat like sandpaper. Smoke fills our lungs. The entire forest is burning and we are lost inside it.

"Then don't follow us," Suzy snaps. She's had enough of him.

Lin keeps pace with Suzy and me, but Rhett and Jasper are slower, second-guessing every turn.

I pause at a place where the forest is divided in two. Pine trees on one side, a grove of hemlocks on the other. And I've lost sight of the moth again.

"Where the hell are you taking us?" Jasper shouts when he catches up. He steps closer to me, like he's going to reach out and grab my arm, but I move away.

"Leave her alone," Suzy says to him. "She's the only chance we have of getting out of here."

"Unless she wants us to die in here," Rhett says. His eyes have taken on the shadow of someone who is desperate, willing to do whatever it takes. Someone who will fight to survive. "She is a witch after all," he says. "Maybe she has something to do with this."

"Jasper started the fire," Suzy says, meeting his gaze. "Not Nora."

Flames tear through the trees behind us, cyclones of hot, ashy wind whipping closer, right at our heels. *We need to move.*

"Maybe she cast a spell to make the forest angry," Jasper says, his mouth flattening into an unbroken line. "Maybe she doesn't want us to find our way out, and it's all a trick."

"Maybe I did," I spit, eyeing him now, anger coursing like black ribbons through every vein. "Maybe I'll make sure you never leave these woods." It's a lie, but I don't care. I want him to think I could conjure up death with the curl of my index finger.

Jasper moves toward me but Suzy steps between us, pushing her small hands against his broad chest. "Don't fucking touch her," she says.

Jasper shakes his head but keeps his eyes on me. "I vote we sacrifice her to the forest, let her burn in here like the witch she is."

"Shut up, Jasper," Lin interjects now, his face flush, the flames working their way up the pines only a few feet away from us.

"You're both assholes," Suzy says, her gaze flicking from Jasper to Rhett.

I wipe at my forehead, smearing away the gritty layer of ash sticking to my skin. Maybe I was wrong to follow the moth. Maybe it's only leading me toward death. *Into the fire.* But my eyes catch on the line of hemlocks, parted by a row of pine trees. The ground slopes down where the trees come together: a ravine. A familiar shape in the ground.

I bolt away from the group—before Jasper can reach out for me—and I run down the row of pines. I only go a few more strides when I know it's the right way.

Ahead of me is a break in the trees.

I sprint to the edge of the forest, my heart hammering, eyes weeping from the smoke. I slow once I reach the boundary—pausing to look back. Suzy catches up to me first. Her eyelids blink mutely, out of breath, and I think she's going to say something, but she can't find the words, so she steps past the threshold and out into the open. Free from the Wicker Woods.

Lin is next, and he jogs straight past me, his gaze meeting mine quickly before he ducks through the row of trees.

I don't see Rhett and Jasper, only a wall of smoke and flames reaching up into the sky, spirals of fire licking from the tops of trees, trying to burn the stars. But maybe Rhett and Jasper deserve to die in here, to meet their end. Penance for everything they've done.

But then they come into view, breaking through the smoke.

Rhett is stumbling, coughing, and Jasper looks no better.

Then something happens.

I see Jasper trip. He staggers a moment—as if struggling against something—then falls forward, landing hard on his side, a stunned gasp escaping his lips.

I move away from the edge of the trees—unsure what's just happened—but then I see, he didn't trip. He was pulled down.

Something has woven its way around his foot—the ground moving beneath him.

"What the fuck?" Rhett asks, now standing beside me. But Jasper is strangely silent, his hands clawing at the charred soil—in shock.

A root is wrapped around his ankle, and it's drawing him back into the woods.

I hesitate, the boundary of the forest so close—only a foot away. I know I shouldn't care, I should just flee with the others and leave Jasper behind. But I can't. I can't see the terror in his eyes and walk away.

I can't let Jasper die in here, like this.

I scramble forward and drop to my knees, grabbing Jasper's arms. The tree root has spiraled tightly around his left ankle and is tugging him back, retreating into the soil. His hands grasp at the forest floor, at twigs and moss, nothing that will help him. His eyes wide.

"Rhett!" I call behind me. "Come help me!"

But Rhett doesn't move. He's standing at the edge of the forest, his expression slack.

"I can't pull him up by myself." Still, Rhett refuses to react.

I dig my feet into the ground, bracing myself, and pull back on Jasper's arms. But the roots are too strong, his legs sinking into the soft, ashy ground. "Shit," he starts saying, over and over in disbelief.

Even for everything he's done, I don't want to see him die out here. Not like this.

"You have to help me!" I shout back to Rhett, but it's useless, whether out of fear or stupidity, he won't move from his place beside the boundary trees, so close to freedom. He watches as his friend is being pulled under.

"You have to empty your pockets!" I yell to Jasper. "Whatever you took from the forest, you have to give it back."

His eyes stall on mine, then he releases one hand from my grip, reaching around to his coat pocket. Clumsily, he pulls out whatever is inside, scattering the items across the forest floor. Silver buttons, a hair barrette that looks like it's made of white pearl, the belt buckle tarnished and covered in dirt.

And then I see it.

A single thing among the others.

Metal glinting up at me. A gold band, a stone at the center.

It can't be.

I want to reach out for it, but I can't release my hold on Jasper. I squint, bending forward, and then I know for sure: The moonstone glimmers a pale milky white, even in the darkness.

My grandmother's ring.

The one that fell into the lake when I broke through the ice. *An offering to the forest*, just like Mr. Perkins had said.

Jasper found it on the forest floor, among the dirt and rot and patches of snow, inside the Wicker Woods. Returned.

Lost things found.

My head throbs and I look away from it, back to Jasper.

But it's already too late—he's up to his waist, twisting, thrashing. The nose on his stupid reindeer sweater is already beneath the soil, patches of snow filling in around him. The forest is swallowing him up.

I'm not strong enough, and I meet his eyes, blinking wide—panic in them. *The forest doesn't want us to leave.*

More dirt caves in around him, and he gasps for air—he's sunk up to his chest now. He blinks up at me one last time, like he's still unsure of what's happening, like he's still a little buzzed—and he thinks maybe this isn't real. Only a dream, an awful, awful nightmare.

He doesn't speak, doesn't cry out, and I hold on to his arms until they are the only thing still aboveground. But then they too are swallowed up by the cruel, dark soil.

Gone.

Gone.

Gone.

I sink back onto the earth, staring at the space where Jasper had been, my own lungs heaving. *What the fuck*, I want to scream, but no sound comes out. Only the absence of air.

Above me, trees are burning, sparks raining down. And I scramble back, pushing myself to standing, afraid I will be next—just like Jasper. But the roots don't come for me. Jasper was the one who started the fire. Jasper stole lost things after I told him not to—when the forest was awake. He was the only one who placed things in his pocket to take home, to keep.

The trees were never going to let him leave.

I wipe at my face, dirt and soot coming away, and brush my hands against my knees. Wanting to be rid of the dirt, any memory of what just happened. Of what I just saw. *Jasper is dead. Jasper is gone.*

On the ground, only a foot away, is my grandmother's ring. My heart swings wrongly in my chest. *Something isn't right—why is the ring here, inside the woods?* But I don't bend down to touch it, I don't lift it from the soil. I won't take it from the Wicker Woods, not now, when the forest is awake—I won't give it reason to hunt me.

The trees wheeze and croak, flames growing larger, and I push myself up, stagger a moment, then turn and run to the edge of the Wicker Woods.

"I—" Rhett stammers when I reach him. "I'm sorry. I couldn't—" But I don't let him finish. I shove my hands hard against his chest, hard enough that it knocks him back and he slams against the tree behind him. He doesn't say anything else. His mouth flat, eyes to the ground.

I step over the threshold and out of the Wicker Woods.

The Black River churns ahead of us, water roiling beneath the layer of ice. Suzy and Lin stare at me—like they heard what happened, like they know Jasper isn't going to appear from the trees. But then I realize they aren't looking at me; they're staring up at the woods, at the way we came.

I turn and see. Against the backdrop of the night sky, fiery red sparks rise in dizzying circles, flames ripping apart the forest. The Wicker Woods are burning.

We watch, mute, as the flames expand, moving toward the Black River.

It's spreading.

It isn't contained inside the Wicker Woods. And it's hurtling down toward Jackjaw Lake.

"We have to go!" I say, grabbing Suzy by the arm to get her attention. "We can't stay here."

Suzy nods and I glance back at the woods one last time. Perhaps for the *very* last time.

A brick sinks into my stomach.

The place I have known my whole life—where Walker women rose up from the soil so long ago no one can remember the year—won't survive the night. I've feared these woods, but under a full moon, I have felt at home inside them too.

I turn away, unable to watch it burn.

I have to find Oliver.

OLIVER

The night sky is electric.

The mountains to the north, the Wicker Woods, set alight.

I stand on the shore of the lake watching the flames raze down through the trees, a sound like thunder.

I know it's my fault. I couldn't face her—I left her room while she slept. I snuck out like a coward because I couldn't tell her the truth and now I feel the dark pulling me under. The forest always there—clawing at me, bones and teeth, trying to draw me back in. She was my only remedy, and I left her alone.

She doesn't deserve what I did. She doesn't deserve the lies I told. But what else could I do?

Fuck.

I might be the villain. I might be all the awful things I didn't want to be. I might have fury inside me I can't contain. Revenge resting just behind my eyelids.

I am not who she thinks I am.

I squeeze my palms against my temples. I rake my fingers through my hair.

I left her alone. I hurt her. But not as bad as it will hurt when she learns the truth.

I thought I would leave and never see her again. But now I stand at the shore, watching the fire tear down through the snow-covered pines, and I can't seem to make my legs move.

My heart beats only in broken measure now—hardly at all.

I have to find her.

I won't let her die out here. Alone.

NORA

We run, cutting trails through the snow, the fire chasing us down the Black River. The fire a monster at our backs.

I don't look behind us—I don't need to. I can feel how close it is. I can feel the sparks burning my skin, my hair, catching on my lashes.

We reach the shore, the frozen lake already reflecting the eerie glow of the fire. The sky turned the color of blood, of smoke. Of not enough time.

The four of us exchange a quick look, but no one speaks. Even Rhett looks as mute as a tomb.

Jasper is dead—a death none of us will be able to explain.

"The fire's moving too fast," Lin says. He pushes back the hood of his coat and I see his full head, his shorn hair, for the first time. The air finally hot enough that he doesn't need his hood. Ahead of us, the trees are already beginning to burn on all sides of the lake. *There's no time.* Lin looks to me and then Suzy, his breathing ragged, and says, "Good luck."

I nod to him, understanding what he means: *We're each on our own now. We've reached the lake, and now we each make our own path. So run.*

Rhett breaks away first, turning west toward the boys' camp. And shortly after, Lin follows, two figures sprinting around the lake as the trees catch flame only a few yards away, closing in.

Suzy looks unsure, like she doesn't know where to go. Who to follow. Which fate she will choose—with me, or the boys back at camp.

"Come on," I say, when her eyes start to water, when she looks like she might sink down into the snow and give up. I grab her hand and she looks relieved.

Together, we hurry toward my house.

The fire hasn't reached the row of summer homes yet, but it's growing closer, devouring the forest along the shore. It's only a matter of time.

We sprint through the pines, and before I've even climbed the porch steps, I see that the door has swung open, slapping back against the wall. It was never fully shut when Jasper closed it—the knob and hinges broken. And now Fin is gone.

I yell into the trees, calling out for him—my heart beating too fast, my throat gone dry—but he doesn't come. *He'll be okay*, I tell myself, my eyes starting to sting with the threat of tears. *He knows the forest.* He'll outrun the fire, he'll escape these woods long before we do.

I glance back into my home—my thoughts swimming and colliding like honeybees when they're drunk on their own nectar. Unable to focus. *What should I grab? What should I take?*

"Let's go," Suzy urges behind me, tugging on my sleeve. "There's no time."

Across the lake, I can just see the boys beginning to flee their cabins, running around the shore, heading for the road. Behind my house, the flames have started moving down the hillside—the fire got here faster than I thought.

"Wait," I say, and I bolt through the front door. I take the stairs two at a time, I stumble at the top but push myself up. Beneath the bed I find the spellbook, I reach for it and tuck it under my arm, scrambling back downstairs and out through the door.

Suzy glances at the book but doesn't ask.

"Okay," I say, giving her a nod, and we rush down through the trees, running along the shore.

"Here it comes," Suzy says.

I swivel around to see the fire making its way down the slope behind the row of summer homes, tearing through the trees. It sounds like a train roaring down tracks. The flames are so hot now that the snow is beginning to melt all around us, dripping off the eaves of roofs, forming puddles at our feet.

The fire won't stop until everything is gone.

I should have grabbed more, I think. Some of my mother's things. Photographs. Her jewelry. Her favorite seafoam-green sweater hanging in her closet.

But now there's no time.

The stars overhead slink into the background, no longer visible through the smoke and ash and embers swirling all around us. We run through the trees, back to the shore, until we reach the marina.

"What are you doing?" Suzy shouts when I dart toward the boathouse.

"Keep going!" I yell back. "I have to warn someone."

She shakes her head and stops in the snow, refusing to go without me. I rush up the porch steps and pound my fist against Mr. Perkins's door. I hear him cursing on the other side, ambling to the front door. A second later it swings open, and for a moment, the breath is caught in my lungs as I gasp for air. "A forest fire," I manage, pointing out at the lake where the trees are burning on all sides.

Mr. Perkins steps out onto the porch, holding a hand over his eyes. "What the hell?" he asks in disbelief.

"You have to get out—now."

"I'm not going anywhere," he answers, lowering his hand and shuffling back toward the door.

"It's going to burn everything," I say.

He nods, wrinkles pinching around his mouth. "And if I'm lucky, it'll burn me right along with it."

"Please," I say. My lungs rasp with each inhale, smoke in my throat, suffocating me with every breath. "You have to go."

He lifts his gaze and stares out over the water—the place he's lived his whole life—then he points a long bony finger up into tree line. "Why don't you go warn whoever's been holed up in the old Harrison place?"

At the line of summer homes, where the Harrison home sits hidden in the trees, I can just make out a narrow spire of smoke rising from the chimney. "No one should be in there," I say. The Harrison place is rarely used, a small single-story cabin that sits vacant most years.

"There's been light in the windows at night—candles, I think."

I swallow and step down from the porch. *It could be Oliver.*

He was gone from my room when the boys broke in. Maybe he went to the Harrison house, maybe he's been hiding out. Although I don't know why.

Still, I need to be sure.

I look back at Mr. Perkins. "If you won't leave, then I won't either." A threat, a way to force him into coming with us.

He levels his gaze on me, testing me, to see if I'm serious. "Just as stubborn as your grandmother," he says, grumbling, before reaching behind him and pulling the door shut with a bang. There's nothing he wants to take with him, nothing to save. But at least he's coming with us. He's fleeing these mountains.

I grab his arm and help him down the steps. "Go with Suzy," I tell him. Suzy shifts from one foot to the other, impatient, ready to run.

"Where are you going?" Suzy asks.

"I have to check that house, then I'll be right behind you."

She raises an eyebrow like she doesn't believe me.

"I promise," I say. "You get a head start."

She blinks, powdery ash drifting away from her lashes. Even her soft russet hair is now a charcoal-gray. "Okay," she says, nodding, and she and Mr. Perkins continue away from the lake, through the dirty gray snow. If they don't slow down, they'll make it down the mountain. They'll make it out before the fire reaches them.

But my heart won't let me leave until I know *he's* safe.

Adrenaline roars through me.

The fire has already started tearing apart several of the other homes set farther back in the trees, roofs burning, windows broken out, curtains billowing with the wind while flames lick up the walls.

The fire is a storm now. Sparks instead of snow. Ash instead of cold. It's blown down from the mountains, from the north, and it won't stop until it's devoured everything.

Until there's nothing left.

The snow in front of the Harrison cabin is still deep, and my boots sink in up to my knees with each step. My breathing is quick, lungs like daggers scraping against my ribs. When I reach the porch, I grab the railing and use it to pull myself up—hand over hand—the spellbook tucked under my arm.

I know I'm running out of time; flames have already reached the trees behind the house. Limbs snapping, snow melting from leaves, bark wheezing as it peels away.

A light shivers from the front windows, a dim glow—hardly visible through the smoke.

I don't bother knocking—there's no time—I yank open the door and burst into the living room.

The room is dark, woven with shadows. A long dining room table that must seat ten people sits against one wall, and a broad fireplace burns hot on the other.

And on the couch, someone is asleep—a boy—a blanket half pulled over him.

Oliver.

My heart stops beating and I take a step closer, hope rising dangerously up into my chest.

"Hello?" I ask. I can't make out his face, partially covered by an arm, but then he rolls onto his side and the arm drops away. The motion startles him awake and he flinches upright—pale-blond hair pressed awkwardly to one side.

It's not Oliver. *Not Oliver.*

It's someone else—a boy I don't recognize. With a narrow face and bright-blue eyes.

Disappointment sinks through me.

"Who the hell are you?" he asks.

"Who the hell are you?" I ask right back.

He tilts his head, confused. And I feel my expression draw tight—both of us unsure of the other. I survey the house quickly: the small kitchen with plates stacked high, cans of food on the wood counter, cupboards left open. He's pilfered whatever he could find—which surely wasn't much, considering the Harrisons rarely visit their summer home. Expired dried beans and stewed tomatoes left behind. Emergency food. A bottle of bourbon sits on the coffee table beside the boy, only a few sips left at the bottom. He's been in here getting drunk. Maybe he ran away from the boys' camp, maybe he's been in here since the party a few houses down—still wasted, no idea what day it is.

I scowl and he scowls back.

"You have to get out of here," I tell him sharply, turning away to head for the door—whoever this boy is, I don't care, he just needs to leave.

But he doesn't move from his place on the couch. "Why?"

"There's a fire heading down the mountain." I point to the window, so he can see for himself.

He scratches at his head, messing up his unwashed hair even more, and he squints—eyes groggy, cheeks flushed. "Doubt it," he answers, sinking back into the couch. "You're just messing with me." And then his eyelids snap open wider and he lifts a finger to the air, like he's making a point. "Wait, are you that moon girl? The one who lives down the shore?" He doesn't wait for me to answer, he just assumes I must be. Who else could I be—a girl way out here in the forest? "I heard you curse boys and lock them in your basement." He laughs to himself, rubbing his face with his palm. "And I'm not going anywhere with you."

I blow out a sharp, irritated breath and walk back to the door. "I don't give a shit what you do, but if you stay in here, you'll die."

He sucks in his lower lip and looks hurt—a little kid who was told he can't play in his tree fort anymore. "Wait!" he calls before I step back outside. "Is the road clear?" he asks. "Did the cops come?" His eyes flash to the door still open behind me, the strange biting wind blowing inside, a mix of winter air and ash.

"What?" I turn back to face him, head throbbing—I need to get out of here, there's no time. I need to find Oliver.

"I mean, did someone come looking for me?"

"I don't know," I answer. "You just need to leave."

He stands up suddenly and looks past me again. He's wearing green sweatpants and a gray sweatshirt that reads ▨ ▨▨▨▨ ▨ ▨▨▨▨▨▨ ▨▨▨ ▨▨▨ ▨▨, and I'm almost positive he didn't bring this outfit with him but likely found it inside the house. Buried in a dresser drawer, mothballs rolling around inside. His expression sinks—a shade of darkness slips across his face. "Did they find the body?" he asks grimly, voice hardly more than a scratch.

"What body?" I ask, afraid I already know what he's talking about.

He squints at me like he's sizing me up, trying to figure out my *true* intention for busting into his hiding place.

"Who are you?" I ask again, something beginning to thread its way along my spine, vertebra by vertebra. Brittle bone by brittle bone.

He hesitates and shifts his jaw side to side like a saw. "Max."

Max, Max, Max.

"You're Max?" I ask, and I can feel the color leave my cheeks. The heat slipping out through my toes.

"Yeah." He narrows his focus on me, his skin pale and sunken. He needs a shower. He needs sunlight.

Max is alive.

Not dead. Not dead at all.

* * *

Every inhale burns my lungs, and I clear my throat, blinking. *Blinking away the smoke. Blinking away this boy who can't be Max.*

"You're supposed to be dead," I say.

His mouth snaps shut. His face corkscrews together.

"They *said* you were dead," I continue. "The other boys. They said you drowned."

Sparks begin to tumble in through the open doorway, blowing across the wood floor—the fire close now, right outside. *We can't stay here.*

"I'm not dead," he answers—stating the obvious—as if I couldn't see for myself. But his tone is off—something not quite right. Something else just beneath the surface of his words.

My hands begin to tremble. "I don't understand," I say. *Maybe he's the wrong Max*, I think. *A different Max.* I slide my shaking hand into my coat pocket, feeling for the smooth surface of the watch, and I pull it out, holding it in my palm. I touch the back, where Max's name is inscribed into the metal. "Is this yours?" I ask, holding it out for him to see.

He steps forward. "I thought it was gone," he says, but he doesn't reach for it, doesn't try to take it from me, as if he is glad to be rid of it. A memory he didn't want. A thing he's been trying to forget.

I close my hand over it. He's the *right* Max.

The one who should be dead.

"Where did you find it?" he asks.

I slide it back into my pocket—I've grown accustomed to the weight of it, the subtle vibration of the hands ticking forward, the measurement of time. "Oliver had it. He's had it since the storm."

But if Max is alive . . . then Oliver didn't kill him.

If Max is alive, then Oliver isn't a murderer. He didn't let him drown in the lake.

Max raises an eyebrow. "Oliver Huntsman?"

I nod.

"What the hell are you talking about?" He steps around the coffee table, and his jaw is pushed out, his shoulders a rigid slope. I can see the confusion growing inside him, along with something else: anger. "You came here to get me to admit what happened," he says, his eyes wide and unblinking. "You're trying to trick me."

"What?" I don't understand what's happening, what he's talking about. And I take a step back toward the open door. Away from him.

"Where do you think you're going?" he asks, words slicked with spite.

A wave of sparks rolls across the wood floor, pushed by the wind.

Max moves closer to me, his bloodshot eyes refusing to blink, to flinch away.

"I'm not trying to trick you," I say. But he reaches forward and grabs me by the wrist.

"Why do you really have my watch?" he presses, squeezing my wrist tighter, stopping the flow of blood into my hand.

"I told you," I say, tugging against his grip. "Oliver had it."

His fingers dig deeper into my skin, and he pulls me closer, his face only a few inches from mine. "You're lying."

With the spellbook tucked beneath my arm, I manage to push my other hand against his face, his chin, and force him away. "I'm not lying," I spit, yanking my arm free from his grasp and starting toward the door.

"So they did find his corpse?" he asks, his voice hollowed out, thin and strained.

I stop and look back at him. "What?"

"In the lake?" he says, as if this clarifies it, raising a single blond eyebrow. "They recovered Oliver?"

"Oliver isn't dead," I say, a sour taste forming at the back of my throat.

A quick bark of laughter escapes Max's lips. And when his mouth falls flat, he leans in close to me again, brows slanted, his teeth grating together. "I watched him sink beneath the ice." His upper lip curls into a disgusted grin, his nostrils flare.

I shake my head. "You're full of shit," I say, but still, I reach out for the edge of a chair, my knuckles turning white where they grip the striped, navy-blue upholstery. "Oliver didn't drown." But even as I say it, the room begins to spin, the watch inside my pocket begins to *tick* impossibly too loud, beating against my skull.

One boy missing. One boy dead.

Which boy is which?

Max shakes his head and says something, but his voice feels too far away, the room tipping on its side, the merry-go-round moving too fast and I want to get off. I need to get out of this house. I dip my eyes to the floor to keep the walls from spinning, and I stare at a beetle turned up on its back near a couch leg—dead. I feel myself cracking apart, little tiny fractures in the shell of my skin. And once the first fissure splits open, the rest will shatter.

Max didn't die that night.

Max didn't drown in the lake.

"What the hell is wrong with you?" he says now. His face sways just out of focus, a blur of hair and bloodshot eyes and a cruel grin, but he's still too close, and I release my hold on the chair. I step away from him, reaching for the open doorway, feeling bits of ash sticking to my skin. Like they will never be washed off. Like I will never escape these flames.

But then there's someone in the doorway, blocking my path. Hands reaching out for me. I look up into his too-green eyes and I feel my pupils narrow to tiny pricks.

Oliver.

Oliver is standing in the doorway.

I choke back a strange, terrified sob. Relief flooding through me. "What are you doing here?" I ask, gasping for air, ash spilling down into my lungs.

"I've been trying to find you," he says, his voice urgent, panicked. "I saw the fire. You have to get out of here." He holds out a hand to me, but I don't take it.

"I thought you were here," I explain, "in this house. But—" *But instead I found Max.* I swivel back to face Max, and Oliver's gaze lifts too, seeing Max for the first time. His expression sinks, fury and hatred seething behind his eyes. Forming a line that runs from his temples to his chin. I want to ask him what's wrong, what he sees when he looks at Max that makes his jaw constrict.

But I wheel my gaze back to Max. "I told you he's alive," I say, the words choked out. Like a part of me doesn't believe them.

Max's face softens and he looks from me to the doorway. "What?" he mutters.

"You were wrong," I say. "You didn't watch Oliver drown."

Max rakes his hands through his hair, as if pulling out the strands from his scalp. "What the fuck are you talking about?" he barks, eyes scanning the doorway where Oliver stands, anger thudding through him. "You're just as strange as everyone says you are," he adds, his grin turned sour. "They say you should be locked up, that you've lived in this forest too long—that no one can stay sane in these woods."

I scowl at him. "I'm not insane," I answer, wishing I had a better comeback, wishing my head wasn't so full of smoke. "Oliver's not dead," I snap, but when I turn back to look at Oliver, his expression has changed. He's no longer looking at Max—he's looking at me, his mouth flattened, eyes pouring through me with the deepest kind of sadness. With guilt and regret and maybe even pity.

"Nora—" Oliver begins.

But he's cut off by Max. "There's no one there, witch girl," Max says, pointing to the door. "You're talking to yourself."

I shake my head, confusion and fear suddenly clattering down every joint, and I step away from Oliver, holding a palm in the air.

I don't know what's happening.

"Weird little witch girl has lost her mind," Max jeers, laughing now. He says something else, but I can't hear. He laughs and more sparks skitter through the doorway, smoke filling the house. The fire is close now. But I don't care.

Max can't see Oliver. He's standing right beside me, but Max doesn't see him.

I was wrong.

So fucking wrong.

I take another step away from Oliver, trying to swallow, trying to find the right words, but they never form.

I thought the boys were worried I would find Max's body. But they were worried I'd find him in here, *alive.* They were worried I'd turn him in, tell the counselors where he was hiding—a boy who drowned another boy.

One boy missing, one boy dead—a girl who couldn't see the truth.

"You drowned," I say aloud, staring up at Oliver, not caring if Max hears, if he thinks I've lost my mind. The thoughts are spiraling fast now, too many moments, too many things I missed. All this time. *I didn't see. I didn't know.*

Oliver's jaw tightens. "Nora," he pleads.

But I shake my head. I don't want to hear my name on his lips. I don't want to hear anything.

"Nora," he repeats. "Nora, please."

I move past him in the doorway before he can stop me, before he can touch my skin with his. The air is humming around me, sparks whirling through the trees. The fire is close now.

I waited too long.

Oliver says my name again, but I'm scrambling down the steps into the snow, into the chaos of cinders.

I'm running down toward the lake, away from the flames, away from Max Caulfield who isn't dead at all.

From Oliver, *who might be.*

I know that moths bring omens not to be ignored and that brooms should never be kept on the second floor of your home. I know windows opened to the east can bring bad dreams, but windows to the west can bring fated love and good fortune. Carry an acorn in your pocket to stay young forever, plant chicory root beside your kitchen window to keep the flies away. Throw salt over your left shoulder. And eat dandelion honey on toast before bed to help you sleep.

I know these things because my grandmother knew them too. And her grandmother before her. These things are as true as the North Star, as sure as a beesting will hurt and then itch.

But what of the things I don't know?

The riddles I can't decipher.

The strange conjuring that made a boy appear inside the Wicker Woods? A boy who shouldn't have returned at all. A boy like Oliver Huntsman.

The trees sag and drip.

Snow melts from limbs—a winter forest set ablaze—and the air whirls with sparks. The fire is all around me, burning the wilds and the woods and everything green. Tearing down the row of summer homes.

I reach the lake, and my breath is a wheeze, sparks singeing the sleeves of my coat, my hair. One even lands on the tip of my nose and I swat it away. Everything is burning and I waited too long to leave. The night has come alive—bursting—a carnival of firelight, of soot and sparks and heat.

And then I see it, bobbing through the smoke, weaving between the embers like a needle stitching through fabric.

The bone moth.

Death is a winged creature who won't leave you alone—not until it gets what it wants, a passage from the spellbook reads, one I've recalled over and over in my mind.

It's beautiful, I realize for the first time: a rare white moth from some deep part of the forest.

But it doesn't flutter closer to me, it quivers just past my shoulder into the trees, where Oliver is moving quickly toward me. But he stops short when he sees me looking up at him.

"The bone moth," I say aloud, finally understanding.

It draws closer to Oliver, hovering, meeting his gaze.

"The moth was following you," I say. "Not me."

Its wings flutter softly, paper-thin like fabric brushing together. Flammable. And then it lifts up, higher into the trees, and shivers out toward the center of the lake—escaping the flames, disappearing into the eerie golden light. It was never following me. Never a warning of my death. The moth had been a warning that death was in my home, death kissed me in my room, death slept beside me with his hands against my ribs. Death kept me warm.

I was wrong about the moth. And I was wrong about *him.*

Oliver moves closer to me, and maybe I should back away, sprint up the shore, but I let him come stand beside me, his shoulder just barely touching mine.

Another burst of déjà vu pours over me. He looks just like he did the morning after I found him inside the Wicker Woods. A boy about to set off on a journey—or perhaps he is a boy who has just returned from one. Weary and threadbare, with aching feet and sore shoulders, but with wild stories to tell. Of the places he's been and the vast oceans he's seen. Villains he narrowly escaped. A boy who left and then returned. *Who came back.*

Except now we might be at the end of the tale. Ash spilling down around us. The moon above stained a savage shade of red from the flames—a blood moon.

I hold the spellbook to my chest and close my eyes, squeezing them shut so tightly I might be able to blot out the sky and the fire and everything that couldn't possibly be real. But when I open them, Oliver is still there. Standing beside me beneath the crimson moon.

"Did you drown?" I ask. The words come out a syllable at a time—tasting strange on my tongue, like sandpaper and wax. Like fairytales. *A thing that cannot be true.*

I hear him breathing, the inhale and exhale of lungs contracting. *Breath in his lungs—the breath of a boy who sounds alive.* But what do I know of dead boys' lungs? What do I know of any of it? His skin smells of pine and fern—the scent of someone who is more wilderness than boy.

He nods. "Yes."

My eyes want to well up with tears, but the air is too dry and it saps the moisture from my skin. "I don't understand," I say. *Any of it. All of it.*

"Neither do I." He shifts slightly, every motion like the battering of wings—an inch too far away, an inch too close. *Never close enough.* "After you found me in the woods," he says quietly, as if it were a confession, "you told me that I shouldn't have survived that long—two whole weeks in the forest. You were right."

Because he was already dead.

I don't know if I want to touch him or scream. Pound my fists against his chest and claw at his skin until he bleeds—*I'll make him real. I'm make him bleed and feel pain and then he'll be a real boy again.* The anger is a jagged lump in my throat.

A knife in my back.

His gaze slides to mine, heavy lidded and familiar while the world burns around us. Fire and heat and lies. "I didn't know," he tells me, like it's something he *needs* to say. To get off his chest. "Not at first. But no one could see me, like I wasn't even there. Except you."

Flames devour whole trees on the farthest shore, licking up into the sky, and there is a fire inside my gut, burning me alive. "Why didn't you tell me?"

"Would you have believed me?" he asks. "Do you believe me now?"

"No." *How can I believe you.*

His gaze lowers and his mouth dips open, his throat fighting against the words. "I didn't want you to be afraid of me."

The roar from the fire behind us fills my ears, a beast coming for us—a creature set loose from the woods. It ignites the summer home where Max had been hiding, the trees around it already glowing red-hot as flames chew them apart. Max might still be inside. Or maybe he fled in time. But I don't care either way. Or maybe I want him to burn—for what he did. *He is the killer, not Oliver.*

"I'm not afraid," I say, I admit, even though I know I should be. *Of what you are. Of what you aren't:* alive.

But Rhett and the others were afraid: They heard things in their cabin, something that terrified them. It wasn't Max. It was Oliver all along, moving among them, unseen. Even Suzy never saw him—not once. Not in the house. Not at the bonfire. I thought she was lying, a cruelty I didn't understand. Now I know she was telling the truth.

She never saw Oliver. *I was the only one.*

He looks out at the lake, and my heart is splitting into halves. Severed in two. *The before and the after.* "I don't know why you can see me," he says. "And they can't."

I grip the spellbook tighter and feel the air leave my lungs. "Because I'm not like them," I say. "Like any of them." Walkers have always been able to see shadows—*we see what others can't.* Mostly in the graveyard—those slipping between this life and the next. The ones who aren't entirely sure they're dead. The night my grandmother passed away, she woke me in my sleep and sat at the edge of my bed. With trembling hands, she removed the moonstone ring she had worn most of her life and slid it onto my hand. "My gift to you," she said, before she sank back in with the shadows. Hours later, Mom told me that Grandma had passed away during the night, long before she gave me the ring. I had seen her phantom passing through the house on her way out. Mom saw her too, long black hair braided down her back as she pushed out through the front door. But she was only a ghost moving among us, passing through the in-between.

A talent all Walkers possess. To see the ones who have gone.

And the night I found Oliver inside the Wicker Woods, I saw him plainly—our eyes meeting as soon as he woke. Nothing dark or ghostly—*ghastly*—about him. Maybe *I* have made him more real by finding him, touching him. *My found item.* If there had been nothing rooting him to this forest, this lake, these mountains, he might have slipped away just like my grandmother, just like the other shadows I've seen. Here and then gone.

But instead he stayed.

Again, I feel the urge to reach out and place my hands along his temples—to see if he is flesh and bone. Roots and knees. To know for sure if he's real.

But I'm too afraid, so I swallow down the urge. I push it into the back of my mind.

"The others were there too?" I ask, my lungs struggling to find air among the ash. "When you drowned?"

Another nod, his skin turning pale—the memory of that night flickering across his eyes, slicing over his skin, cutting him open where he will bleed dead-boy blood.

I meet his gaze, needing to see, needing to ask the question I've wanted a real answer to since the day I found him inside the woods. "Do you remember what happened that night?"

A long icy breath leaves his lungs. "I remember everything."

OLIVER

I don't want to go to the cemetery. But the others insist.

"It's your initiation," Rhett says coldly. "Everyone who arrives at camp has to be initiated. It's tradition."

I've only been at the Jackjaw Camp for Wayward Boys one week, and up until now they've left me alone, barely even said hello. And that's how I prefer it—to be a shadow, to be someone they don't remember. Whose name sinks into the background whenever they try to draw it up. But all day, during breakfast and after lunch, when the snow started falling from the sky in sheets, I've had the sense that something is coming. My cabinmates eyed me with renewed interest, whispers made just out of earshot. *They're planning something.*

And now that the sun has set—the rest of the camp asleep and the counselors no longer checking cabins—the boys stand over me and prod me from bed.

Max is with them too, standing rigid beside the door, waiting.

"You don't have a choice," Jasper says, wearing his ridiculous reindeer sweater. The first day I arrived at camp, the reindeer's eyes blinked red, until one night during dinner the blinking began to slow, a twitch and a shiver, and then they stopped completely. And have never blinked again.

I rise from bed and pull on a coat—what other choice do I have? I don't want to make enemies so soon. In a place where I might be stuck for some time. Months. Even a year.

We leave the cabin and march along the shore, the boys laughing when someone trips on a branch, followed by urgent *shush*es to be quiet. We reach the cemetery, and Jasper pulls out a bottle of whiskey from his coat, passing it around the group. The dark liquid burns my throat.

I expect them to make me chug too many beers or blindfold me and spin me around and force me to find my way back to camp on my own. But it isn't any of these things. They lead me deep into the cemetery, to a row of graves. Some are old and some look like they've been placed in the ground only a few years ago. But they all have the same surname: Walker.

"Walkers are witches," Jasper explains, as if he is giving a history lesson, running his hand over the top of a gravestone.

"They've lived here longer than anyone else," Rhett interjects. "Back before there were trees or a lake. When it was a desert."

Max frowns. "That's not true. This place was never a desert."

"Whatever," Rhett balks. "It doesn't matter."

"You have to tell it right, or it doesn't sound true," Max argues.

Rhett rolls his eyes and looks away.

"They're witches," Jasper continues. "That's all you need to know."

Max steps closer to me, his blue eyes unblinking. "And there's one that still lives across the lake."

"I thought no one lived in those homes," I say, my arms crossed, not wanting to be here. "I thought they were all boarded up for the winter."

"The Walkers stay during the winter," Max answers. "They're the only ones."

I swallow sharply, certain that whoever lives across the lake isn't actually a witch, but I keep my mouth shut. If they want to believe a witch lives in one of those homes, I couldn't care less. I just want to get this over with.

"You have to say her name three times," Jasper instructs now, resting his long, gawky elbow on the edge of a gravestone.

"Whose?" I ask.

He points a finger at the grave below him. Etched into the stone is the name WILLA WALKER.

"If you say her name three times, you'll summon her up from the grave," Rhett says, wagging an eyebrow for effect, as if it makes his words more creepy. Or more true.

"Legend says that Willa Walker wept into Jackjaw Lake and made it bottomless," Jasper adds, as if reciting it from a book—perhaps the very thing a boy said to him when he first arrived at camp.

I make a sound I don't intend, a sound of cynicism, and Max steps closer to me, shoulders rigid. "You don't believe us?"

I pull my jaw tight—I know how these things go. How initiations work. They want me to keep my mouth shut and obey whatever they say. The sooner I fall in line, the sooner I'll be back in my bunk asleep. And if I do what they ask, they won't pick on me after tonight. I'll be *one of them*. And when the next new kid arrives, they'll want me to make him do the same stupid shit.

Max backs away from me and even Jasper stands up from the

grave where he had been slouched. They give me room to summon this old dead witch. I exhale through my nose and say the name three times. "Willa Walker Willa Walker Willa Walker."

A hush settles over the graveyard, and for a moment, it feels as if the wind stops blowing. As if time falls still. My eyes skim the cemetery, the old dead trees and the snow falling between the markers, and for the briefest moment I think maybe they're right. *Willa Walker has been summoned from her grave.* But then Jasper breaks into laugher, followed by Rhett, and it echoes over the gravestones.

"Dude, you should see your face," Jasper says, slapping me hard on the shoulder. "You look like you actually believe a hand is going to rise up from the dirt."

Rhett shoves the bottle of whiskey at me, as if it were my prize for doing what they said. I take a slug, then hand it back.

I think we're done, that we'll head back now. The snow is falling in thick sheets, and I follow them out through the cemetery gate. When we reach the shore, I turn left. But Jasper calls out to me. "Where you going?" he asks. "Did you think that was it? All you had to do was say some dead lady's name three times?"

Rhett laughs beside him, but Max looks just as serious as ever.

This next part is why we really came out here.

This is what they've been waiting for.

I walk to the edge of the lake where they stand, snow blowing sideways through the trees. A storm is coming. The counselors warned us at dinner to add more logs to our woodstoves, to shut our doors tightly so the wind wouldn't blow them inward.

But now we stand out in it, the mountains to the north obscured by black clouds.

"You have to walk out on the frozen lake," Rhett says, his voice buoyant and light, enjoying this. *The main event for the night.* "All the way out to the center."

"And then you have to twirl in a circle like a ballerina," Jasper explains, grinning so wide the gap in his teeth seems broader than usual.

I don't look at them—I stare out at the frozen surface of the lake. At the dark water still visible beneath.

"You're getting off easy," Rhett says. "We could make you sleep outside in the cold."

I shake my head slowly. "The ice won't hold me," I say. I can see that it's still too thin—not frozen solid. Only a month or so ago, I'm sure there was water splashing onto the pebbled shoreline.

"You don't have a choice, newbie," Rhett answers, his voice cold now, his mouth grinning with self-satisfaction. He enjoys this part of initiations—he enjoys the brief sense of power.

"I'm not doing it," I say, refusing to look away from Rhett. I want him to know that I'm serious. Saying the name of a long-dead witch three times is one thing. But this is something else completely. I'd rather sleep out in the cold all night—I'd rather fight all of them—than risk walking out there.

"He could drown," Lin offers—the only one who seems to recognize how dangerous it is. That someone could actually die. "No one's ever had to go out on the ice before," he argues. "We usually make them swim in the lake in the summer, and see if Willa Walker pulls them under."

"He's not going to drown," Jasper interjects, scoffing and brushing a hand through his shaggy hair. "The ice will hold."

"And if he does, it's his own fault," Max says, his eyes like two black orbs, as if something is boiling beneath the surface. The others might still be unsure whether they're going to let me into their little group. But Max knows that he hates me. I stole his bunk when I first arrived. I didn't want to, I would have preferred to go unnoticed, to be the boy whose parents died, who arrived late in the season but kept to himself and hardly took up any space at all.

But Max hates me for it all the same. Blames me for him having to sleep in a one-room hut near the counselors and the mess hall.

And now, standing on the shore, I know he won't let me get out of this initiation. He wants me to suffer. To a pay a price for his eviction.

"If he knows how to swim, he won't drown," Max adds. In his hand, he holds something—a small silver pocket watch—turning it over between his fingers, the chain swinging like a pendulum. Each time I've seen him, he's had the watch, always fidgeting with it. His dad gave it to him, the others told me. It was a birthday gift before he was sent here—*so he could track the hours he was stuck in this shithole*, they had joked. It seemed like a cruel gift, in a way. A reminder that time would continue on without him in the outside world. That he was losing time. We all were—trapped in these mountains.

Jasper laughs, a hearty, side-splitting laugh, and takes another long gulp from the bottle.

Still, I stand at the shore, refusing to move.

Then Max crosses the space between us, before I can brace myself, and he shoves me toward the lake. I take several steps back, then I spin around—my hands balled at my sides. Max and I stand only a foot from each other, both of us ready to make something of it—to not let it go. Bloody knuckles and broken jawbones and bruised flesh.

But then Lin says, "Come on, man, just walk out on the ice and get it over with." My gaze flashes to him, and he shakes his head. "It's fucking freezing out here. Do you guys really want to get in a fight and try to explain black eyes to the Brutes in the morning?"

I feel my fists relax, but Max keeps staring at me, willing me to make a move toward him. I've only been at the camp a week, and Lin is right—I really don't want to start something that might not end. Always checking over my shoulder to see if Max is following me through the trees. Never able to sleep. And I have no idea what sort of punishment we'll face with the Brutes. A punishment that might follow me for the rest of my time here.

So I turn away from Max, my arms rigid, snow blowing sideways in gusts now, and I take a step out onto the ice.

It creaks and settles, but doesn't give way.

I move toward the center, each step a slow shuffle, until I feel the ice thinning beneath me—a layer of water soaking through my boots. I stop and look back at the shore.

"Keep going!" Jasper shouts out at me.

But I can't; I know the ice will break. I shake my head.

"That's not the center!" Jasper calls.

I turn and see that I still have several more yards to go. But I'll never make it. The ice is way too thin. When I turn back to face them, Max has left the shore. He's moving quickly out toward me— rage bottled up inside him, chest puffed, arms clenched.

I brace myself for whatever is about to happen next.

Max doesn't speak when he reaches me, he just shoves me hard in the chest and pushes me backward on the ice. "We said you had to go to the center," he spits, blood rushing into his face.

The ice moans beneath our feet, but Max won't stop—he wants to go to the middle of the lake, where the ice is thinnest. To prove a point. To prove I'm afraid but he isn't. He forces me farther onto the lake and the others on shore laugh—shouting things I can't make out. Voices echoing up into the trees. Urging Max on.

But I know this won't end well. For either of us.

We're near the center when I hear the sound: the cracking of ice.

Max's gaze swings up to mine and his shoulders drop. He looks frightened for the first time, and his head snaps back to shore, gauging how far away we are.

Too far.

"We have to run," I say, out of breath. But Max seems frozen in place. The ice is too thin, and fractures weave along the surface, little spiderwebs expanding beneath Max's boots. It pops and bends, starting to give way.

His eyes dip to his feet, going wide, and there is a low vibrating shudder that rises up from the ice.

I don't know why I do it.

Maybe it's just a reflex. Or maybe it's the burst of memories that flare through me: of my parents the last time they said goodbye, my mom smiling as they strode out the front door, and then the image of their car, destroyed a few miles from our house. The memory of that day, of death so close I could feel it.

And it's here again. Making fissures in the ice.

I bolt forward and push Max away, knocking him hard to the surface of the ice. Something slides out from his pocket: the silver watch with the long chain. We both eye it for a second, only a foot away, and then the ice breaks beneath me.

Whoosh. And the ground drops away.

The cold stabs its talons into my skin like a thousand little cuts with a serrated blade. My head sinks below the surface at the sudden impact, and it sucks the air straight from my lungs. Panic surges up into my brain. My arms reach for the surface, lungs tightening, and I fight to pull myself back above the waterline, drawing in a quick, cold breath of air. I try to yell but can't. No air left. No function beyond staying above the surface.

I grab for the edge of the ice, but my hands slip off. *Too cold.* My arms too weighted. I look for Max and find him standing several feet away, staring down at me, like he is observing a creature in an aquarium. A curiosity in his eyes—but not panic, not shock or fear—only an eerie, calm resolve. He doesn't drop to his knees and try to pull me out, he doesn't yell for the others to come help, he just stares—his jaw set in place. His eyes pinholes of black.

I claw at the ice, and my hand grabs something, something cold and smooth. I clutch it in my palm and then Max is suddenly there, reaching for me. But he doesn't grab my arm to pull me out; he snatches at the thing I hold—the silver watch—and his fingers catch the chain, yanking it back. It snaps apart between us, the watch still in my hand.

I blink up at him and suck in my final breath, knowing it's the last one—the stormy night sky blurring around me—my vision going as the cold sucks all the warmth from my skin, my eyes, my lungs.

I blink and try to grab for the ice one last time, but my arms barely move, and Max only watches. *Cold, cold stare.*

I close my eyes and the dark pulls me under.

One swift gulp, and everything goes numb.

The lake is just as bottomless as the boys at camp said it would be. An immeasurable depth.

I sink and there is no light. No quality of time. Of how much water can enter a person's lungs.

I sink until I open my eyes again.

Until I reach the bottom of the lake that is not the lake at all.

The cold still bores through me, my skin still feels the chill of the lake, but I shiver beneath a thick canopy of trees. Snow falling over me, breathing air into my lungs.

Alive. Inside a winter forest.

And a girl is there, kneeling in the snow and dark. A girl who bends over me with hair long and black.

A girl. Who just might be a witch.

NORA

A soft pain forms in my chest, darkness running through me like a river.

Max was to blame for what happened that night.

He forced Oliver out onto the ice. And the others, Rhett and Jasper and Lin—they were there too. And when Suzy told them I had found Oliver—*alive*—they forced me into the Wicker Woods to see if it was true, if Oliver had somehow survived and had been hiding this whole time. If he was alive—if he didn't drown—it would change everything.

It would mean they weren't responsible for his death.

Max could come out of hiding, and they could all laugh about it: *Remember the time we thought you were dead?* A pat on the back and everything would be okay. No one goes to jail for murder. No one has to pretend they didn't know what happened—he simply vanished from his bunk. No one has to carry the lie with them for the rest of their lives, knowing a boy died one night when they were away at camp.

But I was wrong. I didn't find Oliver alive.

And everything that happened that night couldn't be wiped

away or forgotten. A boy is still dead. *And only I can see him.* Only a Walker can see ghosts in the darkest kind of dark. Our eyes are different, strange, able to see what no one else can.

"I'm sorry," Oliver says, like it's all his fault. Like he's sorry he's dead and sorry he let me believe he wasn't. Sorry that now my skin craves his, that he kissed me in my room and slept in my bed and breathed real-boy breath and let me think it could always be like this.

Bad things happen, I think.

A missing boy is found in the woods. A dead boy.

I lower the spellbook in my arms and watch the sky rain down in scattered bits of ash. I breathe and it feels like razors in my lungs. The fire too close, blazing down toward the shore. *So close now.* But my heart is caving in, and that hurts worse.

"None of it matters," I say. It's too late now anyway. He broke my heart and the forest is breaking around me and there's no time left.

He reaches out and tries to touch me, to run his fingers down my cheek, but I flinch away. He's dead, and even though it's not his fault, he's still dead. *Dead dead dead.* And nothing can undo that. No Walker spell inside the book can bring him back, return real air into his dead-boy lungs.

Nothing can change what's been done.

I glance up the shore, where the trees between us and the road are already engulfed, flames winding up into the skyline, catching on treetops, cyclones of heat and ash. Even the path back to my house is blocked. There's no way out now. We waited too long. *I* waited too long.

The snow has melted away along the beach, revealing black pebbles and ash-coated sand.

"Nora," he says. But I won't look at him because nothing is okay. Because everything is burning. Because the fire is too close, surrounding me now. *And he is dead.* Tears spill down my cheeks.

"I never wanted to hurt you," he says, reaching out to wipe away the tears with his dead-boy palms. A boy I can touch and feel but no one else can. "I'm so sorry," he says. "I wish I could make this right."

"But you can't," I say, bitter words from bitter lips.

He's so close he could kiss me. He could blot out everything with his mouth on mine. But I don't want him to. *Flesh and bone.* I don't want to feel the heat of his skin knowing it's not real. None of this will last.

He was never mine to keep.

I shrug away from his touch. My heart seizing in my chest, my lungs burning so bad it feels like they're on fire, encircled by flames. And I am surrounded by flames—the fire too close, the heat unbearable. Singeing my flesh, my hair swirling up into the cyclone of ash. I can't stay here. I won't survive.

"Where are you going?" Oliver shouts.

"Out there," I answer.

He tries to grab my hand, but I slip away, stepping out onto the ice. It's my only option now—the only place where the fire won't burn.

On the lake.

"Nora, no," he calls, his voice broken, crumbling beneath his tongue. "It's too dangerous."

"Only for me," I answer back. I'm the only one who can die, who still has something to lose. I know there's no time left. No escape. I'll suffocate from the smoke or burn from the flames if I stay here.

I move quickly, before he can pull me back. I sprint out onto the ice, through the low layer of smoke, slipping once and dropping to my knees, but I push myself up and keep going. The ice is thinner than before—than the night I fell through the surface and the water was needles on my skin.

The lake snaps and creaks like old wood, like ice not as thick as it once was. The heat from the fire is melting it, turning it back to water. I shuffle and slip, but I keep moving forward until I reach the center—where the shore is nearly the same distance away on all sides. I press my hands to my knees and try to breathe, but the smoke is too thick. My eyes burn, my lungs rasp with each inhale. And I feel a sudden certainty that I'm going to die out here. That this is really the end.

This is how I will be remembered inside the spellbook: Nora Walker died on the lake, her body never recovered. The long line of Walkers ended with her.

I cover a hand over my mouth to keep out the smoke and I lift my head, standing up straight. The view across Jackjaw Lake is of a forest in flames. *A forest burning.* Started by a boy named Jasper who is now buried in the ground. Swallowed whole.

At the boys' camp, several structures are already gone—torched to their bones. And I can't tell if anyone is still there, trapped in their cabins. The wilderness is on fire and there's nothing I can do to stop it.

I look to the sky, the shade of gunpowder, and I remember the feeling when I fell into the lake, when my skin felt like it was peeling open, when my grandmother's ring slipped free from my finger—sinking down into the dark. *To the bottom of a lake without an end.*

But Jasper found it inside the Wicker Woods. The ring returned.

Just like when I found Oliver.

Both sank into the lake.

I breathe, chasing down the memories as quickly as they skitter away.

Mr. Perkins said that miners used to drop things into the lake—they were offerings to the forest, to calm the Wicker Woods. Because they believed the lake was the beating heart of this place.

The pieces begin to settle in the back of my mind. Dust falling through rays of sunlight—finally visible.

I never knew why things appeared inside the Wicker Woods. What foul form of witchery or mischief was at work. But now I see: *If it falls into the lake, it will return again inside the Wicker Woods.*

A notation I will make inside the spellbook, if I ever get the chance.

And on one fateful night, during a bad winter storm, a boy fell into the lake—he sank to the bottom and was spit back out inside the Wicker Woods. An offering made the night of the storm.

And then I found him under a full moon. Mine to keep. *Finders keepers.*

Now I understand, now I see. But it doesn't change a thing. *He's still dead.* The forest brought him back, but it didn't bring him back whole.

The cold from the frozen lake rises up through my boots, and I begin to shiver. I think I hear Oliver calling for me, searching, but the smoke is too thick now, swirling in strange gusts across the lake, and he can't find me.

Fire spits up into the sky from the tops of trees along the shore. Devouring, angry, hungry. It sounds like a monster, sucking up all the oxygen. And I know my home is gone. Nothing left but a scar across the ground. Only piles of soot and brick.

Tears break over my eyelids and fall to the ice, becoming a part of the lake.

I was born in that house—where every Walker before me has lived—and now it's gone, only ash.

And it's my fault.

I was wrong about so many things. I was wrong when I thought Oliver had killed Max. I was wrong when I thought my death was near. Or maybe I wasn't—maybe death will still find me. Out here on this lake. In this burning forest.

Is it better to burn alive or to drown? Which will hurt less? The ice shifts beneath me, bending away from my weight. An inch of water now at the surface. I squeeze my eyes shut and push away the cold, pushing away the sound of trees cracking and falling to the ground in the distance. The sound of flames roaring along the edge of the lake. Ash in my hair, embers falling at my feet, melting the ice.

I waited too long, I think again. I should have left with Suzy and Mr. Perkins.

Eventually the ice will crack and give out beneath me. Eventually I will sink into the lake and drown just like Oliver.

Another offering to the lake.

A wilderness covered in snow shouldn't burn. But fury can fuel strange things—tonight, it fueled a forest fire. If my grandmother was here, she could fix it, she would wave her finger in the air and the trees would listen. She would make this right.

Through the smoke, I glimpse the boys' camp across the lake and see several boys running from their cabins. They haven't all fled

yet. Some of them are still there. "The forest wants to burn," I think,
I say aloud to no one. And it wants us all to burn with it. Maybe the
forest deserves it. Maybe it's lived too long. I squeeze the spellbook
against my chest and think about all the Walkers who sprouted up
from these woods. All the stories that live in the soil, live inside these
pages. And now it will all burn.

My head begins to buzz, and a familiar sensation skims through
me: I've been here before. I've stood on this ice and thought all
these thoughts and felt the ash in my lungs. The feeling of déjà vu
rattles over me again so quickly that my head tilts back to the red-
stained sky.

Tick, tick, tick, tick, thud.

I blink and refocus. I squeeze the spellbook tighter.

The ice shifts beneath me, so thin I can see the deep black below
my feet. I hear Oliver somewhere in the smoke, calling my name.
He's close now.

I grew up in these woods, I think. Every Walker has. *It belongs to
me, and I to it.*

The forest heaves and whines and screams along the shore,
flames spurred on by spite and revenge. The ice snaps below me.
Fear claws up into my throat.

Oliver shouts again from the smoke, but I don't listen. I don't
shout back and tell him where I am. Instead, I peer up at the awful
sky, at the tips of trees I can just see above the smoke. And I sense the
forest watching, listening. *It knows who I am.*

"I am Nora Walker," I say softly, just as I have each time I've
entered the Wicker Woods, but now my words seem tiny. No magic
in them at all. No meaning. I think of my grandmother—how sturdy

she was. An anchor that could not be moved against her will. Many feared her, the strong tenor of her voice, her wild dark hair—I never saw her take a brush to it and it often caught in the wind and tangled into knots, but moments later it was silk down her back. She was a marvel. And I wish I was her right now, I wish I knew what she knew. How to command the trees around her.

I grip the spellbook tighter, knowing the power inside its pages, the weight of so many words handwritten by all the Walkers before me. I know the meaning in them. That they once commanded these trees, these dark skies. The woods and Walkers are bound to one another. We cannot be divided, stripped clean of the other.

I swallow and say, "My mother is Tala Walker." An invocation, a reminder to the trees of the blood that courses through me. "My grandmother was Ida Walker." I breathe her name, let it linger on my tongue. "I am a Walker." Magic once poured through our veins, *real magic*. We breathed and the forest listened. We shed tears and the forest wept sap down its bark. Many of the old ways have been forgotten, slipped through cracks, but our blood is still the same. Still a fire inside us.

I feel Oliver is close now, nearly to me, but I don't look back. "I belong to this forest," I say aloud, willing the trees to listen. To calm their fury. To stop the flames from burning, from devouring what- ever is left. "I am a Walker," I say again. "You know my name. You know who I am." It sounds like a spell, like a remnant of real magic rising up inside me, burning my fingertips.

I breathe and lift my chin. Certainty pulsing through me. "I am a Walker!" I scream, commanding my voice to grow louder than the raging fire pummeling around the lake.

I am not afraid.

I hear Oliver only a few yards away. "Nora!" he shouts, more urgent this time. And then there is another sound. A change in the air. A crack and a *whoosh*.

That's when I see it: the falling embers, the mammoth pine tree completely engulfed in flames. It must be two hundred feet tall, and its trunk has been uprooted from the soft ground along the shore, fire burning from roots to tip. And now the tree is tipping, leaning, falling. Careening toward the lake, toward me. I stare at it like it's fireworks erupting in the night sky. *In awe.* Everything is happening in slow motion—knowing I need to run, but somehow caught by the dazzling sight of such a massive tree, upending, pitching forward.

A second later, the tree crashes across the lake, breaking through the surface of ice in one violent blow. The sound is tremendous and terrifying. Like a thousand glass chandeliers shattering at once. The lake shudders beneath me.

Only a couple yards away, the tree sinks into the black water, into a gaping hole. Ice fracturing out around it. *Run!* my head screams. But my heart has stalled in my chest, my legs afraid to move. The ice makes an eerie sound beneath me, like metal bending to the point of breaking. Like a long, pent-up howl. I suck in a breath just before it happens.

My eyelids blink.

Time slows.

And then the ice snaps—a quick giving way—and I drop into the water.

The air is pushed straight from my lungs. My head dips all the way under and the spellbook slips free from my grasp—sinking into the deep, just like my grandmother's ring—and I scramble to the surface, fighting for air. I try to scream, to call Oliver's name, but no words come out. My throat is too dry, the air too thick with smoke. My hands slap against the surface of the water as I try to swim to the edge of the ice, but there is no edge. The lake has shattered, broken apart, and now only chunks of ice bob at the surface—just like me.

The shore is too far, not even visible through the smoke.

Again I try to scream, but a wave of numbness pours through me, the cold too cold, the weight of my wet clothes too heavy. *How long have I been in here?* A couple seconds, an hour. *Too long.* My eyes blink up at the ash-choked sky and my arms become useless. My legs stop kicking. *Everything numb.* Everything a smear of black.

Without even realizing it, my head slips below the surface. Slips beneath the waterline.

I sink.

It's worse than before. The cold feels razor-edged, my lungs swollen in my chest, burning against my ribs—needing air. When I fell in before, it had seemed like a dream. Like I wasn't really there. But this is sharp and painful and terrifying.

I pinch my eyes shut and feel the depth carrying me down, sinking to the bottom without an end. But still I hold my breath, afraid to let the water spill in. Afraid to feel it in my lungs.

I won't die like this, I think.

I won't be an offering to the lake, to the forest. I won't drown like Oliver and become a phantom in these woods. This isn't how it ends.

This isn't my story.

I am a Walker.

My eyes flutter open. And see only dark.

A ticking sound enters my ears, soft at first and then louder. The water vibrates around me, like a kite whipping in the air, lashing across the sky. *Something isn't right.*

I sink deeper. Into the coldest cold I've ever felt. I sink and my thoughts spin quickly. Too fast to catch them, but also slow and lazy, pinging between my ears.

The ticking grows louder, and I feel for Max's watch in my pocket. It trembles in my palm, the hands clicking nervously forward and back.

I wait to feel the rocky bottom of the lake, for my lungs to give out. But the watch quivers, seconds that thud against my skin, and the water feels like air, like I'm floating, sent adrift among dark clouds.

I pretend I'm not cold.

I pretend I'm not sinking endlessly into a lake without a bottom.

I pretend a fire doesn't burn along the shore and I never went into the forest with those boys. I pretend the moth never thumped against my window and Suzy never asked to stay at my house. I pretend I never found Oliver inside the Wicker Woods and he never placed his lips on mine. I pretend he didn't drown.

I pretend I am a Walker who is just as powerful and brave as the women who came before me.

I pretend I can make things right.

I am a Walker, I think again. The words sliding across my skin like oil.

I squeeze the watch tight, the cold metal branded against my palm, the only thing I have to hold on to.

When you need it, your nightshade will come, Grandma told me once.

611

My heart rises and then collapses. A ball inside my ribs.

I know what I am.

My eyelids blink and everything, *everything*, tilts off axis, the lake tumbling toward the sky. The silver watch pulses in my hand, tiny infinitesimal movements—*tink, tink, sputter*. The hands click once, twice, in the wrong direction.

Little prisms of light scatter across my eyelids. I squeeze my fingers tighter around the watch, my nails against the glass.

And I let the dark take me.

Spellbook of Moonlight & Forest Medicine

TALA WALKER was born under a buttermilk moon at the end of October.

Honeybees dozed at the edge of her crib, and their fat, winged bodies got tangled in her soft cotton blankets while she slept. When she learned to walk, she tottered out into the woods, sticking her fingers into the hives of wild bees and waddling home with honey stuck to the bottom of her white lace-up ballerina slippers.

But she was never stung—not once.

Tala Walker could enchant wild honeybees with the quick flutter of an eyelash, and they fell into a deep, restful slumber whenever she was close.

Tala left Jackjaw Lake when she was nineteen, wanting to forget what she was, to go somewhere the Walker name had never been uttered. She fell in love swiftly with a boy whose face was covered in sun-made freckles, and when a baby started growing inside her, she knew she needed to return home. To the place where all Walkers are born—in the old house beside Jackjaw Lake. And her daughter would be no different.

She gave birth to a sable-haired girl she named Nora. A girl with starlight in her galaxy-colored eyes. But Tala hoped her daughter would never know magic, never need her shadow side. The thing that made all Walkers different. Strange. Outcasts.

But she was wrong. Her daughter did possess a nightshade—perhaps the most powerful kind ever written about inside the spellbook.

Tala Walker had tried to escape what she was.

But her daughter, Nora, wanted nothing more than to be who they really were: pure-blooded witches.

How to Train Honeybees:

Wear netting over bare skin.

Burn two hickory twigs, let smoke drift into hive.

Count to eleven, then whisper Tala Walker's name into
    smoke.

Collect honeycomb in glass jars before twigs burn down
    to nubs.

NORA

"W ake up, Nora," a voice says, clear and sharp like bell. "Wake up."

It's my grandmother's voice. Chasing me up from my dreams, up from the dark of the lake, the soft tenor of her words whispered against my skull.

My eyes snap open and I feel the snow against my cheek. Cold and wet. The scent of silty earth and green filling my nostrils.

I'm no longer in the lake.

Moonlight peeks through the trees, pale and lonely, bathing my skin.

My fingers push into the snow, into the soil, hands burrowing up to my wrists. I need to feel the earth, feel rooted to something that isn't the endless sinking of the lake. My mouth hangs open a moment, and I want to speak, just to hear my own voice—to know that I'm real—but no words fall out. My body heaves, shivers, and I think I might be sick, but I draw my hands out from the dirt and roll onto my back, staring up at the black, starless sky. I can't be sure of the hour. But it's well after sunset—the darkest part of night.

A ringing fills my ears, and I suck in air like it's never felt so good inside my lungs, greedy for it. Desperate. The wind howls through the trees as if it's coming from straight up inside me. A wailing cry. A hiss and a sputter.

But I'm not inside the Wicker Woods.

Not deep inside the cruelest part of the forest.

I'm in the trees outside my home, near the shore, near the old, slanted woodshed. The pines towering over me. But I can't be sure how I got here. Can't be certain how much time has passed since I fell into the cold, cold lake.

I sit upright, my head wobbling. Snow falling around me.

Yet, if I'm not inside the Wicker Woods, then the lake didn't bring me back—I am not a lost thing returned, not like Oliver.

Something else happened.

Something that makes my eyelids quiver, drops of lake water suspended on each lash, tiny glassy orbs. While sparks swim across my vision.

There is no smoke in my throat. No embers tumbling through the pines, burning my skin. The trees above me are a deep, mossy green and the air is clear.

There is no wildfire roaring through the forest.

I stand and press my hand against the trunk of a tree, breathing, the cold air tickling my neck. My skin pricked with gooseflesh.

A storm is coming. And the air seesaws at the edge of my vision, vibrating—like déjà vu. The sky a familiar shade of dusky black. A feeling, a memory I can't pin down, classify, or catalog like one of Mr. Perkins's framed specimens hanging on his wall.

The ringing in my ears becomes a wail, becomes a scream inside my head. I've been here before. I've stood in these trees. Snow coming down in thick washes of white.

With trembling fingers, I brush the hair away from my face and feel the weight of something on my finger—my grandmother's ring. The moonstone a pearly gray, reflecting the sky, as if I never lost it in the lake. It never slipped from my finger.

Something else has happened.

My eyes flick to the ground, looking for the spellbook I held in my hands when I went into the lake, but it's not here.

The ring has returned. But the spellbook is gone.

Something's happened—to me, to the forest, to everything. I don't remember drowning. I don't recall the cold of the water rushing into my lungs. The pain of death.

I spin in a circle, but there is no sign of Oliver, of anyone else.

I'm alone.

On shaking legs, I push myself away from the tree and start down the slope toward the lake. I can feel the trees bending away, giving me space. I force my lungs to breathe, to determine north from south, to orient the sky from the ground. But the seconds totter strangely around me, slippery like a silverfish swimming through reeds.

If Grandma were here, she would look at the trees, the dark snow-filled sky, my eyes, and she would know if this was all a dream. She would know why I didn't drown in the lake. Why ash-clouds don't rise up beneath my feet.

But right now, she feels very, *very* far away.

I stop at the shore and cross my arms, my mouth dipping open. There are no blackened trees, no spinning sparks weaving through the sky. The row of summer homes and the boys' camp at the far side of the lake have not been reduced to ash. And up in the pines, my home still stands.

Nothing has burned.

I inch closer to the shoreline, the air crackling and settling, and through the falling snow I hear voices, boys shouting, laughing.

It's coming from across the lake.

Maybe I should go back to the house, get warm beside the fire, let my skin and hair and clothes thaw. But I don't. I follow the sound of the boys. The familiar pitch of their voices. Because something is wrong. Something has changed.

Everything is terrifyingly different.

I pass the marina and the boathouse and Mr. Perkins's cabin. Light gleams from inside—not just candlelight, but buzzing, humming electricity light. The power has come back on. At the window, Mr. Perkins is gazing out at the snow, and he waves a hand at me, smiling. *He didn't flee down the road to escape the fire—because there is no fire.*

I'm not dead. I didn't drown in the lake. Mr. Perkins can see me. *But something is wrong.*

Something that flickers across my mind—just out of reach.

Something I can't explain.

I move quicker toward the sound of the boys, toward a voice I think might be Oliver's. And when I reach the cemetery—the odd-shaped land where the dead have been buried—the breath hitches in my lungs.

The boys stand among the graves. All of them.

Shadowy figures in the falling snow: Jasper and Rhett and Lin. They laugh, passing around a bottle and taking long gulps of the dark liquid inside. Max is there too, leaning against a gravestone, blond hair nearly the same color as the snow.

And Oliver: his arms crossed, standing apart from the others.

They're all here. *Even though they shouldn't be.*

I pause near the gate, my heart wobbling against my rib cage, unsure why they've gathered in the cemetery. Why the trees aren't burnt. Why nothing is as it was.

"You have to say her name three times," Jasper coaxes, his bony elbow resting on the grave of my ancestor. *Jasper,* who is alive. Not buried in the soil inside the Wicker Woods. The scene before me swims in and out of focus, thoughts muddled—unable to pinpoint a memory, a moment that makes sense.

"Whose?" Oliver asks, and Jasper points a finger at the gravestone. The place where Willa Walker has been laid in the ground— the Walker who wept into the lake and made it bottomless. The same grave that Oliver told me the boys made him stand over and whisper her name three times—the first part of his initiation.

"If you say her name three times, you'll summon her up from the grave," I hear Rhett say, a serious measure to his voice. A grimness that reminds me of when he broke into my house and pulled me from bed.

"Legend says that Willa Walker wept into Jackjaw Lake and made it bottomless," Jasper adds, smirking.

Oliver makes a sound, and Max moves closer to him, his shoulders pulled back. "You don't believe us?" Max asks. And my head starts to vibrate again, hearing their words, watching as Oliver peers down at the grave and reluctantly speaks Willa's name three times—I know where I am.

I know: This is the night of the storm.

This is the night Oliver breaks through the ice and sinks into the dark. This is the night he drowns.

When the electricity will spark and then die. When the road will be snowed in.

Time has spun and tottered and turned itself inside out. Or *I* have unraveled it. I have done this. Brought myself back to this night. *Back, back, back.*

I am at the place where it all began.

Little pops of light break across my vision—the now familiar prick of déjà vu. The air wavers against my eardrums, as if I'm falling, tumbling, losing all sense of gravity. *This has all happened before.*

On that awful, awful night.

And I feel like I might be sick.

"Dude, you should see your face," Jasper says now—just like Oliver described. And he claps a hand on Oliver's shoulder, laughing, the sound carrying up into the treetops, startling a blackbird that caws from a nearby spruce tree and takes to the sky.

This has all happened before.

The boys begin to move through the cemetery, passing the bottle of booze among them. Rhett and Lin hop over the low wood fence, laughing to themselves. Jasper staggers behind while Max moves slowly, fidgeting with something in his hand. The watch. *The silver pocket watch.* The same one I found in Oliver's coat pocket—the one that broke just before Oliver slipped beneath the water while Max looked on. Air bubbles rising to the surface.

Anger scrapes up inside me, imagining Max standing over the hole in the ice. Refusing to save Oliver's life. To reach down into the water and pull him up.

He watched Oliver die. He *let* him die.

I feel the sudden urge to stride across the snow, out of the cemetery, and wrap my hands around Max's throat. Stare into his eyes and know that he deserves it. Maybe even push him out onto the ice and wait for it to break—make him suffer just like Oliver. Atone for what he did.

But he hasn't done it yet.

Not yet.

I watch as the rest of the boys scale the fence and tromp through the snow to the lakeshore.

But Oliver is last to the fence, his hands in his pockets, gaze turned away from the blowing snow. He doesn't realize he's following them to his death. That when he reaches the lake, they will force him out onto the ice. Max will shove him in the chest, hands coiled into fists, adrenaline in his veins. And in the end, Oliver will break through the surface and sink down *down down down* into the lake.

That soon, before this night is over, he will drown.

My footsteps are quick through the snow, my breathing heavy, and I reach Oliver before he climbs over the fence after the others. He doesn't see me, not at first, his eyes squinting away from the wind, but when I'm close enough, he must sense me because he whips around, startled, and his eyes go wide—a verdant, wild shade of green.

"Oliver," I say softly, my voice terribly small. Terribly, impossibly weak.

He is slow to react, his gaze sweeping over me, stalling at the curve of my lips, the wet strands of my hair, but there is no recognition in his eyes. No flicker of memory. He doesn't take my hand and pull me against his chest and ask if I'm okay.

He only stares.

The trees surrounding the cemetery begin to shake just a little, and I can't tell if it's the wind or my eyes. If things are still trying to snap back into focus—the lake separating itself from the sky.

"Oliver," I say again, lifting my fingers and hovering them only a few inches from his chest, afraid to touch him. Afraid to know if he's real or not. *Alive or not.*

His skin is not pale or sallow, his eyes do not look tormented by his memory of the forest. He looks strong. Different. Not how I remember.

But his face twists when I say his name, arms stiffening at his sides. *He doesn't remember me.* He doesn't know who I am. And the realization breaks me apart. Makes me want to scream. To cry out. To grab him and dig my fingernails into his flesh.

I breathe and each inhale is a rattle.

The other boys are almost to the lakeshore—they haven't yet seen me. And Rhett is shoving Lin playfully, laughing, their voices muffled by the falling snow.

"We can't stay here," I say to Oliver, snapping my eyes back to his. But still, he sways away from me. Just out of reach.

My head begins to clack and drum. My jaw chattering. I know I need to get warm, I need to get inside. My body is too cold. But Oliver only looks at me with the distant look of a stranger. Who won't reach out and touch me. Who doesn't remember anything from before, who looks into my eyes and sees only a girl. Nothing more.

But the silence is broken by another voice.

By Rhett, shouting through the snow. "Who the fuck are you?" he calls. My eyes lift only briefly, to see that Rhett has moved back to the cemetery fence—probably having realized that Oliver didn't follow them out.

I open my mouth, and my lips begin to quiver. *Oliver doesn't know who I am.* None of them do. "I'm—" I start, but my voice catches at the back of my teeth. *I'm a witch.* A witch who might have moonlight in her veins after all. Who jumped into the lake and woke on a night that's already happened. A witch who has felt time slipping around her, who believed she didn't have a nightshade. But maybe, *maybe*, I was wrong. Maybe I can't bring back the dead—maybe no witch can. But I can do something else.

The wind grows stronger, and it blows my hair away from my neck. Up toward the sky. Wild and woven into knots.

Maybe I wanted it bad enough. My heart cracked so deeply it split open and my shadow side spilled out like black mud. *When you need it, your nightshade will come.* Maybe it's been there all along. The part of me that felt time tumbling just out of reach. The moments when I was certain I had been there before, the déjà vu. Over and over and over. A thing I couldn't hold on to long enough, a thing I didn't understand. A thing I couldn't control.

Until now. *Now.*

"She's that moon girl," Jasper answers, and he's standing at the fence now too, watching me. In his hand is the lighter, and he flicks it open, letting the small flame burn a moment before closing it again. "She's a Walker," he says with confidence.

My eyes skip back to Oliver, but he doesn't soften his gaze. He only stares, as blank and heartless as the others.

"What are you doing here, moon girl?" Rhett asks.

I ignore him.

623

"Oliver," I say again, to keep his attention on me, even though he hasn't once looked away. "Don't go out on the lake," I hiss quietly, so the others won't hear. I feel myself inching closer to him again, wanting to touch him, to run my fingers up his jaw to his temple. To pull him close and make him remember. "Promise me, okay?" I suck in a deep breath, my head spinning, eyes having a hard time focusing. As if I'm still in the lake, water pressing against my pupils.

But Oliver's expression doesn't change—his mouth a stiff, puzzled line.

He has no idea who I am.

"What's she talking about?" Lin interjects.

"She's a witch," Jasper says, grinning. And for the first time I notice his left cheek—where the tree branch tore through his skin the night of the bonfire and left a deep, bloody gash. But it's gone. The skin pale and white. No scar marring the flesh.

It hasn't happened yet.

"She's probably casting some curse on him," Jasper continues, swinging himself over the fence and taking several sloppy steps toward Oliver and me, eyebrows raised. "She's going to drag him back to her house and bury him under the floorboards. Like all Walkers do."

Oliver's breathing turns swift and strange, but still his eyes don't pull away.

"Shut up, Jasper," I snap, swiveling around to point a long finger at him. He clamps his mouth closed, like he actually thinks I might turn him into a sad little toad or stitch his lips together with spider-webs and string.

624

"How the hell do you know my name?" he asks, his voice suddenly shaking, his lower jaw pulled down in shock.

Because I am the witch they think I am. I am the one to fear.

I look back to Oliver, breathing so deeply I feel dizzy. "Please," I say. I smile a little, and for a moment I think he's going to smile back, his eyes turning a soft, sunrise green. "Come with me."

His lips part just slightly, the tension in his shoulders drops.

But then Jasper barks from behind him, "She's definitely messing with you, man. Don't let her touch you."

"I know you don't remember me," I say to Oliver, ignoring Jasper. "But I remember you. And if you stay here with them, something bad is going to happen." I swallow and find my voice again. "Please."

I know he doesn't understand, I know none of this makes sense, but I lift my hand, slowly so he won't flinch away, and I touch his cheekbone, his neck, hoping he will see. Some part of him will know that I've touched him before. That he's looked into my eyes just like this and leaned forward to put his lips on mine. Some deep, unknowable part of him will still remember.

"Dude," Rhett says, his voice pitched. "She's probably hexing you right now. Stealing your soul. You won't even remember your own name by morning."

But I keep my gaze on Oliver, willing him to remember, and he finally does touch me—yet, it isn't soft and gentle and kind. He grabs my hand and lowers it away from his cheek, firm and quick. Then releases me.

"Get the hell out of here, witch!" Rhett says, at the same moment my heart sinks into my stomach. He clambers over the fence and starts moving toward me, waving his hands in the air as if I'm a bird he can frighten back up into the sky. Scare back into my roost, into my hovel in the forest. Small and cold and alone. "Or we'll tie you to that tree over there and light a match and see how flammable witches really are."

I know now that Rhett will actually do it. That all of them are capable of awful things. They broke into my house and dragged me up into the woods—I wouldn't be shocked if they actually tied me to a tree and started a small fire, just to see. Just to see if black smoke poured from my mouth and ears when I burned. They're just drunk enough. And stupid enough.

"Oliver," I whisper again, taking a step back, away from the boys—my heart cleaved into halves. A muscle that beats too fast, that has lost track of time. While my head wheels forward and back to the things that haven't yet happened. The things that still might if Oliver goes out onto that lake.

The wind blows up through the trees, and the sky is full of snow. The storm is getting worse.

"Told you she's dangerous," Jasper remarks, just loud enough that I can hear. I take another step back, and another, keeping my eyes on Oliver. I want him to say something, to yell at the boys to stop, to leave me alone. I want him to come after me. But he stands mute. Everything he ever felt for me, everything he ever said, now lost. Slipped away into the darkest corners of his mind.

The Oliver I knew is gone.

Rhett follows my movements, and for a moment he looks like he might come after me, grab my arm and pull me back into the cemetery. Like I am just the thing he needs to occupy his buzzed mind.

626

So I hurry through the snow, around the lake, until I can no longer see them through the blowing wind, and I swear I can hear my heart break—the fizz and crack of it.

I stop when I'm almost to the marina and press my hands to my eyes to keep the tears from coming. *This isn't how it's supposed to happen.*

This isn't how the story ends.

A deep scar is branding itself inside me—a place that will scab over but never heal. I hold in a breath, I hold it until my chest aches, until my lungs burn for a fresh gulp of air. The storm thrashes overhead and I exhale, long and deep, a chill shuttling down my spine, tucking itself firmly between each rib bone. I've always been afraid I wasn't a real Walker. Afraid I would end up like my mom, cynical and scared of what she is. I always thought I wanted to be alone, alone in these woods. Where I can't get hurt, where no one can call me moon girl and winter witch and wild.

But I was wrong. I don't want to be alone. I don't want sleep in my room in the dark and never feel Oliver's hands on my skin again. I don't want a life without people in it. Without Oliver. Without my heart rapping wildly inside my chest and knowing someone else's is doing the same thing.

My life feels spare and thin without it.

I am a Walker who found her nightshade. I am a Walker who wants to be called more than a witch. More than a girl who is feared. I want to be a Walker who can trust her heart, who will chase down this feeling welling up inside me every chance I get. I want to be loved.

Loved.

Loved.

Loved.

Recklessly, foolishly. Without reason or caution or always looking for ways to ruin it.

I want *him*.

I drop my hands from my eyes and take a step back toward the cemetery, back through the storm. Because I don't have a choice. Because I have to drag him away and keep him safe and not let him drown. Whether he remembers me or not, I won't give up on him. Because I am a Walker. And my story doesn't end like this.

But I only make it a few steps, *I only blink once*, when I see someone moving up the shore, through the blizzard—an illusion. A boy.

I blink again.

Him.

I stop and a humming begins in my skull.

Doubt and fear make nests beneath my skin. I want to cry.

He reaches me and time slows. He lifts his head and my heart climbs back up into my chest, braiding itself together—thin fibers of thread to make it whole.

His eyes rove the ground at first, then click to mine. We stare at each other, and I see him searching my face for memories. For moments in time he won't find. Because when I peer into his eyes, I know he doesn't remember me. The girl who pulled him from the Wicker Woods and let him sleep beside her. He lifts his hand and I hold in a breath; I watch him without blinking. I think he's going to touch my neck, my face, my collarbone, but his fingers graze my hair, so gently I hardly feel it. My eyes flutter closed, and his hand draws back again.

When I open my eyes, I see he's holding something between his fingers—a small twig, a green spiny leaf clinging to one end, as if it were awaiting spring.

"The forest sticks to you," he says. Without knowing it, he repeats what I told him the first time he pulled a bit of the forest from my hair. The morning after I found him and we walked back to the boys' camp.

A sob catches in my throat and a smile splits across my face.

He holds the leaf in his hand, a remnant from when I woke in the trees, my hair lying across the ground, and maybe, *maybe* he remembers some small part of me. Something that nags at him.

His eyes narrow, and for a moment he looks pained, like he's trying to pick apart the bits of shadows from forgotten memory. The things that haven't happened yet.

"Maybe we met once before?" he asks, his eyebrows sloped down, his hair curling just behind his ears as the snow falls around us.

My fingers want to touch him again, but I only let myself nod, afraid he'll slip away. "I think we did."

"I think I liked you then," he says.

Tears begin spilling down my cheeks, unstoppable, heavy tears. Salt and sweet. "I think I liked you too."

He holds out his arm, and with the tips of his fingers, he wipes away the tears from my chin. He smiles just a little, and I feel like my legs might give out.

I can't stop myself, I shift forward and press both my hands to his chest. He doesn't jerk away. I feel the steady *thump, thump, thump* pulsing from inside him. *A boy who is alive.* I could never find his heartbeat before—his lungs breathed, his eyes blinked closed, his skin went warm and then cold. Yet, his heart had been missing. As if it were unable to recall the cadence it once strummed. But now I can feel it beneath my flattened palms, and my whole body begins to shake.

An exhale leaves his lips, and he steps closer to me, only a few inches away, and he takes my hand in his. He doesn't remember any of it—not really—but he knows that I do.

And maybe that's enough.

"You're shaking," he says, cupping my hands in his and drawing them up to his lips where he blows warm air against my fingers. "Can we go somewhere?" he asks.

I nod but my legs don't move, my heart clattering too fast, the trees swaying and snapping back.

"This storm is getting bad." He looks up to the sky, and snow lands in his hair, the tips of his ears, his cheekbones.

I smile and more tears come. I smile and know that maybe, perhaps, everything's going to be okay. "I've seen worse," I say, smirking.

The black at the rims of his eyes recedes—the darkness I remember from before, that was always inside him. The cold has slipped away—*as if it were never there at all.*

And with his hand in mine, we walk around the shore of the lake, past the boathouse, where inside Mr. Perkins's cabin I can see him at the window, watching the snow come down. He waves again and gives a little nod, and I wave back.

Time has been undone. Sent back in reverse.

A storm is coming, the worst we've had all year. The road will be blocked and the power will flicker out and we'll be trapped for weeks.

But we'll have time. Plenty of it.

I always will.

OLIVER

Her name is Nora Walker.

I don't know anything about her, yet somehow I remember the arch of her smile. The soft river of her hair. The flutter of her eyes when she watches me. The scent of her skin like jasmine and vanilla. And when her lips purse together and she hums a song under her breath, memories I can't possibly have pour through me.

She is a name and a heartbeat that lives inside me. In a way I don't understand.

The snow falls and the power blinks out and the road down the mountains is blocked. But she doesn't seem surprised—not by the storm, not by any of it.

The lake freezes and Nora takes me up onto the roof. She tells me stories—fables that couldn't possibly be real. About a boy who drowned, who appeared again inside a dark wood, how he couldn't escape the memory of the trees. The cold. And sometimes I think she's talking about me. She tells me how the boy saves a girl from inside a room, how he believes she's a witch but he's not afraid. How neither of them fear the other even though they should.

She recites her tales, and we peer up at the stars and wait for spring to settle over the lake. For the seasons to change. We listen to the night insects buzz from the tall beach grass. We listen to the spring flowers bursting from the cracked soil, nights growing long and warm. We lie on the roof even when the summer rain pelts from the sky, cool drops against our heated flesh. I tuck a wave of hair behind her ear and she kisses me on the lips—and I'm certain there's nowhere else I'd rather be.

I'm certain that love can be a wound, deep and saw-toothed and filled with salt. But sometimes it's worth it. Sometimes I'm certain I've loved her before. That this is the second time my heart has knitted itself too tightly around hers.

The second time I've kissed her for the first time.

The second time I've placed my lips on her neck and let my hands drift up her spine. The second time I've fallen in love.

The second time I've known that I'll never leave these mountains, the cold dark of the forest, the bottomless lake beyond her room.

The second time I've known—without question—I'll never leave her.

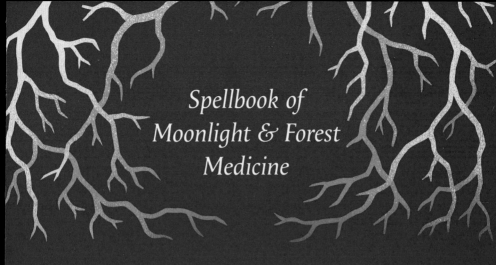

Spellbook of
Moonlight & Forest
Medicine

NORA WALKER was born beneath a paper moon at the end of February, during an especially windy leap year.

Her birth was quiet—her mother, Tala Walker, barely made a sound—while her grandmother, Ida, hummed a tune from an old nursery rhyme to draw the baby into the world.

As a child, Nora preferred pomegranates over strawberries, midnight over midday, and she often trailed after her grandmother, tugging on her skirts, begging for the ginger candies Ida kept in her pockets.

Nora's mother assumed Nora had been born without a night-shade. The first Walker to lose the old magic completely. But during one cold winter moon, Nora and her wolf found a dead boy inside the Wicker Woods, and while trying to flee a wildfire, she slipped into the lake and discovered her shade hidden inside the black hollow of her witchy heart.

Nora Walker could bend time as if it were a prism of light on blue-green sea glass.

Time had never moved in a straight line for Nora, but on that night, she learned it could slip forward and back when her heart begged it to. When she asked.

She could undo the mistakes of the past.

She could make right her wrongs.

She could bring boys back from the dead.

And she would use her nightshade many times.

Nora Walker fell in love only once, with dizzying ferocity, with a boy who knew precisely what she was. She remained at Jackjaw Lake for the remainder of her life, in the old house set back in the trees, and she wrote many stories within the spellbook. Like the winter a storm blew over the lake and not everyone made it out alive. Not at first. She became a storyteller, not just of her own tales, but of the lost items she found inside the Wicker Woods. Of the people she met. She told their stories so they wouldn't be forgotten.

Her own death, however, is a blank spot never noted here. For time was not easily measured for her—the year and age of her death, of most events in her life, could not be certain.

But Nora is said to have lived the longest, strangest, most whole-hearted life of any Walker who ever lived.

Some even say her tale might not yet be over.

That the story of a witch, one who slips through time, can never really have an end.

<u>How to Bend Time:</u>
Light a black candle beside a south-facing window—let
    it burn for ten winter minutes.

Hold a piece of green glass over the flame, casting a prism
   onto the floor.
Write the desired date and time on a white sheet of paper
   and burn over candle.
Close both eyes, then blow out flame.

EPILOGUE

There is no such thing as a common forest.

A place of ordinary trees and unremarkable terrain.

Woods are formed of mischief and misdeeds, thorns to bite at exposed skin, roots to catch a loose shoelace dragging down a path. Malediction lives in the dark, it festers beneath thick canopies of evergreen limbs, burrows into the damp wood like needle worms.

But some forests are older than most. *The oldest kind.* Some forests grow hatred in their bark and moth-eaten leaves so that no safe passage can be made through such a place.

Unless you are built of the forest. Unless blood as black as tar swells through your veins.

Unless you are a Walker.

Walker women have never feared the trees—the ancient sway of limbs clawing at their long, sooty hair.

Locals say they were sprouted from the ground itself, pushed up like green saplings greedy for sun and warmth. That their bones are built of roots and briars and stinging nettle.

They belong to these woods. To the Black River where gold was found along the rocky shore. To Jackjaw Lake, dark and bottomless.

To the fattened moon, tethered in the sky—awaiting the whispered words of a Walker's furtive spell.

The history of Walker women is strange and storied and woven in folklore.

And that's how they prefer it—to be made into legends.

Acknowledgments

At times, writing this book was like losing myself within a dark, dark wood. I might not have found my way back out if it weren't for a few spectacular people.

A ridiculously huge thank-you to Nicole Ellul for venturing into the Wicker Woods with me. For conjuring spells and unexpected endings and word magic. There is surely moonlight in your veins! Thank you to Mara Anastas and Liesa Abrams for providing a home for my dark, twisted tales. To Jessi Smith and Thandi Jackson, thank you for reading countless drafts. Thank you, Sarah Creech, for designing a perfectly spooky cover; Mike Rosamilia, for designing an equally spooky interior; and Jim Tierney, for the magical art. Thank you, Elizabeth Mims and Sara Berko, for making sure stories become books. Thank you to Clare McGlade for rounding out the rough edges. Thank you to Caitlin Sweeny and Alissa Nigro for your marketing magic! Thank you, Lauren Castner, for all the top secret work you do! Thank you, Cassie Malmo, for juggling schedules and making sure this story gets into the hands of as many readers as possible. To Anna Jarzab, Emily Ritter, Jill Hacking, and Chrissy Noh—you ladies are superheroes. And thank you to all the fellow book nerds at the S&S office who make this book possible in all the little/big ways that are never seen!

Jess Regel, you've read an unnameable number of my stories—ones that no one but you or I will ever read, and you have been the greatest ally I could ask for. Cheers to the books buried in both our old inboxes. Thank you for everything. Truly.

To Mom and Dad, thank you for all the bedtime stories. To Sky, thank you for distracting the animals while I write and for eating only cereal when I didn't have time to cook. Love you endlessly. To Mel and Andra and Andee, still the best friends a girl could ask for.

To Ann and Nicky, Jeanie and Tyler. I was on deadline during our trip, but you guys still made sure I got in that turquoise water and played cocobocce. I heart you all. *Banana*.

To the readers of this story, if you find yourself in a dark wood, without a match to light the way. Be your own light.